Praise f[...]

"Cayouette crafts an engaging story tha[...] [...]g onists' high school days and the present. . . . The emotional aspects of the romance take center stage in this heartfelt first novel."   —*Library Journal* (starred review)

"Cayouette makes a memorable debut with a second-chance love story that is equal parts heart-wrenching and inspiring."   —*Publishers Weekly*

"Deeply romantic, *One Last Shot* dazzles with second-chance romance so sweeping it's picture-perfect."   —Emily Wibberley and Austin Siegemund-Broka, authors of *The Roughest Draft*

"*One Last Shot* has everything I look for in a great romance read . . . making for a whirlwind ride that will have you swooning one moment and welling up with tears the next."   —Bridget Morrissey, author of *A Thousand Miles*

"A sweet and heartfelt debut romance that has me itching to book a flight to Italy."   —Hannah Grace, author of *Icebreaker*

"Betty Cayouette's debut novel is an intoxicating romance. . . . Surely just the beginning of a great career."   —Stephen McCauley, author of *My Ex-Life*

"Full of swoon-worthy chemistry and raw emotion . . . I devoured Emerson and Theo's love story in a single bite."   —Annabel Monaghan, author of *Same Time Next Summer*

"*One Last Shot* is a delightful summer read, and a debut not to be missed."   —Hanna Halperin, author of *I Could Live Here Forever*

"Glamorous, tension-filled, with a heaping side of wanderlust! *One Last Shot* pulls off that perfect minute of butterflies-in-the-stomach romance with a few serious moments that will have you reaching for tissues."   —Emma Noyes, author of *Guy's Girl*

"With *One Last Shot*, Betty Cayouette proves that she can do it all! I didn't want to put this book down."   —Jessica Saunders, author of *Love, Me*

ALSO BY BETTY CAYOUETTE

One Last Shot

TELL ME HOW YOU REALLY FEEL

A Novel

BETTY CAYOUETTE

ST. MARTIN'S GRIFFIN
NEW YORK

First published in the United States by St. Martin's Griffin, an imprint of St. Martin's Publishing Group

www.stmartins.com

Designed by Gabriel Guma

All emojis designed by OpenMoji—the open-source emoji and icon project. License: CC BY-SA 4.0

The Library of Congress Cataloging-in-Publication Data is available upon request.

ISBN 978-1-250-29112-7 (trade paperback)
ISBN 978-1-250-29113-4 (ebook)

Our books may be purchased in bulk for promotional, educational, or business use. Please contact your local bookseller or the Macmillan Corporate and Premium Sales Department at 1-800-221-7945, extension 5442, or by email at MacmillanSpecialMarkets@macmillan.com.

First Edition: 2025

10 9 8 7 6 5 4 3 2 1

This one is for all the readers that supported my first book.

Thank you.

TELL ME HOW YOU REALLY FEEL

ONE

Maeve

"You two are just going to have to find a way to work together. There's no way around it."

Even though I can hear the words coming out of my agent Shazia's mouth . . . they're not registering. Because they just *can't* be what she means.

"Sorry, sorry, question here," I interject. I catch Finn's eye for a moment and . . . *Is he smiling? Smirking?* He doesn't get it. I am here through some massive fluke in the universe and need to desperately clutch this stroke of luck while keeping everyone happy with me. He, on the other hand, is a nepo baby who didn't even want to work in entertainment. He would walk away tomorrow, like it was nothing, if he didn't want our millions of listeners to stroke his ego every Sunday. I tear my eyes away from his arrestingly blue ones and continue to plead my case to Shazia. "There has to be some work-around. I get that it needs to be *our* show, but can't we do solo episodes? It's not in the contract that we have to record together, right?"

Finn's agent, who looks like he's a member of every old boys' club out there, stops texting. Apparently, he has deigned to answer this one. "No solos. Both members of the party have to contribute to each episode."

My ears perk up. "Contribute! Not record together." I glance at my agent, who's flipping through the contract that is spread out across the massive boardroom table. The table that Finn and I, and our respective teams, are sitting at opposite ends of.

"Maeve is correct. They don't have to record together."

Finn scoffs. "There's video! It's not like we can just Frankenstein our voices together."

Which is true. But since when does he care about, or even *know* about, our production value?

Finn's eyes are still locked on me. I look out the window. Because I *can't* keep looking into those eyes. They are so pale blue it shocks me. They're the eyes everyone and their mother grew up watching since *his* mother has starred in every rom-com under the sun. But on him—with his square jaw and wavy dark brown hair and freckled skin and a mouth that I had become so used to seeing smile an extra-wide grin that, until Cassidy, was reserved for me—it's lethal. He takes my breath away, even now.

Back in college I was surprised he wanted to talk to me. Now, I'm desperate to avoid having to say two words to him. I still can't believe he let our friendship implode like it was nothing.

Tell Me How You Really Feel started as something fun for Finn and me to do on Sunday afternoons. We'd both moved to New York after graduating from Carnegie Mellon, and since we both lived in the city, we'd gone from being in the same college friend group to being genuinely close. After completing my MA in clinical psychology at Columbia, I was scraping by during my supervision years in the Columbia Counseling Center while he was rebelling against his actor-screenwriter parents by living with his frat brothers and working at Morgan Stanley in a soul-crushing consulting job. I was tired of giving relationship advice to rich eighteen-year-olds who wouldn't take it anyway, and so I decided, why not put my psychology degrees to good use with a sex-and-relationships-advice podcast? I was obsessed with true crime podcasts; every day I walked around New York with stories of grisly kidnappings running through my ears, jumping when someone turned the corner too fast right when I was hearing a woman describe how she escaped death. With my anxiety, it didn't quite make sense that *that's* what I liked to listen to for fun, but for some reason getting wrapped up in an episode made me feel relaxed rather than on edge. I loved when the storytelling was so good that I audibly gasped or laughed aloud on the subway. But I had no idea how to start my own show, or if anyone would even want a sex-and-relationships podcast from me. So, I asked Finn if he wanted to join and jazz things up with a guy's perspective. At least if we did it together it would be fun even if it was a total flop. If he had said no, I don't know that I would have had the guts to actually sit down and record.

In episode one, we sat in my closet of a room and recorded on our iPhones as we dished on first dates we'd been on and gave advice; in episode two, we talked about our past relationships and . . . *drumroll please* . . . how we really felt about each other's exes. But it was episode three that went viral. Like, *really* viral. Because while he was baked and I was buzzed, we recorded an episode that was everything anyone needed to know about how to go down on their partner. We hit Upload before we'd sobered up, it went viral, we got fired from our day jobs, and now, two years later, we have one of the biggest podcast deals in the world. Because suddenly, podcasts are *cool*.

"Since when do you know how the recording works?" I snap at him. "Last I checked, I'm the one setting up the cameras and mics. You don't even care about the show." We started out filming on our phones, then in the brief period before I was fired from my counseling job I signed out cameras from Columbia for us to film on, and once we got the first few big sponsors (Trojan, Airbnb, and Urban Stems, thank you very much), I upgraded us to Sony cameras, Sennheiser lav mics, and one giant SkyPanel light. I had never been so grateful to have taken Intro to Film Production as my creative arts requirement back in undergrad. Finn leans back in his chair and shakes his head, his dark brown hair falling into an agonizingly perfect flop when he returns to glaring at me. "Don't be mean, Maeve, it doesn't suit you."

What an arrogant prick. From the way my heart is pounding in my throat, I can tell a panic attack is on the horizon if I don't get out of this room in the next few minutes. "Do you even hear yourself?" I whisper. "Just let me do this my way because I cannot deal with your bullshit anymore." We said the show was about helping each other find Mr. and Mrs. Right, and I thought it also gave him a creative outlet he was secretly desperate for, but now . . . I think maybe it was all just an ego boost for Finn. I don't know him anymore.

"You can't be serious. Our fans want to see *us*. Maeve, we're good together, and you know it."

I lean across the table, positively snarling at him. "Save. Your good guy act. For. Cassidy."

Finn's jaw drops, and I can tell he's seeing red. "Are you fucking serious right now? I can't believe this. You—"

"That's enough," Shazia interrupts smoothly. "There is nothing in the contract that says you can't record separately. It's my understanding that Maeve takes the lead on tech, while Finn, you take the lead on social, so if she can find a way to do it, I see no reason why it wouldn't be amenable to everyone."

Finn completely ignores her, his eyes still locked on me. I stare right back at him, and even as I start to feel like I might cry or combust, I keep at it. I've spent the entire summer preparing for this, and I don't want him to see me falter.

"Maeve," Finn says finally. "Come on. You've worked so hard on this show. Don't you want to make it the best it can be?"

And just like that, he's playing on all of my anxiety and insecurities. I still can't believe he's *that* awful. "I can't believe you," I whisper. And then I stand up and stalk toward the door.

Right as my hand touches the doorknob, Finn calls out to me. "Maeve, Cassidy is—"

"Save it!" I shout. I know they're done. But it doesn't fucking matter. I *slam* that door behind me and wish I could erase the past few months from my memory.

And this is why we shouldn't record together. Because we don't have a spark; we have a forest fire. And we bring out the worst in each other. Or, rather, Finn brings out the worst in me, while he gets everything he's ever wanted and more. I can't believe we went from . . . *something* to desperately trying to not be in the same room— even though we're being paid millions of dollars to do exactly that.

Once I'm outside the CAA conference room, I have no idea how to get out of the building. I lean against the wall down the hall and do the breathing exercises I learned in therapy years ago. I arrived in LA approximately one month ago, and instead of celebrating this life-changing three-year deal, I've spent most of that time crying into my brand-new overpriced pillowcase while my sister Sarah tells me what trash Finn is. She's a sophomore at USC on the premed track, and thanks to this podcast deal I can now pay her tuition and live in an awesome house. Actually, I can do a whole lot more than that ever since the first installment hit my bank account. But I can't wrap my head around that amount of money and that is a champagne problem I don't think I'll make it to in my weekly Zoom therapy sessions for at least a month, given my current state of affairs. I walk in the general direction of where I think the reception desk is, but before I get too far Shazia catches up to me, her Nikes silent behind me until suddenly she's pulling me into another conference room and kicking out the people who were eating lunch in it.

I shift my gaze toward the ceiling and try to blink back the tears that are forming. "I'm sorry," I offer immediately. "I don't know what it is about Finn; he gets to me." Except I do know. It's that until exactly 105 days ago, I was in love with him. And he threw me out like I was some one-night stand gone wrong, to date Cassidy, who was actually girlfriend material.

"That was nothing," Shazia laughs. "You should see what some of my other clients pull. Besides, he deserves a few doors slammed in his face. It's a novelty for him."

I laugh in spite of myself. When we first started getting big, Finn's mom tried to set me up with the same agent she arranged for him. But I could tell he just wasn't as interested in *me*. He viewed me as someone who was lucky enough to be adjacent to Finn. The average-looking girl he deigned to podcast with, which is exactly what I'm sure much of the world thinks. Even though, in reality, this show was *my* idea, that he *joined*, and together we lit up the airwaves or whatever. I hate that I don't think it would've worked without both of us. I never would have been engaging enough to grow a fanbase without him. But I am the one that actually cares about the show and making it a success, and Shazia's the only agent who actually *got* that. Probably because as a Dominican woman who doesn't come from cushy generational wealth like half of LA, she's used to her contributions being overlooked too.

"You're right, maybe it'll be good for him. But just know I never would have done that if one of the Streamify reps were in the room." I want her to understand that even though he's getting to me, I'm not going totally off the rails. I want to be an asset, not a liability.

"Maeve, I know. It's okay to be enraged sometimes. Guys like him run entertainment without ever working for it. It's infuriating." Shazia pours fancy, pH-balanced sparkling water into the espresso cups sitting on the table, and we each take a long sip. "After you left, I told them that there is to be absolutely no talk of Cassidy. Or of your relationship with each other. On or off air, or you walk." My eyes widen, but before I can protest she jumps in. "I know that you're not walking. No one is walking. But they need to know we're serious. And once Finn heard that, he agreed."

"Really?" I'm shocked. The first two months of our hiatus were radio silence as paparazzi photographed him gallivanting around Europe with Cassidy. But the past month he's been calling me daily and leaving lengthy voicemails, desperate to talk. I've deleted them all because I don't want to hear it. We already talked and he has said absolutely everything I ever need to hear from him. It was both too much and not enough.

"Really. Now, let's talk about you. Where do you want things to go with the show? Or even after the show?"

Shazia and I haven't talked much since I agreed to the official Streamify deal months ago. At the time, it felt like I had finally made myself into something. I thought Shazia was being ridiculous when she told me to start thinking about what my next move would be. I wanted to keep doing *Tell Me How You Really Feel* with Finn forever.

Yeah, it was more graphic than I wanted, but I understood. Go viral now, get the deal, then do the show exactly as I wanted. With Finn. Because together we are so *alive*. When we were working together to brainstorm and record, it felt like the best idea I'd ever had was constantly on the tip of my tongue. I was on fire and constantly lit up inside with adrenaline and inspiration. With desire. Until suddenly I was crashing down into the lowest low I'd had in years. Now I wonder if Shazia saw the writing on the wall.

I take a deep breath, then blurt out my idea, ready to be told it's unrealistic. Even though I've built something that has value and have gone to school for the better part of a decade, in meetings with agents and producers I still feel like a little girl who's playing dress-up. And the problem is, when I played dress-up as a child I'd always look to my right or left and see my sisters doing it better. "I want to do a solo show. I want to do serious couples counseling and record it, and let it air. I think I could make something really powerful, that really helps people. I know *Tell Me How You Really Feel* isn't exactly viewed with quite that level of gravity . . ." Ever since that fateful third episode, people wanted to call us the sex show and discount any serious advice I had. And the content that went viral was always the graphic segments, so in order to grow we had to talk about sex, especially once I was fired from my counseling job because of our show and needed the income. But it was beyond frustrating. Especially because even with the sex advice, it's not like I was doing ASMR porn; I was giving research-backed and experience-based advice. Why can't a woman talk about sex and still be considered serious? Haters petitioned CMU and Columbia to take back my degrees and called me a whore, while Finn got a *GQ* cover that said he was dismantling toxic masculinity one podcast episode at a time. "I really feel like I could do something good here. I want to show people how to have healthy conversations. About sex, but also about finances, children, trauma. All of it."

I wait for her response with bated breath. Because I've never been the talented one. My twenty-four-year-old sister Sarah is a future surgeon, my twenty-three-year-old sister Claude is a pageant queen, and seventeen-year-old Tiffany is about to go to college on a full ride for D1 soccer. I'm thoroughly average, despite striving to be great. I got lucky with this show, but no one tunes in to watch just me.

Shazia mulls over the idea for a moment, and my heart is in my stomach. Until she breaks into a grin. "I was *hoping* you'd say a solo show." Now I'm the one grinning. "I think you'd be great at it. Maybe as a reality show?"

I frown. "I mean, I figured it would be a podcast. With video, but still a Streamify production."

Shazia winces and dread rises in my throat. "Once you told me about all the problems with Finn . . . I asked about separating the deal into two solo show contracts. They aren't interested at this time."

I swallow and finish her sentence. "In a solo show with me." Because they already asked Finn to do a solo show. When we were in negotiations, they wanted to add a show to his contract, a weekly rewatch show of all his mom's rom-coms. He declined, telling them that he was only interested in podcasting with me.

"Once *Tell Me How You Really Feel* grows under their marketing dollars, I'm sure they'll change their tune. But maybe in the meantime, we think about different formats. Because, Maeve, it is a *great* idea. Truly. Someone will want it. I want it!"

I can only podcast with Streamify. That's why we got this meaty deal, because we're exclusive to the platform. They bought a few shows in historic deals, hoping to force listeners away from the other platforms. And while there's nothing wrong with making my idea a TV show—some reality shows are really just higher production value podcasts, now that we do video episodes—knowing they don't think I have the talent to host a solo show stings. It makes me doubt whether I even do. I try to do a strategy my therapist taught me and follow the self-doubt with three affirmations. *I don't have the talent for this*, is replaced with: *I made something great. I have changed listeners' lives. I deserve this.* But it can only do so much given how much the past few months have worn me down.

I force a smile. "You know, a show doesn't sound so bad. Let me think on it. I want to get the podcast going before I commit to something else."

"Of course. Once again, you're my smartest client." Shazia pours us each another tiny espresso cup of water and throws hers back. "Listen, if things don't go well with Finn, call me. I'll sort it out. I have to head across town for another meeting, with a supremely irritating client who went viral for gluing her eyelids shut and now has a beauty show on Netflix."

And that is why I can't help but think I probably, maybe, didn't earn all this. Because even people like that have a Netflix show. "Have fun!"

I wave Shazia off, then slip my feet out of my heels and slump back in my chair, all of the energy drained out of me. But to my dismay, when I shut my eyes, it's Finn staring at me that runs back through my head.

TWO

Finn

Doesn't she know I'm only doing this for her? I'm well aware that this is all my fault, but this is her podcast. I've gone along with everything the past two years because she *deserves* all this success so fucking much. And, selfishly, because I know that right now doing the show is the only way she'll let me be in the same room with her. But without her, what is the point of any of this?

After Maeve slams the door behind her, her agent stands up. "The only way this will be possible is if there is no talk of what happened between the two of you. No talk of Cassidy. Or else my client will walk."

My agent, Mark, snorts in disbelief without looking up from his phone.

"I need to apologize to her," I try to explain.

Shazia quite literally shushes me. "No. You've explained enough."

She exhales and glances at Mark, who is ignoring us. She beckons me over, and I walk to her side of the long table, so she can lean in to whisper. "If you care about her at all, then you will agree not to talk about it. That is the only way to make this situation manageable."

I blow out a puff of air in exasperation and stare at the ceiling. I hate knowing how much I've hurt Maeve. I am such an idiot. I thought I was just doing what she wanted. I was sticking to the premise of the show by trying to find Mrs. Right! Dating Cassidy was *great* for the Streamify deal negotiations, and it got us a ridiculous amount of positive press. And since Cassidy is such an It girl, being together elevated me from being famous but also not quite *it*—a child star from a celeb family that flamed out—to a genuine A-lister. Something I didn't even want, but which benefited the podcast and Maeve significantly. And bonus: dating her made my parents happy for once. At first, it just felt easy. For me, Cassidy was always the one that got away . . . or the first one that got away, anyway . . . and I really thought that dating her could really be the start of the rest of my life.

But if this is what Maeve needs, then I'll do it. I'll do anything to make this right. "Fine. Agreed." I nod once at her agent, shake her hand, then try not to flinch when she also lets the door slam on her way out.

I sit down and turn to my agent. "I am not doing this without her."

Mark pauses his constant stream of texts and puts his phone face down on the table. "Finn, I know you like this girl. But she's . . ." He waves his hand flippantly as though the thought of Maeve is an annoying gnat, and my blood starts to churn. "You don't need her. You can't break the contract, but you could record an hour a week remotely and we can get you on a movie set. You can be the next Batman. With your face and the scripts your dad has already written for you to star in alongside your mother, you're golden. Just think of Maeve as the girl who got your head on straight, and got you out of the Wall Street gutter, and leave her behind. She's a nobody without you."

I want to fire him on the spot. But Mark has been a friend of the family since I was in diapers. He works for my mom, the revered Evangeline Sutton, and he's known my dad forever, so he'll be at every dinner party my parents throw. But I can't let him talk about Maeve like that. And I am so tired of my family pressuring me to get into the business. "That's not true. This show is all Maeve. And I *don't want* to do movies, or shows, or whatever. I'll do this with her, and that's it. But isn't there some way you can make sure we have to record together? I need to at least talk to her." Even if our relationship is off-limits for now, I have to apologize in person. Then I know I can get us back to where we were, at least.

Mark actually rolls his eyes at me. "You're a good-looking kid. Send some flowers. A car. Purses, perfume, whatever she's into. She'll come around."

Except, that isn't Maeve. She's fiercely principled and doesn't give a shit about bags and shoes if it's coming from the wrong place. But Mark isn't going to have any good advice for me. "Whatever. I'll see you at dinner next week."

My mom is throwing a huge party next week, which she's calling an equal pay gala. Her foundation is a passion project, and I'm sure the party/gala will raise a ton of money for women and minorities in production, but, as I heard her explaining to my dad the other night, it also has the added benefit of reintegrating me into the Hollywood crowd and celebrating my move back to LA. Every A-lister in the industry will be there. Even though Maeve isn't talking to me, I invited her and all three of her sisters, although Sarah is the only one of them in the area. None of them RSVP'd.

"Speaking of dinner, you should make sure Maeve is at that gala. There's rumors that you two are fighting, and Streamify isn't happy."

"We are fighting," I retort. "There's no way she'll go. And I thought you said not to worry about her."

"Fine. You got me. Streamify doesn't give a shit, but your mom wants her there. She's irked they haven't met." Mark stands and drops his untouched coffee in the trash, then holds the door to signal me out.

"Now is not the time for them to meet."

"Flowers. Purses. Perfume. See you next week."

I've heard through *Architectural Digest* that Maeve is renting an expansive Hollywood Hills mansion. I, on the other hand, am living in my parents' guesthouse because they were so horrified by the rental I picked last week that my mom called the real estate agent and sweet-talked her into firing me as a client. Which is exactly why I liked living in New York.

When I walk into our house, I hear music blaring from the home gym, where my mom is undoubtedly working out with her trainer. Ever since she turned fifty she's been relentless with the workouts, although her fears about her popularity and roles drying up appear unfounded. My dad's been writing for her since they met on her breakout movie set, when she starred in the first adaptation of *Malibu Rising*, and he's never going to put her in a secondary role. Unless I'm the primary, despite my protests that I don't want to act again. Acting is off-limits. I've seen the press rip my own mom apart, and I've experienced firsthand how critics and the paparazzi treat nepo babies. It's *harsh*. I can't go there again. Podcasting is a happy compromise.

"How was the meeting?" My dad, Richard, is in the kitchen, making an elaborate salad for lunch for himself and my mom. And by the

looks of it, for me as well. Whenever I come home, they forget that I'm twenty-eight, and start acting like I'm sixteen.

"She hates my guts. So, same old."

My dad dumps fresh-cut peaches into the massive bowl he's mixing everything into. "Did I ever tell you about when your mom hated me? It was that first set and—"

"Yes." I cut him off. "Only a million times, half of which were in the last week. Tail between my legs, I've got it. Except I'm not even going to be able to record with her, let alone talk to her. We're recording this week's episode separately."

"How will that work?"

I shrug and start prepping bruschetta. My parents might be able to be practically carb free these days, but I need more than a pound of kale. "I don't know. I'm sure she'll figure it out, since she's the smartest person I know. I don't think it'll perform, though."

"You might be right about that. You can't fake chemistry. You two have it on-screen, and talking to a wall and piecing together close-ups won't cut it."

"She'll probably make it look like we're in the same room. She's that good."

My mom sweeps in, dripping sweat and beet red, in a workout set that shows off that she has a better six-pack than I do. She kisses my dad on the cheek, and I duck away from her, not wanting to be drenched in secondhand sweat. "Is Maeve coming to the party? What a regal name. She's made for the spotlight. And so *young*. Have you seen her skin?"

"Yes," I hiss. "No need to tell me how good she looks. Trust me, I know." She looked amazing in today's meeting. Her hair was still the slightest bit damp, as though she'd just gotten out of the shower before driving over, so it looked more brown than auburn. Her skin was slightly red, the remnants of a sunburn, since it's virtually impossible for her to tan, and she wore a dress that I'd never seen before. It was bright red, which she knows is the color I think she looks best in. When we met in college, she was wearing a red minidress and was adorably self-conscious because she thought it was too much for her as a quasi-redhead. I told her it wasn't too much. She was outshining the dress, hands down.

My mom steals a slice of peach from the salad and eats it, giggling at my dad when he tries to push her hand away. They're like newlyweds, truly in love, which is a rarity in Hollywood. "Well, just so you're aware, Cassidy will be at the equal pay gala. Her mom is my best friend, she's such a fierce advocate for equal pay on set, and our new movie launches next month. I had to invite her."

I groan. "Just kill me now." Cassidy also thought we made sense together. Which is true. We're the kind of couple magazine editors and fashion houses dream about. Nepo babies with arresting looks and talent to back it up. I've known her since we were kids, and ever since that movie we did with our moms, pictures of us out together always get picked up. But we always have had a great time together. When we tried dating this summer, the dates were all fun. But we both realized quickly that we didn't actually connect in that "talk until four a.m., share your hopes and dreams, text ridiculous GIFs, push each other to be better, and laugh until you throw up" kind of way.

"Relax, honey, she doesn't hate you. It was good of you to take all the blame in the press, and her mom said she always had a hard time sleeping with you since you two used to take baths together."

"Mom! Too far. Way too far. Getting together was Cassidy's idea! Anyway, I'm not worried about Cassidy hating me. We're good. I'm worried that if by some miracle Maeve shows up, this will only make things worse." I start stress eating bruschetta.

My dad serves up the salad. "Maybe Cassidy can talk to her. Tell her how she really feels and all."

"Your puns are awful corny for a screenwriter," my mom chastises.

"Tell that to my Oscar."

My mom fakes a cough. "*Our* Oscar."

"That's what I said!"

They're too much. This is why I need my own place. I'm going to find my next apartment on Zillow, where the real estate agent will think my mom's a catfish if she reaches out. I pick up my salad and the cutting board of bruschetta, only to have my dad snatch two pieces off and hand one to my mom. "See you two later. If you think of some romantic grand gesture I can use to get Maeve to forgive me, please don't use it in a movie, just tell me."

THREE

Maeve

I spend the next two days testing out how we could make an episode together without actually *being* within a hundred yards of each other. Typically, we have a three-camera setup. I set a close-up on Finn, a close-up on me, and a wide shot that shows the two of us together. In the edit I cut between the three cameras, depending on who's talking, our body language, gesticulating, reactions, all that— and the audio is pristine thanks to the lav mics that are clipped to our shirt collars. I think we *could* make an episode with just close-ups and hide that we're not in the same room . . . but the problem is, our episodes aren't scripted. We prepare what we're talking about, and always have a list of Questions of the Week to end the episode, but we're typically improvising.

Because together we're hilarious. And smart. And maybe sexy? All of my good qualities increase tenfold when I'm in the room with Finn.

I write a script for this first episode, which is something I've never done before. I spend hours laboring over jokes, thinking about how Finn would talk, how he would answer the questions I pull from our online form and DMs. How he would tease me. And then I try to play both parts and piece it together. And it sucks.

I hit Pause on the practice video and get up from my editing bay to start pacing. It's an awesome setup that used to be a laptop in my closet in New York, but now has a full room in my ridiculously large house. I have two forty-inch color correct monitors, a completely tricked-out laptop, and an ergonomic chair that set Streamify back five grand. It all showed up wrapped in a giant red bow the day after I moved in. Finn got a five-thousand-dollar bottle of whiskey.

I need to make this work. I text my group chat with my sisters.

sos! I'm trying to make an episode with both Finn and me in it . . . but without actually doing it together

and it sucks

help please, I'm out of ideas

Sarah starts typing, then stops, and I groan and hit Play on the episode again. It's so stiff and awkward. It would be marginally better with Finn in it. But I don't think we'd be able to pass it off as a normal episode. And I can just imagine what the articles would say if people discovered we were pretending to record together. Our fans are incredibly loyal . . . but also figure out *everything*. They are basically FBI agents. They've tracked down my high school prom photos, who Finn's first kiss was (Cassidy, obviously), all of my family members, and where my hometown is, even though we use code names for everyone and everything important. Give them a month and they'll probably be mailing vibrators to our new home addresses. They'd know we're faking it.

My phone starts vibrating with a flurry of texts from Claude and Tiffany. They're probably together, sending these dueling texts from opposite ends of the couch. I don't miss home, but I do miss them and the chaotic energy of having three sisters, which surrounded my entire childhood.

Claude: I say record with him again. Pretend he's a teammate you don't like

Tiffany: F for effort

Not helpful, I reply.

Sarah: Can't you each just do your own half

It's too awkward, I type quickly.

Tiffany: Bridal shower game!!!

You each have to separately answer questions about the other and see if you get it right

Now this I like. We can lean in to not recording together, acknowledge it, and make it part of the fun. This could work. Finn and I actually played that game on *The Today Show* once, and, shockingly, he got every single one about me right. I missed two, but to my credit they weren't softballs. How would I know the name of his Little League team? Unlike the rest of the women and gay men in America, I'm not obsessed with him.

I think this idea could actually work. I pick up my phone instinctively, to call Finn and tell him my idea, only to stop myself. For the past two years he was the first person I told everything to. He was always so excited for me. It was the first time that I felt like someone really appreciated and believed in *me*. I really thought he felt the same way I did about our connection. Everything we did was better with each other. With him, eating takeout on the floor of my bedroom wasn't depressing, it was incredible because we were laughing and coming up with ideas and building on each other's thoughts and creating an awesome episode about it that went out to millions of people. And then reading messages from people who dumped a toxic ex because of us, or orgasmed for the first time, or came out to their best friend. And falling asleep with my head on his shoulder while he was listening back to the episode, and thinking it all meant something, when to him it was just a fun thing to do. When he was always looking for someone like Cassidy, who's shiny and perfect and famous and doesn't talk about blow jobs on a podcast.

So instead of calling him, I text Tiffany a thank-you GIF, then get in my car and drive to the studio.

"Maeve! We weren't expecting you today. Is Finn coming in?" The receptionist looks surprised to see me. Previously, Finn and I recorded in stellar locations like Finn's living room floor, my bed, his bed, my fire escape, and occasionally a friend's apartment. We had offers from production studios in New York, but once we started getting big I didn't want to sign over our IP. I didn't know we'd get a deal like this . . . but I knew I hated the idea of a middle-aged man owning any part of this show that I'd worked so hard on. Even now, we're licensing the IP for three years, exclusively, and at the end of the term we could walk away with it. But in the meantime I'm definitely going to enjoy using Streamify's super professional studios whenever we want.

"He's not! Just testing something out, and he's busy with family. Would you mind helping me set up?"

The receptionist presses "1" on the phone she had already half raised to her ear as she talked. "I'll get a PA sent over to you right away! Want some snacks? Coconut water? Cappuccino? Wine?"

It feels strange to have someone fussing over me like this. I've always been on the sidelines while my sisters prepared for big events like pageants and soccer tournaments, and despite our success with the podcast the past few years, since we recorded alone, it never felt like as big a deal as it was. "An iced coffee would be great. Thank you so much." I shove my beat-up CamelBak deeper into my bag.

Before I have time to sit down, a young man is opening a hidden door in the wall and motioning me toward him. For a second, I wonder if it was unprofessional to do our first recording session without Finn. He's more used to being catered to than I am, but he loved the offices when we toured during contract negotiations and would get a kick out of this VIP treatment. But he made his bed, and now he has to lie in it.

"I'm Leo. It's great to meet you," the PA says as he leads me down an elegant hallway. "I've actually been working on the *Tell Me How You Really Feel* set for the past month, psyched to see what you think of it. I'm here five days a week, so I'm your lead PA, anything you need I'm here. I don't know how you two roll, but if you prefer to record in the middle of the night or something, just say so, I'm there."

"Oh wow," I stammer. "Thank you. We usually record . . ." I think back to the past year and a half. "Well actually, we have no set schedule. But I think we'll be getting much more organized now that we're at Streamify." We'll have to, if we're going to keep recording separately.

"Sweet, sweet. Can't wait to see how the magic happens."

I would be wincing if I said something that cheesy, but Leo appears to be dead serious. He presses on what looks like a bookshelf that houses solely sex-related books, and the door slowly opens to reveal what is clearly the *Tell Me How You Really Feel* studios.

"You like it!" he exclaims, and I realize my jaw had dropped. Except it wasn't in a good way. The table is designed to look like a massive vagina, and the walls are painted with line drawings of naked people of all shapes and sizes kissing. There are regular mics and penis mics sitting at the table, and the flower arrangements are in vases shaped like butts and busts. The room does have a strangely expensive vibe . . . but is also so "in your face" sexual that my blood curdles. Now that we have the big deal, I want to gradually make the show more serious, not more viral through sex and shock value.

"It's . . . it's definitely a lot," I manage after a moment of Leo clearly waiting for my response. I drop my bag on the table and start examining things. The camera equipment is nicer than what Finn and I have been using, and the room is entirely soundproof. But it's *a lot*. I turn to Leo and smile winningly. "We actually use lav mics." At least that gets rid of the most egregious thing in the room: those awful penis mics that would inspire a thousand GIFs. Again, my hand twitches, instinctively wanting to send Finn a picture of them. "But when Finn comes in . . . definitely put it back out."

"For sure," Leo agrees smoothly. He opens a hidden compartment and pulls out lav mics. What is with all the hidden compartments? It's like Streamify decided showing they had drawers, doors, and closets in this massive building was gauche. "I know the room really pops. But I thought it would help, you know? With the goal."

"What goal?" I ask immediately. Does he know I want my own show? To never be in the room with Finn again?

Leo starts testing the lav mics as he talks. "Beating *The Paul Myers Show?* Since both shows are going Streamify exclusive and relaunching the same week, it's kind of intense competition. I would love to see Paul Myers get knocked down a peg. I hate the guy. The stuff he says about immigrants is wack. Once I heard he was coming on too, I practically begged to be reassigned to you guys."

My blood runs cold. No one has said anything about *The Paul Myers Show* going exclusive with Streamify. I don't know if I would have even signed the contract if I realized that was happening. "Why wasn't there a press release about his show going exclusive?"

Leo shrugs. "I assume he's worried about the ratings and wants to save the publicity for the first week out. So you'll be easier to compete with."

"Right . . ." I trail off. "Would you mind giving me a minute?" I feel blindsided and need a moment to regroup. A jolt of anxiety has shot through me, and I need to get my bearings so I don't spiral.

Leo makes a swift exit and I drop into the chair with a dull thud. *The Paul Myers Show* is the most popular, and the most problematic, podcast out there. It's bigoted, extremist, inflammatory, and downright dangerous if I'm being honest. Paul Myers is obsessed with making the world a more hateful place. He's taken aim at us more times than I can count, calling me everything from a whore to an uneducated hick, and spewed all sorts of homophobic and transphobic names at Finn, just because he knows the slightest bit about feelings, nice clothes, and personal grooming. It's truly disgusting. And I have no idea what his problem is with us. Ever since the literal one time we overtook him in the ratings, with episode three, he has been relentless.

I pull out my phone and dial Shazia. She picks up on the second ring. "Maeve. What's up?"

I swallow hard. "Did you know Paul Myers is exclusive to Streamify too?"

"What?" I can hear the surprise in her voice.

"Apparently, they held the press release. He's launching the new season of his show the same week we are." I take a deep breath. I want to keep the quiver of panic out of my voice, but it feels like I'm hearing my own voice, small and tinny from afar, through a haze of fear. Dread is heavy in my gut. Ever since we've inked this contract I've been waiting for everything to come crashing down. I *knew* there had to be a catch. And now my anxiety is finally validated. "I don't know if we'd have signed if we knew."

"They should have disclosed this. We could argue it constitutes reputational damage to you and Finn, to be so closely associated with Paul Myers, since he's part of this new Streamify-exclusive campaign. Both sides have an option to cancel in the event that anything in the contract is found to have the potential to cause reputational damage."

"I don't want out of the deal. But I just . . . I don't know." There's a long pause. I don't want to end the contract, despite everything. It's sixty *million* dollars. That's a life-altering amount of money. But I do feel duped. "Do you think he's getting paid sixty million too?"

Shazia's tone is steel when she speaks. "I think he could very well be getting paid more. I'm going to see what I can do about this. Maybe they can sweeten the deal. They knew this would upset you; that's why they kept it secret. They have to be prepared with something they're willing to give."

I end the call, eyes smarting as I blink back tears. There's nothing I can do about this, and I feel like I have my emotions under control now that I've taken a minute to assess the situation, so I might as well get to work. I knock on the wall so that Leo knows he can come back in, and he returns and resumes testing the lav in silence. Once he's done, he presses a button under the table that results in an immediate knock on the door/bookcase. He opens it through touching the wall in a specific (but completely unmarked) spot, making me very worried I'll get stuck in this orgy of a room, then grabs an iced coffee from a young woman and turns. "Everyone is rooting for you. Literally everyone here hates him, except the execs that he's about to print money for." He hands me the coffee. "Iced oat milk latte, one pump cinnamon, half a vanilla creamer."

It's eerie that he knows my order. But it's also good to hear that he's in my corner. "Thanks."

"So, do you need a run down on how the equipment works? It's all ready to go, keep the mic set to phantom power so it pulls power from the camera. Cameras each have eight hours of run time on, four hours recording power since while it's recording you halve the battery capacity. I'll switch out the batteries if need be, but thought that would probably be enough. You basically just have to hit Record. Any questions?"

I shake my head. These cameras are souped up models of the ones we've been using. Not having to stop everything to switch out batteries every thirty minutes will be a huge plus, though. "This is all amazing, thank you."

"Do you want me to monitor the camera and audio feed?"

I glance around the room, suddenly worried it's full of hidden cameras. It feels strange to know someone's watching, although it's undeniably helpful to have someone checking that nothing cuts out or glitches. But Finn and I have always recorded just us. It was intimate, and sometimes I still blush thinking of the conversations that we uploaded for the world to listen to. I tell him things during our recordings that I never thought I would share with the masses, because it really does feel like it's just for us when we're recording.

"No need," I say ultimately. "If you're still here when I head out, you could check it over for technical issues. And would you mind sending me the footage afterward?"

"On it. I can't believe you actually self-edit. I thought that was a myth."

I smile for real now. "I enjoy it. I want to make the edit perfect. And Finn likes to—" I cut myself off. We're not going to be spending twelve-hour stretches hunched over Premiere on my MacBook together anymore. "It works for us."

Leo leaves me to it, opening the hidden door by placing his hand on a totally different area. I run my lav mic under my shirt and clip it to my collar, then double-check that the shotgun mic is on phantom power. Next, I check my close-up on the camera opposite me and cut in slightly. It would normally be an over-the-shoulder shot, but I want it to be so tight on my face that our viewers forget they don't see Finn's shoulder and the side of his head as he looks over at me. I'm always surprised by how many of our viewers tune in to the video version of the show. We get tagged in Instagram stories of people throwing it up on their TV or having weekly wine nights with their roommates while they watch on their biggest laptop. More than half of our viewers watch the video, which makes this so much harder to get away with. But I have to try because I don't think I can sit here with Finn and talk about relationships without bursting into tears, screaming at him, or both.

His words from our last real conversation echo through my head. It was the day after his first date with Cassidy, and it took place through my apartment's intercom because I didn't want to see him and wouldn't pick up his calls.

Cassidy's the kind of girl I've always been looking for.

Of course I love you. You're my best friend.

What we did doesn't have to mean anything.

Fuck. Him.

I hit Record on my mic and the cameras trained on my close-up and the wide shot, and I turn Finn's close-up camera off altogether. Then I open my laptop to the list of topics I want to cover this episode—cuffing season, which dating app to use, and who pays on a first date, the questions I've chosen for Questions of the Week—and start recording.

"Hello everyone, we're back again with another episode of *Tell Me How You Really Feel*. I have missed you all literally so much. Today we're doing something a bit different—Finn and I are recording our hot takes separately, then comparing, so get pumped to see how he *really* feels about all of your questions. There will be no walking it back when I raise my eyebrows at him this week . . ."

"Maybe I don't want to know," I moan from my pool float. I'm on a giant unicorn in the pool in my rental house's backyard, and Sarah is on a flamingo, phone in hand. "You're using your 'bad news' voice."

Our episode aired yesterday, Sunday, at 12:01 a.m. After I finished recording, I sent Finn a terse message explaining what he needed to do for his half. Normally I'd be concerned about leaving him to record solo, but I'm sure Leo walked him through the entire process, or just handled all the equipment for him. I edited it alone, and Finn approved it without listening, which I *know* because he texted me back faster than it would take to watch the episode.

I know it's not our best. It was decently entertaining. And Streamify has no approval authority over our episodes, so I hit Upload last night without a fight. But our spark, the chemistry that makes me laugh aloud while listening to us . . . it wasn't there. We both sounded pressed, fake, as though we were recording under duress. Which we basically are.

On Friday morning the articles about Paul Myers's deal dropped, so I'm sure he'll get more listens than ever this weekend since he's top of mind. I hate that during this first week of competition I know that our episode wasn't that strong. Because this is now a clear-cut challenge. In the space of a week, Shazia renegotiated our contract to include a hefty sixty-nine percent bonus if we can overtake Paul Myers in the ratings for twelve consecutive episodes. He's making one hundred million over three years, but with this bonus we'd overtake him. To get the network to close the updated deal, I also agreed to a minimum of one event or vlog per month with Finn. Just this morning I got the Docusign notification that the contract has been signed by all parties; so it's official. I am now contractually obligated to act like I enjoy spending time with Finn.

I don't like it, but if we want to hit this goal, we'd have to do that anyway.

And I desperately want to hit the goal. Because making more than Paul Myers would make me and Finn the highest paid podcast hosts ever, full stop. It would also make me the highest paid female podcaster ever, since even at my currently outrageously high salary, several other popular podcasts (including my favorite crime junkies show) have hosts that are paid commensurately. But the (co)highest paid podcaster would be a woman, for the first time ever. I've struggled with imposter syndrome my entire life, and it would feel good to have quantitative proof that I am the best at something, for the first time ever.

But beating Paul Myers for twelve episodes straight will not be easy. Especially with this start to the season.

Sarah doesn't say anything, which means the situation is worse than I thought. "Just tell me." She floats farther away, as though having an extra few feet of water will protect her from my feelings. "Well, technically, the ratings aren't bad. A *lot* of people listened. You're the number two–ranked show." This makes sense. It's our first episode back, after our first ever hiatus, and Finn did his job and promo'd it on social. Solo. "But the response . . . is not ideal."

"They hate it," I say flatly.

Sarah wavers for a moment. But she's more logical than emotional, which is why she'll be a very competent surgeon. "They hate it," she agrees. "The general attitude is, *What the fuck*. PopSugar posted, wondering if it was AI generated. And *The Paul Myers Show* released a parody TikTok of you two recording with water guns to your heads. Fans want to know why you're suddenly not, you know, doing your thing. Real talking about each other's dates. About his breakup with Cassidy. Who you're seeing. Whatever."

"Fuuuuuck," I moan. This has been my fear the whole time. That suddenly everyone will realize that I actually am totally average and not worth listening to. That this house, this life, this audience, and any potential for a solo show will all go away. Lately it doesn't matter how many affirmations or meditations or therapy sessions I do. Even though I'm pushing forward, I just can't shake these fears.

"It's not that bad," Sarah offers. "It's only the first episode. You two could do the next one normally."

I flip my tube under and hold my breath until I see stars. When I come up for air Sarah claps. "That was almost two minutes. New record. Desperation looks good on you."

"Thanks." I get out and wrap a giant towel robe around myself and pour an oversized glass of rosé. "Even if we record together, I can't talk about Cassidy. It's honestly even worse that he dated her just to dump her. Like, what, is no woman good enough for him? I can't talk about us. About any of that."

Sarah's quiet for a minute, running her hands through the water. "I mean, Maeve," she says finally. "That's the show."

"There has to be another way," I mutter. I pull out my phone and start reading the comments on the Insta teaser Finn posted for the episode. He did a good job, playing up the gamified aspect of the recording style. But the comments are brutal. Girls say I was boring but that at least Finn was hot. I know I was a bit stiff solo, but it burns that even though I gave great advice during the show, they didn't want it. I put real thought into what I said, while Finn joked around, clearly not having prepared at all. I expected him to put more into it. It's almost like he's trying to sabotage this format, since I know he wants to record together.

"Maybe they just need to get used to it," I hedge. I don't know what to do. I want to beat Paul Myers. I want to make a show that I'm proud of. But I really feel like recording with Finn will destroy me right now. I need more time. Maybe three years or so.

"Finn is not worth ruining all of this over." Sarah gestures to the house behind me. She doesn't say it, but I know she's also thinking of the family expenses I've picked up: her tuition bills, our parents' mortgage, the pageant dresses and soccer cleats. I'm happy that I'm able to help out, even if I had to switch the full family group chat to "Do Not Disturb" and make the new one with just my sisters because I was so tired of seeing my mom send photos of the dresses and soccer trophies instead of screenshots of my place in the podcast charts. "Why don't you just go to the party and talk to him? See if he can make it five minutes without talking about the off-limits topics. Maybe you two can call a truce. I feel like if you recorded some episodes together, even if they're about random stuff like this one was, they'd go over fine. And I'll go with you."

What Sarah doesn't get is that even if he obeys Shazia's terms and doesn't bring up our personal lives . . . knowing he doesn't love me like I loved him makes my insides feel like they're being wrung out every time I look at him. Every time we talk and it feels like what we had before, it *hurts*. But she's right. What else can I really do? "Fine, we'll go."

FOUR

Two years before the Streamify contract

Maeve

I try to roll over in bed and nearly fall onto the floor. And then it hits me. *Fuck. This is not my bed.* I gather myself and with surgical precision extract myself from the bed without waking the man next to me. He's some sort of Chad . . . or maybe it was Brad. Or Pete? I don't know, but he works in investment banking and paid the tab for not just me but both of my roommates last night. And given the pounding headache I have, and the fact that I didn't slink away to my own place last night, I'm guessing it must have been quite the tab.

Once I've gathered my clothes from the floor and am safely in the bathroom with the door locked, I pull out my phone. Five percent battery. Fuck. I knew this guy wasn't a keeper. I *always*, no matter how intoxicated I am, plug my phone in. And when I got up, it was his that was attached to the cable on the nightstand. I use my last few percents of battery life to text Finn.

walk of shame and Jamie's?

battery is dying so meet me there

Somehow sending those measly two texts have dropped me from five percent to one. I go through the bathroom drawers until I find a ten pack of toothbrushes and rip one out of the plastic. By the time I've freshened up and tried and failed to make my crop top and mini skirt look less . . . small, my phone dings with a text from Finn.

be there in twenty

And then my phone dies. I throw my shoulders back and walk into the bedroom, where the quasi-unidentified man is still snoring. I let the door slam behind me. He doesn't flinch. I sigh heavily and poke him in the back firmly.

He rolls over. "Babe, get back in bed. I'll Uber Eats us something."

There is literally no way. "I actually need to head out . . ." I smile apologetically as I hand him his phone. "My phone is dead. Can you call me an Uber?"

He fumbles to unlock it then just hands it to me and rolls over. "Put your number in too," he mutters.

I don't do that. But I do spring for the Uber Black.

Fifteen minutes later I'm walking into the diner and dropping into a booth with Finn. We started this tradition not long after moving to New York, and I'm always pleasantly surprised by how much I enjoy it. Back in college we were definitely in the same friend group, but we weren't the kind of friends that hung out one-on-one. But ever since we moved to the city and most of our friends dispersed elsewhere, we've gotten much closer. Finn did flashcards with me for my clinical psychologist licensure exam, and I bring him a homemade dinner when he works late into the night at

Morgan Stanley. But our most consistent tradition is the walk of shame brunch.

Before I can say anything, the waitress is bringing over food. "I already ordered," Finn explains as she sets everything down.

With someone else it might annoy me that they ordered for me. What if I wanted to change it up? But we have a strict diner tradition that holds firm regardless of the time of day. Milkshakes, two of the strangest dishes on the menu, and if we're really hungover, one normal breakfast item.

Once everything is on the table, Finn begins narrating his choices. "Coffee, because duh. Chocolate shake for you, strawberry for me. Fruity Pebbles French toast, and veggie chicken and waffles but with reaper seasoning. I thought these were close enough to normal that we didn't need more."

"Definitely not," I agree. "But honestly, if the waffles are too spicy from the chicken, I might throw up."

Finn raises an eyebrow. "That bad? Let's debrief."

"Well, for starters, I really don't remember his name. He had an amazing place, and if it's all coming back to me correctly, he actually did go down on me. Like, really well. But rich, cocky, boring, and probably trying to overcome all his childhood insecurities by dropping a ton of money on women and nights out. We didn't actually connect at all."

Finn smirks, his tone teasing. "Well, what do you always say . . ."

"'You're never going to meet the one after ten p.m.,'" I recite dutifully. "Ugh. I wish I hadn't stayed over. I passed out and didn't wake up in time to leave."

"No! *You* stayed over? I thought that was a third-date-only privilege." He widens his eyes in mock horror before shoving a giant bite of the purple-crusted French toast into his mouth.

I nod woefully. "I *know*. And he unplugged my phone from the charger and plugged his in. The audacity! But I didn't leave my number, so nothing too crazy." I take a long sip of milkshake, then coffee, still skeptical about the chicken and waffles. "Your turn. You had a real date!"

"It didn't exactly turn out that way . . . I bought her dinner, and everything was going well, so I was going to whip out one of your tricks and—"

"Tricks? I don't have tricks. I have tips," I correct primly. I cut the tiniest bite of wing and waffle and pop it in my mouth, only to be hit with a wave of spice so strong that I think I might have a heart attack. I immediately take such a giant sip of my milkshake that suddenly my grimace is due to both spice and brain freeze.

"Whatever. I was going to take her for a walk and get flowers from a street vendor. But she wanted to go to Marquee."

"No!" I exclaim as tears run down my face from the spice. "Not Marquee. Anywhere but Marquee. Don't tell me you went and ruined a perfectly nice date by clubbing. You're horrible at clubbing."

Finn nods grimly and cuts his own bite of the chicken and waffles. "I clubbed. Or I tried." He starts to chew and winces, his eyes immediately turning red. Within a few seconds I can see his face sweating from every pore.

"Finn, you are amazing at dinner. You're good at a speakeasy or cocktail bar, where you can talk, and charm, and use your knowledge of fancy drinks. But you dance like a broken marionette."

Finn snorts into his milkshake, which he's started chugging to try to assuage the spice of the chicken and waffles. "Please, like you're any better," he chokes out finally. "You faked food poisoning to get out of clubbing two weeks ago."

I roll my eyes dramatically. "How'd you end the night? Did you kiss at least?"

Finn sighs and rolls his shoulders. "I think she got the ick. After like an hour and a half I got her an Uber. We didn't even kiss goodbye. In bed before midnight, and I doubt I'm getting a second date."

"Give me your phone. And what's her name?"

"Kelsea." He hands the phone over and begins to plow through the remainder of the French toast while I compose a text.

Hey Kelsea! I had a great time last night. I know my dance moves are horrible and I hope they didn't scare you off. I'd love to take you out again and hear more about

"What is Kelsea's passion? Or job? Hobby? I need something you learned about her."

"Taylor Swift needlepoint," Finn responds quickly.

Hey Kelsea! I had a great time last night. I'd love to take you out again and hear more about your Taylor inspired needlepoint and get to know you better. I know my dance moves are horrible, but I hope you can shake it off and give me a shot at a second date ☺

I hand the phone back to him before hitting send and he reads it over. "Are you sure it's not too much? Like, why bring up the dance moves, can't we just leave the awkward in the past? And I don't want to seem like her stalker with the needlepoint."

"You need to show her that you care and pay more attention than the average guy she goes out with. And I made the dance move thing lighthearted with the Taylor pun. You can't not say something; otherwise, the ick will be too strong. Just send it! You have literally nothing to lose."

Finn shrugs and hits send.

Within five minutes she's responded, agreeing to a second date, *and* sent a pink heart emoji. "I should do this for a living," I exclaim.

"Um, Maeve, you literally do."

"A living is a stretch. I need to find a private-practice job now that

I've finished my supervision hours, because I am done making no money. The Columbia kids never take my advice anyway, and I don't get to work with any one patient long enough to make a difference. In therapy I want to help them come to their own answers, but I can't do that if I don't have the time to actually work with them week after week. With you I just get to tell you how I really feel about all of it, help you fix the problem, and then you learn from it for next time. It's giving advice not therapy, but honestly, I love it. And you know I'm good! I should have a podcast." I take the French toast plate away from Finn and try the last bite. Who knew Fruity Pebbles could be so . . . delicious?

When I look at Finn, his eyes are wide and he's gone still. "Maeve. That's it. You actually do need a podcast. And you need to call it *Tell Me How You Really Feel*."

I laugh. But something about that title sends a chill down my spine. It's actually not bad. "Don't be ridiculous. Podcasts are for, like, true crime detectives, which, I mean, we love. And middle-aged white guys who have nothing to say, which, like, we hate. But I'm nobody. I'm not the kind of person who starts a podcast."

Finn shakes his head adamantly. "No, no, no. This is your future. I'm so serious. Podcasts are huge now, and you would be so good at it. And you *love* podcasts! You send me clips of that crime one literally daily. Every block we walk down, you've listened to a podcast episode about a murder on it. You could have a show where you'd give relationship advice, but 'real talk' style like this. And it's actually smart advice because you're a real therapist."

I take a huge gulp of coffee. This is suddenly sounding like too good of an idea, and I need my hangover headache gone so I can think about it properly. "Who would I even have on the show? I don't know enough people."

"I don't know. Maybe you could just tell our stories. Or people can write in with questions."

I drain the rest of my coffee cup, so energized by this idea that my hangover feels like a distant memory. "Do it with me," I say. "Let's record just like this. We can literally record our morning-after debriefs, and then put it out on Sunday afternoons."

Finn's face breaks into a huge grin. "Let's do it. *Tell Me How You Really Feel* starts now."

FIVE

Finn

Seeing Maeve in our living room quite literally knocks the air out of my lungs. She's with her sister, who is shooting daggers at me. If looks could kill . . . But I can't look away from Maeve in that dress. The skirt is black, but the top is the *exact* color of her skin, with black lace flowers creeping upward from the skirt. Everything is covered, but it also looks like she's wearing almost nothing.

Suddenly a hand is on my shoulder, although I barely register it. Maeve still hasn't noticed me, and her sister is subtly moving in front of her so she won't see me. "She looks good, doesn't she? I had my stylist send over dresses for them."

My mom's voice is low in my ear. Sarah blocks my view and I turn toward my mom, finally listening. "You did what? Mom! You need to stay out of it."

"There's no reason I shouldn't be able to meet such a talented young woman in entertainment just because my son acted like an idiot. Now introduce me." She starts walking toward Maeve, and I seriously consider tripping her. Her heels are so tall, it would definitely look like an accident. I hesitate for a moment, then rush after her because she's already wrapping Maeve in a hug. She towers over her, and Maeve's face is quite literally smashed against my mother's half-exposed chest. This is humiliating. "It is so great to meet you! I'm Evangeline," my mom gushes. "I have listened to every episode, and you are a genius. The talent! And Finn tells me you handle the recording and editing. I have people for that, if you want them. . . . But anyhow, it is incredible and I am so happy to meet you."

She finally stops for air and I speak into the lingering pause. "Maeve, this is my mom. Mom, Maeve." Maeve always feels awkward at parties. Usually we're a unit, chatting with people, sharing snarky comments, getting inspiration for episodes. I'm sure she feels especially out of place here since everyone is an A-lister except her and Sarah. Despite the success of *Tell Me How You Really Feel*, she's still more like celebrity adjacent than a true celebrity, although I suspect our Streamify deal will soon change that.

Sarah opens her mouth, probably to take the opportunity to ream me out in front of my mom, but Maeve jumps in. She smiles, and if I didn't know her better, I would think it was real. "Of course. It is so great to meet you. My sister and I grew up watching you. And thank you so much for the dresses, the styling . . . we had so much fun."

"You deserve it after what he put you through." I think I'm in a waking nightmare because Cassidy has somehow materialized on my other side. She cuts me a glance, then continues. "Finn, just leave. Let us all talk."

I think I am going to throw up. Or die, or combust. Is this real? I look to Maeve, because whatever she wants me to do, I will. She's the only person I can read in a glance. I always thought that was a myth in books: that one look could tell you exactly what someone was thinking. But with Maeve, I've spent so many hours staring at her, at her bony knuckles while she edits, at the slight gap in her left eyebrow, from when she fell off her bike, the way she pushes her hair behind her ears when she's uncomfortable, widens her eyes just the tiniest bit before narrowing them when she's shocked but won't say it, the one silver filling in her back teeth that's visible when she laughs genuinely. I know more from one glance at her face than an entire conversation with anyone else.

She gives me an almost imperceptible nod, or maybe it's just a flicker of her eyes, and I turn and leave them, my hands shaking. I used to think I was so confident. But really, I just had nothing I cared about losing.

I pour myself two fingers of whiskey and take it out to the pool. Yes, the pool. The infinity pool that my parents put in even though we live at the beach. Actually, they likely put it in because we live at a *public* beach. I didn't realize it was strange to put in a pool when you live on the water until I mentioned it to Maeve and she promptly laughed in my face at the decadence. It's hard for me to know whether Cassidy is helping Maeve plot my imminent demise or telling her that I really do love her. I'm desperately trying to eavesdrop when the CEO of Streamify plops down on the pool chair next to me.

"Finn, my man. How's it going?" Derek is pushing sixty-five but likes to pretend he's twenty. And his girlfriends actually are. Streamify's was the only offer we seriously considered, since they wouldn't take our IP because what they wanted was platform exclusivity. But knowing that they also signed Paul Myers makes me want to back out of the contract altogether. I would, if I didn't know Maeve actually needs the money.

"Ah, all right." I do my best to appear chill and not like I'm watching my life combust. "You?"

Derek claps me on the back. "I'd be better if one of my biggest buys of the year didn't just bomb their first episode back. Those memes? That we're forcing you two to be here? Not funny."

I drink the rest of my whiskey in one gulp. "We're just getting into the swing of things."

"No, you're not. You two are on ice. But it's not too late to sign the solo show. If you two drop below the top one hundred in the first three months, we can terminate the *Tell Me How You Really Feel* contract."

My blood runs cold. I'm not cutting Maeve out. This show is the only shot I have at turning things around with her. And she *deserves* all this and more. "We can turn it around. We just had a scheduling conflict. It was my fault."

This time the hand that touches my back makes me jump. Because I know Maeve's touch. So light that it almost feels like a soft puff of wind or a butterfly. Her hands are always ice cold, and she uses this maple-scented lotion that makes me crave pancakes. She sits next to me on the chair, and it's like every cell in my body breathes a sigh of relief to be allowed next to her again. I don't know how I've made it through this many days without her next to me.

Derek smiles widely, even though seconds ago he was telling me he wanted to axe her. "Maeve! You look stunning. We need to get you out to more events. You two look great *together*." He raises an eyebrow pointedly.

"Thank you, Derek," she says sweetly. I hate how he's looking at her.

"Derek was just saying that if we drop below the top one hundred in the first three months, they can terminate the contract." I've spent enough time talking to my mother and Maeve to know how often women are left out of the important business meetings because they happen at boys' clubs and golf courses. Even though my instinct is to keep her from worrying, I'm not going to leave her on the outside of these backdoor meetings about the show she started. Especially not when the theme of the night is pay gap equality.

I feel Maeve stiffen almost imperceptibly next to me, but she doesn't visibly react. "Well, I wouldn't worry about that. We have a *great* episode planned for next week. Finn's mom is coming on the show!"

Derek brightens considerably. "Finn! You should've just said so. This will be great stuff, maybe we can get some photos of the three of you here to promo it. I'll get my guy on it."

Before we can argue, he's lumbering away, barking orders into his phone. Maeve and I are left sitting alone, so close I can feel her shiver. I turn toward her and she looks down at her wineglass, hiding her face from me. "Is that true? About the cancelation?" Maeve asks.

I'm surprised she has to ask. Even though I typically took charge of contract negotiations with our old sponsors, she always read them so carefully that I joked she should just take over. I take advantage of her being so close to me to examine her. She looks as beautiful as ever, but I can tell she has dark circles under her eyes, shielded by makeup. And she has a smattering of acne along her temple, where she always breaks out when she's stressed. I hate that her pain is my fault. "Yes. But that isn't going to happen. Is it true that my mom wants to be in an episode?"

"Yes," she says, and she tears her eyes up to look at me. And it kills me, because they're wet. No tears have fallen, but I can see her blinking them back, see the agony in her dark brown eyes. Because she has to talk to me.

"I'm sorry," I blurt out. "I—"

"Finn!" Her voice cracks. "Stop. Shazia meant what she said. I *can't* be always worrying about everything coming up. I can't talk about it. If we're going to work together at all, our relationships have to be off-limits."

I don't know how we're going to bring the ratings up long-term if we do that. But I would agree to anything she wants right now to alleviate even a fraction of the stress she's feeling. Although I know Maeve's been managing her anxiety pretty well the past few years, I can tell that she's on the verge of a panic attack. "Whatever you want. I won't bring it up, I promise."

"Thank you," she breathes. One tear starts to fall, and when I go to dab it with my napkin, she flinches.

I pull away, chastened. "Sorry."

She ignores me and wipes it away herself, just as Derek barrels out of the house with a photographer, Cassidy (bearing her phone), and my mom in tow. "Photoshoot time!" he commands.

I want to tell them that now is *not* the time. But when I look to Maeve for permission, she doesn't make eye contact with me, and instead she turns to them and pastes a smile on. "Let's do it!" She offers me a hand, and I help her up because apparently when we're faking it, touching is okay.

The sun is setting behind us, and the view is gorgeous. We let the photographer arrange us. First, we do a few shots with me between my mom and Maeve. Then he takes a few of Maeve and me, her tucked into my chest. I let my chin rest on the top of her head, which is possible thanks to her heels, and for a moment I feel her lean into it, and her eyes flutter shut. It hurts to look at her because I know it feels right for her too, but I've ruined it. I've ruined everything. Without her, I feel directionless, untethered. I look up, and right as I do the camera flashes.

"Those eyes," the photographer mutters. He turns the camera toward us, and Maeve breaks away to look at it. I feel exposed, like everything I feel is written on my face. But Derek just takes a picture of the preview with his cell and texts it to someone, then starts giving more instructions.

My mom takes my hand and squeezes it once, quickly. For the first time since all of this has happened, she looks worried, and if I had to hazard a guess, I would say it's because now she realizes Maeve isn't just another girl to me. She's everything.

We launch into a series of goofy shots, Maeve and my mom tugging on my arms, them whispering to each other while Maeve holds me off with a palm to the face, us playing rock paper scissors, and me picking her up and throwing her over my shoulder. Cassidy takes videos and air-drops them to Derek for social, but she looks more pained by the second. Even though we're doing fun-looking things, the mood is more somber than playful.

"Can we get one more? Maybe you two with Cassidy?"

"No." Maeve and Cassidy say it simultaneously.

My mom jumps in too, speaking directly to the photographer. "We're done here, thank you."

Derek rolls his eyes. "Whatever. Thanks all, great stuff. Can't wait to see those ratings!" He's walking away before we can say anything else, and the four of us are left there, the request looming.

"Finn, honey, can you help me in the kitchen?" I follow my mom out gratefully, after checking that Maeve isn't giving a wide-eyed "please don't leave me with her" look. She pointedly is talking to Cassidy and ignoring me.

My mom leads me to a spare bedroom, since the kitchen is actually full of caterers and bartenders. She takes her heels off and starts massaging her feet. I sit next to her on the bed, but it's at least two minutes of silence, just her groaning as she gives her feet a break from the heels. "Maeve is lovely," she remarks finally.

"She is."

"If this was one of my movies, I'd tell you to make a huge gesture, sweep her off her feet, and apologize. But this is real life. So you need to start by being happy with just being her friend. With potentially always just being her friend. If you can get that foundation back, you can work from there."

"That's not very romantic." My voice is pinched.

"That's because what you two have is real."

I nod. I can do this. I can be her friend. I'd rather be that than nothing to her. "I can start there."

"Good. Now get back out there and let her sister yell at you. You won't get anywhere if her family still hates you."

SIX

Maeve

My head is spinning as I walk out of the party. I *cannot* lose this podcast. I've worked too hard on it. It's supposed to be one for them, one for me. A few years of in-your-face content that exploits my privacy, and then my own show once fans care enough about me to watch me without Finn. But that's never going to happen. I grab my keys from the valet Evangeline hired and start to get into my car.

"Maeve! Wait, wait." Finn is running out of the house, chasing after me. "Can we please talk about this?"

I sit in the driver's seat, and Finn grabs my door, stopping it from closing. It shouldn't be so sexy, seeing his palm straining against the door I was about to close, the other arm braced against the car. My stomach twists despite myself as I remember the last time those hands were on me . . . but I push the thoughts away firmly. "What more is there to say? We'll record with your mom, get the ratings up, then get back to normal." Or a version of it.

"*Maeve*. Please. Don't let hating me keep you from making *Tell Me How You Really Feel* great. Let's go to a diner like we used to in New York, have a brainstorm sesh." Before I can interject, he rushes to continue. "I know it's not like it was. But let's find a new way to make this work, instead of putting a Band-Aid on it. Come on."

I let go of the door and clutch the steering wheel with white knuckles. I hate that he's right. "Fine. Get in."

Twenty minutes later, Finn has directed me to a tiny diner on the outskirts of his neighborhood. It's inside of a vintage cable car that they've restored to be the tiniest of diners. It's cute. I wish it were a soulless chain restaurant so I wouldn't have to, for the millionth time, be charmed by the places Finn took me to. We used to go to diners all the time in New York during our walk of shame debriefs, the twenty-four-hour kind, not the hipster avocado-toast brunch places our college friends frequented. Finn would spend hours researching, finding the most unique places. Once, he even rented a car to take me to a speakeasy-style diner in the Hudson Valley. He took me to the diner from *When Harry Met Sally* and reenacted the orgasm scene in reverse, inspiring viral videos from other customers and invoking a lifetime ban for both of us.

The moment we sit down, Finn scans the menu, and when the waiter comes to take our order, he places it without consulting me. Which would have been sweet before, but now it irks me. "We'll have the crab rangoon omelet, a chocolate shake, a strawberry shake, and coffees please."

The waitress winces when he orders the omelet. "And scrambled eggs with toast," I add.

She nods eagerly at this logical half of the order. "On it."

When I look away from her and toward Finn, he looks hurt. "That omelet is going to be awful," I say.

"I know. That's why we have the milkshakes."

I stare at him. He doesn't get to be the person who knows me best anymore. I need to keep space between us because I won't be able to do this if I feel like he still occupies half of my brain. "So. You wanted to brainstorm?"

Finn wipes the crushed expression off his face. I really can't take his hurt feelings seriously because I know he doesn't hold my feelings as carefully as I've always held his. I always thought that everyone else just didn't understand how sensitive and thoughtful he is. That his brasher, bolder, naïve nepo-baby spoiled persona was just that, a persona. But in reality, he was acting with me.

"Right. So, just to lay it all on the table . . . our relationships are off-limits. Our show is giving each other relationship advice so we can find love. My mom is coming on this week, and she is famous. No one wants to hear us do our show separately. No spark, yada yada." I roll my eyes to hide how much it stings that our fans hate having me solo. That I'm not talented enough. That without Finn none of this would have happened. "If we drop in the ratings, we're axed, and—"

"I'm axed," I interrupt. "You're fine."

"There's no me without you, Maeve." Finn's tone is earnest, heavy with emotion. He'll be a great actor once he's done with this show. Done with me. "I'm not going to do a show without you."

I don't say anything for a moment, and the waitress arrives with our milkshakes and food. She wrinkles her nose at the offensive omelet, which reeks. After she leaves, I lean toward Finn. "Don't eat it. You're going to get food poisoning. You need to be alive to record."

Finn grabs his fork and cuts a piece directly from the center. Crab mush drips from his fork. He holds eye contact with me as he puts it into his mouth. He stifles a gag as he chews and swallows. "I'm not going to ruin our streak. We've tried everything else."

We used to count as one. If he tried, it would count for both of us. "Your streak now." The smile in his eyes dims, and for the first time since all of this, I feel a tiny bit bad for refusing to let him back in. But I know what Sarah would say. What Shazia would say. *Fuck him.*

"Maybe we should have guests," Finn blurts out. "Beyond my mom. Other shows have guests, and it really boosts them."

I know he's thinking of *The Paul Myers Show*. Paul Myers will have anyone on, the more extreme the better. And he goads them into saying inflammatory things for ratings. But, each guest does bring their fan base with them, and many of those people stay. And having celebs on the show generates press. Previously, we held off on guests despite people begging to come on, because we didn't want to let anyone disrupt our dynamic. But there's no dynamic left.

"Starting with Evangeline is huge. Seeing her on it will make other A-listers want in. Do you think they'd actually be willing to talk about their sex and relationships with us? I don't want to go so off topic, talking about their movies and random stuff."

"If that's our requirement for them to come on. And if my mom does it." Finn smiles, and I'm reflexively grinning back before I can stop myself, which only makes him light up more. I forgot what it was like to brainstorm with him. How *alive* it makes me feel, like every brain cell is firing and we can only go up.

"I could provide more serious advice. Tap back into how I used to be a real therapist at the counseling center. And you could offer a guy's perspective like usual. Banter, keep them comfortable. Thank god I finished everything so I can say I'm a fully licensed therapist now."

"You mean your five thousand hours of supervision? That was brutal."

"It was only three thousand."

"Ah, only three thousand. That's nothing."

I smile in spite of myself. Back when I was completing my master's and getting my clinical and supervision hours, it felt like I would never be done. I remember Finn comforting me at a diner a lot like this while I went down an anxiety spiral over not being a full therapist and making real money until I was twenty-five, almost twenty-six really, as I liked to point out when I was feeling especially anxious. Little did I know that basically the moment I finished supervision the show would take off, and at twenty-seven I'd have an amount of money in my bank account that I couldn't even fathom. I take a huge sip of my chocolate milkshake as though sugar will make me forget all those years that Finn was truly my best friend, and I recoil with brain freeze.

"You always do that," Finn whispers.

"I can't help it. I need to wipe away the thought of you throwing up that omelet in your mouth. It's revolting."

"Guilty as charged." Finn takes a much more reasonable sip of his shake, then goes to reach for mine. And stops himself, folds his hands in his lap. He's probably getting grease all over his expensive tux. I'm going to destroy this dress with how much I'm sweating in it, from the stress and exhilaration of being around Finn. "I think this is a great idea, though. We'll get that celeb boost. It's a transition, so it explains why we're not talking about . . . us. And Maeve, you'll be so amazing at this. You're great on the show now, but you could be doing so much more."

"I was actually thinking about doing my own show at some point," I blurt out. "I want to do like, serious therapy, with regular people. And let listeners in on every minute of it, plus add some commentary of my own so it helps the listeners more." A blush rises on my cheeks. I wish I had more makeup on. I'm so pale that I can't hide anything when I'm embarrassed; even my ears turn pink. I shouldn't be telling him this. It's extra, beyond the talking we need to do to work together.

"I think that's brilliant. Why aren't you already doing it? I'm sure Streamify would fund a second show for you."

I shake my head. Of course, Finn thinks everyone has the same privilege he does. He's never understood when I or friends of ours worried about things, whether it was the cost of an Uber to the airport or not being able to get in to a master's program. If he wasn't so generous, he'd be infuriating. "We're not all a celebrity, Finn. They won't. They want us together, not me solo. Maybe in a few years when we've proved ourselves."

He looks angry. His jaw flexes and I can tell he's grinding his teeth, a flash of irritation in his clear eyes. "That's such bullshit. You're smarter than anyone on their roster now. Your show would be the best thing that ever happened to them. Why don't I talk to Derek, I think—"

I feel a burning sensation in my nose and the back of my eyes and try to convince myself it's brain freeze, not impending tears. I blink rapidly to keep them from spilling over my lashes and leaving black streaks down my cheeks. When I get anxious like this, I cry easily, and despite all these years working on myself—the time I spent in therapy is what made me want to be a therapist in the first place—I feel embarrassed that I'm so emotional around Finn now. I hate that this is what our relationship has turned into. I don't know why I ever thought Finn and I would work together. He doesn't understand what it's like to be a real person. Right now, I feel like I'm cosplaying at being a low-level celebrity, but the last few years he was cosplaying at being a normal guy while he took a break from being *famous* famous. It's all been a lark for him; I'm twice as serious and still never going to catch up to what he was born into. And I *don't* want him fighting my battles for me. I'll earn the show through hard work and good ratings. And even then, I won't get the respect; everyone will still say it was handed to me, or that I just talk about sex, or whatever disparaging, sexist thing is brought out next to disparage women like me who actually care about our careers and striving. "You don't get it," I snap. "We don't have to talk about it. And don't talk to Derek."

I take one more long sip of my milkshake and put it back down on the table. "I'll see you when we record." And then I clomp out in my heels, and it only burns slightly more than it would've before we talked when I look over my shoulder and see that Finn is shamelessly watching me leave.

In therapy this week I found myself lamenting the fact that I've never felt anything *close* to what I've felt for Finn with anyone else. My therapist suggested that maybe he's the one person I actually let in, and that seriously dating other people could help. But I lasted all of five minutes with my dating apps downloaded before the anxiety got to me and I deleted them all again. I don't have it in me to open up when I'm already going to have to reopen my deepest wound every week when we record together.

And the mood in the studio on Tuesday is *tense*. I go in early and set up a fourth and fifth camera with Leo so that we have a close-up on Evangeline and a duo shot of her and Finn. Seeing them next to each other is eerie. Although Finn has a lot of his dad's features and a more masculine jaw, he's definitely a pretty boy. And their light blue eyes are absolutely stunning. I would tune in just to get to see them together.

Finn teased the episode with a few of the photos of the three of us from the party, and our fans freaked out. We got thousands of messages, with questions people wanted us to ask Evangeline during Questions of the Week, and fans wanting to know if Finn and I were on the rocks. And then when Streamify shared the money shot of Finn and me . . . it was picked up by every outlet and shared over a hundred thousand times by fans speculating that we've been keeping things quiet because we're together. Fat chance. They don't know that Finn would never *seriously* date someone who isn't of his pedigree. That he'd only ever be into me for fun while he kept looking for the real deal.

"Wow, I feel like I'm on a movie set. In someone's wet dream," Evangeline jokes.

"Mom!" Finn flinches. "We're recording already."

"What! You two said you wanted me to talk about the ole razzle dazzle."

Finn moans and drops his head to the table, which is sans penis mics. "Oh my god. Don't ever call it that again."

I jump in. "And we're back with another episode of *Tell Me How You Really Feel*. Today we have our inaugural guest . . . Evangeline Sutton!"

"AKA, my mom," Finn adds.

"I think they *know* that, Finn. You're basically her clone," I tease. It is much easier to play nice with him when we have a chaperone present. Evangeline looks pleased by our back-and-forth, her gaze traveling between us while her eyes twinkle.

Finn leans over and wraps his arm around his mom so their heads are next to each other. "I just don't see it." Now I'm the one rolling my eyes. "But anyway, you're right, Mom. We did bring you here to get into the nitty gritty. Sex, relationships, all of that. No need to keep it PG, even though I may have to go to therapy to get this wiped from my memory."

"Aw Finn, you have a therapist sitting right in front of you. I think you'll live." I sound flirtatious. I've listened to a lot of our old episodes this past week, to try to make sure I can emulate the old version of me, and not sound like I would love nothing more than to pulverize Finn's heart like he did mine. In all of our episodes, we sound like we're seconds away from turning off the mic and taking off our clothes. The chemistry is frankly oppressive.

"Agreed!" Evangeline remarks. "I didn't raise you to be afraid of sex talk. And since I'm your first ever guest, I'd love to kick this off with a bang. I am all about eliminating the gaps in our society. The pay gap. The academic achievement gap. And . . ." She hits the table, right in the center of the vagina, where the clit would be if it was more anatomically accurate. "The orgasm gap."

Evangeline makes eye contact with me meaningfully. We did a precall to talk through what she would be comfortable discussing, and she told me she was willing to talk about how she and Richard overcame a glaring orgasm gap. I jump in. "For those of you listeners who haven't heard of the orgasm gap—"

Finn coughs into the mic. "Heterosexual men!"

"It's referring to the disparity in orgasm frequency between men and women. Studies vary, but some show that in heterosexual relationships ninety-five percent of men orgasm during sex, while only sixty-three percent of women can say the same. Which is strange, because men and women are *equally* as likely to orgasm while masturbating."

"So basically, men suck and aren't focused on female pleasure," Finn jumps in, with the layman's perspective.

"In a way, yes," I agree. "But it's not entirely their fault. Media, from movies to books to standard porn, all depict sex in a way that focuses solely on male pleasure. It doesn't pass the clit test, so to speak, since they don't acknowledge the clit at all. And did you know that if a movie has a female orgasm, it's often rated NC-17 instead of R, while a male orgasm can get away with a PG-13 rating? Anyways, for most women, the clit needs to be stimulated for them to orgasm." I turn toward Evangeline. "So Evangeline, what is your experience with the orgasm gap?"

Evangeline smiles widely, knowing that this clip will go viral. "For the first year of my relationship with Richard, my husband of thirty-one years, I *never* orgasmed. Not once."

Finn's jaw drops. "Dad! Come on!"

Evangeline nods. "I know, right? But back then, no one was having conversations about sex like you two do. I was in my twenties, and I'd only had a bit of good sex. And when I met your dad, we fell hard for each other. We're still falling for each other every day, as I'm sure Finn knows."

"I can confirm. Since moving back to LA I've seen them make out more times than any son should have to. It's like they forgot how to shut the door." Finn turns toward his mom. "So I know dad must have figured out how to get something right. What changed after that first year?"

"What changed is that we started talking about sex. He thought he had to act all macho and try to please me like he'd seen in the movies, especially since I was a literal movie star." Evangeline flicks her hair. Maybe I'll throw up a few paparazzi or premiere photos of her here in the edit. She was huge after their *Malibu Rising* adaptation came out, right when she started getting serious with Richard. "He didn't even know where the clit *was*, since there was almost no sexual education back then. And I thought I was supposed to act like he was doing a great job, even though he wasn't even close to getting me to orgasm. Which irked me! Because it's so much easier for guys to come, he was batting a thousand. And most of my friends, even other married actresses who were so gorgeous and successful, were used to almost never orgasming with their partners. They just advised me to buy a great vibrator and use it while he was in the shower afterward. So I didn't know what to do, especially because everything else in our relationship was perfect. He was my soulmate, I was completely certain. But I didn't know if I could commit to a life without orgasms. I remember when I brought it up to him, I was so nervous that he would take it badly and that it would be the end of us. But now, I'm *so* happy that I was open and fought for my pleasure. Because Richard loves me and wanted to learn how to make me feel amazing. It turned out it was actually a relief for him to be told exactly what I liked so he wasn't fumbling around in the dark."

It's hard to believe that Evangeline is willing to be this open with us. To let us air this. Even now, although sex is much less taboo, I speak much more openly—and graphically—about it than other women do publicly. And household name celebrities just don't. This will break the internet. "What exactly did you say to Richard back then?"

Evangeline tilts her head, thinking. "I think it was something like, *'Babe, you know how I said I always come when we have sex? I lied. It's never gonna happen unless you figure out how to touch me.'* Not very eloquent. I think I definitely could have gone about it better. But after we had a heated conversation initially, we were able to talk about what I actually needed from him and it worked better from there. Even now, we're still learning new things about each other. But Maeve, I'm curious. Since you are a licensed therapist, what would you have said?"

We hadn't discussed this, but I appreciate the question. It gives me a chance to show off my actual skills, and edges me a tiny bit closer to my solo show. "Well first off, let me say that having the conversation at all is better than holding it in. It's amazing that you brought it up and advocated for your O, even though your friends were accepting way less. But, what I would say is to have the conversation out of the bedroom, and to keep it positive. The bedroom should be for fun stuff, sleeping, sex, cuddling—"

"Does that mean no more podcasting and takeout in bed?" Finn asks with a pout.

"Maybe if you ask nicely . . ." I tease. "But seriously, I'd have these conversations on the couch, in the car, at the dinner table. Somewhere private, but less intimate. And it's easy for a partner to feel attacked or emasculated when they find out they haven't been doing it for you. So, a great way to have the conversation can be to frame it in a positive way. So instead of saying, 'What you're doing is *so* bad. I literally never come,' you could say, 'Babe, I love you so much, and although sex does make me feel close to you, I'd really love to come every time. What you're doing now does feel good, but can I tell you, or show you, what would feel incredible and make me come so hard?'"

Finn leans into the mic. "Maeve, I think you're a genius. If a girl told me that, I wouldn't even realize she's saying I'm not doing it for her yet. I'd be turned on!"

"You heard it here first, people," Evangeline jokes.

We spend another hour recording with Evangeline, and I step back and let Finn take more of the lead on Questions of the Week since I was all in on the beginning. And even though it's hard to jump back into this teasing, flirty dynamic with Finn, I leave the studio with a smile on my face. I *know* this week's episode will be a hit.

SEVEN

Finn

"I'm sorry, but this is ridiculous." Maeve should be excited, but instead she just sounds stressed. "Since when do podcasters get to go to the Met Gala? That has never happened. Did your mom set this up?"

"Um, no. Maybe now that they're dropping movie money on us, we get that movie star treatment."

Maeve is right. Our episode with my mom was the most listened to episode ever on Streamify. All of her famous actress friends shared it on social, it went mega viral, and we've been at number one in the ratings ever since. We usually do well. Really well, like top three or top five. But not most listened to ever well.

Now, there is no way Streamify is even going to considering axing the show. In fact, they want to pour money into PR for it, and their first big idea was sending the two of us to the Met Gala for one of our mandated events together. And these aren't side entrance Met

Gala tickets . . . we get to walk the carpet. We're under strict orders to 'act like we like each other' and not to confirm or deny a relationship, despite Maeve's vehement protests and declaration that she wants the world to know she is *not* with me. Derek wants to play up the speculation, and said that when we're ready to talk about our not relationship on the show we can be honest. Until now, we do the mandated monthly appearances and lean into this gray area of almost (but not quite) fake dating.

I'll take it.

We're in the car that's taking us to the hotel, where we each have separate glam teams to get us ready. Or, rather, Maeve has a glam team and I have a groomer, the decidedly creepy name Hollywood uses for men's glam artists so we don't feel emasculated. "Think about it like this. We get to go to the Met Gala. How awesome! It'll be fun even though I have to spend time with my cohost, whom I hate. Maybe I'll hate him less after a few drinks. How's that?"

Maeve turns completely away from me and stares out the window. "I feel like we're on *Punk'd*. There's no way this is real."

"Maeve, come on. I know you felt overlooked growing up and all, but now you're the star. Can't you just enjoy it?" I sigh loudly, exasperated. I know Maeve isn't being a brat; she's genuinely suspicious that she was invited. But she needs to start realizing that she's creeping closer to being a true celebrity every day. I just want her to enjoy this.

Maeve inhales and exhales slowly, and when she speaks, I can tell it's through gritted teeth. "My childhood isn't for you to talk about anymore, Finn. I have anxiety, and I can't always control when I feel anxious. I *know* it's not always rational."

Now I feel like a total asshole. Maeve is still staring out the window, leaning as far away from me as possible, but she doesn't realize I can see her reflection in the tinted glass. Her mouth is tight with tension, and I wish I could lean over and ki—I need to get myself in check. "We're at the Met Gala because you made an incredible show, our episode knocked it out of the park, and Streamify arranged tickets to capitalize on the publicity. That's it." I take care to soften my tone in hopes she actually believes I'm being genuine and it alleviates some of her anxiety-induced imposter syndrome.

She doesn't respond. But I do see her shoulders relax slightly.

We're still not speaking when we get to the hotel, and although our suites are adjoining, I hear Maeve test then engage the lock on the communicating door as soon as we enter our rooms. After a few minutes, "Karma" by Taylor Swift starts blaring, and I know she's freaking out. She never leans on other people, as though if she does everything alone and doesn't let anyone know when she's struggling she'll somehow earn bonus points. I know if I knock on the door, she'll refuse to open it, or open it just so she can slam it in my face again. But I want to be there for her. I need to find a way for us to get ready together so I can build her up a bit before we're thrown onto the red carpet and she gets *really* anxious.

I pull out my phone and dial Lavender, our head stylist. She's also my mom's stylist, but happily, Streamify is footing the bill for her tonight. She's in charge of the glam team, made up of makeup artists, hair stylists and groomers, and I'm hoping I can work something out with her.

"Finn, is everything all right?" It sounds like Lavender is in the middle of a spin class. Or at a concert. Music is blaring and I can tell she's screaming into her headphones. I can vaguely hear someone in the background telling her phones aren't allowed.

"Hey! Yes, well, kind of. I was just wondering if you could cancel my groomer?"

Lavender laughs at me and ignores the continued requests to put away her phone from the person who I am now sure is a spin instructor. "No. You're cute, but not that cute. Listen, all men wear makeup at these events. It's normal! Ask your dad—"

"No, no, I'm fine with the makeup. I just . . . I want to get ready with Maeve. And if my person canceled and we have to share, then I can get ready in her suite." I can hear how pathetic I sound. But I don't care. I've used up my lifetime quota of not being there for Maeve, and now I need to be there even though she's mad at me.

"Are you ten? Just ask her to glam together."

"I pissed her off in the car; she'll say no. Please? You could even just put the groomer in her room and say he's a stylist so he doesn't lose the work, and we'll all just pretend some imaginary other groomer canceled. And I'll double everyone's tips. And post! On Instagram, TikTok, YouTube, wherever and whatever pictures you choose." I'm laying it on thick. But her silence means it's working.

"You're lucky your mom is my best client," Lavender grumbles. "One minute!" she yells suddenly, to the instructor. "I paid to be here! Relax! Frowning creates premature wrinkles." Then her attention is back on me. "Listen, I'll be there in an hour and on your behalf I'll ask Maeve if you can join her glam party if she's comfortable with that. And if she says no, your groomer is back in your room and I tell her the whole deal. Fair?"

"Fair. Thank you!"

An hour later, it turns out Maeve still has enough of a soft spot for me, and our mutually assured good press, to let me into her room. I've gone to enough events with my mom to know that the pre-event glam is the real party. But this is Maeve's first celebrity event, and I want to make sure she has at least some fun.

Lavender has set up stations in Maeve's suite, two for hair and makeup since I'm there too, one for mani-pedis, although I'm totally crashing that, and then the dress and shoes that Maeve selected back in LA are hanging in a garment bag. I don't know what the dress looks like, but I do know that it's her classic red, since the theme of this year's gala is camp, and we've dressed to evoke classic slasher films. And, presumably, sex, lipstick, romance, all that, since we're us and Streamify wants to hit the world over the head with the fact that we're a sex show.

"Wow . . . this is a lot." Maeve and I are both in fluffy white robes, and she's surveying the room with wide eyes. Her gaze is half fear, half anticipation, and I want it to be all excitement.

I walk over to the black chair, which I assume is mine, and plop into it. "Remember in college, when the pregame was the best part of going out?"

"Finn, the pregame is *still* the best part of going out. I hate going out."

If this were a year ago, I'd pull her into my lap and we'd take a goofy video for our fans. Now, she's hovering three feet away from me. "Mmmm true, good thing tonight we're actually working. You love working."

This actually gets a smile out of her. "Good thing."

I can't imagine what my life would be like now if I hadn't gone to college and met Maeve. I went to Carnegie Mellon completely on a whim, because Pittsburgh sounded like such a random city where no one would care that I was Evangeline Sutton's son. It also had an incredible theater program, so I thought that *maybe*, if it seemed like I flew under the radar enough, I could act. Just for fun. Low stakes (no stakes really), totally for fun, not in a professional way at all. Just acting. Of course, it didn't exactly work out like that. Apparently, even in Pittsburgh I look too much like my mom to fly under the radar, and I dropped out of the acting program the first week of school. But it didn't bother me because, for the first time in my life, I had met people like Maeve, who—even though they knew who my mom was—didn't care. And for four years I got to act almost normal, so long as I stayed away from the theater kids who were desperate for an introduction to my parents. And most importantly, over the years I broke through Maeve's guardrails and got to know her. Which is why it's *so* frustrating that in the space of a few months I undid years of history.

Lavender sweeps into the room and, just like that, what could have become a *moment* is swept away. But Lavender is ready to pump everyone up and her energy is contagious. "Maeve, thank you so much for being flexible. You're an angel! With cheekbones to die for, I might add. Now let's get this party started!"

She pops a bottle of champagne and pours for each of us, while her assists turn music on and start setting out their tools. Maeve and I sit next to each other in the chairs and Lavender turns to us. "So, tonight. Go big or go home, right? You two are stunning together, you complement each other so well, especially in the outfits we've put together for you. We'll start with hair for Maeve, so it can set, while we prep your skin and do Maeve's nails." Lavender eyes my expression. "Both of your nails," she amends. "And I do have one special request from Derek . . ." Maeve and I glance at each other, already knowing what it is. "Maybe some fun content? Getting ready? Something? Anything?"

I look to Maeve. This is our contractually mandated appearance for the month, so while the extra videos are technically a request . . . they're really a command. "Fine," she agrees. "But let's get this started for real."

My eyebrows shoot up. "Tequila?"

She nods. "Tequila." We've taken and shared approximately a million and one videos together taking tequila shots before going out, during particularly graphic episodes, and at bars with fans. We always cross arms and give them to each other, so close that if we turned a few inches to the side we'd be kissing. More often than not, I'd wrap her in a bear hug after, and she'd lean into me, and it would feel—"Finn! Take the cup."

Maeve is waving the shot glass in my face. Lavender takes a video as we stand in our robes and cross arms. I haven't been this close to her in months. I could count her eyelashes, which are impossibly long, but almost totally blond. Back in college she wouldn't leave the dorms without mascara, but once we moved to New York and started hanging there she got more comfortable with going au naturel.

I lock eyes with Maeve, and it feels like time stops for a moment. We should be throwing back the shots, laughing, acting, hamming it up for the camera. But for a second, it feels like both our guards are down, and there's no animosity clouding the air between us. I want to kiss her. I don't want to kiss anyone else who isn't her ever again. I want to hold her and love her and build her up every day. I don't think I'll be able to go on without her.

"Ready?" Maeve whispers, so quietly the phone won't be able to pick it up over the music that's blaring.

"Always. But Maeve . . . you deserve all this, okay? Try to remember that tonight. Unlike me, or almost everyone else on the carpet, you earned it."

Her eyes never leave mine. She blinks, and I can see the veins on her eyelids, the stray hairs that will soon be plucked between her brows, the flush of her cheeks since we've already had half a glass of champagne, or maybe because we're this close. She doesn't respond to what I said. Because I'm the asshole that says shit like that after making her feel like she wasn't special at all. Instead, she just counts down. "Three, two, one." And we take the shots.

The next three hours pass in a rush of hairspray and nail polish fumes, makeup, champagne, and laughter. Lavender and her team do a great job of making the lengthy experience fun, and Maeve and I endure some good-hearted teasing about early episodes of the show. Maeve and her hairstylist bond over being from outside of Pittsburgh, and by the time we're done with the hair, face, and body styling, everyone has shared about their love lives but us. And they've clearly been instructed not to ask, probably by my mom via Lavender.

I go back into my room to change into my outfit, which is a play on a classic tux, but with red creeping up the sleeves. When Maeve is ready, Lavender knocks three times on the connecting door, and I walk back in. My jaw drops.

Maeve is wearing a *Carrie*-inspired outfit, which suddenly makes my own outfit make a lot more sense. Her dress has a pale pink base, but the top is red and it drips down, almost like blood, but classy and artistic. Her hair is styled as if it's wet, which I had found strange but didn't comment on, and now it all clicks. It's slicked back to be reminiscent of Carrie's after the blood poured down on her. And her lipstick is a bold red.

"I was thinking of one finishing touch," Lavender explains before I can say anything. "It's a bit 'out there' . . . but I was thinking Maeve could kiss your cheek. And leave the lipstick imprint there."

Maeve looks surprised. Before she can answer I jump in to say *something* about her dress. "Maeve, you look amazing. Truly. You were made to take over the Met Gala, clearly. Whatever you think on the kiss."

She cocks her head. "Let's do it." She walks up to me, reasonably steady in her heels, but still only coming up to my shoulder. She places a hand on my arm to steady herself, and I catch her lower back.

"Is this okay?" I ask, my voice low.

She nods. And then arches her neck up toward me, clearly going in for the kiss. I'm frozen, not turning my head away to give her my cheek like I should for this. The last time we were this close . . . *How could I have thrown it away?* Maeve reaches up with her other hand and turns my face for me, cupping my jaw gently with soft hands. She plants a firm kiss on my cheek, then leans back to inspect her handiwork.

"You outshine the red too."

EIGHT

Before the Streamify contract

Maeve

I roll over in bed, which is practically my entire room in my tiny New York City apartment, and pick up my phone. It's been buzzing incessantly, so loudly that it woke me up even though I didn't go to bed until two a.m. and it's now only seven. Last night we got slightly too fucked up and released our third podcast episode, which verged on inappropriate and got five hundred downloads in the first three hours, a new record for us.

But now my phone is positively vibrating with more notifications at once than I can count. Episode download alerts, people tagging me in Instagram videos and TikToks, threads, tweets—everything that could be going off is.

I lean over the edge of my bed and throw a pillow directly at Finn's face. "Finn! Wake up!"

He groans and throws an arm over his eyes. "What time is it?"

"Doesn't matter! You need to see this."

He must hear something in the tone of my voice because he sits up very fast, very suddenly, and turns those light blue eyes toward me. For a moment, with him looking at me so intently, his hair mussed and the imprints of my spare sheets across the side of his face, it feels like we're having a first "morning after." That would never happen. But I falter, thrown, because for an instant I wish we were having a morning-after moment. Even though we're having a moment that is much better, more irreplaceable, our fifteen minutes of fame per Andy Warhol's wise assessment. But I'm stunned by the intensity with which I briefly want that something more, something that I thought I'd convinced myself I don't need.

"Maeve. What is it?" His words cut through my thoughts. It's just his eyes that make me think confusing things, really. I need to get my head on straight.

I hold up my phone. "We're viral. Like, *really* viral."

Finn leans in to look at my phone and pulls himself up on the bed. I'm under the covers and he's on top, our legs tangled but with the thin barrier of my sheet between, his arm behind me as he watches my phone. He's so close I can smell his morning breath, and I'm sure he can smell mine. But we're close enough that it's okay, I don't care, even though in the back of my mind I think maybe, just maybe, I might start to.

Suddenly Finn reaches out and covers the phone. "Wait. Let's guess."

"Guess what?"

"How many downloads," He leans his head back in thought. "I think five thousand," he says as he climbs under the covers with me.

Without saying a word, I tuck myself under his arm, against his bare chest, me in my tank top and boxers. "I guess fifty."

"Thousand?"

I turn toward him, so close with the way we're lying that I can barely see him, only the details of him. The slight scar on his chest from when he fell into a fence, the stubble on his chin, the underside of his eyelashes, longer than a boy's lashes had any right to be. I always assume I look worse like this, at a strange angle, so close. But maybe if you like someone enough, they always look good. "Look how many notifications I have! I don't even want to see your phone."

Finn looks down at the floor. "It's probably dead."

I'm sure it's dead, because he would be getting ten times as many notifications as I am. I open my phone and it feels like time stands still for a moment while we check the downloads number. I don't feel Finn exhale under me until I'm looking at the screen and trying to figure out if this could possibly be a practical joke. Maybe one of my sisters learned to code? There's seemingly nothing Claude doesn't excel at, so it's totally possible.

"Is that real?" I refresh the page, and the number goes up by five thousand: 3,567,310 downloads.

"Fuck," Finn swears quietly.

I turn my phone face down. Then when it keeps vibrating, Finn reaches out and powers it down all the way. He throws it onto his makeshift bed on the floor. A twin-size air mattress that we only half filled last night before collapsing, drunk on the episode and too many glasses of wine and weed seltzers. I want him to say something. His parents are certifiably famous, and he's adjacent to that in the way that all children of celebrities are. He can make it through four years at a normal college with me, but if he steps into a nice club in New York or LA, he's getting photographed by the paparazzi. He's one fall or jump away from actual fame. And this was a fucking leap.

So when he wraps his arm around me and pulls me close before letting loose a fake scream, my body sags with relief. I giggle, but then push forward and ask my real question. "I guess we're viral. Are you disappointed?"

Finn tucks my head in close to him. "No. It was inevitable with you; I knew that. You just didn't believe me."

"You never said that. Why would you have done it then? It's the opposite of your whole 'I'm not my mother' vibe."

He squeezes me tighter. We were never like this in college. But somehow, since coming to the city, we went from having walk-of-shame brunches to telling three and a half million people how to give oral sex to cuddling half clothed in bed. Maybe now that we've pledged to the world we're just friends and looking for Mr. and Mrs. Right, we don't have to do that awkward dance that most male-female friendships have. I just need to tell that to the chills running up and down my arms.

Finn notices my goosebumps and rubs my arm absentmindedly while he thinks about what I said. He must think I'm cold. Because it would be laughable to think we'd ever be together. "With you, I thought it could be fun. You want to actually help people, not just cash out and have your face on a billboard. For that, with you I'll let the fame happen."

Finn has the kind of face that is destined to be on a billboard. It's always been obvious to me that he would ultimately become *someone*, and when we're hanging out alone it feels almost criminal that I get to stare at him for hours, just me. I'm pretty. I know that I am, and on good days, most days lately, I do feel that way. But sometimes intrusive thoughts sneak in and I start thinking things like I am now: *You could never be on a billboard. You're not your sisters. Your face is forgettable. People are just tuning in to watch Finn.* And I have to stop and consciously remind myself that, no, I love my hair. I love my freckles, that multiply in the summer, that just the other night Finn tried to count but gave up after 237. My skin is clear and bright, which back in middle school I would have given anything for. I like myself. I try to repeat it in my head in moments like this. *I like myself. I am beautiful. I am grateful.* But I hope there's a day when I don't have to remind myself to do that anymore.

"Should we get brunch?" I ask. "I think I need coffee and a massive amount of grease before I confront the contents of this episode."

Finn sits up, and my shoulder feels cold where the warmth of his chest was just flush against it. "Let's leave the phones off. I don't want to hear what anyone else has to say about it."

Our episode detailed *exactly* how to give oral sex. The descriptions were graphic and our arguments over technique were heated. At one point I thought Finn might demand we prove the validity of our strategies. I had planned on the show being more relationship advice than sex how-tos, but I was fresh off talking to my sister about yet *another* man who didn't know how to get the job done, and then Finn tried to say that not all women knew their stuff either, and suddenly our iPhones were propped against cups, cameras on, and we had the rented recorder I signed out from Columbia flashing red. If we had waited until the morning to put the episode out, I never would have.

So, phones off sounded pretty good to me. "Agreed. I don't want to know if I'm fired until Monday."

I walk to the bathroom while Finn pulls his clothes from the day before back on in my room. I have four roommates, since on a college therapist's salary I can*not* afford a New York City apartment. I can barely afford a room in one, and my parents think it's ridiculous that I didn't move back home and find a job in Pittsburgh. I don't know what made me want to bleed money on New York, but being here feels like possibility. I don't have the special something my sisters so clearly do—I spent my childhood trying to do my homework in a moving minivan as my mom shuttled us between their various events and awards ceremonies—but here, maybe, I could find a place that was different than the one on the sidelines I'd always thought I would have.

And so when, senior year, Finn asked if I was moving to New York after school, I said, *Of course, I move next week.*

This podcast . . . it's definitely *something.* Alone in the bathroom I dance around, overcome with euphoria at how absolutely wild this is. Suddenly, Finn flings open the door.

"I could have been naked!" I shriek.

He just laughs and steps into the tiny bathroom with me, and I see he's holding my laptop. "I could hear you dancing. You need music."

I reach over and give the computer my fingertip, then he opens YouTube and types P-A, and that's all it takes for my favorite song, "Paper Rings," to pop up. He hits Play, and it's blasting, definitely waking up my roommates, but I couldn't care less, because we're dancing wildly, and he's taking my hands and spinning me around, trying not to knock my computer off the toilet seat, and we're laughing. Because *Tell Me How You Really Feel* is definitely the start of something.

NINE

Before the Streamify contract

Finn

"On this week's episode of *Tell Me How You Really Feel*, we're going to be spilling our guts about the one that got away," Maeve says with a smile at me from her side of the couch.

I don't want to hear about Maeve's one that got away. Hearing about dates and one-night stands is one thing. It won't be as easy to hear about some guy that Maeve still has feelings for. But I play along. "Ooof, this will be a tough one. What are we calling your guy? Mine can be . . . the girl next door."

Maeve snorts. "As though you've ever dated the girl next door. We should be calling her Miss Dior."

I roll my eyes good-naturedly for the camera trained on my close-up. We've only been doing *Tell Me How You Really Feel* for a few months, but in that time our setup has gotten significantly better. We have a lot more time now to focus on creating high-quality episodes, since Maeve was fired from her job at Columbia and I quit mine under duress from my manager, and we also used our first brand sponsorship check to buy used cameras off eBay. I would have been happy to buy us new cameras months earlier, but Maeve insisted that we only pay for show-related things with show earnings. Regardless, now we have a wide shot, plus close-ups on each of us to capture any particularly funny facial expressions.

Maeve's right, though; anyone with access to the internet will be able to find out that the ex I'm referring to is Cassidy Cross, my childhood best friend, who is an It girl and much more famous nepo baby, and currently the face of the Miss Dior perfume line, among other things.

Maeve's ex, on the other hand, is a total mystery. "So? What are you calling yours?"

She tilts her head thoughtfully. "The homeroom charmer."

"He sounds like a real guy next door."

Maeve nods, a small smile playing on her face. "Oh, he was. Generically good-looking. Kind, with these deep green eyes and long lashes. He's a catch."

"So? Why didn't you catch him?"

Maeve draws her feet up onto the couch and I pull them into my lap, adjusting a blanket over us. My hand rests on her bare calf and I can tell she must have shaved this morning, her legs are smooth and still slightly sticky from lotion. "Well, we went to prom together. We had a great night, we actually—"

"Did you lose your virginity to him?" I interrupt. "On prom night? Like in a movie?"

Color rises on Maeve's cheeks. "Finn! I was getting there."

"I'm sorry, I'm sorry. I just got excited that we're basically in a Hallmark movie right now." I squeeze her leg reassuringly under the blanket. If she decides she doesn't want her virginity story on the podcast, we can always cut it later.

"They don't have sex in Hallmark movies," Maeve corrects me authoritatively. "They just kiss, chastely. Anyways, we did have scx on prom night, after the most perfect night. And I *thought* we were losing our virginity to each other. But it turned out he'd had sex with my friend literally two weeks prior."

My heart drops for her. I know how inferior Maeve always felt to her siblings as a child, and even though this was a friend, I can't imagine it helped. She was just telling me the other night that it's only now that she has her master's and is the one living in New York and starting a podcast that she's starting to actually feel like she measures up. "How'd you find out?"

Maeve scrunches up her face in a cheesy "woe is me" expression, but I can see in her eyes that the memory really is painful. "He had a birthmark. Like, right above his dick. And I was so excited to tell my best friend about losing my virginity. She was my only friend that I didn't share with any of my sisters too. And before I told her my big news, she told me about a guy she had sex with at a party, and when she mentioned the birthmark, I just knew. I didn't tell her for years. I didn't tell him back then either; I just blocked him. But a few months later he showed up at my summer job at the ice cream shop, which was in our small town, not Pittsburgh, where he and I were both moving for different schools. I called him out, he apologized, said he really liked me, that it was just sex at a party with her, yada yada. But I didn't want to hear it. He chose her over me for that big moment, and I just didn't believe him about actually liking me at the time."

I pause before speaking, to make sure she's finished. "So why is he the one that got away? He doesn't sound that great. Was the sex that good?"

Maeve exhales strongly. "No. He does not pass the clit test. But also, we were eighteen and hadn't discovered lube. But he's the one that got away just because I really did like him. He was the first person I've had that head-over-heels feeling for. We had not just homeroom but almost every class together, and we really did have a great time. I wanted to be around him all the time. He was smart, and funny, and I've always kind of wished I'd given him another chance. My friend had even said the sex was just sex, that they wanted to lose their virginity with someone they trusted but didn't like so they could get it over with. Maybe he was telling the truth. But also, like . . . he knew she was my friend."

"Do you know what he does now?"

This brings a change over Maeve. She actually bites her lip to keep from laughing. "It's too identifiable. You've actually seen him."

My jaw drops. "Did he go to CMU with us?"

She shakes her head, eyes dancing. "No . . . but remember that guy from Pittsburgh who was on *The Bachelorette*?"

It takes me a minute, but suddenly I do know, because I watched every episode of the past season with Maeve. "No! The professional walker?"

She nods gravely. "Yes. He's doing the very important work of getting people in Pittsburgh to walk more. The gym? It's too big a goal. Just put that beer in a coozie and *walk*. And don't worry, at home walking in place in front of the TV still counts."

Now I'm the one who can't hold it in. I start laughing and Maeve joins in until we're both tearing up. "He is, like, superhot, I'll give you that," I say finally. "But trust me, you can do better."

"He is who I still think about, though!" Maeve exclaims, more lighthearted now that we've broken the tension of the story. "Like, I think if I met him now, we wouldn't have anything to talk about. But also in high school? He was every girl's dream. I hope he's found love. He actually lasted a long time on the show. But anyway, tell us yours. It's a sweeter story."

"I guess I can let you off the hook this once," I tease. Maeve and I have talked about Cassidy off the podcast several times, so she already knows all the details. "So mine is also my first love. But I wasn't such a late bloomer—I first fell in love at nine years old."

"I'm sure you were a heartbreaker even then," Maeve remarks with a grin.

"I can't confirm or deny. I'm not *that* vain. But anyway, the girl next door—"

"Miss Dior."

"Fine! Miss Dior." Everyone knows exactly who we're talking about when we talk about our exes. Fans have compiled relationship timelines for everyone I've ever dated, and done their best to cobble together Maeve's dating history. "Miss Dior and I were in Croatia, costarring in a movie with our mothers. So romantic, I know. Our moms were playing former best friends that had a falling out and then are brought back together when their children fall in love in the beach town they spend summers in."

"Weren't you nominated for an Emmy for that?" Maeve interjects.

My stomach twists. "I was." That Emmy nomination ruined everything. Until then, acting was something that was so pure and fun for me. I wanted to be just like my mom and loved every second of doing that movie with her. But after the Emmy, the paparazzi were relentless. I was asked to leave my Little League team, I was excluded from every birthday party and afterschool hang because me being there caused a disturbance, and I couldn't do anything normally until I'd hidden away for years, getting homeschooled with Cassidy on set while she and our moms filmed movies.

Maeve must be able to tell I'm reluctant to talk about it because she presses her foot into my stomach gently to show she's with me, but she doesn't ask anything. "Just start again. I'll edit out my question."

I nod gratefully. "The movie was set in the beach town they were supposed to have grown up in, and it was Miss Dior's and my first time acting. The whole movie was a family affair, since her stepdad was the director and my dad wrote the script. I'd known Miss Dior my entire life, but because we were that little, and the movie was with our real moms, the lines started to feel . . . blurred. Like between reality and the movie.

"But we knew that for this one scene in the movie we were supposed to kiss. And Miss Dior came to me and said we needed to practice, so we didn't ruin the movie with our bad kissing." I smile now just thinking of it. "She brought me a Hershey's Kiss and asked if I would be her first real kiss before we do it for the Academy."

Maeve can't help but laugh. "That should've been in the movie. It's the cutest thing I've ever heard."

"It really is. But anyway, I agreed, obviously, and I told my mom I had to take her on a real date. So our moms took us to a fancy restaurant and sat at the table next to us while I 'took her out to dinner' at nine years old. We had a blast. Honestly, best dinner date of my life, and then when I walked her to her hotel room, our moms hung back at the elevator and I kissed her. It's still the most romantic night of my life, I have to say. I peaked at nine years old."

Maeve reaches out and squeezes my hand, her eyes wet. "Finn. You hadn't told me this whole story! What happened after that?"

"Oh nothing. I mean, we were nine after all. We just went back to being friends and finished the movie. I think the next day on set I asked if I was her boyfriend now, and she was like, 'No way, silly. I'm nine.'"

"That's crushing. Wow. Have you ever talked about it?"

I shrug. "We've joked about it over the years. We're great friends, and our families are still super close."

Maeve frowns. "Why have you never gone for it with her? You obviously like her. And come on, she is drop-dead gorgeous."

I hesitate, considering. "I haven't really considered it, I guess. We're still young, and she is definitely the one that got away, but I haven't felt like our time is up, you know? Like, if I got together with her, I think it would be endgame, since we are such good friends. I mean, she's the perfect woman, right? I could never do better than her."

"What if she's the one, though? You're not going to try?" Maeve's voice is barely a whisper, her eyes wide.

"I really don't think she's interested," I say lightly. Why have I never tried with Cassidy? I feel almost stupid for not trying, but it's never really occurred to me to. She's been such a supportive friend over the years, and our lives look really different now since she's leaned into the spotlight and I ran away from it. "I mean, her most recent ex is Ja—Oscar-winner-whatever-fake-name," I fumble. "Let's bleep that out. But talk about high profile. I heard he keeps his three Oscars in the bathroom."

"The only word I just heard is *ex*. Real talk for a sec: I say go for it if you have the chance," Maeve says firmly. "The whole point of our show is to help each other date to our fullest potential so we can find the one! You should at least try. I mean, I would date Miss Dior if given the chance! She's literally the coolest woman ever."

"I'll see if she wants your number."

"We're back, back again with another episode of *Tell Me How You Really Feel*, and this week we will be getting *into it*, because both Maeve and I went on dates last night."

I grin at Maeve. We're sitting in my living room, mic'd and recording. In the last nine months the show has only gotten bigger every day. It would be almost scary, but since Maeve is alongside me the level of success barely feels real, like this is some inside joke between us that we could call off at any time. But more often than not, when we step outside together, someone recognizes us, and networks have tried to buy the podcast IP from us for sizable amounts of money.

"That is *right*," Maeve agrees. "And as much as I want to hear about your date . . . I need to tell you about mine, like, urgently, before he becomes a Netflix special in the next five hours."

"Don't tell me you went out with Jeffrey Dahmer. Or a Trump?" I talk a good game, but hearing about Maeve's dates, which more often than not are awful, makes the hair on my arms stand straight up and something twist in my gut. I worry about her going out with guys we don't even know.

"Not quite. This guy, let's call him . . ."

"Netflix Special?"

She nods, smiling widely. "Netflix Special. He calls me a car, good, takes me to Nobu, great, and everything is going well. He doesn't have, like, a third eye, or a penis tie, or anything strange. He's even employed! He's an exec for a bank or something. And, obviously, he claims he hasn't heard of the show, but then lets slip that he listens every week."

"So pretty standard."

"One hundred percent. But the date goes *well*." Now this is something she has not said before. And even though I should be happy for her, my smile suddenly feels very forced. "So well that I agreed to a nightcap."

"No. Really? I thought you said, and I quote, 'Basically, if you want to date, go without sex as long as humanly possible so that he falls in love'?"

Maeve nods, dead serious. "And shame on you, Finn, for thinking that a nightcap automatically means sex."

I roll my eyes. "Fine, you got me."

"Anyway," Maeve continues, with a dramatic hair flick and a grin. She thinks that people watch for me, but I know approximately *all* of our male listeners are tuning in just to watch her flick her hair, adjust her tank top straps, or cross and uncross her legs after we've been sitting for too long. Men are disgusting. "He calls an Uber Black, and it takes us back to his place on the Upper East Side. He's been shockingly interesting to talk to, he likes Nathan Fielder, is well-read, athletic, all the things. And then when we get to this place . . . it's *nice*. Old money nice. And you know all my other dates have sucked, so I'm thinking, 'Oh shit, what if *he's* Mr. Right? What will we talk about on the show if I find *the one* right now?' And so we go inside, I'm looking around, and he shushes me in the living room." She pauses for dramatic emphasis, her eyes huge. "Because he's thirty-six and lives with his mom!"

"No!"

"Yes! And she heard us come in, and she walks out of her bedroom holding this cat, that's, like, a jungle cat? You know those cats that are, like, illegal to have? Like celebrities can still get them for a ton of money, then get canceled for it? Anyway, she recognizes me! And tells me that she bought the vibrator I recommended last month."

My jaw is on the floor. I would have shriveled up and died. "What did you say?"

"I thanked her, and this morning I mailed her a *Tell Me How You Really Feel* bottle of lube!"

The laugh I've been trying to hold back bubbles over, and I can't stop. "You didn't," I choke out.

"I did!" Maeve insists. "I'll show you my credit statement, seriously. She deserves lube!"

"What did you say to Netflix Special? And wait. Why is he called Netflix Special and not Momma's Boy?"

"Aha! Great question!" Maeve grabs my forearm and looks into my eyes. "Because I did not make my exit then. I had to see what his plan was! After this whole situation he's clearly embarrassed, and when his mom won't leave, he takes my hand and, like, leads me away. Down the hallway. To a fire escape. Which can be romantic!"

"I don't like the sound of where this is going . . ."

"We got out on the fire escape, but instead of sitting, talking, opening a *really* nice bottle of wine (because I need it at this point) . . . he starts climbing up. Like, to the apartment above us. And so I follow him!"

"No! No, Maeve. You can't follow men into strange apartments up fire escapes! It's so creepy. I'm going to have to, like, watch from outside like a stalker or your security each week." Not a bad idea, now that I'm thinking about it . . .

"I had come that far . . . So, I follow him upstairs to the next apartment, and it's completely barren. Except for a cage." The way every inch of my body gets a chill when she says "cage" is uncanny. But before I can jump in, she holds up a hand. "The cage was full of cats that he was illegally breeding. For Mother's Day. But next to the literal cage of sad, sad wild cats . . . he had laid out a blanket and charcuterie board, like five hours earlier, before he left. And next to that . . . was another empty cage, that he *claimed* was for the kittens, but who really knows . . . So then I basically sprinted out of there. Now. Tell me how you really feel. Let's go."

"Well, one, terrified that you would follow him up that fire escape into his room of cages. Please, never again. Literally just call me and I'll kill off one of my already deceased grandparents so you have a reason to leave to comfort me in my time of need. Two, disgusting.

Everything about it. That cheese could have killed you after sitting out that long, even if he decided to wait a few hours. Three, good job on sending the car man; you know you need to do shit like that since you live at home." I sound lighthearted, but the thought of Maeve being around men like that is horrifying to me. Especially because I know she's partially doing it for the show. This week is the first time, though, that for a moment I thought she might actually like the guy, and that pull in my gut when I realized it was a bad date . . . I think it might be relief.

Which I probably shouldn't think too hard about, since our show is dependent on us dating other people for content. Something Maeve wouldn't have suggested as the premise if she wanted to date me, like, at all. I need to get my head on straight and just be grateful that I get to be the one to do this with her.

"All fair points," Maeve responds. "Now, tell me. How was your date?"

"You know, mine was much less eventful. But there was something strange, once we got to the bedroom." I flush. I feel strange talking about sex with these women. I'm not typically one to kiss and tell. But I try to do it in the most respectful way possible, and let Maeve be the one to poke fun if something is really ridiculous. And mainly, we're using these escapades we share as teaching moments.

"What's her code name?" Maeve interjects.

"The choker," I say immediately.

"Ooooh, I like it. A little spice!" This makes me blush even harder. The thought of Maeve getting choked out, or having sex at all, is too much for me. I've seen her in her bikini, and there is so much good stuff happening under all her turtlenecks and long sleeve shirts that I have to seriously focus on maintaining professionalism.

"We were starting to hook up, and everything was normal. The

date was good even! And she initiated the hook up. I'm going down-
town, when all of a sudden she yanks me up by the hair and tells me
to tie her up and choke her while I fuck her."

"Wow. She knows what she wants! I think that's kind of nice."

I frown. "It is! If she finds someone who's into all that. But I'm a
bit more . . . vanilla. And I wasn't comfortable with that stuff. And I
couldn't pretend I hadn't heard her, since she literally pulled my face
off her clit to tell me."

"Finn, you can't pretend not to hear her. That's, like, so childish."

"It was awkward!"

"Well, what did you say? I hope you didn't make her feel bad
about it."

"I said, 'On it,' then went to the other room to pretend to get rope
or whatever, and then came back and said I had to go, my mom just
called and one of my grandparents has died, could I call her a car?"

Maeve shakes her head and laughs. "Finn, your entire family history is on the internet. Next time, I give you permission to pretend
I'm having an emergency. But not a dead grandma! I'm trying not to
jinx mine like that."

"Thank you, I appreciate that. Now tell me, how did I do?"

"I'll give you a solid five for dishonesty. Want to know what I
would have said?"

"Uh, obviously." And I really do. Maeve is a genius with relationships, which is why it's so baffling she's not in one. She's literally the
perfect partner. She's not just talented, smart, funny, and caring,
she's also a knockout. The whole package.

"I'd say, 'Baby, thanks for telling me what you're into. I haven't
done anything like that before, and I'm not ready to jump into it tonight, but I think it's so fucking sexy that you know what you want,
and if you're open to holding off on that stuff for tonight, I'd still love

to try and make you feel good.' It sets a boundary for that night, but doesn't make her feel dumb, and leaves the door open for the future. I think it's a good compromise."

I raise an eyebrow. "And when I never want to do that stuff after thinking about it?"

Maeve laughs. "Text her. Way less awkward, for everyone involved. 'I had a great time the other night, but I think we're looking for different things. I wish you the best!'"

"How do you always know the right thing to say?"

"Eight years of overpriced education."

TEN

Maeve

It shouldn't feel so good to pretend things are normal with Finn. That what we were doing was *ever* normal. But as we pose on the Met Gala steps and cameras are flashing and people are shouting and I should be panicking . . . all I really notice is the feel of his palm on my back. The warm weight of it is quietly reassuring, in a way that I only ever feel with him.

I look up toward him. "Thanks for doing all this with me."

I know he doesn't need to. Didn't ever need to. The only reason I can think of that he stayed with the show (since after last summer, I know it wasn't for me like I'd secretly hoped) is that doing the show scratched the creative itch I know he has. He's tried to suppress his creative drive for the novelty of a normal life, but I know it's in there somewhere, because when I was looking for a charger at his apartment one day, I found a whole drawer of annotated scripts. No one acts as masterfully and joyfully as he did at nine years old just to never think about doing it again.

Finn looks down toward me. His height makes me feel both dainty and protected by him. I always said height didn't matter. It's not a deal-breaker. But with him, it definitely adds. "Don't be ridiculous. I should be thanking you. Sub me out for any other guy with half a brain and decent looks, and Maeve, you'd still be here."

"I wouldn't bet on that."

"Kiss! Kiss!" a few people have started yelling. "Can you confirm or deny your relationship?"

I raise an eyebrow at Finn, and he smiles mischievously back. This might be the tequila talking, but I know we're both thinking it—*game on*. He leans down as though he's going to ravish me with a dramatic kiss . . . and then stops short, to whisper in my ear. "I would."

We make it through the rest of the red carpet, pictures, interviews, and press, with minimal fanfare. After all, there are people like supermodel Karli and the most decorated actress ever, Sandra Streap, here. We're a fun moment, but they're *famous* famous. Inside, we accept cocktails and meander through a gorgeous exhibition of blown glass in vivid colors. After the gala, the exhibition will be open to the public, but right now I'm getting chills seeing every celebrity I've ever watched on my TV or phone screen casually looking at the artwork and mingling in absolutely outrageous outfits.

I see my favorite singer leaning in to read the plaque next to a hot pink sculpture, and I almost drop my drink. How did I end up here? Suddenly I feel Finn's hand on my exposed back and jump.

"You're staring," he whispers.

"How are you *not*!"

I let Finn pull me closer to him, his hand on my hip guiding me as we walk through the exhibit, and tell myself it's just for show. I can feel his palms sweating, but he's just overheated in his jacket. He couldn't be nervous. What has he ever had to be nervous about? And the heat is definitely cranked up in here to accommodate all the women in their provocative and often skin-exposing outfits. Outside, there were space heaters, something that I never realized were there based on the media coverage of the event, but was very grateful for. "You know, this is a social hour. You could talk to them."

I take a long gulp of my drink. "Maybe right after my personality transplant. Come on, you're the social one, you go for it. I'll be fine by myself."

As much as I still am angry at Finn . . . I am so relieved when he shakes his head immediately. "I'm not going to leave you at the Met Gala. We're working tonight, remember? We have to present a united front."

Of course. That's why he wouldn't leave me. I need to stop letting myself believe for even a second that the connection we have is anything. We're not friends anymore, we're coworkers. We eventually make it to our table, which has a range of famous people at it. An actor, an NFL player, a singer who's been nominated for New Artist of the Year, a popular YouTuber, a tennis star and her tech billionaire husband, and us. The Met Gala is famous for seating people strategically, next to people that they might not know they have much in common with, but actually do, so I'm curious to see how our evening will go. We're set up in the atrium, and although it's light outside, they've made the room dark through overlays on the glass ceiling, giving the entire atrium a reddish tinge. In contrast to that creepy vibe, the place settings are ornate china and lace doilies, while the centerpieces are made of literal Barbies, dressed as each of us in our typical non-Met Gala outfits. It's creepy and awesome all at once. And I'm definitely snagging my Barbie on the way out.

We're the first to make it to the table, so rather than be stuck alone with Finn in terse silence or, worse, sparkling conversation that makes me doubt everything, I make my excuses and duck out to the ladies' room.

I thought that I would be alone in here . . . but it seems that the reason the atrium is empty, is that *everyone* is in the bathroom. I have to swallow a gasp when I see an entire reality TV dynasty in front of the mirror touching up their makeup. I subtly pinch my elbow, one of the few places of my body without makeup on it, to make sure I'm not dreaming. I grew up in a lower-class household outside Pittsburgh, where the epitome of luxury was eating out at a restaurant on our birthday. And that restaurant was Primanti Bros, a greasy sandwich shop. My parents poured everything into my sisters' pageants and soccer fees and MCAT prep, and so there were months where we didn't even have Wi-Fi in the house, and if I wanted to see the antics of all of the A-listers in this bathroom I'd have to walk to the local library. How did I end up here?

"Maeve!" Syma, the star of a hit HBO show, turns around to look at me. "Oh my god! I'm such a fan of the show!"

"Oh wow!" I smile at her while trying to look around to see if we're being filmed by someone for an elaborate viral joke. "Thank you so much! I mean, I'm such a fan of *your* show."

Then her costar Renee walks out of a stall. "I recognized your voice! I listen *every day*. I think I memorized your oral sex episode. My fiancé should send you a fruit basket." Renee was a former *Bachelor-ette* contestant—who was famous for her conservative upbringing and waiting for marriage—but left the show alone and ended up engaged to a lesbian pop star and starring in *The End of Us* with Syma.

"Forget the fruit basket; you two should come on the show!" This is inappropriately bold of me, and as I get a side-eye for my overt soliciting from an actress reapplying her eyeliner, I start to sweat from every pore in my body.

But Renee squeals in delight. "Really! You're having guests? I assumed it was just Evangeline. But yes, please!"

The excitement on our side of the restroom, and the promises of publicity on our show, gets several more friendly and recognizable faces turned my way. Just as I'm adding the last cell phone number to my phone, which feels like a dangerous game in itself—like, what if I accidentally text *How to End a Love Story* star Sarah instead of my sister Sarah?—Syma starts motioning everyone in the bathroom toward the mirror.

"Selfie time. We have to do it, it's iconic."

The reality TV family immediately position themselves in the front, clearly having been waiting for this moment. Is this why everyone was in the bathroom? For the famous Met Gala mirror selfie? I look behind me for the exit, because I am sure I am not meant to be in this photo, but Renee grabs my arm and tucks me into the front, dead center. The cell phone clicks, airdrops are sent, and suddenly I'm pouring out of the bathroom with all of the most famous women in the world. I look at my phone, half expecting the photo to be gone. Snatched by someone's publicist from the dark web, so that lowly me, a random girl from PA who has been viral for all of two seconds, can't post a photo that in any way associates me with the most famous female rapper in the world, who's giving a sultry pout in the upper right corner, one hand on her pregnant belly. But the photo is there, as are texts from all the women I connected with in the bathroom. My Instagram notifications start going off wildly, because I've been tagged in three different photos, and I turn my phone on silent and drop it into my clutch.

I drop into my chair, still in shock, and Finn's arm is immediately across the back of mine. "Are you okay? You were gone for so long." His brow is furrowed, and he's leaning in so close to me I can smell his cologne. When I don't answer, he grabs a glass of water and pushes it toward me. "We can leave if you want."

I take a long sip. "I'm fine. But you should really go to the bathroom and start networking. I think I just lined up the next six months of our podcast in there."

"Ah, I don't think that's how it works with guys. But Graham said he'd totally come on." Finn gestures to the NFL player who is hulking over the table across from us. He nods and gives a small wave. "He needs your advice, like, yesterday."

I smile at him and extend a hand. "I'm Maeve; it's great to meet you. I think I may have just booked next week. But how about the following?"

"I'm there."

The rest of the night passes in a flash, and actually is surprisingly brief. Our publicist from Streamify had warned us it was a quick night because we'd have to get to the after-parties. After the gala ends, Finn and I sneak out and into a car that drives us approximately one block to our hotel, where Lavender and her team are waiting to touch us up and help us into new outfits. We're no longer dressing for the theme, but we are coordinated. At this point we're several drinks deep, and this sneaking around and changing clothes feels both thrilling and ridiculous.

When Finn comes out of his room in a completely clear tux, with a hot pink undershirt and pink silk boxers underneath to match my hot pink dress, I can't help but laugh. "Tell me you picked that."

"They said it was cool!" he exclaims. "What! I'm taking risks. You know there's paps outside. Real men wear pink and all."

"You're basically in men's lingerie." He pouts, then pulls a few poses. Lavender is filming our outfit reactions for social, but unlike earlier, I'm not faking anything. I'm tired of reminding myself to hate Finn and want to enjoy the rest of the night. Even if it will hurt when I've sobered up in the morning. "Okay, initial shock aside, I love it. That you're scantily clad, and I get to be covered up."

Finn's gaze rakes up and down my body, and I see him swallow. His voice is hoarse when he speaks. "I don't know that I'd call that covered up."

I glance down at my dress. It's tight, but thin enough to still be comfortable. Which means that my nipples are basically on full display, and the dress shows every curve I have. It's a two-piece, so a sliver of my stomach is showing, and the monster heels make my legs look amazing. "The important bits are."

Finn exhales sharply. "I have something for you." He ducks into his room and returns with a pair of Air Force Ones that match my dress exactly. "Your feet are going to kill you in an hour, if they don't already. You hate heels."

I take them, already admiring them. They're a gorgeous color, and I have a sneaking suspicion he got them custom-made. Which is confirmed when I turn them over and see our logo on the underside. "Finn. These are incredible. But I already look like a hobbit next to all these models and actresses. I don't know . . ."

"I know, I know, you're fun size." He takes the shoes back from me and ties the laces together, then puts them over his shoulder. "I'll carry them, just consider them my accessory. And then we can put your heels in the coat check once we're there, since there are no photos inside. And we'll match."

He sticks out his foot, which is clad in an identical pair. Why is he so thoughtful? These shoes shouldn't be making me feel all warm and fuzzy inside. But after the bathroom, I told myself I was going to embrace this, put aside my hurt feelings for the night, and try to just have fun. And so I find myself nodding. Stepping toward Finn and wrapping him in a hug. "Thank you."

We shouldn't fit together as well as we do. He's a giant and I'm barely five feet. But somehow we always click, no matter the height of my shoes. I let my body relax into him, and he cradles the back of my head tenderly. When I pull back, his eyes are moist. "Ready?"

Outside the hotel, cameras flash as we walk hand in hand to the after-party, my sneakers bouncing against his chest. I can feel my smile threatening to crack my face in half, because it feels so *nice* to be able to be best friends with Finn again, even for a night. I glance at him, and he's watching me, his smile just as big, and I hope someone got a picture of this moment, because even though it'll sting when I've sobered up and remembered that for him we're best as friends, I'll want it.

Inside, it's nice to have privacy after all of the shouting and flashes on the street. My feet are killing me, so within thirty minutes Finn has checked my heels and I'm dancing my heart out in the sneakers. If I was still in heels, I'd be either sitting or on my way out the door already. The party is somehow even more star-studded than the actual event, because all the celebs who didn't attend the actual event but still wanted to party are now here. I spot Cassidy on the other side of the room, as well as every supermodel I've ever followed, all of my favorite singers and actors, ranging from a newly eighteen-year-old starlet on a CW show to the legacy stars my parents grew up watching. Many of them know who we are, or at least who Finn is, and make a point of saying hi.

But Finn never leaves my side. We dance and snack and take shots with Graham and Renee and dance some more. After a few hours I'm ready to drop, and I follow Finn to a couch in the back room, where a bar has popped up. We collapse onto the couch, and without any discussion, Finn folds me into him and I relax. It feels so good to be tucked against him again; his shirt is soft, and his plastic-y clear tux has long since been discarded after his sweat made it fog up. He leans his head against mine, and I wrap my arm around him and—

I jolt awake. Finn is shaking my shoulder, and around us employees are cleaning up. The venue is completely empty of partygoers, and the music is off. "Maeve, we gotta go. It's six a.m."

"You should've woken me up," I murmur.

"You looked too peaceful."

Finn pulls out his phone and starts tapping away. "Car's outside." He helps me up and we walk out. My legs are aching, sore from all the dancing and the hours in heels, and I almost want to ask him to carry me. He's scooped me up on the way out of countless clubs in New York and frat parties in college, when I was more than done with my heels. The coat check guy is gone, and Finn's suit and my heels are sitting on the counter. He grabs them and ushers me outside.

You'd think that given that the party is over, all the photographers would be gone. But a lone paparazzo is still standing outside and snaps pictures of us as we walk out. Finn tries to shield me against his side, and given how sweaty and rumpled he looks, I have to imagine I'm just as bad. Maybe we can buy these photos and keep them from going out. But probably not, since it looks like we're doing a walk of shame after doing something illicit in the venue.

Inside the car the driver hands Finn a bag, and I know the smell instantly. "You didn't."

"Oh, but I did." He's gotten my favorite hangover food: bagel sandwiches from Russ & Daughters.

"Oh my god, I love you right now." And then my cheeks light up. We used to say things like that all the time, since we really were friends. But after I said it and meant it . . . and he didn't mean it, not really, clearly, I haven't said it since. Now that the buzz has faded and we're in the light of day, I feel stupid for thinking I could forget about everything with Finn and be friends like we were. It feels too *good*. I'll never be able to move on and get over him if I let him get this close.

Finn can feel the change come over me. When we get to the hotel, he tries to help me out of the car and I brush him off. When we get in the elevator, he presses the button for our floor, then looks at me when the door closes. "I love you too," he says softly.

"Except you don't," I choke out. My eyes are welling with tears. I practically run to my door and open it, refusing to look at him. He follows me, takes his bagel out of the bag, and holds the bag out to me. I snatch it from him and shut the door, desperate to get inside before the real waterworks start.

"Maeve!" I hear him call through the door, and his footsteps pace back and forth for a moment before the door to his room slams shut. I hear the water turn on in his room, and I follow suit.

I strip my sweaty dress off and leave it in a pile on the bathroom floor, then step into the shower and sink to the floor. While the water hits my back and washes the night off me, I start to sob. Being around him, letting myself enjoy it, just reminds me that what we have feels too good. To me it feels like a once-in-a-lifetime connection, but it isn't for him. So I can't let him in because doing that will destroy me. I have to protect myself.

ELEVEN

Finn

"Haven't I *shown* you I care?" I hiss at Maeve. We're sitting in the studio waiting for Renee to arrive. "I have done everything I could think of. Not call. Call. Not talk about what's off-limits. Try to apologize. But Maeve, I *do* love you! I care! Just *look* at me."

Since coming in today Maeve has completely iced me. She'll only answer me when I speak directly to her, and won't make eye contact. Everything felt so normal at the gala, and then when we left, somehow me getting her her favorite bagels set her off? I don't *get* her. She is so much harder to understand than other women, and usually I love that about her, but right now it's killing me. Can't she do the bare minimum and communicate? For god's sake, she's a therapist and I'm literally begging her to tell me what to do to make things right between us.

"No. We need to keep things professional."

"Was that what we were doing when you fell asleep in my lap at the after-party?"

My tone is harsh, and I regret it as soon as I say it. But Maeve's eyes flash, and she actually engages with me, so maybe it's better that I said it. I'd rather her be screaming at me than ignoring me. "That was a momentary lapse of judgement. My sincere apologies. Next time I'll make sure to vacate the position for Cassidy, or some model."

I triple check my mic pack to make sure that we're not recording. "*How* can you discard our entire friendship just because I fucking dated Cassidy?"

"*I* am not the one who discarded our friendship. And I told you I'm not talking about this. And you know what? Fuck you, Finn. Fuck. You. I know not getting exactly what you want is a new experience for you. But you can't just have me and discard me like I'm nothing. Go fuck yourself. Or fuck literally anyone else. Whatever, I don't care anymore."

I shake my head. "I can't believe you." That's how all our friends saw me. As some sort of fuckboy, because I took a lot of different girls out on dates. They assumed because I'm me I couldn't actually be interested in finding someone I connect with, and that I must be sleeping with all of them. I wasn't, and it hurts to hear Maeve make me out to be a horrible guy when she actually knows me. I was just trying to navigate a complicated situation and be fucking happy. Being a rich celeb doesn't magically make you feel fulfilled. I needed something more, and I thought that something was the show. But, as it turns out, it's not the show, although it is better than my finance job, so what made me happy for those two years must have been Maeve. Maeve, who has always seen me for who I actually am and now thinks I'm trash. I open my mouth, ready to say who knows what, because this just pisses me off, but I slam my jaw shut when the door opens.

Renee walks into the studio in a rush of fruity perfume, with a tray of iced coffees labeled with our names. "I grabbed these from your helper! I'm so excited to be doing this." She sets the tray on the table. I met her briefly at the gala and at the after-party, but spent last night watching her show and YouTube videos of her *Bachelorette* highlights to try to familiarize myself with her. "I feel like I'm basically your first guest, since Evangeline is family."

"Ah, I buy that." I sound tense. Maeve, on the other hand, is smiling angelically like she doesn't have a care in the world. She's the one accusing me of not caring, but she turns feelings on and off like a switch whenever something is work related.

Maeve gets up and hugs Renee, helps her put on the lav mic under her shirt while I avert my eyes, and instructs her on where to sit. By the time we've all settled in and I'm getting up to hit Record on the cameras, I'm still reeling from our conversation. Maeve removed the duo shot from last week, and so now we just have four cameras, three for our close-ups and one wide shot of all of us. She also got us even more upgraded lav mics, ones that attach to our shirts with a tiny pin instead of a clip and are virtually invisible.

I launch into the intro this week, since we typically rotate. "We are back again with another episode of *Tell Me How You Really Feel*, and we have our next guest, Renee Jones. Renee here is a pro at telling people how she actually feels, whether it's men she's axing from *The Bachelorette*, or her fiancé, whom she proposed to just this past month."

"Oooh, are you introducing me or roasting me?" she teases. "Thank you both so much for having me. When I say I *screamed* when I saw Maeve in the bathroom at the Met Gala . . ."

Maeve jumps in. "I can confirm. I had the words 'oral sex' ringing in my ears all night."

"How do *I* get into the ladies' bathrooms? Sounds like a party! We are not having those types of convos at the urinals."

"That's for sure," Maeve snarks. "Renee, let's dive right into it. In the Met Gala bathroom you told me that I would be getting a fruit basket from your fiancé because of our viral third episode, which dives into oral sex. And I have to admit, Finn might be the one who's actually due the Edible Arrangements in this case."

I pretend to dust off my shoulders. "I'm doing the good work, what can I say."

"No, actually," Renee interjects gleefully. "His tips in episode three were great, don't get me wrong. That position shift to go at her clit sideways? Game-changing. But it *wasn't* game-changing until after I listened to episode seventy-one, where Maeve talks about the O face."

"Tell me more." We've gotten a lot of compliments on that third episode. It went viral for a reason, because no one ever breaks down exactly how to go down on someone, and a lot of people are left fumbling in the dark. But this I've never heard before.

"Well, basically, I couldn't come. My girlfriend is amazing in bed, but I was too self-conscious about how I looked to actually get there. As everyone and their mother knows, I was a virgin when I was on *The Bachelorette*. I was saving the goods for marriage, and my parents, bless their hearts in Alabama, believe that because I'm with Candice, I am still a virgin. They haven't gotten the memo that there's more types of sex than penetrative. But basically, even though it felt good, I just couldn't relax because I was so worried about looking cute. Like Maeve said, my whole life I was expected to look good for men. Somehow that transferred over, and so even though Candice is a woman, I still was trying to perform, rather than be in my own pleasure. And I didn't even realize it until Maeve talked about it in that episode."

"I remember that one. Vividly. I changed what I do because of it, that's for sure," I comment.

Maeve nods. "For anyone who hasn't listened to that episode

yet, I basically begged men not to stare us down while they go down on us. I want their eyes shut or glued to my nether regions so I can come without worrying about having the perfect cute O face. I only feel comfortable enough to look completely gross and not feel self-conscious about it with like six people, and a new partner is not one of them. I want to look cute for them and don't want to be in my head about it!"

"Who are the six?" Renee pipes up.

Maeve blushes. "My parents, two, my three sisters, makes five . . ." She hesitates, the pause loaded. She never said who the six were during the episode, and I hadn't thought to ask if it was a literal number. My heart rate spikes as I wait to see who it is. Her high school boyfriend? Some guy from college? "And the sixth is Finn. I tend to look my most grimy around him, when we're editing or just hanging."

This isn't true anymore. The only time I've seen her without makeup these past six months was during the Met Gala prep. And she's been wearing nice clothes like armor around me, instead of her usual *Tell Me How You Really Feel* sweat sets.

Renee cocks an eyebrow, so I jump in before she can pop a question we don't want to answer. "Wait. So, Renee, why is your fiancé the one sending the fruit basket here?"

Renee tilts her head theatrically and smirks. "Because now she doesn't have to have a complex over not making me come. Don't worry, world; she's great. No orgasm gap here."

"That's what we like to hear!" Maeve claps lightly. "Now, Renee, you mentioned that your family has some views on sex and sexuality that are different from yours. What was it like to go from being the bachelorette and looking for a husband to proposing to your wife?"

Renee takes a long sip of her coffee. "You all should drink up too. This is going to take a while to unpack."

I laugh, and Maeve nods encouragingly. "We're all ears."

"It made falling for Candice really confusing. It took me months to realize what I felt for her was something more than wanting to be her best friend. That maybe I've had a few crushes that I thought were just wanting to be best friends with people, because my up-bringing raised me to think that being gay was for other people. Or that because I genuinely liked guys, I couldn't also have the same intensity of feelings for a woman."

Maeve spends a while unpacking feelings with Renee, and while I jump in here and there, I can't help but be distracted by the situation between Maeve and me. She doesn't feel comfortable around me any-more. At the gala I thought I should just jump on any chance I got to progress things with her: holding hands, dancing, cuddling. But I broke her trust, and it seems like doing those things makes her more overwhelmed and pissed at me later. I want to convince her that I really do care. But maybe the only way to do that is by taking a step back and showing her that we don't have to be the same as we were before, so intimate, for us to be close. I'll respect her space and try to take things slower, rebuild the friendship, instead of trying to race ahead and pick up where I fucked up.

We record with Renee for over two hours, but the time flies by. "Can I come over to edit it with you?" I ask Maeve as we're packing up.

She shoots me a withering glance. "No. I'll get Leo to drop a hard drive off at your place after I cut it together. Send me a timecode if there's something you want to change."

Streamify is way too paranoid and doesn't want us upload the footage to Frame.io, which is what we would usually use to share episodes if one of us was out of town or something. But leave it to Maeve to find a way to still make sure we can edit separately. I take a deep breath. I want to fix things, but she's being so dismissive of me, and it really pisses me off. "Wouldn't it be easier to just edit together?"

"Um, no. It's actually faster for me to do it solo. Find a hobby, Finn, that's not watching me edit." She walks out without a backward glance, and for the second time today I feel like I got punched in the gut.

On my drive home her words are echoing through my head. Ever since the podcast stopped being something we really did *together*, I've felt untethered. Getting to do something more creative like that was a relief after trying to make the finance world work, but it's not truly fun when I can't be collaborative with Maeve. Maeve has been my direction the past two years. But I can't be carried along by her momentum if she won't let me into the boat with her, and I miss having a creative outlet that feels safe.

My parents are constantly trying to pull me over to their next project. But I can't do acting. I read the scripts Cassidy has been sending me in secret, and before our relationship blew up in my face, I used to be her scene partner on FaceTime. And I loved it. Ever since that first movie when I was little, I have loved acting. It makes me feel lit up all over; it's an adrenaline rush. The only thing I've felt that parallels it is the spark I have when I'm with Maeve. But I can't handle getting stalked by paparazzi twenty-four hours a day again. Having men banging on my car windshield and chasing my car. That experience as a child was excruciating, and just thinking about it makes my palms sweat and my throat close up. Acting isn't worth everything that comes with it.

I need to fix things with Maeve because being with her, doing the show with her for real . . . I know it can be enough. It has to be.

TWELVE

Before the Streamify contract

Maeve

I reach over and turn off the mic definitively. "I cannot do one more take."

Finn laughs and throws it onto the coffee table. "It has been a bit of a challenge today."

Every single time we tried to record this week, there was a huge disruption to our audio. First, at Finn's place, construction workers started doing maintenance on the bricks, pounding directly on the wall next to us. It sounded like someone was trying to knock down the building. Then when we tried again at my apartment, my next-door neighbor decided to embark on a Harry Potter movie marathon, blasting the first three in a row through our shared wall. And now, at the gorgeous brownstone Finn's mom's friend owns, there is some sort of emergency happening right outside our window.

"Today? Try this entire week."

Finn starts packing up the mics as I put away the cameras. "Maybe we should try recording in the dead of night," he suggests.

"With our luck there would be a flash mob club directly outside our window. Or, like, in our own apartment somehow."

"Let's get out of the city. Have you ever been to the Hamptons? Montauk?" Finn's eyes have lit up and he puts the bag aside.

I laugh and turn off the third camera. "Do I look like I summer in the Hamptons?"

"Come on, let's do it. I'll rent a car. In four hours we'll be in the Hamptons. Yes Way Rosé is one of our sponsors this season! It's on brand; we have to do it."

I roll my eyes and take the batteries out of the camera, and put them on charge. "It costs like a million dollars to go there." I'm happy that we now make enough that I can get by in a studio without roommates, but I still have barely any savings and am far from well-off.

Finn holds up a finger in the pause gesture. "So, if it were free to stay there, you'd go? Like right now?"

"If you can get us a place in the Hamptons, for free, then after we pick up clothes from my place, yes, I will go."

Finn is the kind of guy who knows everybody. Who can make something happen, who goes to Cannes and within three hours is on a yacht with the most famous actors there, even though he planned to just drop in. I forget sometimes that he's ridiculously well-connected and his family is obscenely wealthy. So when, within an hour, we're in a borrowed convertible on our way to a family friend's place in Montauk, I'm still slightly surprised.

He drives confidently, only one hand on the wheel, his dark hair blowing in the wind and sunglasses sliding down his nose. In fact, in his partially unbuttoned white linen shirt he looks like he's already *in* the Hamptons. When he turns to me, grinning, my breath catches in my throat for a moment. The way he looks over at me, for the briefest moment, at a red light . . . if I didn't know better I would think he felt something for me. Something more than friendship.

But the whole point of our show is that *we're* just friends. Who help each other find the one. And who go on friendly trips to the Hamptons to record, then sleep in separate rooms.

"So tell me, what's the dream studio?"

"What?" Finn likes to lob questions at me with no warning. You'd think that, as a therapist, I'd be the one doing the asking, but with him all bets are off.

"Your future podcasting studio. What's it look like?"

I've never thought much about it. But I can play along. I stick an arm lazily out the window and feel the wind wrap around it. We have the top down now, almost in the Hamptons, and I can smell the impending rain. I love it. And more than anything, I love that I'm here with Finn.

"Soundproofed, for starters. And very cozy, you know? I want it to feel like we're at home in the living room. But, like, a super nice living room. With brown leather chairs, but then lots of bright white, so it doesn't feel too manly. And pink accents on, like, the coffee table, the picture frames. And . . ." I trail off, thinking. "And artwork on the walls that's all by women. Sexy artwork, but still a bit reserved. Classy, since I see the show becoming a bit more elevated once we're not selling our sex life for a viral week."

"I like it!" Finn remarks. "Sounds very elevated. The most elevated. How about some sort of plaque that says TELL ME HOW YOU REALLY FEEL?"

"Maybe in a subtle way," I agree. "And I want the studio to feel like it's golden hour, beautiful morning or evening light. But actually be completely artificial lighting so it looks consistent, and we could record easily at any time without having to relight as the natural light changes."

Finn throws his head back, laughing, and I flush, pleased. I don't think of myself as at all funny, but I relish when I make him laugh. Every inside joke we share feels like a building block in the story of us. It makes me wish, sometimes, that there could be an us that isn't possible, that wouldn't work with the show. A version of us where tonight we'd get into bed together instead of brushing our teeth together and then texting from separate rooms. "Now that sounds like you," he remarks. "Amazing vision, but also practical to your core."

"It's the dream combo! And I'd have a room in front for social content. And a *huge* editing bay, and a kitchen with every snack imaginable."

"Sounds like an entire house at this point."

I nod, then remember he's driving and can't see me nod. "Basically. Think like, super-fancy pool house vibes. Like a techie pool house! And, we'd get to leave the cameras and mics up at all times so we don't have to break down."

"Now that sounds like my dream. Although, we'll be so rich and successful by then, we can just hire people." Finn pulls the car into a long driveway, of a house that is directly on the water. "We're here."

Let's always keep it just us. The thought was on the tip of my tongue. But now, I'm busy taking in this house that was apparently sitting empty. "You can't be serious?"

"Oh, but I am." Finn jumps out of the car and grabs both of our suitcases. "They had the housekeeper bring us some groceries and wine, so we should be all set on food. But there's lots of good places around here, we should really go out tomorrow."

I follow Finn into the house and my head is spinning. This is a huge mansion. There are floor to ceiling windows in the living room, revealing a massive infinity pool with an outdoor grill and built-in marble tables, and a private beach entrance. The kitchen, the entire interior really, is real estate porn. "Why do they not spend every waking minute here?"

Finn shrugs. "I think they're doing a movie. In like, Antarctica or Alaska, or somewhere remote."

I open the fridge, which reveals fully stocked shelves, with organic produce, premade meals, anything I could think of. And on the counter are bottles of red, white, and rosé, all of which look more expensive than any wine I've ever bought.

"Remind me. Why are you bumming around in the city again? Living with four roommates? Working?"

Finn grabs chips and guac out of the fridge, ignoring my questions. "Their chef's guac is legendary. You have to try it." I follow him outside and we sit on the deck, enjoying the sunset and the guac, which is indeed delicious. Because of course it is. Why would they have anything that isn't incredible?

"So? Why are you doing CMU and the corporate life?" Maybe I shouldn't press it. But I suddenly really do want to know.

Finn is getting the full golden-hour treatment. He looks like a Pinterest photo come to life. His eyes are so blue they're stunning, especially in this light. "I wanted to live like a normal person."

I look around us: at the view, the house, everything. "But like, why? I'm really asking." And I am. Because I grew up in the tiniest house imaginable, in the shittiest little town. Our water would get turned off if my mom didn't get enough shifts that month. I can't imagine choosing to live in dorms and rat-infested post-college New York shoebox apartments when you have other options.

He sighs, heavily. "First off, I'm not complaining. And I'm telling this only to you."

"Finn, of course. I'm actually asking."

He looks away, toward the water. "My first really vivid memory isn't my mom, or dad, or some fun time in the pool. It's paparazzi chasing us out of a store, my mom pushing the stroller and then abandoning it and pulling me into the car. She had an assistant get the stroller later because she was so scared of how close the guys were getting to us that she didn't think she could stop to put it in the car. It was a whole crowd of men with cameras, and they were so *aggressive*. In California it's now a misdemeanor to photograph the children of celebs, but we were actually here in the Hamptons. Where it's fair game. And then that same thing, basically, was my entire childhood. *Especially* after the movie. I couldn't take a walk, go to the park, do anything really unless we were in a private area or abroad. It's just not a way to live. And the older I got the worse it was. They really hound you, you know?"

I don't. I actually can't imagine growing up like that. But I nod, encouraging him to keep sharing. He almost never talks about this. Finn looks back at me, and I can see in his eyes that these memories hurt. "My first real girlfriend, not Cassidy, but when I was a teenager, dumped me after every detail of her life was in *People*. When I failed my driver's ed test, it was in five different tabloids! I couldn't have anything for myself. People kept asking when I would act again. And as a kid I actually did *love* acting. I would put on little skits at home for my parents, and doing that movie was one of the best times of my life. But I knew that whatever I did would lead to my life being ripped into tinier and tinier shreds until there was nothing left for me. So I decided to be as boring as possible. And go to the most boring state, Pennsylvania, where there's no paps. And make my life entirely unexciting to photograph so that I could actually live."

My stomach twists, because what he's calling too boring to

photograph is my real life. My home. But this is his moment, and I understand what he's saying. "But the show . . ." I trail off. Because I know. He did it for me. "Are you okay with it all?"

He nods. "I chose to do the show with you, Maeve. You didn't force me. You didn't even try very hard to convince me. And I love doing it with you. It was unrealistic to think I could stay out of the spotlight forever anyway."

The sun has almost set now. It's a tiny ember on the horizon, and there's a chill in the air. I'm about to suggest we go inside since it's getting dark, when tiny fairy lights turn on, triggered by the setting sun. This is what being rich is like. Your every need is anticipated without you having to think about it. I never yearned to be rich, but now that I can see complete financial security in my future, and all of the ease it brings . . . I catch myself wanting it. "I'm sorry, Finn, that sounds awful. No child should have to deal with all that."

"But I get all this," he says with a dark smile. "It's a trade. But my parents are the ones who made it."

We watch the last of the sun fade away. I reach out and squeeze his hand once, then drop it. "Well, I'm glad we have the show together."

For the first time since we came out here, he looks at peace, his smile genuine and his eyes soft. "Me too, Maeve. Me too."

THIRTEEN

Maeve

"You know, this is nice. I could get used to it." I'm lying on Sarah's twin-size dorm room bed, looking around at the string lights and polaroids taped to the walls. "It's, like, minimalist. Maybe we should start chilling here instead. We can film *Tell Me How You Really Feel* college edition. 'Is the fuckboy who won't answer my texts my soulmate?' will be an easy week for me."

Sarah lobs a pillow directly at my head. "Next time, that will be a textbook. I know this isn't up to your Met Gala McMansion standards, but some of us are in college still."

I raise my hands in surrender. "Comments withdrawn. Can we go the dining hall, though? This is making me nostalgic for freezer-burned froyo and living on fries because the rest of the food is inedible."

Sarah shoots a withering glance at me from her roommate's bed. "No. You're famous now. And way too old to go to the dining hall. It's creepy until you're like fifty with your own kids. But you can take me to La Barca."

Twenty minutes later we're sitting outside at La Barca's patio and staring down flights of dragon fruit, hibiscus, pineapple, and rosé margaritas. Sarah rests her head on her fist and pretends to push a pair of glasses up the bridge of her nose. "So, Maeve, tell me—how do you *really* feel?"

"You're giving . . . cringe. Seriously, gross." I take a long sip of the dragon fruit marg. My sister introduced me to this place soon after I moved, after talking it up the past few years. And surprisingly, given that she typically subsists on ramen and pizza bagels, it did *not* disappoint.

"I'm just teasing! But seriously, how are things with Finn? The new episodes are really good. I missed you two together." She catches my narrowed eyebrows. "But I hate him, obviously. Ready and waiting to key his car, slander him online, put Nair in his shampoo, whatever it takes."

Sometimes I hate my sisters, but in moments like this I remember that I love them even when I hate them. "Thanks. I mean, we look good on camera or on the mic or whatever . . . but it's awful."

Sarah raises an eyebrow. "Your drunk texts from the gala say otherwise."

I drain the rest of the dragon fruit marg and move on to the pineapple. "Trust me, I paid for thinking we could go back to normal after I sobered up. Knowing that I'm disposable to him . . . I just can't trust him. And having fun with him hurts! Like, seriously. Laughing with him basically feels like purposefully poking splinters directly into my heart, because I want it to be as real as it feels to me, like, so badly. Wanted. Because now I hate him, and you can't love someone you hate, unless they're family. But it really does hurt. You know, heartbreak causes the same reaction in the brain as withdrawing from hard drugs. It's science."

The waiter brings out our food, and we dig into our fish and shrimp tacos ravenously. Through bites of taco, Sarah responds. "Well, that sucks. But real talk: you have three years on this contract. And it's going to be way too tiring to hate him the entire time, so you really need to find a way to be friendly. Or at least call a truce. Maybe the gala was too all in. Just treat him like Claude after she's really pissed you off, but she also won her soccer match, so you can't be a total brat."

"I have to be nice to Claude, though; she's family. It's not that easy with him." Claude might destroy my favorite shirt, but Finn got me to open up about every insecurity, to show him all of my soft spots, just to have him stab them with a fork perfectly designed to hit each and every one.

"Well, he's your ticket to literally making history as the highest-paid female podcaster, beating Paul Myers, getting your solo show, basically all your hopes and dreams. I mean, no biggie. But talk about incentive." Sarah reaches over to my side of the table to steal a taco, and I bat her hand away.

"Maybe you should be a therapist too." My tone is light, but her words are ringing in my ears. *He's your ticket.* She must not think I have what it takes to do this on my own either. *Fuck.* I know this is just an intrusive thought. She's my sister and she believes in me. But it rings through my mind anyway. *She must not think I have what it takes to do this on my own either.*

She grins and swipes one shrimp from my taco and adds it to her own. "Too easy. You did what, six years of school? Eight? Try fifteen years of school and residency."

"That highest-paid spot is looking sweeter every day," I mutter. Sarah's face drops a bit, and I falter. I don't want to make her feel guilty or indebted just because I'm paying for her school. Well, maybe just indebted enough that she'll be my on-call source for all medical questions. But not actually indebted. "I'm kidding. You know I'm happy to pay it."

"I appreciate it."

Sarah looks like she's about to say something touchy-feely when my phone chirps loudly. Earlier, I'd set it so emails about the show go to a special inbox, with notifications on so I don't miss anything. Now that I'm not worried about the show getting canceled, I'm trying to get my head in the game and capitalize on the good ratings to hold our spot long enough to beat *The Paul Myers Show*. I pull out my cell and open the email, only to be greeted with a five-paragraph essay.

"What? You got all bug-eyed." Sarah leans across to try to read the message.

"It's from Graham, our guest this week. The football player. He had told Finn he had a specific problem he wanted help with, and he wasn't kidding." I scan the email quickly. The sum of it is that Graham is deeply in the doghouse with his girlfriend.

"Why don't you prep with Finn?"

I roll my eyes. "Why would I do that? He's basically the comic relief." Sarah just stares me down, not saying anything. She knows that's not exactly true. I would call her the two years we did the show, buzzing from spending hours working on an episode with Finn, glowing from building on each other's ideas and making something great. "Fine. I'll text him."

Saw that email. Want to come over and brainstorm?

I look up at Sarah. "Done, but he's pissed now too. You should've heard us last week. There's no—"

My phone buzzes. Be there in thirty

Sarah lunges across the table and grabs it out of my hand. "Don't!" I say.

"'See . . . you . . . then . . .'" Sarah types. She glances up. "Should I add 'Fancy a truce?'"

I stand and grab the phone back from her. "I think he gets the memo. I've got to go. It'll take me thirty minutes just to get there." I look down at my outfit: a sweat set, greasy hair, and no makeup—and Sarah snickers.

"If you don't care about him, you don't need to dress up for him."

I signal a waiter and tap my watch against his card reader to pay. "Enjoy the walk to campus," I shout over my shoulder as I dash out. The drive to my place in the Hollywood Hills is a theoretical twenty-eight minutes, but in actuality is at least forty since LA has hellish traffic at all times. When I pull into my driveway, Finn is already there, sitting on the doorstep with his head lolling back against my door.

"Sorry I'm late," I say as I get out.

But Finn has perked up considerably at my arrival. "I thought you ditched me."

I unlock the door and let us both in, and he immediately starts walking around and looking at my things, making himself overly comfortable in my space. "Wow, Maeve, this is a great place. It's exactly what you always talked about."

"Almost." I used to fantasize about having a giant marble kitchen island that my sisters could sit at while I cooked, a huge pool, and an at-home theater. And that's all here, it's just that this place was—

"Whoa!" Finn's shout tells me he found exactly why this place was a bargain. "Maeve! This is the house from your crime podcast, isn't it?"

I follow him into the living room. Which is *very* recognizable because before I started renting this place the owners let Netflix film in here for the first-ever video episode of my favorite crime podcast, which just happened to focus on the horrific murder that happened in this very living room.

Finn turns to me, his eyes wide. "It isn't . . . Is it?"

"Sarah hasn't noticed yet. It was a fantastic deal . . ." I look around. The room has a sparkling paint job, and they let me keep the awesome furniture Netflix used in here for filming. But I've seen the crime scene photos, and the wall my TV is on used to be covered in guts from when a woman axed her neighbor to bits after finding out she hadn't vaccinated her children, which led to her baby dying of complications from the measles. "And, I mean, in a way . . . the woman killed her son first?" I wince as I say it. "I didn't say that; strike from the record. But I swear it's not haunted. And maybe it's cool podcast history? And it has a pool!"

"I can't believe you didn't tell me this. You know I love that show too! They're making a dramatization too; my dad's working on it, and the podcasters are producing." Finn grins at me. "It's cool, seriously. I mean, they could be like friendly ghosts."

"You know, that's basically what the real estate agent led with. Shazia was horrified that I took this place, but I kind of like it. And who knows, they want to sell it. Maybe if I last a year with the spirits, I'll buy it and get a great deal." Even though I now make more money than I ever have dreamt of, it doesn't feel real. I still agonize about the cost of getting my dinner delivered instead of picking it up, and I can't imagine paying for a first-class plane ticket. The other day I added two thousand dollars of items to my Reformation cart, but I couldn't check out. Instead I just favorited them and decided to wait for the sale. Maybe at some point the money will feel real, but after living frugally my entire life, I still feel like I could lose everything in an instant. I flop down on one side of the couch, and Finn sits on the other, leaving a comically large amount of space between us. "So, that email."

He snorts. "The novel you mean? Graham isn't going to need a ghostwriter for his eventual memoir. He's ready to go."

I put my feet on the ottoman and Finn follows suit. Our socked toes touch for the slightest moment while adjusting, and we both pull back. He moves his feet to the very edge and I look away uncomfortably, opening my computer that was tucked into the corner of the couch. I never thought we would be like this. I thought we had a bond that couldn't be degraded down to awkward glances and snipes that go for the throat. It just shows that even though I'm great at giving other people advice, it doesn't mean I necessarily have my own house in order.

"So, basically, he is in deep shit," I summarize. "He showed up baked to his daughter's christening. Bad. And he didn't propose when she got pregnant because he was waiting to do it when he won the Super Bowl. And then they lost, so he didn't do it. So she already thought he wasn't serious, and he made it even worse with the christening. She's not speaking to him, and he's staying in the guesthouse and wants to not only fix things but propose because he knows he's waited too long already."

Finn whistles. "He is in *deep*. And I assume he's already tried apologizing."

"Well, who knows if he did it right," I counter. Finn raises an eyebrow, and I elaborate, mimicking a guy's voice. Finn's voice, really. "I'm sorry, but you just don't understand, I meant X, Y, Z and yada yada bullshit bullshit."

"Ouch. He seems like he meant well. And he loves her!"

"Well, actions have consequences."

Finn pulls on the neck of his T-shirt. I can see beads of sweat forming on his temple. "Do you have water?"

I stand to get him a glass, then pause. "Want to go in the pool?" I still can't believe I have a pool. And that it's an inground pool, not a plastic six-foot-deep aboveground situation. I never thought I would be the kind of person who has a pool, which when I was growing up meant you were *rich* rich. But the people I'd considered rich rich as a kid are probably people that Finn considers poor.

"I didn't bring trunks." He glances down. "But I won't look if you won't."

I speak slowly, since clearly he's an idiot. "If you think we're skinny dipping, you're insane. Wear your boxers. I'm going to go change. Brita's in the fridge."

I practically run up the stairs and lock my bedroom door behind me. I squeeze my eyes shut, trying to forget the last time I saw Finn naked. How good he looked. How he looked at me. The way my stomach dropped when I saw how he looked at her just weeks later. I take a few deep breaths, pop half an edible to calm down and hopefully stop the panic attack I can feel brewing, ready to unleash if he says one more idiotic thing, and start digging through my closet for my cutest bathing suit. I want him to see what he's missed out on.

When I walk downstairs, I see that Finn is already in the pool, floating on the flamingo in his underwear. They're tight gray Calvin Klein briefs, and instead of looking like an idiot, he looks like a male model. It's so irritating. As is the way my nipples tighten and I feel something low in my gut at the sight of him. But I'm gratified to see that I'm not the only one reacting.

Finn's blue eyes look darker as he watches me walk toward him. And if I'm being honest, I am walking a bit slower than usual. Letting my hips move. I may not be a six-foot-tall model like Cassidy, but I am fit, and just like my sisters, my curves are in some *great* places. And this tiny Inamorata bikini isn't leaving much to the imagination.

I jump in, splashing Finn and holding on to my top for dear life, then climb onto the unicorn float. "So, solutions for Graham."

"Right." Finn's voice is rough and he coughs. "Maybe you tell him exactly how to apologize. So he can get it right and take accountability. And then we focus on how he can show her how much he cares."

I let my float spin lazily and lean back on the neck of the unicorn, my feet dangling in the water. "And he has to make it clear he loves her. And has this whole time, that he's not just doing this because they have a child. It's about her."

"Why would it be a bad thing to want to be a family now that he has a kid?" Finn's spinning his float by sculling with his hands so he can stay facing me.

"It's not a bad thing. But a marriage, at least a good one, is a lifetime. Why would she want to marry someone who isn't actually choosing *her*?"

"Maybe he just doesn't know how to make her believe she's who he chooses."

I'm not sure we're talking about Graham anymore. But I continue as if we are. "Not taking something that's important to her seriously, like the christening, isn't a good way to show it. I don't think he can propose right away. I think he needs to earn his place back in her life, then go for it. And have the moment be about her, not about him, like the football plan was."

Finn is quiet. I hope he doesn't think I'm saying he still has a shot. Because we are *done* done. I reach a hand toward him, and he paddles toward me, then reaches out tentatively. I take his hand firmly and start to tug, not realizing until he's tipping over and I look up and notice that his mouth was open, about to say something, his eyes wide and earnest.

FOURTEEN

Finn

I surface, sputtering. I thought we were having a *moment*. "What was that for?" And I'm immediately hit in the chest with a beach ball. I serve it back at Maeve, and it hits her leg with a sharp smack, knocking her off-balance.

She rolls off the float, and I try not to look too hard to see if that completely impractical bikini slips. "Whoever gets the first point gets to ask the other whatever they want. Honest answers only."

Game on. "Where are the goal posts?"

Maeve points to the two opposite sides of the deep end. "Seven-foot markers." She tosses the ball to the middle of the deep end, and pushes her float to the shallow end.

"You're on," I say, eyes narrowed. "Three, two, one!"

We both lunge for the ball, vicious in our intensity. We've been tiptoeing around each other for months, not touching, barely talking, but now she's elbowing me and I'm pushing her away. At first I'm slightly worried about hurting her, since I'm twice her size, while we fight over the ball. But after she holds me under for at least ten seconds, ending it with a kick to the ribs, I realize that with her fighting dirty and me fighting fair, we're a pretty even match. Playing this impromptu, scrappy version of water polo should be sexy, considering we're both practically naked. But I forgot how competitive we are. There is not an ounce of sexual tension here, just months' worth of frustration coming out, on both sides.

Right as it seems like Maeve is going to launch the ball over my head and make a point, I lunge at her and bring her down by the arm, dunking us both underwater. For an instant I'm afraid I've hurt her. How many hours have I spent watching that arm hold a mic, or her wrist poised delicately over the computer, editing? But she shakes it off and uses my momentary concern to her advantage, laughing in my face and grabbing the ball back.

We fight over the ball until my legs ache. We both have scratches on our arms, and I may have bruised a rib. But finally, I throw the ball and it hits her seven-foot marker. "Yes!" I bellow. "Take that!"

"Best out of three?" she tries. We swim over to the edge of the pool and both hold on, heaving.

"Nice try. I know my question."

"Ugh, fine. But let me get out of the pool."

Maeve pulls herself out with effort and lies down directly on the deck, not even bothering to make it to a chair. Her chest rises and falls dramatically as she catches her breath, and I lie down alongside her but opposite, so our heads are next to each other, but our bodies are facing in different directions. Personal space, since I'm taking the slow and steady route now.

"You know, this is *exactly* where she dragged the body," I point out. "Or the big chunks anyway. She dissolved them in a bucket on the lawn."

"They bleached it, relax."

I laugh shortly, unable to really get into it since I'm still gasping for air. Maeve is the only person I know who would be this unperturbed about living in a murder scene. "Do you miss us? Like how we were before?"

"That's your question," Maeve says. A statement, more than asking. I nod, and she seems to feel the movement of my head, or the splatter of my hair, or just know what I mean, because she continues. "Yes. I do. But we can't go back; it's not possible." The silence is heavy for a moment. I turn my head, but she keeps looking up, and all I can see is the side of her face. Her auburn hair is darker since it's wet and slicked back, bleeding water onto the pool deck. Her cheeks are flushed, and she's biting her lip, a nervous habit she has. Tiny droplets of water are falling off her lashes. At least, I think it's water. I'm not sure. "But you were right. The point of the show was for us to find the one. It was time for us both to date seriously; it was the whole premise. And Cassidy was a good fit for you. She's always been the one that got away; it would have been ridiculous not to try."

The show did help me find the one. But it was you, not Cassidy. That's all I can think. But it's not the thing to say right now. Maeve won't believe me.

"Can we be friends again? Like actually friends. I miss you. We don't have to be cuddling and touchy. But Maeve, I miss us." I'm whispering, my entire body craning toward hers.

She turns her head, just the slightest bit, and catches my eye. "Just friends?" I nod, barely, and she looks back up at the sky and even though I can't hear her exhale, I see her chest rise and fall. "Fine. Just friends. Normal friends."

I don't know what normal is for us. Normal is giving her everything, every last bit of me, all the best parts that I didn't even know
were there until I was around her. But normal is better than having
her hate me.

I stand up and offer her a hand, pulling her up. "Thank you." We
walk over to the chairs set out by the pool house and I point to a sec-
tion on the middle of lawn where there's a patch of grass that has
clearly been freshly put down. "That's where they found her?"

Maeve nods. "I kind of want to dig it up. They say at least ten
small bones were never recovered."

I drop into my chair and look over my shoulder at it while Maeve
grabs waters from the outdoor fridge. "I'll do the grunt work if you
want. You can just hose off the potential bones."

"I'm in."

We sit in silence for a few minutes, chugging water. Only once
I've had a bottle and a half and am at serious risk of dry drowning do
I stop. "So where did the water polo come from?"

"Oh, my sisters used to play when we were really mad at each
other. Breaks the ice."

I nod, my chest warming. That means Maeve wanted to make
things at least somewhat better between us too. "You had a pool?"

She shakes her head. "We played at the public pools. So there's
a limited number of runs, since the lifeguards banned us afterward
each time. We worked through all but one public pool in the Pittsburgh area."

"Well, I hope you saved the last one for a really big fight."

"Of course."

I steel myself, then chug the rest of my water. I know I sweated
out way more than two bottles during that match. "We've been in
number one for two weeks, you know."

Maeve splashes me with the remnants of her bottle, and I shake my head like a dog, soaking it in. "We dropped to number two today."

"Fuck. Them?"

"Yeah. He got an evil tech billionaire on. Being number one for six straight months is going to be really hard."

"I think we can do it. Maybe he'll get canceled."

Maeve shakes her head. Her hair is starting to dry in the heat and some strands are becoming redder. I always love seeing her like this, in the in-between states, when I know that I get to see her in a way our fans don't. Although, right now, I can see so much of her that I'm having to think unsexy thoughts like, mic cutting out, canceled contract, wide shot stopped recording, temporary ban on social for inappropriate content, to keep myself from showing how attracted to her I am. My briefs don't leave much to the imagination, but she's not looking. "Paul Myers could turn getting canceled into better ratings. I hate him, and I hate how good at manipulating the ratings he is. But we have time. The guest thing is working for us." Silence lingers for a few minutes. And it's easy, not the tense, *don't talk to me* silence we've been having. "So what have you been up to?" Maeve asks finally.

It's the first time she's asked me about myself since the "incident," as I think of it now. I try not to show my surprise. "Like aside from the show?" She nods, and I can tell she's actually asking. Listening. "Nothing really, to be honest."

Her brows furrow. "What do you mean? You haven't been editing, so you must have some spare time."

"Trust me, I do. But I just . . . I don't know what to do."

Maeve is quiet for a moment while she takes this in. "We're in LA now. You could just think about acting aga—"

"I can't," I cut in, my stomach twisting with a familiar anxiety at the thought.

Maeve raises her eyebrows at my strong reaction. "The paparazzi are more regulated than when you were a kid."

"And the fans have smartphones. It evens out." I sigh, long and heavy. I've thought about all this too, mostly late at night when I'm feeling unsatisfied and alone. But I always come back to the same thing, which is the visceral memories I have as a child of just feeling so *scared* by all of the shouting and chasing and flashing lights.

"We're already famous now. The show is big and you're you. And you made yourself much higher profile this past summer. I really think it won't be that different of an experience than the life you're living now." She purses her lips, holding back whatever else she was going to add.

"Think about the women from your crime podcast," I argue. "They're super famous, for podcasters. They have almost a million followers, they go to award shows, the whole thing. But they can still go out to eat unnoticed if it's a random spot, go to Target, whatever. Then think of what would happen if my mom tried to walk into a mall."

"She'd be mobbed," Maeve acknowledges.

"Exactly. And to their million followers, I have thirty million, ten of whom have stuck around even for the decade I never posted. Acting would make everything infinitely worse. It would be like when I was a kid again, being hounded." Just the thought of living like that again makes my skin crawl. "I'm not ready to give up being able to use a Starbucks drive-through. But you're right, I know I'd enjoy it. Until I couldn't tolerate it."

Maeve is quiet, just listening. Not pushing. And not saying we don't need to talk about it because it upsets me. She's the only person I ever talk about this with. After a few minutes of silence, just us and the breeze, she finally speaks. "If you ever decide it's worth it and want help learning to sit with your anxiety surrounding it, I'm here. And I know that if you decide you want to you can. You'll find a way you can still live a full life with it, like your mom has."

"Thanks," I say tersely. She doesn't understand how hard it was seeing the press decimate my mom's confidence for years, stalk our family, harass me wherever I went. Podcasting is one thing. If I started acting . . . it's a massive amount of risk. With *Tell Me How You Really Feel*, I knew what I was trading for, and it was time with Maeve. This is a whole different story. But I break the tension, more concerned with keeping us on track than talking out my existential crisis. "Who should I make the bill for this session out to?"

Maeve giggles and splashes water on me. We spend the rest of the afternoon working on our plan for Graham's episode, and for the rest of the season. Planning what guests should come on when together, how to make the episodes pop. Cool social content we could film. I really believe that if we can actually work together, we could take that top spot.

When I get into bed later that night, for the first time in months I actually relax when my head hits the pillow. I feel so much better now that I've gotten to a better place with Maeve. Just as I'm drifting off, my phone dings.

It's a text from Maeve. I think you activated the ghosts. I've been feeling a chill in the air

One text shouldn't make me smile like I'd just won the lottery. But I can't help it. I thought they could be friendly ghosts?

Good point, I'll ask them to stream the show.

Maybe we can do a special episode-advice from beyond the grave

SOLD!

I fall asleep clutching my phone, a smile still on my face.

FIFTEEN

Before the Streamify contract

Finn

Maeve and I are on our way to a restaurant in DUMBO, after spending the day at a rooftop pool, swimming, reading, and drinking with fans who showed up after someone posted about us being there. It's in the nineties in New York, which feels more like the hundreds, and despite having showered off the sunscreen and chlorine only an hour ago, I'm sticky again with sweat.

"What do you think we should talk about this week?" I ask Maeve halfheartedly. It's hard to even think about the episode when it's this hot, and we're both scrolling through our phones mindlessly.

"Blow jobs? Anal? That's all anyone wants to hear about." She starts ineffectually fanning herself with her purse, and I join in, flapping hot air toward her with my paperback. "Let's check the DMs."

Since we end each episode with Questions of the Week, our fans are constantly DM'ing us questions and topics they want us to cover. At least, at first it was just questions and glowing messages. Now, we also have *a lot* of solicitations, and a variety of complaints, largely from fans of *The Paul Myers Show*, egged on by the host himself. Maeve gets the brunt of those, disgusting men with no followers or posts or profile photo, telling her she's a slut, going to hell, and a variety of other awful things. It's unclear why he hates us so much, but ever since we bumped him from the number one spot during our third week, he's been constantly running his mouth about us, and getting rewarded with tons of views.

I open my Instagram and navigate to message requests, then start scrolling through. The first three messages are women asking me on dates, which I ignore. Next, there's a very graphic photo (block and delete). I glance at Maeve's phone and see her systematically delete ten messages in a row with dick pics. I definitely have it easier. Back on mine, I scroll through questions about who should pay on dates, whether their boyfriend can stay over at a female friend's house, anal and oral sex questions, as well as a few about what to wear on a first date.

"We haven't done this yet," I offer. "Are shorts acceptable to wear on a first date? What about polo shirts?"

Maeve looks up from her phone, brow furrowed. The subway door opens and more people get on, packing the car so tightly that we can barely see each other's face despite sitting next to each other. "That's tough. I'm inclined to say no to both. But also . . . maybe some girls are into that?"

"I'll keep looking," I say. I continue scrolling until I get to a message that makes my stomach drop.

Go kill yourself. U r disgusting. No talent, prob not even from ur parents. Going to hll.

This person can't even spell. They have no posts and don't know me. But the message still makes my pulse race. The moment when I first read it, I get a jolt of pure adrenaline.

Talentless hack. DIE. Your movie sucks 2

I block and delete. But after a few more nice messages, there's more.

I'm gonna kill you and Maeve. I no where u live. Your show is disgusting, making women whores. Devil's work.

U think ur funny? Show sucks. Nepo baby w no talent. Mommy nd daddy bought ur fake fans. Loser

"People are awful," I complain to Maeve.

"Tell me about it," she agrees. "This guy told me he hopes I choke on a dick and die. Like, what is wrong with them? At least five of these are verbatim from lines Paul said during an episode."

In a recent episode, Paul Myers gave his fans word-for-word hate mail lines to send us, about how our show is corrupting the youth, is un-Christian, and contains bottom-of-the-barrel talentless content. He's going after the two of us in an alarming way given that we've never said a word about him. At least since it's Maeve and me together, we can laugh about it sometimes and try to make it seem more wild than scary.

"Maybe we should do one about what the ideal first date looks like for each of us," Maeve suggests finally. I've stopped scrolling and am just trying to ignore the sweat dripping down my back, since with each person who gets onto the train it gets hotter. "Show that they're different but talk about the similarities. And the things people should absolutely not do. We can ask for bad date stories for Questions of the Week!"

"I like that." I would like anything at this point. It's too hot to think.

Maeve posts a photo of us at the pool with a Q&A feature asking for bad-date stories and first-date noes, and then I post the same question but with a selfie of us jammed between the thighs of subway riders standing, our hair disheveled and faces shiny. By the time I've done mine, Maeve's is already getting responses, but we both put our phones away.

"Only five more stops," Maeve remarks listlessly.

I don't answer. I feel like I'm sweating more than I should be, even in this heat, packed into a subway car like sardines. And I feel a pressure in my chest, like my heart is being squeezed and it's getting harder to breathe. I try to take a slow deep breath but it just makes it worse.

Another stop comes and goes and the feeling gets worse. It feels like an elephant is sitting on my chest and I feel both cold and hot, drenched in sweat. We get to another stop and suddenly I just have to get off this packed train. "I've got to go," I say, too quietly. Why am I speaking so quietly? I push through the crowd, leaving my book on the bench and into the still muggy air on the platform. I want to get outside, to the real air, but I don't think I can. I drop into a seat, gasping, and drop my head between my knees.

"Finn! Finn!" Maeve spots me and runs over as other people filter away to the exit. She's holding her things and my book, and drops to the dirty ground in front of me. "Finn? What's wrong? What's happening?"

"I think I'm having a heart attack," I choke out. Is that possible? Can day drinking and a life of excess drugs, alcohol, and good food give me a heart attack in my twenties? I'm sure it happens.

"What? What does it feel like?"

"I think I'm dying," I gasp. "Can't breathe." It feels like this will never stop, like there's no air, and the tight feeling, this weight on my chest, is going to kill me.

"Take a deep breath," Maeve says as she pulls out her phone. "Try to breathe."

A cop walks over to us. "Is everything alright here, miss?"

"I think we need an ambulance," Maeve says, her voice panicked. "I have no service down here."

"Langone Health's emergency room is right outside. I'll help you get him out." The officer puts his arm under my shoulder. "Can you stand?"

Maeve tries to get my other shoulder, but she's way too short. She keeps an arm pressed to my back, steadying me as we make our way outside the station and across the street to the automatic emergency room doors. The cop deposits me on a gurney in the hallway, then leaves, and Maeve stays glued to my side. "Just try to breathe, I'm going to get someone."

I still feel like I'm dying, although the walk didn't make me feel worse necessarily. Within minutes Maeve has returned, pulling an alarmingly young-looking doctor behind her. "He's having a heart attack or something," she yells. "Help him!"

The doctor looks at me skeptically, then starts taking my vital signs. I'm hunched over and my chest feels like it'll explode, like I might die before we see a doctor who's not ten. I've never felt anything like this, and it's terrifying. Maeve takes my free hand and squeezes it, looking between me and the doctor expectantly.

"Is your chest pain sharp or dull," she asks me.

"Sharp. I feel . . . it's crushing."

She nods and holds her stethoscope to my chest, listening. "I don't think you're having a heart attack. But let's get you checked in, we can do an ECG to be sure."

"Are you a doctor? Or, like, a *Grey's Anatomy* intern?" Maeve asks.

The doctor glares at her as she helps me lie down and starts wheeling my gurney. "I'm a resident. And more than qualified to help your friend here. You can do the paperwork in the lobby while I administer his ECG."

Maeve opens her mouth to argue, but before she can I'm whisked away into another room. The ECG feels like it takes a year while my chest is caving in, and I'm sweating more than humanly possible. "How long has it been?" I ask Maeve when she's back by my side.

"Ten minutes," she says, her voice tight as she looks toward the doctor expectantly.

"He's not having a heart attack," the doctor says firmly. "I believe he's having a panic attack."

Understanding flashes over Maeve's face and she takes my hand. "Are you sure? Do you have any other tests you think you should do?"

"I can order blood tests. But I don't think it's necessary."

"Please order them," Maeve commands firmly.

"Happy to. It might be an hour or two, though. We just had two gunshot victims come in, and it's all hands on deck. Someone will come by."

She opens the curtain and leaves, and Maeve turns to me and climbs onto the tiny bed. I'm just wearing underwear and a hospital gown, and feel mildly ridiculous. My chest is still tight and uncomfortable, in a way it's never been before, but now that I know I'm not dying . . . it's embarrassing.

"It'll be okay," she says as she rests her head on my shoulder.

I put my arm around her, and having her there, holding her against me, starts to make me feel marginally calmer. We lie like that as I try to breathe, the even rise and fall of Maeve's breath the guiding light for mine. It feels like no time at all, but when I check my watch, it's been over an hour.

"I'm sorry," I say after a while.

She sits up. "For what?"

"Um, dragging you to the ER." I glance at my watch. "Our reservation was like two hours ago now."

"Don't be an idiot. I don't care about that." She lies back down on my chest. "You scared me. I'm just glad you're okay."

"I've never . . . I've never felt like that," I say finally.

"I know."

I've seen Maeve have a panic attack and helped her through it. I just didn't realize it felt like *this*. Like you're dying.

"I don't usually even feel anxious. I don't know what happened."

It's silent for a while. When Maeve speaks, her voice is quiet. "Death threats and hate messages could give anyone a panic attack, Finn."

I know, logically, that I should just ignore the horrible messages. If you had asked me yesterday, or even a few hours ago, if they bothered me, I would have laughed it off. But reading messages from strangers saying they're going to kill Maeve and me, or that we should kill ourselves, that I'm nothing, worse than nothing . . . it's hard to shake off. My parents and I, especially my mom, have dealt with the press my entire life, which is why I wanted nothing to do with it. I've experienced the vitriol that one bad paparazzi photo can cause. So I thought I was prepared for this. I thought by podcasting instead of acting again I was avoiding the brunt of it. But nothing really can prepare you for what it feels like to hear how much people hate you.

"People suck," I say quietly, wearily. My entire body is exhausted, and the nurse who popped in earlier said it will be at least another hour before the blood tests, since more pressing cases have come in. "Want to go home?"

"You don't want to stay for the blood tests?"

I nestle my head into the top of Maeve's. "No. I want to be doing this at home on the couch, fully clothed, with pizza and a movie. After a shower."

And that's exactly what we do.

SIXTEEN

Maeve

"Wow, Maeve, this setup is wild." Finn is scanning the room, marveling at how I've rearranged things. We're still in our sex dungeon of a studio, but with Leo's help I've hidden the cameras inside of the walls. You can see small cutouts where the lenses are, but otherwise they're unobtrusive and it makes the room feel less like a recording studio, more like somewhere we're just hanging out.

"I think it'll inspire our guests to open up even more. These big name guests are media trained, so I feel like it's harder for them to be vulnerable in front of the cameras. Now they'll hopefully forget the cameras are even here."

Finn walks up to the wall and peers inward toward the camera. The cutout is perfectly sized for the lens, so he can't see beyond it. "How do you adjust them?"

I walk forward and press on the wall to the right of the camera, in the same way we've learned to press to open the door. The hidden door slides open gently, revealing the camera on a tripod. "Voilà!" I exclaim.

Finn golf claps. "How long did this take you? I would've helped."

I close the door, then walk around the table and drop into my seat. "That's the best part. It took maybe an hour of me explaining my vision to Leo and the Streamify in-house team. And then they just did it."

"Well, as always, you're ten steps ahead of me."

Before I can respond, Leo knocks on the door and then leads Graham in. "Graham! How are you?" Finn pats him on the back.

Graham looks mildly awful. He has dark circles under his eyes and looks thinner than when we last saw him, but his face is puffy, as though he's been either drinking too much or crying. "Nice to see you again," I add.

Graham nods morosely. "Did you get my email?" His eyes are glued to mine, as though he thinks I'm the one person who can get him out of the doghouse.

I nod as I grab Graham's mic pack and hand it to Finn. "We did! And we think we can help." Graham's focus remains directed on my response as Finn snakes the lav mic cord under his shirt and pins it to the inside of his collar. He clips the mic pack to Graham's waistband and ushers him toward his seat facing us.

"Really?" He reaches into the pocket of his sweats and pulls out a Tiffany's box and pops it open. There's a monster ring inside, at least five carats with diamonds studded around it. "I got a ring. Should I propose? Maybe that'll sweep over it?"

Finn quietly gets up and starts opening the camera compartments to check if we're recording, while I reach over to Graham and gently close the ring box. "Let's not jump the gun here, Graham."

Finn sits down and leans toward me. "Recording," he whispers.

I catch his eye for just a second, so he knows I'm on the same page. No intro, diving straight in. We can film a pickup intro at the end, since clearly right now Graham is an anxious wreck. It feels good to be working together again. "So, Graham, I just want to recap the situation to make sure we're all on the same page about exactly what happened." And so our listeners know what the heck we're talking about, since they won't have read his letter. "You and your girlfriend, Tif, were going strong. You were planning to propose at your first Super Bowl. Before you even know if you're in the playoffs, Tif gets pregnant. You decide to wait to propose, hopefully after winning the Super Bowl. Then you do get to the Super Bowl, but you, ah, don't win, and don't propose. Tif has the baby, and you two are having a bit more conflict. Then three weeks ago you showed up baked to your daughter's christening, and since then you've been sleeping in the guesthouse."

"Exactly!" Graham exclaims. "I don't know what to do. She wouldn't come to the gala with me. She says she goes off actions, not words, and mine don't line up, and her mom always told her I wasn't serious, and she was right. But I'm so serious. I've loved Tif since we were sixteen."

I nod, my face placid, trying to keep him calm. "Got it. And we know you tried apologizing. Do you remember exactly what you said?"

Graham pulls out his phone and scrolls to the texts. "'Babe, I'm so sorry. I got the date wrong, and then by the time you texted I could only sober up so much. It'll never happen again.'" Finn visibly winces beside me and Graham's eyes bug out in alarm. "What, man! I apologized!"

I pause, giving Finn a chance to jump in. "I know, I know," he says.

"Before meeting Maeve I might have said the same thing. But you didn't take responsibility for your actions, you know? I mean, come on, I'm sure she told you when it was. Maybe you had an invitation on the fridge too? And if I had to bet, I'd guess she told your assistant, who put it in your calendar. You explained how it happened, instead of acknowledging her feelings and that you understand why your actions hurt her."

"Do you want to try rephrasing the apology?" I ask. "Not to send; just as an exercise."

Graham tilts his head. "Sure, sure. I think I see what you mean. How about, 'Babe, I'm sorry. It was messed up of me to be careless with the times. It won't happen again.'"

"That's a good start!" I say encouragingly. "Mind if I tell you what I might like to hear?"

"Yes, *please!*"

I glance toward Finn for an instant, without meaning to, then tear my eyes back to Graham. If Finn knows how to apologize so well, how come he never managed to do it with me? But I take a deep breath and force my focus back to the episode. "A good apology acknowledges what you did wrong, how it impacted the other person, and how you'll change what you did in the future. So something like: 'Babe, I am so sorry. I love you and our daughter so much, and I recognize that not showing up to a once-in-a-lifetime milestone like this makes it seem like I'm not serious about this family, and it probably makes you feel like all the hard work you're putting in to raise our amazing daughter is not appreciated. I will not act this carelessly with your time and feelings again. I know words are cheap, and I will make sure that my actions in the coming weeks, months, and years reflect how I feel, which is that you and our daughter are the most important part of my life. I will prioritize family time, take initiative and plan things for us to do, and make sure to express gratitude for you and your work.'"

The room is silent for a moment after I finish, and I wonder if this apology was too much. And then I try to quash that thought. Women are always made to feel they should downplay their emotions, try to placate their boyfriend's negative feelings that are a result of their own bad behavior. He should be giving a thorough apology! Graham breaks the silence first. "Can we play that back? I want to write it down."

I smile. "You can listen to the episode when it airs if you want. But the point of this is to help you develop your own skills. It's better if you think about acknowledging her feelings and how you impacted her and create your own apology from there."

"And then whip the ring out?"

"You know, let's talk about the ring, the whole proposal," Finn says. "Why didn't you propose at the Super Bowl?" He looks genuinely curious as he asks this. I wonder if he ever thought he might propose to Cassidy. Their summer in Europe was so romantic, and given that she's been his *maybe someday* since they were nine, it's not that outrageous to think he might have brought a ring to Rome. I was more shocked to hear from TMZ that they'd broken up than I'd have been if he'd dropped to one knee.

"I lost man. I couldn't propose after losing."

"Do you think her answer would have been different?" I ask. I like where Finn is going with this.

"No. But I wanted to show her how great our life together will be. That I'm a winner." I bump Finn's knee under the table. During our negotiation meetings with networks, this was our signal to let the silence sit, to see what the other person says when we let them talk themselves out. Finn presses his knee back into mine and I feel a thread unravel somewhere deep inside me, because I know that even though this is supposed to just be a truce, he's slowly working his way back in. And at my core, I want him to.

After a moment of silence, Graham continues talking. "I wanted it to be perfect. Back in high school, she wouldn't date me. She said she was too smart to be spending all her time and energy on a boy when she could spend it on her own dreams. Even in college, she only let me take her out once she had a job offer for after graduation. And now . . . this life is hard for her. Being a WAG is a lot of work, which people don't realize. I don't want her to think I'm expecting her to put her dreams aside for me. That's why I told her we should hire a nanny! So she can go back to work. I want her to know I'm not a loser who will bring her down. But at the Super Bowl I literally lost, so I couldn't propose then."

I nod, keeping eye contact with Graham. "It sounds like you might have some nerves over whether Tif will accept your proposal. And so by proposing after a literal win, you wanted to show her you bring value to the relationship." Graham nods, blinking rapidly as the rims of his eyes become red.

"What do you think bringing value to the relationship looks like from Tif's perspective?" Finn asks. "Like, when you're not fighting, do you think when she thinks to herself, *wow, Graham adds so much to my life, I'm so happy we're together,* she's thinking about you being successful at football? Or something else?"

I nudge Finn's knee with my own. That was a great question. He gives me all the credit, but he's great with people. And sometimes, when I want to tell a guy what to do after hearing a Question of the Week, or a story from a friend, because I think they're making bone-headed decisions that make no sense, Finn is able to break through to *why* they're thinking that way. And together we can give both halves of a perfect response.

"She doesn't give a shit about the money or the football stuff, other than that she wants me to achieve my goals. She tells me what she cares about. She likes that I listen to her talk about her work—she's a journalist, and she's so talented. I love hearing her talk about it, she gets so excited and it's amazing. And she likes that we travel to new places together during the off season. And that we both care about our families and our faith."

"And what do you value about her?"

"She makes me a better man every day. She helps me think about things I never would otherwise, like about people who are different from us. My charity work with The Human Rights Campaign is all thanks to her. She's kind. She has her own thing, you know? Her own passions. She's smarter than I'll ever be. What I love most about our daughter is that she's half Tif, and that Tif is raising her and teaching her how to be a good person. No one is a better mom than Tif."

I'm tearing up now. I blink rapidly. "Graham. Don't propose now. But don't wait for a Super Bowl win either. Football is not an important part of your relationship. Your best proposal is one that is honest, where you tell her what you just told us. And I'm not saying do it now, because first you need to apologize properly and win back her trust, so that when you propose she knows it's because you want forever with her, not because you want to sweep a fight under the rug."

"Can I do it here?"

"Do what?" Finn asks.

"Apologize. On air."

Finn and I look at each other. "Sure. But when you call her, you have to tell her you're on air. If she wants to keep it private, then you should respect that."

"Of course." Graham pulls out his phone to call her and I see that she's his pinned contact. It's a small thing, but navigating to her number is so intuitive to him that I can tell he calls her constantly, and I love it. It's the little things like that that make up a great relationship. I point at the table and he rests the phone on it.

"Graham? Aren't you on that show right now?" Tif's voice is quiet through the speakers, and I take my lav mic off and place it next to the phone speaker so it'll pull her sound while they're talking.

"I am. Baby, I've been talking to them about how badly I messed up. We're still recording, but I was wondering if I could apologize."

Tif snorts. "This should be good. Go right ahead." She sounds pissed. I wonder how many times he's made the fight worse through poorly constructed apologies and lack of communication.

Graham inhales deeply. I can see the tension in his shoulders. "Tif, I am so sorry. You are the best thing that has ever happened to me. You make me better every day. I am so sorry I disappointed you. You work so hard to raise our daughter, and I can't imagine a better mom. I pray every day that our daughter is as passionate as you are about her goals, as smart as you are, as focused. It was so careless of me to forget about her christening and to show up in that state. There is no excuse for it, and I shouldn't have tried to give one. That was about me trying to feel better about dropping the ball, not apologizing for not being there for our family. I will spend every day with you going forward trying to be the man you deserve, because I know you're the best woman on this earth."

"Graham," she says softly.

"I have more!" he interjects. "I know the past year has been hard. You're an amazing mom, but I also can't wait to see you working again, because it lights you up. Baby, I never want you to doubt for a second that I'm always going to be committed to you and our family. Forget football, you and our little girl are my life. I am so sorry for my actions, and I hope over time you can forgive me as I earn back your trust. I love you." He ends the speech with a huge exhale, and we all lean into the phone with bated breath.

"I love you, too," Tif says finally. "And I appreciate the apology. I'm looking forward to moving forward from this together."

Graham wipes away a tear silently. "Tif, thank you for giving me another chance. And I'm sorry for all the times I made excuses the past few weeks. I didn't realize what I was doing was a faulty play."

"I appreciate that," Tif says softly. The line is silent for a moment, before she speaks again. "And Maeve? I know this apology was all you. Thank you for teaching him how to express what he means."

Finn pulls his lav mic off and holds it in front of me, so my audio will be picked up cleanly. "That's what we're here for. Teaching men emotional intelligence so their partners don't have to."

Tif laughs, and Graham chats with her for a few minutes longer while Finn and I re-mic ourselves. Once he's off the phone, Finn jumps in. "Now, Graham, since that's out of the way . . . let's talk locker-room talk. What goes down in there? And how do you respond when someone says something that isn't cool?"

We dive into the next segment, with Finn leading the way, and for the first time since we started recording together at Streamify, it feels good to be working together again.

SEVENTEEN

Finn

I follow Maeve into the Chargers box, and my pulse immediately skyrockets, I start sweating from every pore, and my mouth goes dry. Because this box is clearly set up for a romantic evening for two.

After the episode, Graham reached out to let us know that he and Tif were better than ever, and he insisted on giving us box seats for the game this weekend. I persuaded Maeve to accept, even though she couldn't care less about football, but now that we're here it's clear these aren't just box seats . . . I speed walk over to the bucket of champagne and rose petals and snatch the note that's in front of it. At the gala I had confided to Graham that I'd fucked things up with Maeve too. I didn't want him thinking he was the only guy who makes huge mistakes! But I do *not* want Maeve reading this note.

I open it. *Thank you both. Now it's your turn to work things out.*

I shove it in my pocket and glance over my shoulder. Maeve is exploring the rest of the suite, which has been laid out with romance in mind at every turn. Instead of burgers and fries, there's oysters and chocolate-covered strawberries, several arrangements of red roses, and matching jerseys with our names on them. She pulls the jersey over her head, and when she pokes her face out, her hair is sticking in every direction, spiky with static. "I think he got the wrong idea about us. I can't exactly blame him after the gala." She tosses me a jersey. "Don't make it awkward."

I pull mine on. "When have *I* ever made things awkward?"

Maeve ignores me and picks up the entire tray of strawberries, bringing them down to the seats and balancing them on an armrest next to her. I pick up the oysters and follow suit, then place the bucket of champagne in the row in front of us. "What are we drinking to? Not actively hating each other's guts?"

Maeve pops the bottle, and the cork flies forward into the stands. "Should I admit I still have dreams about punching you in the face before or after we drink this?"

I grab the bottle from her and take a long swig. "I'm ready. Now, in this dream, do you break my nose and ruin my perfect Sutton bone structure? Or break your own hand?"

"Your face kind of folds in. You know, like a jack-o'-lantern after it has sat outside until November tenth, and it's starting to rot from the inside out?" Maeve snatches the champagne from me and drinks. "It's honestly graphic."

I've had a few graphic dreams about Maeve, especially since she fell asleep in my lap at that after-party. I suck down an oyster, then offer her one and try not to watch her lips as she daintily slurps it from its shell. Her auburn hair falls forward around her face as she leans to eat it, and I want to push it behind her ear. I miss being able to reach out and hold her. Nothing has ever felt as good as her warm weight leaning against me, or the feel of her hand in mine. When I'm next to her, I feel like I actually know my place in the world, because there could be no more important place than by her side. The game is just starting, and although I should be watching avidly, it's hard to tear my eyes away from Maeve. We pass the champagne back and forth, and snack as we try to guess the careers of everyone in the boxes around us, until eventually I realize that not only are we having fun, but I'm pretty buzzed.

"Episode idea," I blurt out. "We have people write in the wildest places they've had sex and then tier rank them based on scandal level and logistics."

Maeve arches an eyebrow. "Are you thinking about fucking me in this box?"

The thought had crossed my mind, but instead of admitting it, I roll my eyes dramatically and pass the bottle to her. I can tell by the flush in her cheeks that she's tipsy too, although we're not quite done with the bottle. "Come on, this entire room is like a neon sign that says GET IT ON."

"Maybe I *requested* oysters, strawberries, and champagne for my sport-side meal, ever think of that? Maybe I eat these every time I watch the Steelers at home." Maeve is half turned to face me, and the spot on the shared armrest where our elbows are touching feels like the most sensitive part of my body.

"Maeve, if you call your parents right now and they can name one time you watched a football game start to finish, I'll go on the podcast and talk about when I couldn't get it up for Stacey Maloney back in college."

Maeve's eyes light up. "I *knew* something went down that night. You couldn't look her in the eyes, like, ever again."

"I'll have you know that Stacey told me that it happens to everyone. And when I saw her in New York on the subway . . . I got off before my stop to avoid confronting my trauma." I press my elbow toward Maeve's slightly, and she doesn't move away. In fact, I think she presses back into me, just the tiniest bit. Maybe touching without recoiling is the next step in our friendship reformation.

"I wouldn't want to force you to open up about anything you're not comfortable with," Maeve remarks primly. "Unless you make a different wager, then I will absolutely yank the full story out of you."

Before I can jab back at her, I tune in to the cheering around us. Because they're not shouting, "Go Chargers!" or anything like that anymore. And they're not fading away like they typically would after a touchdown. In fact, when I listen more closely, the cheers near us are incredibly loud, and it sounds like they're yelling . . . *Kiss*.

Suddenly Maeve grabs my arm. "Oh my god, Finn, look." She points directly ahead of us. "We're on the kiss cam." She looks at me with pure horror in her eyes, as though kissing me will make her turn into a toad, or I have a highly communicable disease.

"Kiss! Kiss! Kiss!" the crowd is roaring around us, now that it's clear we realize what's happening.

I'm going to kill Graham. I would bet a million dollars he set this up. I turn toward her, then even farther, so that my mouth is hidden from the jumbotron camera. "What do you want to do?"

But Maeve doesn't answer me. Instead, she takes my jaw in her hand and turns me toward her. We make eye contact for the briefest of moments before I reciprocate and pull her face to mine, and when I kiss her, I know with every fiber of my being that what was in her dark eyes wasn't disgust or apprehension. It was anticipation.

I crush her face toward me and cradle the back of her head, while she wraps her arms around my neck. We don't settle for a peck. We meld together, falling into exactly where we left off the last time this happened, and instead of feeling strange or awkward or tense, I feel at home. There's no fumbling, and after a moment the sound of the crowd blurs away, and when Maeve's mouth parts, I press deeper. By the time she breaks away I've forgotten this was for the kiss cam at all, and am left blinking into the sunlight. Maeve leans her head on my shoulder, and I remember we're being filmed and wrap my arm around her, both of us grinning.

Once the cameras are off us, I turn to Maeve, hoping that maybe now we can *finally* talk about us. How can we ignore this conversation when we just had our tongues down each other's throat, right? But she's moving the strawberry tray and grabbing her purse.

"Maeve, come on. Where are you going? Are you okay?"

I follow her out of the seats and back into the safety of the booth, where no one can hear us or film us. She sits down on the couch and pulls out her phone, opens the Uber app.

"Maeve!" I'm raising my voice in a panic, and I hate that. She flinches at the escalated tone, and I immediately soften. "I'm sorry, I'm sorry. But please! Don't leave right now. It's just a kiss, right?"

Maeve pauses, her phone in hand, the ride not yet confirmed. "I just need some space, Finn. I know that wasn't confusing for you since you can hook up with me and have it mean nothing, but it's hard for me."

Her words are choked with emotion, and I hesitate, not sure if I should say something or obey our agreement not to talk about us. It's way easier to give other people advice than to know what to do in the heat of the moment. Her eyes flick down to the phone, and I start talking, desperate to say anything that will get her to stay here with me. "It's not meaningless to me, Maeve. I know why you think that after everything, but it's not just a show. I really—"

"Stop!" There's fire in her eyes, and pain. "I don't want to hear this song and dance again. I know not getting what you want is a new feeling for you. The challenge must be fun. But I don't want to hear about it. This isn't even a real kiss. I'll tell Shazia this is our monthly contracted appearance together." She hits Confirm on her app and stands. "I'll see you in the studio."

I can't believe her. Why is she constantly assuming the worst of me? Do I not get any credit for the past few weeks of playing by her rules?

"Maeve, I'm sorry, but you're being a fucking child. I thought you were supposed to be the mature one."

Her eyes flash as she shoves her phone into her bag. "And I thought you were supposed to be my *person*. You know, I wish things had worked out for you and Cassidy. Because now I have to stand here knowing you threw us away for absolutely nothing. I'm *tired* of being mature."

We're absolutely screaming at this point, in our matching jerseys, in the romantic suite that was supposed to make us remember when we liked each other. More than liked. But I can't *stop*. "If you care so much, then engage with me!"

Maeve walks toward me until we're standing face-to-face. Or rather, her face is at my chest and I'm staring down at her while she cranes her neck up. "Finn, not being in love with you is an awful lot of work," she whispers.

"Then don't do it anymore," I counter. "*Please*." My voice cracks, and I don't care. If I thought it would help I would get on my knees and beg her.

Maeve's eyes are dry and hard. She tucks her hair behind her ear needlessly. "Finn, I want you to listen to me. And actually hear me, please. I want to say we can get back to what we were. That we can try again. I wish we could, desperately. But we can't. Because you didn't make a mistake. You made a choice, and it's not the same thing. I am not disposable. When I said I would always be there for you, you know,

I guess I lied. In this world, the world where I had to learn that you never valued me like I valued you, I can't do that. So we are coworkers. And that's *it*."

And then she leaves. I slump to the ground. I don't know how she can give everyone else the grace of forgiveness, but when I make a mistake, I'm persona non grata. We've had this same fight over and over, and not once has she believed a word that's come out of my mouth. So you know what? If she wants me to act like the guy I am in her head, the one who doesn't give a shit about her, who acts like she's a coworker? I can do that.

I pop another bottle of champagne, chug half of it, burping between gulps from the carbonation, then grab my phone and stalk out of the suite. I walk out of the private area and into the stands, and then I wait. It takes about thirty seconds for someone to recognize me, and suddenly girls are walking over, asking for selfies and to take videos together.

"Want to come up to the booth?"

I don't even know who I'm addressing the request to, but suddenly I'm walking upstairs, with at least ten women behind me. And when they get to the booth and see all the champagne and strawberries, the party really gets started. I'm wavering, on the line between drunk and totally fucked up, and the next hour (or two hours? three?) are a blur of dancing and kissing and videos. I have a sneaking suspicion any time I start to sober up that I will regret this. But I take care of that worry with another shot.

Maybe now she'll see there is a difference between who I've been the past few months and who she's been making me out to be. Because now, now I'm acting like someone who doesn't give a shit. Because she's not the only one getting over someone. It's time for me to get over her.

EIGHTEEN

Before the Streamify contract

Maeve

"What are we looking for again?" Finn asks, as he trails behind me while I comb through the racks of the third Housing Works of the day with laser-focused precision.

I don't look up, instead carefully inspecting the seams on a Ralph Lauren sweater. "We're not looking for anything. We're just *looking*, in case we find something."

This is Finn's first thrift store crawl and he clearly is having trouble grasping the concept. I shouldn't be surprised, since I don't think he's worn anything used in his life. "I don't get it," he mutters. "My mom's stylist can source whatever you're looking for. What should I be looking out for?"

I put the sweater back on the rack definitively. "I told you, I'm not looking for anything. I'm just looking in case we find a treasure. And that's the fun part! Having someone source a specific item, one, probably is not a good deal and, two, takes away the thrill of the hunt. It's only fun if you find something that's, like, an obscene deal."

I lead Finn over to the massive jackets rack. "Now just look through."

He halfheartedly starts pushing through the jackets. "Maybe I need an example."

"It literally isn't hard. Just look for something stunning, or from a good brand, then inspect it and check the price to see if it's a good deal." I pull a jacket out with a flourish. "Like this! This is vintage men's Burberry, which is an incredible find. But it's missing the belt and is too big for me, so I would need it tailored. Which is only worth it if the price is incredible, which, at Housing Works, it probably is." I check the tag. "Four fifty. Not worth it. But if it was one fifty? Treasure!"

Finn takes the jacket from me and looks it over skeptically. He winces at a stain on the collar that would totally come out with dry cleaning. "Do you want to go to the Burberry store? I'll get you the jacket as an early birthday gift. And it'll have a belt and be clean."

"That's not the point. This is for fun!"

Before I can dive deeper into the dopamine rush I get from finding something good, I hear a gasp from behind us, and before I even turn around I know what's coming.

"Oh my god! Maeve? And Finn? Holy fuck! I can't believe it's actually you!"

It's a group of three young women, one of whom is now filming us on her cell phone. I grin. "It's really us! It's so great to meet you!"

I hug each of them in turn, and then Finn does the same. We've never met these women, but just like every time this happens—which lately is almost every time we step outside—the vibe is more reunion between friends than fans meeting podcast hosts.

"I've been watching your show ever since episode three and it is literally so epic! I finally confronted my cheating ex and now I'm single and thriving!"

One of the other women jumps in. "You did my question on Questions of the Week last month! I wrote in asking how to explain responsive desire to my boyfriend, and it totally worked. Also, your episode about blow jobs is literally life-changing."

"Well, we're happy to help," I acknowledge with a smile. "It really means so much to meet you all and hear that."

"Want to go out?" the woman who originally recognized us asks. "We were just stopping in here on the way to the Bachelor bar!"

"Let's do it!" Finn agrees quickly.

I roll my eyes. "He doesn't understand the joys of thrifting."

"We've gone to six stores in the last three hours. I think if I was going to find the joy, it would've happened," he retorts as he throws an arm around my shoulder and squeezes it. "Besides, who knew there was a Bachelor bar? This is my first season watching the show with you, so I may as well get the full experience."

"He loves it," I stage-whisper to the women conspiratorially.

Fifteen minutes later, we're in a bar that is completely packed and decked out for *The Bachelor*. There's a bracket made out of print-outs of the contestants' faces on the wall, a kiss tally on a white-board behind the bar, and custom drinks for each of the remaining three contestants. I've never been either and am totally blown away by it, but I can barely take it all in because it seems like every single woman in this bar watches *Tell Me How You Really Feel*.

Finn and I have done shots with seemingly everyone in the place, taken at least a hundred selfies, and heard more stories about how our show has helped people's relationships than I can count. Since we record at home, just us, the size of our audience and the impact of the show doesn't feel real until we're somewhere like this.

Right now, for example, an incredibly drunk couple is crying as they tell me how episode thirty-seven prompted them to both reveal their feelings for each other, and come out to their respective families. "I just can't imagine what our life would look like without the show," one of them gushes. She pulls her girlfriend closer to her. "I never would have said anything to Maria; I'd still be living a lie at home. And we never would have tried nipple play!"

Without warning, Maria launches herself forward and tries to hug both Finn and me at the same time. "We love you! And your custom lube!"

After we've thanked them, Finn grabs my hand and pulls me toward the bathroom. The line for the women's is long, but he pulls us both into the men's and into the handicapped stall. "This is incredible," he whispers. "But we also have to get out of here before another girl asks me to sign her breasts."

I nod and start tearing up. "This is . . . I can't believe it. Every single person here listens to the show. I'm so happy, I just can't believe this is real."

Finn is only inches away from me in the tiny stall. He reaches down and wipes the tear off my cheek. "This is you, Maeve. You're changing their lives."

The tears are coming faster than he can wipe away now, and he pulls me into his chest. Eventually my tears subside, and I pull away, leaving two mascara stained spots on his white T-shirt. "I'm just happy," I say quietly. "This is all so much bigger than I ever imagined."

"It's only going to get bigger." Finn hugs me again for a moment, resting his chin on top of my head. It feels too good for him to hold me like this. We're friends. Just friends. But this podcast has brought us closer than I ever imagined, and although the premise started as debriefing each other on our dates and giving sex and relationship advice, lately we've done more advice and questions and haven't brought up dates. He's probably just busy, or picky, but I haven't wanted to go on dates, because I want to spend every night hanging out with him. It scares me how much I care about him, when I know I can't have him. He's never liked me like that and he could have *anyone*. When he could have the most famous, beautiful, talented, rich women in the world, there's no way someone normal like me stands a chance. That's probably why we've been able to be friends for so long.

But when I stare into his eyes, it always takes my breath away.

I pull away and look up at him, needing to end the hug before I say something embarrassing that I regret. "Should we make our escape? We'll have to basically run out, or else we'll spend the next five hours talking to people."

Finn nods resolutely. "On three. One, two, three!"

He pushes open the stall door and I rush out ahead of him. He wraps his arm around me and helps propel us through the crowd. At the door I grab his arm to stop him and turn around, to see that at least ten people are filming us and almost the whole bar is watching our departure. "Thank you all so much! We love you so much! Also I think Poppy is going to win the show!"

That gets a resounding cheer, and so with that we turn and start running down the street, overcome with laughter. It's now dark, and raining lightly, so when we turn the corner Finn pulls us under an awning while he calls an Uber. "Your place? We still have to see who he sends home."

"Perfect." I'm tucked in front of him, his arms making a circle around me while he's using his phone. I don't think I can remember ever feeling so safe and happy.

NINETEEN

Before the Streamify contract

Maeve

"Do you think we should take it?"

We're sitting in my new apartment, which is at least seventy-five percent nicer than my last one. It's the kind of apartment that isn't clean and white and soulless enough to be a building with amenities, but that has a brick shower large enough for two people, as much outdoor space as indoor, and only a few holes in the wall that I've strategically covered with posters, because although now we're making money, it's not enough that I am even thinking about pretending I have the taste to blow huge portions of it on art that might be bad.

But with the deal we're considering, I could buy whatever bad art I like. Finn rubs his hand up and down my smooth calf, which I shaved just in case I did end up sitting here with my feet in his lap. "Do you want to?"

"I asked first."

"But it's yours."

"It's really not." No matter how many episodes we do, how many articles we pose for together, Finn insists that the show is mine and he is a mere participant. I never know if I should be flattered or offended.

"For sixty million and the IP, we probably shouldn't be debating it. Why aren't you sure?" Finn looks at me, his gaze focused, and my breath catches. His eyes on me, so intense when it's just us, is like that first moment when perfectly warm fresh spring air wraps around me when I step out of an air-conditioned car. For a moment everything is impossibly good and inspiration is in the next breath, and I couldn't imagine anything more beautiful than where I am, even if it's on a couch I rescued from the sidewalk and still am only mostly sure doesn't have bedbugs.

"Even if we have the IP, it won't be ours. Streamify will be telling us what to do."

"If that's what you're worried about, don't be. I won't let any dodgy exec tell you what to do." Finn reaches a hand toward me and holds it there, waiting, not dropping it even when I don't immediately reach out to meet him. I take it. I always take it. "I'll say you're an eccentric creative who can't be controlled. That if they tell you what to do for even one moment, I'll walk because we won't be great anymore. That I'll take a vow of celibacy and shave my head so girls don't like me anymore."

I squeeze his hand tightly and bend at the knees, edging closer to him. He hasn't looked away once, even when he's taken a sip of wine, but now he puts the glass down and interlaces my hand in his. "I mean that. Let them be my problem while you make what you want and change lives and all that."

I don't know whether to believe him. But so far, I always have and he's never let me down once, so why not? "I guess we have a deal, then."

I put my own glass down, and Finn tugs me toward him on the couch until I'm basically in his lap and he wraps me in a tight hug. It's hard for me to believe we're doing this. I never thought I would live in LA; it has always seemed like a bit of a concrete wasteland. Coming from Pittsburgh I'm suspicious of somewhere that always has good weather. We started meeting with Streamify months ago, and in the first meeting I wore a pantsuit and was sweating buckets before I even stepped inside. And the money? It's an unimaginable amount to me. Even once the first payment hits my bank account, I don't think I'll be able to comprehend it. Why would they pay that to make *Tell Me How You Really Feel* exclusive to Streamify without even trying to take the IP? I'm living in a fever dream that I don't want to wake up from, digging my nails into my thigh every hour to see if the moment is real.

I pull back from Finn just slightly and he shifts, pulling me completely into his lap until I'm straddling him in my sundress and I can feel a hard heat between his legs. And it's both shocking and thrilling, because all this time I assumed he just never felt that for me. My logical brain says that I should pull away, walk away, make sure to keep everything as is because I've only just been handed more than I've ever wanted. Why ruin it? But maybe the point of this was him.

So instead, I press myself tighter into him and my gasp meets his rough moan of an exhale as his hands slide down from my waist to my hips and he presses me tighter still. I haven't been looking at him, not really, because we're too close for that, my face pressed against the side of his, but now I pull back. Because I want to know that it's me he sees, not just another woman he'll talk about on the show later. I catch his chin with my hand and pull back, turning his focus toward me, and when his eyes lock on me they're not unfocused with desire. They're alert, looking into mine, almost as desperate to see me as I am to see him.

I nod, once. And he pulls my face to his and kisses me. It's not a pretty, chaste, first-date kiss. This kiss is the last two years of tension, the last six of friendship, and our future all wrapped into one. He crushes me to him and devours my mouth expertly, but not because we teach twentysomethings how to be good at sex, or because he's been getting a crash course in what I like when I spill my guts to millions through a recorder in our living room every week. It's like we click into place, and all the kisses I've had before this one were just practice for this. Like our relationship has been on pause at eighty percent and we just found the missing twenty.

And all of the little anxious thoughts that I usually have, the same ones fans write in about—does my stomach have rolls when I sit like this, do I look good at this angle, can he see up my nose, does my breath smell, are my hands too cold, am I too heavy, is he thinking of someone hotter—not one of them is here. It's like the chatter in my brain has been turned to silent. And for the first time in two years I know I'm doing something that will never make it onto the podcast.

We kiss and kiss and kiss, and if it was just this forever, it would still be better than anything else. But after who knows how long, Finn pulls back. "It's embarrassing to admit how much I've thought about this, Maeve. About you."

"Wow, Finn. I mean, tell me how you *really* feel," I whisper playfully. I should be embarrassed. I mean, did I *really* just say that?

But he just laughs. "Can I take you to bed now?"

I nod and kiss him, and it seems that suffices because he picks me up without a moment's break and carries me to my bedroom, lowering me onto the bed.

He kisses me so gently, so tenderly, it's like he's concerned he'll never get to again. Which is silly, because how could we do this and not have it be the start of the rest of our life? For a moment, I'm distracted by the realization that maybe he was waiting for this. Because the show will change. But it won't matter once the deal is signed. Maybe that's why he was promising to take the brunt of any disapproval changes, to unburden me so I didn't have to worry about what this means.

The thought makes me feel better. Calmer. Less worried about this not meaning all that I want it to.

Finn pulls my dress over my head and discards it on the floor, watching it fall for a moment before turning back toward me and leaning back for a moment to look at me. I hitch forward to unbutton his shirt, bring him to meet me, but he holds out a hand. "Wait, Maeve. Just let me look at you. Fuck. I just never thought I would get this moment with you."

. And it is a beautiful moment. He reaches for me and slides my underwear off, and these last seconds before we're touching, they are what will separate our before and after. I always said I would never take a nude photo, but right now I wish I could bottle this moment, preserve it, have it to look at all those future nights that come afterward. I want to remember this feeling before our bodies are familiar.

Finn's eyes travel up and down my entire body, drinking it in, and there's not one part of me that I don't want him to see. When he reaches my eyes, we lock in, and he leans forward, holding himself over me carefully and leaning down to kiss me, his shirt and belt and shorts rough against my already exposed body. He keeps kissing me while I start unbuttoning him, getting everything halfway undone, all the easiest bits, before he's ripping off his clothes, the restraint gone. He lowers his mouth to my clit and I can confirm that everything said in episode three was more than true.

After a moment, two of his fingers are moving in and out of me rhythmically while his mouth works around me and his other hand holds me flush against him, and I should be self-conscious, because I always am at this point, except now I'm not, and then I'm coming and exploding around him and he's pulling me closer, not stopping until it's happening again, and then I'm limp. He pulls himself up and rests his head on my chest and I play with his dark hair, which smells like the mint shampoo that I keep at my place now because he stays here so often even though until now we were just friends.

I run my nails down his back and feel him shudder, so I pull him up to kiss me, and feel how ready he is between my legs. I'm wet and slick, so wet that this is the first time in years I don't reach for lube, which I always use on principle because we should all use lube, because it makes a woman's orgasm from penetrative sex eighty percent more likely and it has our podcast's logo on it, but now I don't. Because I don't even want to orgasm again, I just want him inside of me to complete this night. To be as close as I possibly can. To feel him lose control.

I can feel how hard he is against me, and when I reach down and touch him, his face clenches and he groans. I grab a condom from the bedside and put it on him, then guide him to my entrance and remove my hand, leaving his tip barely poking in. He holds himself there for so long I wonder if he'll pull away. When he finally does push in, in one slow thrust that should hurt due to his size but doesn't because all I want is for him to fill me and he's gotten me so ready for it, he looks at me. And I look at him, my eyes steady, not breaking the eye contact for a kiss until he's fully inside of me. I have never felt more connected to anyone than I do in this moment.

When he starts moving, it feels so *good*. This is lacking the awkwardness of a first time as we move against each other, and I feel him pressing into me, knowing that the way I move around him is what is making him sweat and moan. It's not that long, but it's perfect, and when he finally releases, I hold him to me tighter. We're sweaty and gross and it's everything. I should get up to pee but I don't, and instead we just lie there intertwined, him still inside of me.

Finn kisses me on the lips, then the side of my head, over and over and over, and I nuzzle my face closer to him. "Fuck. I love you, Maeve," he says as he squeezes me in a tight hug.

I should just enjoy it. But his tone . . . it's too nonchalant. I don't know what it means. If it's a declaration, or just the casual words we've said so many times on the show. I try to measure my own tone when I respond. "I love you too." But I want to know how he means it.

TWENTY

Before the Streamify contract

Finn

Sleeping with Maeve was *not* something I expected to happen. When I wake up next to her, I watch her in the morning light, which is streaming in because we fell asleep without closing the blinds. Her hair looks more red than brown right now, and I gently bury my face in it and inhale the smell of her perfume.

We said we loved each other last night. And this does feel like love. I've been drawn to her for years, I love so many things about her, I can't imagine my life without her. But we've said those exact words a million times before, and I'm not sure what they even mean right now. Something we've talked about on *Tell Me How You Really Feel* is post-nut clarity, those moments after orgasm when you're hit with a rush of realization that either you can't get enough of this person, or you want them out of your bed. And I worry that Maeve and I may have been hit by opposite moments.

I feel great about last night—Maeve is the most gorgeous, kind, smart person. I have *always* thought about what it would be like to be with her like this. I just didn't think a relationship was in the cards for us because I had slotted so solidly into the friend zone back in college. But while I was overjoyed, she seemed slightly distant after we had sex, and it has me in my head. I get up and head to the kitchen to make French toast and try to ignore the tightness in my heart while I desperately wait for Maeve to wake up and tell me this was the start of something.

When Maeve finally comes to the table, her eyes are alert, no post-passion haze in sight. My stomach drops.

"So . . . should we talk about it?"

I serve us each two slices of French toast and sprinkle blueberries over them. "The deal? Or last night?"

Maeve rolls her eyes and takes a bite of her food. "Guess that answers that."

My stomach drops. I don't want to ruin my chances with her because I didn't speak carefully enough. "What? Maeve, come on. I'm really happy about last night, okay? Maybe we should try this. Us." *Please say yes.*

Maeve takes a deep breath. "Is that really how you feel?"

"*Yes*," I say emphatically. "I was surprised, but—"

"Me too," Maeve interjects. "I don't want you to think . . . I don't know. It was a surprise is all. A good one, though."

"Agreed," I say carefully. I feel like I'm walking on thin ice right now. "It's tough timing with the deal, though. If you want, we can keep things between us for now."

Maeve was reaching for her coffee, but pauses, then puts her hand back in her lap. "I think that's a good idea," she says finally. "We don't want anything to jeopardize the deal. Maybe we should take a break, go back to how things were, then try us for real in a month."

"Is that what you want?" I ask. Even though I suggested it, I don't love the sound of it. I don't know why I said it; it just came out. But I want to do what she's comfortable with.

"I think it's the best thing to do," Maeve says.

I nod in agreement. It makes sense, I guess. I can get behind it. "Okay, then. I'll have to spend the next month planning an epic date, I guess."

Maeve finally cracks a real smile. "I guess so."

We both dive into our French toast and coffee with gusto now, and I feel better. I don't know why I was so worried. Maeve isn't like any other girl I've ever been with. I should've known she'd be chill and communicative about this.

We move forward with the deal with a handshake agreement, and our agents start negotiating the terms mercilessly. For two weeks I'm waiting for the moment that Maeve says she's ready now. That we have the money locked down so maybe we don't need to wait a *full* month. Every time we sit and watch TV, her leaning against my chest but not turning the rest of the way to kiss me, I wonder if I imagined how meaningful that night was.

But we agreed to put things on pause. So I don't say anything. Even when a month comes and goes and I fall asleep every night wondering if I let her fall through my fingers and somehow got everything wrong. But Maeve is the more emotionally intelligent one, the one who always knows what to say, so I wait for her to say something.

Which is why now, even though I want to be trying this out for real with Maeve, I'm giving her a bit of space for the night while I meet up with Cassidy while she's in town. She's modeling in a campaign here, so dinner at Carbone it is.

I walk in, slightly late since I spent an extra ten minutes at home charging my phone up from one percent, lest I risk missing *the* call from Maeve saying the ink has dried on the contract and we can actually do this. Cassidy is already seated at a tiny table near the bar and sipping a glass of red wine, a second already set out for me. I make my way through to her, and she stands, kissing me once on each cheek as though we're in Europe.

"I'm French now, don't judge," she admonishes when I raise my eyebrows at the greeting. "I ordered for us."

"Spicy rigatoni, meatballs, veal?"

"But of course!" The restaurant didn't open that long ago, but from the day it did our mothers have been obsessed with it and insist on going at least once each time they're in New York. I think my mom would go every night if she could persuade my dad and me to join her.

The waiter comes by with their version of a bread basket, which involves three types of bread, a chunk of fresh parmesan that they hack off for your viewing pleasure, pickled cauliflower, and salami, and we dive in. I like the garlic toast as much as the food we order off the menu if I'm being honest.

"So, how's modeling treating you?" I ask. Cassidy is, and always has been, completely stunning. Sometimes the children of famous people have a combination of too many arresting features and look slightly strange, but both Cassidy and I had the good fortune to take on a flattering combo of the features of each of our parents and leave the rest.

"Today was fun. But slightly boring, overall. Maybe I'll go back to acting, since I can't sing for shit." Cassidy takes a huge bite of bread and cheese and practically moans in pleasure. "If I could sing and not sell my abs for a living, I would eat here every day."

"You don't need abs to be an amazing model. You're gorgeous." I flush, slightly, from the compliment and the half a glass of wine I just downed.

"You flatter me. But tell me about you! The deal hits the press tomorrow. Why aren't you with your girlfriend?"

"Who said she's my girlfriend?"

Cassidy arches one eyebrow. The waiter brings over our pasta, since we've made our way through the antipasto as though we were famished, and she takes a bite without missing a beat, eyebrow still cocked. "Spill. You know I won't tell. No one here will."

I look around us, knowing she's right. Carbone inspires an exclusive crowd, and the few people who aren't famous and just scored a reservation are seated on the outer periphery. They love being able to see all the celebrities at a glance, but they're really seated there so they can't hear us.

"We slept together. Then the next morning she wanted to put us on ice for a month." I eat a huge mouthful of pasta to distract myself, and for a moment it works, because that spicy vodka sauce is heavenly. But when I finish chewing, Cassidy is still waiting for me to elaborate.

"For a month? That sounds like calling it off. How long has it been?" Cassidy's tone is dripping with skepticism.

"Not necessarily." Even I can hear how weak that sounds, now that I'm explaining the situation out loud. "Maybe though? I'm not sure. She really is *that* practical and chill. It was super bad timing with our deal, since us getting together would basically blow up the premise of the show Streamify just paid a fortune for. But it's been more than a month already, and she still seems like she's not interested in trying."

"You could just see each other in private. There's no reason to completely pause things like you did," Cassidy remarks lightly. She reaches across the table and cuts a piece off of one of the meatballs, then pushes the remainder on the plate toward me.

"I know." She's right. But I've been successfully ignoring that aspect of the situation. I just wanted to do whatever made Maeve comfortable and gave me a real shot with her.

"You want to know what I think?"

Cassidy has always been brutally honest. Scathing at times, although usually right. And quick to be apologetic when she's wrong. This is the first time I've confided in anyone about what's happened between Maeve and me, and I'm desperate for advice. I've known Cassidy since we were in diapers. Even if what Cassidy says is harsh, I want to hear it from her view. "Yes," I say, my throat tight.

"I'm sure she loves you. But if she was *in* love with you, she wouldn't be doing this 'let's hit pause' bullshit. She basically told you she wants out. Don't blow up your show over sex when the whole point of the show is for you each to find your person. Which means, on some level, that ever since you made the show you've known it wasn't each other."

I don't know that I agree. I've known Maeve was someone special to me since I met her; I just didn't want to rush things if it wasn't the right time yet. But maybe I just don't *want* to agree. On some level her words ring true, like she's vocalizing all of my fears in a few sentences. But before I can dive into it, Cassidy takes a deep breath and continues talking.

"But also, Finn . . . maybe it's time. Try us out again for size. We've both dated everyone under the sun and slept with half the A-listers in town."

"What!" I'm waiting for Cassidy to laugh, but she seems earnest. And maybe it's this dim, romantic lighting, but the moment she says it I can't help but think . . . *what if.*

"You were my first kiss. First love, in a nine-year-old way. I've heard your 'one that got away' episode, and now that I get asked about it every time I do press, I can't stop thinking about it. And I think we should really try. If it doesn't work between us, it's okay, we know we can get through that no problem. I have a great hotel in the city the next few nights . . ." She trails off as she reaches across the table and squeezes my hand. Now I'm definitely blushing.

"I don't know if it's appropriate, given everything with Maeve . . ." I say quietly. It isn't appropriate. But what I said isn't no. And Cassidy and I both know it.

If the last month is any indication, it seems like Maeve might not want to be with me. It would be cleaner to stick to our original premise, especially as the fine print of the deal is getting negotiated. Maybe I *should* try things with Cassidy too. Maeve always advocates a roster and getting to know multiple people and trusting your gut. And right now, in my gut, I do want to see where things could go. Because while I love Maeve, I've also wondered what there could be between Cassidy and me since I was nine years old.

"You're literally on pause, a break, whatever, that *Maeve* asked for," Cassidy says softly. "It's not doing anything wrong to try. This isn't some one-night stand; it's seeing if we're each other's second-chance romance. And, I mean, we're all grown-ups here."

I bite my lip. "I'll be right back."

I walk to the restroom, already pulling my cell phone out of my pocket and dialing Maeve.

"Finn? What's up? I thought you were meeting Cassidy tonight."

"I am! I'm there now." I lean against the bathroom door, unsure what to say. "Maeve, do you actually want to be in a relationship with me? Or was that just something you said?"

"Why are you asking me this now?" Maeve whispers after a moment of silence. I don't answer. "Is it because of Cassidy?"

"I want to know," I say finally, which is true. "But it's coming up now because of Cassidy, yeah. She was just telling me she wants to try again, she and I, but I told her you and I were something, but then I wasn't sure, and—"

"You should try with Cassidy," Maeve says immediately.

"Maeve. I really do want to try with you. I just also . . . I don't know."

I hear a sharp inhale on her end. Her voice sounds dull, almost robotic. "Waiting was just an excuse while I sorted things out. You should be with Cassidy. I know that's what you want. It's what's right."

"Are you sure?" I ask again.

"Definitely. Have a good night, Finn." She ends the call faster than I realized and for a moment I'm just holding the phone to my ear in the silence waiting for her to say, *Never mind. Come home. Fight for us.* But she's already gone.

I half know she's just giving me an out. But I also half want it.

I walk back to the table and look across it at Cassidy. I've always thought I'd get another chance with her. That she might be the one for me. When I look into her eyes, I have a pang of nostalgia for that summer in Croatia. My first kiss. That cute little date. And before I can talk myself out of it, I lean in and kiss Cassidy.

On the way out the door at the end of the night, Cassidy squeezes my hand, just once, and I see the flash of a paparazzo's camera. I groan and silently pledge to have my agent buy the photo. But we stay out until four in the morning before falling into bed at her hotel, and I forget the photo completely until I see us on the front page of the *Hollywood Reporter.*

My heart pounds when I see it. I wanted to try things out, not go tabloid official. As I listen to Cassidy singing horribly in the shower, my first instinct is to text Maeve. This is when we'd normally head to a diner to debrief, or record an episode at her place, where we dive into every detail of the night before. I could text her still. But I know in my gut that it wouldn't be the right thing to do in this moment; it wouldn't be fair to her or to Cassidy, and for the first time since I kissed Cassidy last night, I wonder if I've gone after love, or if I got scared and ran away from it.

TWENTY-ONE

Maeve

I lie on my gorgeous white couch in my murder scene of a living room and touch my lips softly. It was just a kiss. Not even a real kiss. It was a fake kiss for a kiss cam, and we put on a good show for them; it shouldn't affect me like this. But I can still feel the ghost of the imprint of his lips against mine. And the memory of the confidence with which he pulled me closer to him and held my face to his makes my stomach twinge.

It was an incredible kiss. But that doesn't mean a thing.

He doesn't love me. I'm the friend he chills with while he looks for the woman of his dreams. Who he fucks, then forgets about. Who he claims to love then throws away. And he didn't just sleep with someone, no, that would be easier. He went on a date with his ex to see if he could find something better than us. He wants to be loved by everyone whether or not he loves them back, and bask in a sea of constant adoration. The only reason he's fighting for mine is because he's not used to anyone withholding anything from him. But I am *not* disposable.

I'm just a challenge to him. I repeat it back to myself, just a challenge, just a challenge, just a challenge, until I almost believe it. If that kiss wasn't seared into my brain it would be a heck of a lot easier.

Just as I'm about to get ready for bed, my phone rings with a Face-Time from my sister.

"Hello?"

Sarah is walking through campus, headphones in, her face scrunched in anger. "Finn is such fucking trash. I'm so sorry, Maeve, he's disgusting."

My pulse immediately skyrockets. "What are you talking about?"

Sarah stops walking and behind her a tall boy with a backpack walks directly into her. "Watch where you're going!"

"You haven't seen it," she whispers. "Ughhhh! I'm so sorry. But I'm sending it to you now."

A moment later I have links to six different TikToks and five Instagram stories in my messages. I watch them one by one, while my sister waits. Within an hour of begging me to talk to him, Finn apparently was having a party in the suite with a bunch of random women he rounded up. They're dancing, eating the romantic food Graham had sent up for us, leaving lipstick-smeared kisses all over him, and generally having a fantastic time.

All of the air rushes out of me. "I can't believe this." The Finn I know has *never* acted like this. This is an elaborate "fuck you" back, even for him. "What about the kiss cam?"

Sarah winces again as she pulls open the door to her dorm and starts rushing up the stairs to the safety of her room. "Well, it went viral first. And these aren't . . . exactly viral. They haven't hit a mil."

"Yet," I correct darkly. I breathe in and out deeply, trying to keep my anxiety at bay. I don't want to let myself feel betrayed by him. This is why I didn't want to let him in in the first place. But it feels like everything is crumbling. I try to take another deep breath, but I can't. It feels like my chest is caving in. I've spent the last decade getting my anxiety in check, through therapy, meditation, yoga, everything. But in this moment I don't think anything is going to help me. And then the doorbell rings.

"Fuck. Is that him?" Sarah sounds panicked. She knows what a journey learning to handle my anxiety has been. "If it is, don't answer it. Maybe you can do an emergency therapy appointment."

"Thanks for telling me about this." I can't tell if I mean that or if my words are jaded with sarcasm. And based on Sarah's face when I hang up, she can't either.

I walk to the door and look out the peephole. Finn is standing there, freshly showered and in a *Tell Me How You Really Feel* sweat suit, in fact, the same merch I'm currently wearing, with flowers and an apologetic frown on his face. He also looks mildly terrified.

I leave the deadbolt done, but crack the door so I don't have to yell. "Finn, just leave. Now." My voice shatters into tears, cutting off my final word. I slam the door shut, not caring if I catch his fingers in it, and slump down to the ground, my back against the door. I try to hold in the sob, holding my breath until the pressure feels like it might explode, then letting out a racking cry that I try to swallow.

"Maeve? Maeve!" Finn is knocking on the door, and once I make a noise I hear him drop to the ground on the other side so his head is closer to my level. "I'm sorry. I was cruel, and drunk and an idiot. Just let me inside. Let me help."

Finn is the only friend that I've had a panic attack in front of. In high school I would lock myself in the bathroom, climbing into a hot bath, shaking. I had a few back home, and then in college it happened again and again, but I hid them from my friends. It felt like I was dying and would never stop and I was embarrassed by my trembling hands and relentless sobs and struggles to gasp for air.

Once we went viral, and Paul Myers started directing his relentless vitriol and militaristically mean fans toward me, I had my worst panic attack in years. We'd been editing and I was trying to ignore the hateful DMs I was getting from *The Paul Myers Show* fans, and suddenly it was too much. When I tried to retreat to the bathroom with a tight smile, Finn followed me and held me when I broke down. And afterward, he didn't look at me any differently. He just asked about my strategies for managing my anxiety, if I still went to therapy, how long this had been happening. He was just *there*. I had never let anyone see me in such a vulnerable state, and it made his betrayal later sting even more. Because *of course* he wouldn't want me.

I struggle to breathe, and it feels like my chest is closing. I'm sweating, my sweatshirt is damp, and when I try to ground myself and focus on the feel of the door behind my back, I can't. I start crying harder, hyperventilating. This will never stop. This *must* be what dying feels like.

Finn's voice is low through the door. "Maeve? Maeve? Just breathe. Slower. I know you're breathing now, but try to take just one slow, deeper breath. This feeling will pass."

Last year, his words might have helped. But now the very sound of his voice hurts. Because I *love* the low gravel of his soothing whisper. And my entire body recoils further because of that, because he continues to break my trust so completely. "Stop!" I manage eventually. I can barely understand my own garbled words through the tears and the snot. I'm wiping a whole range of bodily fluids onto this sweatshirt, leaving dark streaks and sweat stains. "Just stop."

I can hear his inhale through the door. "Okay," he says, chastened. For a few minutes the only sounds are my sobbing and choking breaths. Eventually, as my body starts to wear itself out, Finn speaks again. "I'm not leaving."

Eventually I've cried until there's nothing left. I slide away from the door and walk away from him without another word. Let him sit there. I go into the kitchen and grab my water bottle, then take it upstairs and climb into bed with it, not bothering to wash my face or take off my disgusting clothes. In the past, Finn might have brought a cool washcloth to me, to lay on my head to fight off the inevitable headache. But now I just let the pressure build and try desperately to fall asleep.

I must have succeeded because when I wake up, it's light out and the birds chirping are in aggressive contrast to my splitting headache and puffy eyes. I get up and gently wash my face, then go downstairs to mainline coffee. As the Nespresso machine is heating up, I hear a strange sound coming from the entryway of my house. I look around and grab my water bottle, as a weak attempt at a weapon, then walk toward the door and peer outside.

Finn is out there dragging a lawn chair away from the door. He looks rumpled, and after a moment of confusion I realize that he's been out there all night. I open the door. "You slept here?"

He looks over instantly. "Maeve! How are you? Sorry, I should have picked the chair up. I was trying to get out of here before you woke up."

I don't know what to say, unsure if it's sweet or idiotic that he spent the entire night on my front lawn. But before I say anything, a car pulls up to the driveway. "Uber Eats for Finn?" Finn waves weakly and the driver holds a bag out the car window. Finn looks between him and me, then drops the chair, runs over to the bag and snatches it, then jogs over and holds it out to me.

"I really wasn't trying to be here when you woke up. This is for you. I'm going to put the chair back, then just pretend I'm not here. And I left a note under your doormat."

"I . . . okay." I take the bag and head back inside, reaching down to grab the note on my way. I don't know if he was hoping I would invite him in, or he genuinely meant to leave before I got up. And I don't know that I care. I'm so exhausted from last night that all I want is to relax, and although at one point that would have meant curling up on the couch for a movie marathon with Finn, we're so far from that place that it's not even funny.

I unpack a variety of pastries and bagels from the bag, make my coffee, and take the whole setup to the back deck. And then I open the letter.

Maeve, I am so sorry. For yesterday, because inviting all of those women into a space we had just shared an intimate moment in was childish and cruel. But also for last year. I don't think we can move forward without saying something about everything that happened between us. I'm sorry my actions made you feel used and like I didn't care about you. I never meant for you to feel that way, and I understand why you did. I deeply regret not recognizing that you are the special person that lights up my life. Without you in it, everything I thought I liked before seemed dim. I got scared and ignored that the most amazing person in my life was already right in front of me. Please forgive me for making you feel like you're not the most special person in the room. You will always be the most special person in the world to me, whether you believe it or not. I know I have ruined my shot with you, but please let me be your friend. I promise I'm done

trying to force things to return to how they were. But I
would really like to discover what the new us can look
like, because you are my person. And I swear to you,
that's how I really feel. Love, Finn

I have no tears left to cry as I read Finn's note. I want to believe
that he really does feel like I am his other half. Because for the past
few years my life felt infinitely brighter with him in it every day. He
made it easy to do hard things and made me feel like the best version
of myself. I miss him so much each night that I spend alone that I feel
physically ill. But it's also hard to believe he would have turned to
Cassidy if he really felt as strongly as he says. I don't want to be his
second choice.

But I want him. I really, truly do. No matter how much goes down
between us, in my gut and in my heart I feel some sort of deep certainty that he's the one. And then I need to use every ounce of will-
power I have to hold back because my logical brain knows better.

I fold the note into quarters and shove it in my pocket, then
take a long gulp of coffee. I'm going to need several of these to get
through today. I have a lot of editing to do, and a lot of complicated
feelings to ignore. As I bite into a fresh chocolate almond croissant,
I try not to remember that Finn slept all night on a lawn chair at my
front door, for the entire world to see. We're not nineteen anymore,
and his back is probably killing him. I can't believe he did that. I try
to convince myself he's just being dramatic. Putting on a show. But
I can't.

Because I do believe he cares. And while I still don't think I can be
with him, despite wanting to more than I've ever wanted anything,
I'm ready to try to be friends.

TWENTY-TWO

Finn

Being stuck on the outside looking in like this hurts. To be literally on the other side of the door like that while she breaks down . . . it's awful knowing that she's so upset by my actions that she'd rather go through a panic attack alone than let me in.

I stayed so that I'd be close if she decided she did want me there. She didn't.

And clearly, she still doesn't. I go home and wait all day for a text or a call from her after she reads my note. I saw her pick it up. But the message never comes.

I'm back home, still ruminating on how I manage to make mistake after mistake, when suddenly my phone is ringing with Derek on the line. Which it should absolutely not be, since I've *said* I don't want to do backdoor meetings that exclude Maeve.

"What's up?"

"Finn! My favorite podcast host. I have good news."

I frown. "Does Maeve know about this good news?"

I can practically hear him sigh. "Why don't you dial her in?"

Unfortunately, I doubt she'll pick up. But I give it a try, and to my surprise, after a moment, she does and I'm able to merge the calls. "Maeve, Derek is on the line with us."

"Oh!" She sounds shocked. I probably just fucked everything up worse somehow, but at this point I don't know what to do. "Hi, Derek." Her voice sounds tight, as though she's trying to make her tone upbeat and not able to quite get it there.

"Now that I have both of you on the line, I have some good news." He really likes to make it sound like he was always planning on dialing Maeve in. Such a jerk. "You two are interviewing supermodel-turned-fashion-designer Karli Causeway at Fashion Week in Milan."

"But Derek . . . isn't it already Fashion Week?" Maeve sounds skeptical. I know she already booked a pop star for this week.

"Technically. Which is why we're letting you use the Streamify jet. You leave at six a.m., and the interview is the following day. And we got you both invited to the Prada show. We'll send a videographer with you two too, make a vlog of the entire thing. And, yes, it will count as your contracted event for the coming month."

I wish I could see Maeve's face. Is she excited? Or is it too draining to go after her panic attack? I'm there with her no matter what she wants to do. I send her a text. What do you want to do? I can shoot him down if you don't want to go.

Let's go. They're investing

She's right. Derek is pouring resources into this, and it'll definitely be good for our ratings. We've held the number one spot for several weeks straight now, and the drama at the game yesterday only helped. I wait, letting Maeve speak first.

"Amazing," Maeve says finally. I think I'm the only one who can hear the exhaustion hidden in her voice. "Thank you so much, Derek. This will be some great content."

"Sounds like a blast," I echo.

Ten hours later, we're on the private tarmac at LAX, wind whipping around us while we board the plane. We both drove, since I gave Maeve a heads-up that our cars will show up freshly washed and waxed on the tarmac upon our return. Assistants grabbed our luggage and now the videographer, Chris, is filming us as we board the plane. I know Maeve is turning it on for the cameras . . . but just like at the gala, it selfishly feels amazing to have fun with her, even when I know she's faking it.

When we step onto the jet, Maeve takes in the interior, then turns back toward Chris and the camera and widens her eyes. "When I say I *never* thought I would be on a private jet . . . Literally never! I hadn't even been on a plane until college. I can't believe this! I wish I could take all of you here with me." Our fans love Maeve because she loves them, and she's a totally normal woman who made it big overnight. She's real and relatable, and I'm a perfect foil for that because of my upbringing. With the show in general, I'm in it for Maeve, and she's in it for the fans, and it's a great combo, really, because it means I can, or used to be able to, take care of her, since all she thought about was their needs, not her own. She was mining her life for content, going on dates with guys she might not have looked twice at before, to see if there was a story or a lesson there for our fans. It was brutal because so many men are creeps or had inappropriate expectations because she talked about sex on air. So I just tried to make the experience fun for her. Take away some of the drain. Because, for me, going on dates was never so rough.

We talk about the jet and the trip for the cameras for a few minutes, then Chris puts it away and we start actually getting settled on the flight. A ten-hour trip goes down much easier when there's a chef making you a three-course meal and there are full-size beds to sleep in. But Maeve will barely make eye contact with me once the camera is turned off. There's not tension in her shoulders, so I'm inclined to think she's more exhausted than angry, but whatever it is, we're not going to get through it with Chris and the crew lurking, or cameras rolling.

When we land in Italy, there are several cars waiting to take us to our hotel, and so when Chris moves to get into our van, I stop him. "Hey, man, why don't we regroup at the hotel?"

He hesitates, since I'm sure he's been instructed to film every moment, *especially* if and when tensions get high. But after Maeve gets in the van and slams the door, causing us both to jump, he nods and starts backing away toward another vehicle. "For sure, man."

I slide into the car with Maeve. "I'm an asshole. Please forgive me. I don't deserve it. But I would love to stuff my face with fresh Italian pasta with you with a clear conscience."

Maeve tears her gaze from the window, where she's closely monitoring the drivers loading the cars with our pelican cases of breakable equipment, and rolls her eyes as she looks back over at me. "Wouldn't want you to get indigestion." I wait, hoping she'll say more. Raise a white flag to meet mine. She stares at me, her eyes dark and serious, her hair tucked half into the neck of the oversized *Tell Me How You Really Feel* sweatshirt. She looks beautiful. Seeing her so casual like this makes my stomach twist because these moments, the million in-between moments that make up a lifetime, are what I cherish most with her. But I'm not saying that. Not now. Not yet. "I'm ready to actually be friends again, if you're really ready too," she says finally.

"Am I pushing my luck to ask if you forgive me?" I say quietly.

"Yes," she whispers. And I'm not sure which part of that she's saying yes to. But I don't push it.

At the Hotel Principe di Savoia, Chris is filming again, and we're led up to adjoining suites. For the sake of the vlog we pretend to be staying in one suite together, to keep things spicy for our fans, but in reality the living rooms adjoin and we'll each have our own space, same as at the gala. The rooms are ornate, with lush carpeting and finishes, beautiful artwork, and beds complete with balconies. We *ooh* and *ahh* over the setup for the camera, and Maeve turns toward Chris and looks directly into the lens. "Will Finn be spending the night on the floor or in the bed? Vote in the comments. And if you get it right, maybe we'll tell some never-heard-before stories from our college days."

I playfully jump in front of her and place a hand on the outside of the lens, which will make it look like I'm grabbing the camera, although it's actually mounted to a compact shoulder rig and Chris. "She's kidding. Those stories can never see the light of day. I'll sleep in one of these monster chairs."

"Bed will be cold without you in it," Maeve complains with a pout. Maybe we should have set some ground rules for what we're doing while we're on camera. I know part of the whole deal is that we're meant to flirt, to be provocative. But I just want the cameras *gone* so I can make sure that the two of us are truly okay.

Once it seems like we have more than enough footage of us exploring the room, the hotel, the assortment of clothes that our Streamify team sent for us to wear at the shows, I reach over and hit the button on the camera to stop the recording. I open my mouth to start talking, but Maeve grabs my arm and I stop. She reaches over to a pocket on the side of Chris's rig, pulls out his backup mic, and hits Pause on that.

"Is that everything?" she asks Chris. He nods, and then she gives me a "*now* you can continue" look. We're unnecessarily cautious, but that's what makes us so good. Streamify owns this footage, and we want to make sure that they get only audio and video footage that we're okay with them using, because while we can influence the edit . . . we can't control this vlog like we do the podcasts, since it's for their channel, and their editors are cutting it together.

"What do you really *need* for this video?" I ask him. "You have the jet and the hotel. You'll get the interview tomorrow. No need to get our setup tonight, it's boring. Plus, us getting ready and going to the fashion shows. That seems like a solid vlog, don't you think? It's Maeve's first time here, and we just want a little privacy."

Chris hesitates before speaking, and I see his eyes flick down to the monitor, making sure the recording is truly off. "They want everything from your hotel breakfast to your cab rides. We definitely need the duomo and at least one dinner to fill things out. Maybe, uh—" he falters uncomfortably "—you two in the hotel pool. They noted in the brief that the stylist supplied bathing suits."

Maeve walks over to the closet and starts digging through, then pulls out a few scraps of string that are supposed to pass as her bikini. "Then I guess we're going shopping."

I turn to Chris. "We get it, man. This is a big gig! You want to deliver. We want a popular vlog too. How about we do the duomo and a dinner, and on top of the duomo you can get a shot of us—" My instinct was to say "kissing," because I know something as juicy as that will buy us some privacy, but I spoke too soon. I don't want to push boundaries that far on camera when we're finally settled on genuinely being friends again.

"Having a romantic moment," Maeve interjects. "Maybe someone can help Finn track down some flowers, chocolates, and candles?"

I nod eagerly. "Perfect."

Chris opens his mouth, questions about what's actually going on between us clearly on the tip of his tongue. But then he closes it, regroups. "I'll film Finn calling the concierge while Maeve is in the shower."

Maeve smiles sweetly at him, and he blushes. "Can vlogs be nominated for best original short? Because don't worry about a thing, Chris. This is about to be Oscar-worthy." She hits Record on the mic she's holding and hands it back to him, and he presses Record on the camera.

I turn to Maeve. "How jet-lagged are you? Should we check out Milan?"

She tilts her head. "I don't know. I'm kind of tired, and we have the episode tomorrow."

I step closer to her. "Maeve, let me take you out. There's somewhere I want to show you."

She smiles and laces her hands around the back of my neck, looking up at me. "I guess I'll take a quick shower, then." She takes her sweatshirt off as she walks away, while Chris is panning to her, and just as it's about to reveal whether she's wearing anything underneath, I grab the camera and pull it back toward me. Maybe just a hair too roughly.

"Eyes stay on her face," I say. We're good partners because we can build off each other. She doesn't have to tell me what to do for me to react to it for the camera. When we're filming things together, whether it's silly promotional videos for social, full episodes, or guest spots on other people's channels, it reminds me that I probably would like acting, especially if Maeve did it with me. But that's not an option; she'd never be game.

Once I hear the shower turn on, I raise my eyebrows at the camera, then hold a finger to my lips, and dial the concierge. "Hello, Mr. Sutton. How can I help you today?"

"Hi! I'd like to surprise Maeve. Would it be possible to get tickets to the duomo, a nice bottle of champagne, a few candles, and chocolates and strawberries? And maybe a blanket?"

"Of course, Mr. Sutton. How would you like us to bring it to you? Please be advised that food and drink are not permitted in the duomo."

I wink directly at the camera lens as I respond. "Of course. In a tote bag please. Discreetly."

Chris and I wait five minutes, then Maeve steps out of the bathroom wrapped in a towel, her hair damp. When they cut this together, it'll look like she almost interrupted my phone call. "What should I wear?"

I pick up a garment bag off the bed. "I got you something."

Maeve looks directly at Chris. "Cut please. You can start again when I'm dressed and ready."

"You're not going to open it?" I pretend to pout, although I have no idea what's in the bag.

"That one has my outfit for the show! I'll pick a good one to show off your imaginary taste, don't worry."

Chris sits in the other room's living area while Maeve and I get ready, recording only when the concierge drops off the tote bag and I pretend to get it surreptitiously, only to leave it by the door and walk right back into the room where Maeve is getting ready. I sit on the bed while she does her hair and makeup, like we used to back in New York, although then the apartment was so small that I could sit in the living room and still hear her perfectly while we talked.

"So have you met Karli before?" I can't see Maeve, but I would bet she's putting mascara on. Of her makeup routine, it's what requires the most focus, and her voice always sounds off cadence while she does it.

I lie on the bed and look up at paintings of naked angels on the ceiling. This hotel feels like a historical landmark, someplace that should be a museum, not thousand-dollar-a-night rooms. "I met her once when I was a kid. She and my mom were both repping Chanel perfume, and I went along on a shoot to the desert and watched them roll around in the sand for a while."

"Interesting. And very high end. She got her start on *America's Next Top Model* back in the day, but she's really elevated since then," Maeve remarks. She probably worked up an entire dossier on Karli while I slept on the plane. "Maybe we should get her to dish on that a little. Or ask about the *Playboy* shoot? I've gotten too used to knowing roughly what each person is going to want to focus on."

"Maybe she has something," I offer. "A big reveal. She's very private, so to be honest I'm surprised she wanted to come on at all." So surprised, that I asked my mom if she arranged it. She denied it, then suggested we add on a weekend in Amalfi or Cinque Terre, which didn't make me feel inclined to believe her.

"Maybe," Maeve muses. "Do you think we should put it out off cadence?"

"Why would we do that?"

"The vlog can be our regular episode to fill the week. And getting this out while it's still Fashion Week might build buzz."

I stand and walk to the bathroom. Maeve is curling her hair, the American plug hanging out of her mammoth adaptor, and I hold out my hand for the wand. She hesitates a moment as we stare into each other's eyes through the mirror, then gives it to me, and I start curling the back, so the sections she can't reach look as good as the front. My mom taught me when I was seven, and the first time I offered to do it for Maeve she was so surprised she dropped the drink she was sipping as she got ready into the sink.

I start curling, and she stays still, watching me work in the mirror. "I think that's risky," I say as I curl a long strand in the opposite direction of the previous, so the curls don't all clump together when she brushes it out. "The big names have been helping the ratings."

"So does press," Maeve counters.

"So let's see what she says," I offer. "If it's something that is a huge fashion-related get, that reporters will be all over if it comes out this week, we release early and shock everyone."

"Fine," Maeve agrees. It's striking how different this conversation is from the ones we've been having. Our words are the same, but instead of curt, our tones are collaborative, and it makes all the difference. I finish with the back of her head, then turn the wand off and place it on the counter as she finger combs through to loosen up the curls. "Will you spray?"

"Of course." I grab the hairspray she has out, already knowing which bottle is the right one; she shuts her eyes, and I set her hair. Now that I've dealt with having less, being a team feels better than hoping for more.

"You know, even if we run Karli's early, maybe we shouldn't put out the vlog as the regular episode. It just feels so different than the show . . . What if you did a solo one? Or one with an expert in something—more expert to expert?"

Maeve adds a bit of texture spray to her roots. "We both have to be in the episodes, though. They don't want just me."

"I could read Questions of the Week to you two at the end or something." I think it would be good for the network to see that Maeve is totally capable of pulling off her own show. Even though I don't want to stop doing this with her, I want her to be able to do whatever she wants.

Maeve makes eye contact with me in the mirror and smiles slightly. "I've always kind of wanted to do an episode about anxiety with my therapist. And both she and I could answer questions at the end, show both my perspective as someone with anxiety and a therapist, and hers as my doctor. Do you really think the network would go for it?"

"They don't have approval privileges. If you want to do it, we're doing it."

An hour later, we're climbing the steps in the duomo, Chris trailing behind us. When we get to the top, Maeve launches into a monologue, talking about how exciting it is to be out of the US for the first time, and I speedwalk ahead, beyond the top viewing area and to the back side of the roof that most people rush through on their way out. It's as beautiful as the front, maybe more so since there are fewer tourists taking selfies here. I set out a navy blanket, held down by the candles the hotel wrapped up with it so the glass wouldn't break, light them, then pop the champagne quietly and pour us each a glass. I'm laying out the elaborate cheeseboard the hotel made when Maeve and Chris round the corner.

"Finn!" Maeve calls out. "What is all this?" She walks over to me, shooting a confused glance over her shoulder for the camera. I stand and pass her a glass of champagne. Suddenly, a passerby shrieks.

"Oh my god, is this a proposal?" She pulls out her cell and starts recording, and I look over, panicked.

Maeve reaches for me and turns my face back toward her, drawing me tight and angling our heads out of view of the camera. "Ignore her," she whispers.

I take her hand and lead her to the blanket while Chris and our amateur teenage camerawoman continue filming us. Maeve settles in, adjusting her skirt carefully, since it's painfully short, and then I sit across and take a deep breath. I can play into this. It only feels weird because

I wish it was real. If we get fake engaged, will Maeve consider actually marrying me? Last week I would've said it was well worth the gamble.

"Maeve, you are the best person I know. I know I will never deserve you, but I wanted to make sure your first night in Italy was half as special as you are. But also, we have to eat fast because technically this is illegal, and we can't get arrested before the interview tomorrow." I raise my glass and toast her. "Thank you for inviting me to do *Tell Me How You Really Feel* with you. I hope that you'll be telling me how you really feel for the rest of your life." I reach for my back pocket and the girl gasps, but then I just pull out my cell phone and take a selfie of us.

The disgruntled tourist walks away, swearing lightly, and Maeve laughs. "She really thought you had a ring, huh?"

"Clearly, I dropped the ball here."

Maeve reaches toward me and grabs a strawberry. "I think you did alright." She pops it into her mouth in one bite, and I follow suit with cheese and crackers.

We sit there, chewing silently, eating crackers and strawberries, waiting for Chris to get the hint. He keeps filming. Eventually, Maeve starts giggling. "Finn, I can't eat any more of these. They're delicious, but I want to have pasta our first night in Italy." *Our.*

"You've got it, man, right?" I call up to Chris. I don't know what he's waiting for.

"How about a kiss? Something to really sell it?"

Maeve turns. "Or a strawberry eating competition? See how many each of us can fit in our mouths?"

He glares, but it feels lighthearted. "Make it good then."

"On it!" Maeve laughs. She starts lining up two rows of the remaining strawberries, and I do the same, trying to match them for size. "Let's do this in the style of a western," she instructs. "You can add sound effects of lassos and music and whatever in post. So, Finn, we should start by narrowing our eyes, really serious. Chris, cut in. Get a few options, and then when we start we'll be messy."

We do a few takes of each of us staring down the other, the glittering city and walls of the duomo around us, then Chris counts us in. "Three, two, one, GO!"

We each start shoving strawberries into our mouths, and I push one back so far I gag. Maeve starts to laugh and spits one out, and she watches it roll off the rooftop. Chris is wildly panning back and forth between the two of us, trying to capture everything. I make it through six of my ten strawberries before waving my napkin as a white flag, while Maeve is still trying to fit a seventh in her mouth. She bites down into the tip of it and leaves it dangling out, then pumps her arms victoriously, before making a cut gesture at Chris. He ignores her, and films us spitting out the strawberries.

"You better not use that last bit," Maeve sputters.

"Eh, could've just kissed. Besides, it's funny. And now you get to be done. I'll film dinner tomorrow when you're dressed for the show and not drooling fruit."

I start laughing as I really take in the two of us. Our nice clothes are covered with specks of pink strawberry juice, there are half-chewed berries everywhere, our teeth are covered in seeds. Once I start laughing, it sets Maeve off, and she suddenly is doubled over with giggles. Naturally, now that we're incapacitated, a security guard rounds the corner.

"Fuck," Chris mutters. "Take the food and run!" He shoulders his camera and starts speed walking out, and Maeve and I start throwing food into the tote, as the guard starts yelling in Italian.

"What's he saying?" Maeve asks through laughs, her eyes tearing up.

"You don't want to know." My Italian is limited, but I know enough to recognize that he wants to fine us. I grab the champagne bottle and Maeve's hand, and we start to run around the side of the roof and toward the staircase. The pace we take down the stairs is completely reckless, considering the end of the staircase is the interior of the church, but we turn and burst out the doors and into the piazza. Maeve drops the tote into a trash bin as we run, the guard still chasing us, and out of the corner of my eye I see Chris crouched across the street filming the pursuit. I push the champagne bottle onto a young couple as we enter the galleria and attempt to get lost in the crowd.

I pull Maeve into the Prada store and we hide behind a mannequin and watch the guard run by, still collapsing with giggles. "Can I help you?" the sales clerk asks, interrupting our escapade, her voice dripping with disdain. This is one of the most elegant Prada stores in the world, and we definitely don't look like we belong.

We both attempt to straighten up, but Maeve can't stop giggling and tries to turn her head and hide behind her fist and a fake cough. "We're going to the show tomorrow!" I offer. "They sent outfits, but we'd really love to try something new on."

"Is that so? Could I get your names?"

Before I can give them, since it's completely true, Maeve tugs on my hand. "So sorry, but we must step out. Have a great night!"

She darts around the saleswoman and drags me behind her, dropping my hand once we're out of the store.

"I wasn't even lying! We could have gotten fresh clothes," I protest as we walk out.

"From Prada?! I don't belong in there. One item is more than I've spent on clothes in the last year. They would be uninviting us before we could swipe our card. And we're criminals now! Being arrested in Italy is not on my bucket list."

We walk back out into the night and I look around. "Well, even criminals need to eat. Pasta?"

"Pasta," Maeve confirms.

We should go somewhere nice, since it's her first night, but instead we just duck into the first restaurant we see. "Can we get one of each pasta?" I ask as soon as the waiter comes to ask if we want water.

He hesitates. "Sir, there are six different dishes here."

"Sounds perfect. And wine please, whatever you think goes with . . . all of them."

When he leaves, Maeve leans across the table to whisper. "Now he's going to tell everyone this horror story about how Americans order the entire menu because they're gluttons."

I look at her solemnly. "It's my sworn duty, as an American tourist, to confirm every supersize stereotype. How would you feel if an Italian came to America and said they only ate kale salad? It's no fun!"

Maeve was mid-sip of water when I'd started talking, and she starts laughing so suddenly it spurts out her nose. I give her my napkin so she doesn't have to wipe her snot with her own. Once air is the only thing coming out of her nostrils, she giggles again. "I forgot how much fun we are."

"Someone tell Chris. He thinks we're divas."

"We are divas. We just ordered every pasta on the menu and had an illegal picnic on the duomo with a cameraman."

"Oh right, I forgot," I tease.

The waiter comes back to our table with plates of a *cacio e pepe*, Bolognese, carbonara, pear ravioli, squid ink octopus, and pesto gnocchi. He sets them all down with a flourish. "Let me know if you need more," he adds sarcastically.

Maeve picks up her fork and tries the carbonara, which is directly in front of her, with a moan. "This is incredible. Why haven't we done this before?"

"Come to Italy?"

"Yes." She moves to try the *cacio e pepe*, and I stop her.

"You need a palate cleanser."

She takes a sip of wine, then digs into the next one, and repeats this for the rest. I don't try any because I want to see her reaction to each. I've had all of these, from all the best restaurants in Italy, but coming here, to this random, side-of-the-road place with Maeve, is better than any of that. Her enjoyment is so wholehearted. Most of my friends from LA have eaten at countless Michelin-starred restaurants because they also have famous parents, fancy vacations, and unlimited resources. Good food is a requirement for them, not special, and they don't want to moan over something and seem like a rube. But unabashedly enjoying things like Maeve does is way more fun.

Once she's ranked them all, I dig in, and we spend the next hour debating their merits before doing the same with every dessert on the menu. It's decadent, delicious, and so much fucking fun. I feel so relieved that things feel more normal between us. I will do anything and everything to keep her in my life.

TWENTY-THREE

Maeve

"Do you hear that?" I'm standing in the living room area in Finn's adjoining hotel room's suite, mic out, headphones plugged in, trying to get room tone.

Finn steps into the room and cocks his head. "No? Did something interrupt it?"

Whenever we record an interview, we get one minute of room tone, which is an audio recording of basically nothing, in the room we're in. No talking, no moving things, just as close to total silence as it gets. Which is never actually silent. It feels silent until you have the headphones on, and then suddenly there's the buzz of electric overhead lights, the hum of a fan or AC, someone laughing as they walk by in the hallway—we can hear it all. In our Streamify studio it's soundproofed, so we have no outside noise and all I can hear is the faint hum of lights.

"No, but there's something besides the sound of the lights. And there shouldn't be; I turned the air off."

Finn takes the headphones from me and puts them on, scanning the room slowly. I follow his gaze, and then I think I see it. I pick up the mic and move it closer and closer to the window as he listens on the headphones. When I'm a foot away, I pause and watch him listen. He nods and rips the headphones off.

"It's stuck open, like, the tiniest bit." He presses down on the window from the top, to no avail. Obviously. If it could've been shut farther, I would've done it. I crouch on the floor and look at the crack. The wood has warped over time, since we're basically staying in a museum, and there's maybe half a centimeter of space. Too small to feel a draft, but enough to hear it. I take a breath and stand. "It's fine. I'll get room tone and we'll work with it."

Finn goes to the other room and returns with a T-shirt that he tries to wedge into the crack. We moved all of his things into my room, so that we can film in this one. "Does that help?" he asks once the shirt is in place.

I shake my head. "It'll be in the video. And I am not masking it out in post, so don't even ask." In one of our early videos we had a Truly sitting out on the table, and I spent five hours masking in Premiere, frame by frame, so that I could use the Content-Aware Fill to erase it. In a photo, it's easy to remove things like that, but in a video it's a whole different story. Finn had helped by supplying me with constant snacks and shouting words of affirmation as he watched over my shoulder.

"Fair," he agrees as he pulls the shirt out. "Remember when someone had a heart attack in your building mid-episode? And the ambulance parked outside for hours?"

"How could I forget? I don't know why we didn't stop recording. We had to redo everything."

"It was, like, the tenth episode! We didn't know how loud it would be in post yet."

I walk over to the monitor and gesture to Finn to sit in so I can check the lighting and framing Chris set up for us while we were sleeping off our vats of pasta. He walks over to the chair we're saving for Karli and sits in it, looking to the side toward our seats like she will be. As I adjust the close-up camera angle slightly, I keep talking. It's nice to be able to talk again. Last night broke the tension we've been having, and it's almost too easy for things between us to feel good again. "You know, if I recall, it was *you* who claimed that on movie sets they record through sirens all the time, and mics are designed to weed out extraneous noises."

Finn looks at me with his peripheral vision, not moving his head so I can keep adjusting. Karli is Finn's height and roughly his complexion, which makes this pre-light even easier. "Well, how could I have known the mics we rented for free weren't up to par with my mom's movie sets?"

"Hmm, I wonder. Can you be me next?"

Finn gets in the chair closest to Karli's, but facing hers, and slouches down a foot so I can direct the camera on his face. "Are you sure you don't want to just sit in? I'll do you."

"Yeah?"

He nods and walks over, we switch places, and I barely notice the half second that our arms brush when I walk by him. I sit in my chair and turn as though I'm looking at Karli, and Finn starts adjusting the camera that's for my close-up. It's hard for me to wrap my head around everything that's happened in the past few months. Not even between Finn and me, but the fact that I just flew to Milan Fashion Week on a private jet, am interviewing a supermodel whom I watched on TV in high school, and am going to the Prada show tonight in an outfit a stylist selected for me. Finn appears at home with all of this, which makes total sense, but every time something new happens I'm waiting for it all to be snatched away.

I should be worrying about staying number one in the ratings so we can beat *The Paul Myers Show*, knock Paul Myers down a peg, and make gender pay gap history. And even though that *is* my goal . . . what I worry about at night isn't that *not* happening. It's waking up in the morning and having all of this ripped away because someone realized that I don't belong here, and they could throw someone like Cassidy into my role and have the show do twice as well.

"Dollar for your thoughts?" Finn says softly.

"Shouldn't it be a penny?"

"I'd pay a million, actually."

"Do you think the show's still good like this? I almost feel like, with the celebs, anyone could be interviewing them and it would do well." That's almost my real worry.

Finn walks over and sits down in Karli's chair, facing me. "I think anyone could interview them and people would watch. But not that it would be like this. They wouldn't share these private things with other people. You hold what they say carefully, you know? They trust you not to exploit it in a fame grab, to take it seriously, to use it to advance important conversations. Most people would just try to get them to list their favorite sex positions or something dumb to get an outrageous viral clip. But you're not most people."

Why is it that I believe things only when Finn says them? My therapist, my sister, Shazia, ten million people online—they could all say similar things, and I wouldn't hear them. But when he says it, I believe it. Before I can respond, someone starts knocking on the door, and then opens it.

"Ciao!" Karli exclaims. "I had the desk make me a key for the filming suite. Hope you don't mind!"

"Of course not! It's so great to see you!" Finn rushes to greet Karli and they hug.

"Wow! I can't believe I'm meeting you," I gush as I hug her next. I come up to her shoulder.

"Me? I can't believe I'm here with you! Huge fan! Did you know I grew up in Williamsport? Not too far from you."

"In middle-of-nowhere-PA hours, that's around the corner," I joke. Williamsport is in farmland, hours from an airport, at least a forty-minute drive to a grocery store or mall for most people. Everyone out there gets used to driving long distances to do *anything*. "Finn, would you mind getting Karli mic'd? I just have to run and change."

I duck into the other room and pull on a *Tell Me How You Really Feel* sweat suit and start quickly applying mascara and lip gloss. We're basically set up, but Karli is a half hour early, so I wasn't quite ready. From the other room I can hear her and Finn chatting about Fashion Week, his mom's latest projects, their favorite spots in Italy. But then I hear Karli ask about Cassidy, and my ears perk up.

"How's Cassidy? Is it gauche to ask what happened? You two were always the cutest together. That romance you two did is my comfort movie."

"Clip that to your shirt." It sounds like Finn is mic'ing her. An awkward time to answer a relationship question. I pause, mascara wand still in hand, and listen intently. "You know Cassidy, she's amazing. Gorgeous, smart, talented, the full package. We tried, but dating like that was a huge mistake. We don't have the chemistry and compatibility you need to date as adults. And I realized I had feelings for . . . someone else, which was unfair to her, too. I'm a chronic idiot."

I wonder if Finn knows I can hear him through the wall. He has to be talking about me. I know he is. And he's speaking quietly, but not quite whispering, which makes me think he's trying to answer without me hearing. I cap the mascara quickly and walk out without warning, and his eyes jump to mine with a start. Interesting. The entire situation is a trigger point for us, so I understand him not wanting me to hear. But his response . . .

It seems like he really means that.

This whole time I've assumed that he's been placating me, trying to calm me down by saying what I want to hear, so he can have his cake and eat it too. He got to date Cassidy, and when that didn't work he decided to try to reignite things with me, his sloppy seconds. There's no way he was dating Cassidy, *the* It girl, and dumped her for me. There's no way. In the letter he said he just wanted to be friends again, anyway.

But as I set the wide shot, Karli and Finn still chatting away, I can't help but stare at Finn through the shield of the monitor for a moment longer than I need to. Now that I'm not busy hating him, it's harder to ignore that I've never actually stopped loving him.

TWENTY-FOUR

Before the Streamify contract

Maeve

I'm hysterical. Not in an "oh, she's crying, so men call her hysterical" way. But in an "I can't stop sobbing on the way to a panic attack" way. "We were on a break! Hitting pause! Not *seeing other people*! I can't believe he did this."

"Maeve. Maeve. Can you hear me? Take a breath, okay?" Sarah sounds panicked through the tinny phone speaker.

My mind is racing a mile a minute, and I can't stop it. "We were *obviously* not seeing other people! He went on a fucking date and called for permission when he was already there. He said he *loved* me! I can't believe this. And it was a *date*! And I am not fucking disposable. I can't believe I slept with him. Fuck. Fuck!"

"You're spinning! It'll be okay. Just sit down and try to breathe. Fuck him."

I drop to the floor and rest my head in my arms on the couch and try to get my breathing in check. Tears are streaming down my face and I don't know whether the sleeves of my *Tell Me How You Really Feel* sweatshirt are soaked with sweat, tears, or snot. "Am I being crazy? Like, this is on him, right?"

Sarah laughs shortly and something untwists in my gut. "Uh, no, you are *not* being crazy. Only someone with literally no integrity would say what he did is okay. If he actually cared and wanted things to work and loved you and whatfuckingever, he wouldn't have even considered dropping you for Cassidy. You're not being unreasonable."

I wipe my face and peel off my sweatshirt. The sense of loss is absolutely crushing. I *knew* this was all too good to be true. I can't have Finn, have the deal, have it all. I was so *stupid* to believe that he really loved me. Every day of the last two years doing this show we've been joined at the hip, but not together. If he wanted me, he would've done something earlier. For an instant I let myself believe that I really was that special. The kind of girl he'd want. That the glow of the Streamify deal and making *Tell Me How You Really Feel* had rubbed off and made me special.

As fucking if.

"I hate that it's Cassidy," I whisper.

"We can hate her if you want," Sarah offers immediately.

"I can't even hate her!" I lament. "She was his first kiss. They have history. I'm the evil wench standing in their way in this story. And come on, who doesn't love her! *I* love her! Her modeling-behind-the-scenes TikToks, her movie cameos, her "Get Unready with Me" . . . it's all perfect."

"I became an Armani foundation diehard because she used it in her *Vogue Beauty Secrets* video," Sarah admits somberly.

"This isn't her fault. It's Finn's. It's his choice. Like, his actions have shown me how *he* really feels, and that's that." I try to stay strong as I say it, but I can't. My face crumples and suddenly I'm sobbing again. Sarah murmurs comforting words as I descend into a full-on panic attack.

I've been dealing with panic attacks since I was twelve or thirteen. My first one was after seeing Claude win a pageant and Tiffany win a game in the same weekend. In bed that night my mind was spinning, and I started crying silently as I convinced myself I was nothing compared with them. That I would never amount to anything. That no one even liked me and everyone talked about me behind my back and I could never stop feeling like this. I thought I had died for a moment or was about to. Now I know how to recognize when my anxiety is making me think things that aren't true, and I try to deal with them as they start. I pop a weed gummy and get in a hot bath, Sarah still on the line, while I wait for it to kick in and numb me. I just need to make it through the night, and in the morning I can deal with this.

So in the morning, I accept a date with the first guy I find on Raya and block Finn's number.

TWENTY-FIVE

Finn

"You ready?"

I hold a hand out to Maeve so she can decide whether to take it before we step out of the car and into public. After the interview with Karli, Maeve and I felt normal—joking, laughing, talking—and I want to hold on to every moment of this.

Maeve takes my hand and grins. "We're at Fashion Week. With *Prada*. Holy fuck."

Seeing her light up and smile wide makes me feel warm and light. I want to kiss her. Instead, I squeeze her hand, and lead her out of the car when the driver opens the door. When we step out of the car, the lights are blinding and people are screaming.

"Maeve! Finn! We love the show!"

The shouts are endless, and we should rush past all of the fans like all the other celebs do, but instead, Maeve stops. She turns completely around, so instead of heading inside, she's facing the fans that are pressing against the barricade. She waves, big and exaggerated, and shouts back to them. "Thank you all for listening! We love you! So fucking much!" She looks up at me. "Do we have to go in?"

I glance at the Prada security guard, who's already glaring at us. "Who cares? Do whatever you want!"

"Film this!" she yells to Chris, and he pushes past the guard and around the barrier. Maeve turns to the fans and drops my hand to grab her phone from her purse. She holds it up to her mouth like a microphone and the crowd quiets, straining to hear her next words. "It is time, for a little thing I like to call . . ." I bang my hands on the metal of the barricade in a drumroll, seeing where she's going with this. "Questions of the Week! Rapid-fire Fashion Week edition." Maeve sticks her phone toward a random girl. "Go!"

"Ahhhhh. My boyfriend wants a threesome. With another guy. What do I do?"

Maeve holds the mic up to me. "If you're into it, do it," I say, my words tumbling over each other as I try to rush them out. "Any reservations, don't."

Maeve takes the mic back. "And make sure it's not in your own bed, and it's not someone you'll ever see again. And if you drive them home, *they* sit in the backseat. Next!"

A girl shoots her hand up in the air, and Maeve thrusts the mic toward her. "My best friend is skipping my birthday to go camping with a guy she's been on, like, five dates with."

"Ladies, your friends are who will be there through every relationship. They're your soulmates, and your partners are guests, at least until you have kids."

She offers me the mic, and I chime in. "I hope he knows that he's getting further from the friendship seal of approval with every s'more."

"Next!" Maeve is exuberant, shoving the mic deeper into the crowd. The security guard starts moving toward her, and I step in between them.

"Who should pay on the first date?"

Maeve is talking before the question is fully out of the girl's mouth. "Men! Always. When women are making the same amount on the dollar, and there's no pink tax, and men are doing an equal amount of domestic duties, we'll reevaluate."

The security guard is about an inch away from grabbing Maeve's cell phone. "One more?" I say to Maeve.

"One more!" Maeve yells.

"Are you together?" someone screams.

"And that's a wrap! See you Sunday for the next episode of *Tell Me How You Really Feel*!" I grab Maeve's hand and we run inside, breathless and laughing. The security guard slams the door behind us in a huff, and through the window we watch as he tries to corral the fans who were pressing so hard against the barrier that it moved incrementally closer to us.

"How did they know we were here?" Maeve asks, her eyes shining with adrenaline. She's a natural at this, the mix of entertainment and advice. I really think it's her calling.

I shrug. "No idea. But you definitely just made their day."

"Good," Maeve says with satisfaction. "In New York we got to see fans of the show all the time, and really interact with them. I kind of miss it."

In the two years we spent doing the show before the Streamify hiatus, we interacted with fans in a way that no other celebrities do. It horrified my parents and got us into the tabloids and trending social media posts more times than I could count. Because we *engaged*. When we went out, we'd take shots with fans; at Yankees games we'd join them in the bleeder seats; if we ran into a group of fans on the street, we'd answer their questions, do TikToks with them, join them for lunch. We're lucky we never got murdered, to be completely honest, but it really was fun. And although we gave sex-and-relationships advice centered on finding the one, the crux of the show was really about how to be a good partner, friend, and person, so most of our fans are genuinely super cool.

"We should do a live event. I bet Streamify would be all over it."

Maeve raises an eyebrow. "Streamify would vet the people and suck the fun out. It would be like a *Bachelor* taping, where everyone is a superfan. I want to meet the fans that would never show up to something like that, that we just happen to see out. The ones who just stare at first because they don't want to be cringe and walk up to us."

"Then I guess we better start going places." The reason we haven't seen anyone is because neither of us has been going much of anywhere since the LA move. We used to do everything together, and in each other's absence we've both been wearing a hole in our respective couches.

"Guess so," Maeve says, and bumps her shoulder into me. And it feels pretty damn good. I feel a surge of hope that maybe, in a few weeks, I won't feel the same emptiness I have the past few months, because Maeve and I will be good again.

Both of our outfits are completely over the top. We're in full denim, Maeve in a bralette-type top and flared jeans, and me in denim cut-offs and a jacket with no shirt. I don't know if we look good, or completely ridiculous. But at least the clothes are comfortable, even if Maeve's giant heels look like death traps. She said she would wear anything if she got the bag she wanted, which to my untrained eye looks exactly like her other bags, although this one is Prada.

Now that we're in the atrium, we're with all the other guests, and suddenly I see him. Paul Myers. A jolt of anxiety goes through me, and I instinctively try to turn Maeve around, but she's already seen him. And even worse, he's seen us too and is heading straight for us.

Maeve looks at me, her eyes wide with horror. "What is he going to do? Kill us and live stream it?"

"I'm sure that's his wet dream. I don't know. Why can't he just avoid us like a normal person?" I wish we weren't wearing denim anymore, because I think every pore of my body is now sweating.

But when Paul Myers finally gets to us, he just grins and offers his hand. I shake it reluctantly, and I catch Maeve's hand going to her purse to touch the hand sanitizer I already know is in there. He goes to offer Maeve his hand, but withdraws it as she pretends to fumble with her bag and drink.

"Nice to finally meet," he says brightly. And it's jarring, because his tone of voice, even the pitch of his voice, is . . . it's different than his on-air voice.

"You hate us," Maeve says flatly with a sweet—albeit fake— smile. "If you're here to say something awful, just get it over with."

"Baby, it's just show business."

"Don't call her 'baby,'" I growl. I put my arm around Maeve protectively and she leans in just the slightest bit. She sounded so cool and collected when she just spoke, but with my arm around her I can feel that she's trembling slightly.

Paul Myers laughs. "Relax. You of all people should know that this is just work. Thanks for helping me get the ratings the past few years."

"You mean you don't actually hate us?" Maeve asks softly.

"No. We probably aren't even as far off in our actual beliefs as you think. My *Paul Myers Show* persona? Sure, he hates you. But it's acting. Get over it. You're doing the same thing when you make up all those stories about your dates."

Maeve and I have never made anything up. What we do is nothing like what he does. We teach fans about healthy sex and relationships—he spreads hate, bigotry, and violence. "You know we've been getting death threats from your fans for years, right?"

Paul rolls his eyes. "Grow up. Same here. I just wanted to introduce myself and let you two know—no hard feelings. Your whole bit is great, really. My daughter is your biggest fan."

Maeve and I just stand there in silence. She's still trembling slightly, and without another word Paul Myers turns and walks away. "What the fuck . . ." Maeve whispers. "Did that really just happen? He's . . . pretending to hate us? Whipping his fans into a hateful frenzy over us for ratings? But secretly likes the show?"

My brain feels stuck, like it can't compute what just happened. "I can't believe he'd tell his fans to send us all those horrible messages just for fun. For money, really, since it's all for ratings."

"I don't know that it's for the money," Maeve muses. She drains her drink. "Maybe it's for the fame. The ego boost from the fans that he doesn't seem to agree with or respect. He's using them like sheep to build his throne."

I take a deep breath. My heart is pounding, even though he didn't attack us in any way my body is still prepared for some sort of altercation. "I don't even know what to say right now. Want to get another drink? Repress this and deal with it later?"

"One *thousand* percent," Maeve agrees.

After mingling for a while longer we get shepherded to the hall with the runway, and make our way to seats with our name cards. We've tried to refocus on the fun and pretend Paul Myers isn't here and we didn't just have the conversation. The alcohol definitely helps.

Maeve squeals when she realizes that we're in the front row, albeit off to the side and it's enough to make me feel excited for something I already *know* I find boring.

A model walks down the catwalk wearing what looks like a deconstructed umbrella, and while other people around us nod astutely, Maeve's whispers are hot in my ear. "We call this weather insurance. Because when you have an umbrella, it never rains." Next, a woman dressed in a hot pink leather trench with felt flowers and forest animals on it walks down. "Beanie baby explosion. They have pink guts." I swallow a laugh and try to pass it off as a cough. A man in a coat with fuzzy balls as sleeves walks down. "This is giving. *I always wanted to be a cheerleader but instead worked at JP.*"

This time I can't hold it back. People down the aisle from us shoot disapproving looks, and now I turn to Maeve. "They're going to take back the bag if we keep being a nuisance."

She mimes zipping her lips. It takes roughly three outfits for her to start up again.

The model walks out in only a thong, and a designer runs out and starts spraying on her dress. "The emperor's new clothes," Maeve breathes into my ear.

I can't stifle my snort of a laugh in time, and it cuts through the silence just when they cut the music, so the only sound is the spray of paint. And my stifled snort. A security guard makes a beeline for us, leaning down to whisper as soon as the music is back on. "If you don't stop, you will be asked to leave."

Maeve and I nod solemnly. *So sorry!* she mouths, her eyes wide and angelic, as though she wasn't the one instigating all this. After he turns to leave, Maeve shifts incrementally, so that her knee is *almost* touching mine. I think if I wasn't wearing so much denim I could feel her body heat. After a moment, I let my knee inch closer, until they're touching, barely. And she doesn't pull away.

We don't look at each other for the rest of the show. But our knees stay pressed together.

Chris joins us for the after-party to film, and the evening passes in a blur of good but tiny food, models, laughter, and expensive clothes. By the time we get back to the hotel, my arm is supporting practically all of Maeve's weight as she hobbles in her heels. I help Maeve into her room, then go to open my door, since I need to move all the stuff we stashed in Maeve's during the interview back there. But the connecting door flashes red.

"Try the outer one," Maeve suggests. She takes off a heel and moans in relief. "Next episode: 'Post-heel Orgasms, a New Frontier.'"

"Gold!" I shout back as I head into the hallway, leaving the deadbolt holding Maeve's door open just in case, so she won't have to get up and let me back in. I try the key on my outer door, but nothing happens. I walk back into Maeve's room and dial the front desk. "Hello! Our key isn't working on the second room, five twelve?"

"I'm terribly sorry about that, Mr. Sutton. Let me check on that." I hear the computer typing. "That room is assigned to another guest for the evening. Your team removed the equipment after the recording session and left a note here saying all gear is in your colleague Chris Landry's room."

"I see." I hesitate. I don't want Maeve thinking I orchestrated this. "Are any other rooms available for this evening?"

"I'm afraid we're fully booked sir. Again, I apologize for the mistake. Would you like me to inquire at any other hotels for you?"

I hesitate. I don't want to push any boundaries with Maeve. But it's already two in the morning. I mute the phone for a moment. "Maeve, they gave our room away and the hotel's booked. Can I sleep on the floor? Or should I let them book a different hotel?"

Maeve sticks her head out of the bathroom, already in the hotel robe. "What? It's the middle of the night; don't book somewhere else. We'll figure it out."

I unmute the phone. "No need. Have a good night.

"I can sleep on the couch or floor," I say quickly once I've hung up. "Sorry, they must have thought the second room was just for recording."

Maeve steps out of the bathroom, her face washed clean. "These couches are barely comfortable enough to sit on. They're ornamental. You can sleep in the bed if you make a pillow wall."

"A pillow wall?"

"Yes," Maeve says primly. "It's a big bed. Plenty of room for a barricade. I don't want your sweaty legs near me while I'm getting my beauty sleep."

We've shared a bed more nights than I've slept on her floor on the air mattress. But I start grabbing pillows from the various chairs. "On it."

The next ten minutes, while we take turns using the bathroom and changing, feel charged. We've had a great two days. I don't want this to turn things in the wrong direction. Maeve typically sleeps in some version of a giant T-shirt, but tonight she's wearing a silk pajama set. It's almost lingerie-esque, and I try not to look at it for too long.

"The Prada stylist left it for me," she says awkwardly.

"It's nice," I choke out. I put on a full *Tell Me How You Really Feel* sweat suit so that I'm as covered as possible. I almost ask if I should stay above the sheets, but when Maeve slides into the bed, I follow suit. The wall of pillows looms between us.

"Should I turn the light off?" she says finally. Her voice sounds tense.

"Sure."

We lie there in the dark, and I can tell from her breathing that she's not falling asleep. Not even close. And after a while longer, through the pillows, I hear her open her mouth and inhale, as though she's about to speak. I want to move one, so I can see her face, but I leave them, and instead just turn my head to look at the lace embroidery that I know Maeve is on the other side of. "I only hated you out of self-preservation," she says softly.

Her words hang there. Only when I'm sure she won't add anything do I speak. "I won't give you reason to again." I don't know how much to say. This moment is too fragile to risk. Instead of trying to add more, to push when we're still on the cusp of breaking, I reach my hand up and let it rest on a pillow between us.

Maeve takes it and interlaces her fingers with mine. I'm asleep before I can enjoy feeling her there with me.

TWENTY-SIX

Before the Streamify contract

Finn

Cassidy stares at the ceiling as she lies in bed next to me. "This isn't working, is it."

It's a statement, even though it could be a question. The six inches of space between us on the king all but confirms it. I reach out and squeeze her hand once, quickly. I try to sound reassuring, even though all I've felt in my gut the past few days is dread. "It's not. But I really am glad we tried."

Cassidy and I have spent the past two months going to all of the most romantic places in Europe. We spent time in Rome, Marseille, Santorini, Budapest, Seville, and we're currently in Paris in a hotel room that overlooks the Eiffel Tower. We've ridden Vespas, eaten everything from seven-course meals to questionable street food, gone to spas, on yachts, to palaces and high teas. We've been living in a mashup of every European romance novel and movie, and the paparazzi have been stalking us shamelessly, but we've just ignored them and let the cameras click. Seeing them makes my stomach twist every time they accost us as we enter a restaurant or leave the hotel, but it genuinely doesn't bother Cassidy.

But despite living out what should be the most epic romance . . . our chemistry isn't here. We had more chemistry when we were just friends catching up than we do now that we're dating. It almost feels like another role that we're trying to act out and force to work. The way the press is reporting our every move makes me feel like it *should* work. I want to give everyone the romance they're rooting for! From tabloids, to *People*, to *Vogue*, news outlets are thriving on the coverage of our supposed European romance, and fans write in every day, saying we've made them believe in love and all kinds of stuff like that.

But I can't stop thinking about Maeve.

I miss her snarky texts, the way she tucks her auburn hair behind her ear, her laugh that turns into a snort when she tries to hold it in, the way she always takes a bite of frozen pizza too soon when it's out of the oven even though she knows it'll burn her tongue. I miss who I am with her. Maeve always pushes me to be the best version of myself. I don't think she even realizes she's doing it, but I just always want to strive to be better around her because she works so hard and is so damn smart. I want to be the man she deserves.

I turn on my side to face Cassidy. "I'm sorry. This wasn't fair to you."

Cassidy turns on her side to face me too, her hair falling perfectly around her face as she props her head on her fist. "We're all grown-ups here, Finn. I really mean that. I'm glad we tried. Now we don't have to always wonder. It would absolutely haunt me if we'd never tried. I mean, we had an *amazing* vacation."

"That we did." I stare at the ceiling, trying to keep my eyes from smarting. I feel like I've messed up everything with two of the most important people in my life. Like I'll never be able to come back from this cliff I've dived off of. "Do you think I've ruined things with Maeve?" I say finally. It's not fair to ask Cassidy. But it's all I can think about. Cassidy hesitates to respond, and I rush to fill the silence. "Sorry. I shouldn't have asked that. It's rude. I should be asking how to make sure our friendship isn't awkward now that we've done this."

"No, no, it's okay, really. We're not babies anymore, but it'll be fine." Cassidy lays her head on the pillow and purses her lips. "But with Maeve . . . maybe. But I don't know. I've always thought you seemed good together. With her you're just . . . you're like you used to be. Back when we were nine and acting and having fun without worrying. You seem more *you* with her, if that makes any sense. The you I love most is the you that you are with her. That's why I don't want to keep forcing this. I want that you back."

I nod. I know exactly what she means. She watches as I grab my phone from the bedside table and hit Maeve's contact. There has to be a way that I can make this right. My call goes straight to voicemail, meaning I'm blocked, and I suddenly think I might throw up.

Fuck.

TWENTY-SEVEN

Maeve

I had thought that recording an episode with my therapist back at the Streamify studios would be more anxiety inducing than any previous episode. When I brought it up back in Milan, I hadn't really thought we'd do it, but it had been something that had been percolating for a while, because I thought it could be a good way to establish my credibility as a more serious interviewer, which would help my case for the solo show. It's more personal than anything I've done, and we'll be talking about my most painful, core issues. But as Finn hits Record on each camera, I don't feel nervous at all.

Finn is listening in to the episode from outside the studio, then will come back to do the Questions of the Week segment with the two of us. I would have been happy to have him here for the entire interview, but he insisted that it didn't make sense; and now that we're actually starting, it does feel right with just Jenn and me. But even though it feels right, now that we're good again, I miss having his reassuring presence in the chair next to mine. But I'm looking forward to showing that I can carry the show solo.

"This week on *Tell Me How You Really Feel* I'm doing something totally new. I'm sitting down with someone who's both an expert and someone I have a deeply personal relationship with. This is Jenn, and she's been my therapist since I was thirteen years old. She specializes in generalized anxiety disorder and cognitive behavioral therapy, but I can confirm that she's so knowledgeable in so many other areas as well. Jenn, thank you for being here today."

"Thanks for having me Maeve. This is definitely different from our usual sessions. The setting alone is . . . very whimsical."

I laugh. "That's one way to put it! This already feels strange. Like it's a mix between therapy, an interview, and just chatting." I can tell that this is strange for Jenn too, and I'm sure the different type of episode and guest will feel odd to our viewers, so I want to acknowledge the awkward.

"Agreed. But it's great seeing you in person!"

"It is! Jenn and I first started working together in person when I lived outside Pittsburgh back home. We continued that when I was at CMU, since that's also local. But ever since I moved to New York, and now LA, our sessions have been primarily virtual." I pause, waiting to see if Jenn will jump in. But she seems to be waiting for me to set the tone and get things started. "I've mentioned having anxiety in previous episodes, but I've never fully dived into what that looks like and feels like for me. It's been a lifelong struggle, and Jenn has been my guiding light along the way as it has ebbed and flowed and I've worked on my strategies for dealing with it."

I pause and look to Jenn to jump in. If there are any awkward beats while we get our footing here I'll just cut them out in post, which I told her before we started. "Working with the same patient for such an extended period of time is relatively unusual in therapy these days, and I've really enjoyed getting to know Maeve."

"If you have questions, just ask them," I tell Jenn, since she seems hesitant to continue. "I edit this and can always cut things out."

"I'm used to keeping things confidential. This is all very unusual, and so I feel strange divulging details of your journey."

I nod thoughtfully. I would feel the same way. That's something I would have to balance in my solo show too, so I'm glad we're doing this now, so I can start thinking through problems like this before I present my idea to a network. "I give you my permission to be completely candid. If there's anything that feels too personal, I'll cut it out in post. I know this is unusual, but I think it'll be a great episode and help a lot of our viewers."

"Okay," Jenn says after a moment. "When I met Maeve, she was thirteen years old and was dealing with anxiety in a big way for the first time. It's very common for the onset of anxiety to be in puberty, but as I got to know Maeve more, we learned that she had experienced feelings of anxiety from a much younger age."

"That's true. I didn't even realize it, but the dread I'd feel before going to a birthday party without my sisters, or the stress I felt even in third grade when I had to rush to get my homework done because I had been at my sisters' activities all day, was actually anxiety. At the time, I would mainly just cry, and my mom thought I was throwing a temper tantrum, or hungry, or tired. She would feed me, put me to bed, and let me cry it out. Which is exactly what her mom always did. But in reality, at that age that was just the only way I knew how to express my anxiety. Having those big feelings be overlooked really hurt."

I worry that I sound cold while I talk about this. I'm not crying or tearing up, but I've spent so many hours thinking about this over the years that it's almost old news to me at this point. It's a core wound, but one I already have explored for years. "My parents grew up really blue collar, and they were busy just trying to keep the lights on. Like, literally. We haven't talked about that on the show ever, but I grew up pretty poor. I can't count how many times our electricity and gas was turned off because the money had been used on my sisters' pageants or soccer fees. We were a "toughen up and bear it and support your family" house, and it sometimes made me feel like I didn't matter. It definitely made me think that there was something wrong with me because I couldn't just tamp down my feelings like my sisters could. And I also felt that way because I wasn't good at anything that people in our small town deemed important, and my parents focused all their time and resources on my siblings. I know it was because they understood how to help them excel, like they only had to help in a tangible way. Buy dresses. Buy cleats. Drive them to events. And what I really needed was more emotional support and care, which was just something they weren't educated about."

"Even now," Jenn says, "you seem to carry a lot of guilt. It's okay to admit that your parents hurt you. That their best was not enough in certain moments."

"Putting on my own therapist hat for a moment . . . I love when you give me permission to feel hurt. Because I have anxiety, I struggle a lot with guilt. I am such a people pleaser. I worry that my loved ones will stop loving me if I express my feelings, even though that's irrational. I know they won't. They love me and just were working with the limited tools they had."

"That's true. And it's also true that it's okay for you to feel hurt. Feeling anger or pain doesn't make you a bad person. I think something that we've spent a lot of time on, maybe the most time on over the years, is identifying intrusive thoughts versus true thoughts, and learning how to sit with uncomfortable feelings and work through them in a way that is as healthy as possible in the moment."

"Do you want to elaborate on what that looks like? With me or in general?"

Jenn nods, taking her time. "For example, if you set a boundary and tell your mom that when you're home for Christmas you won't be going to the Miss Pennsylvania pageant, that may upset her. She hasn't spent the same amount of time and effort working on healthy behaviors that you have, so she may say something hurtful and triggering."

I jump in. "Like, 'Don't you want to support your sister?' Even though I spent the first eighteen years of my life supporting her nonstop at the expense of my own time and schoolwork."

Jenn nods. "Right. So that may make you feel anxious. And it could start a whole range of intrusive thoughts that are based on your anxiety, not on reality."

I interject again. "Like that Claude must be mad at me. My mom won't want to talk to me anymore. Why am I such a bad person. I'm a fuckup. I can't do anything right. And on, and on, until I'm having a panic attack."

"Right. That was not your mom's intended result. And your sister has done a million shows and probably isn't invested in whether you're at this specific one. If she knew how draining it is for you, she would probably rather you not go. You know that, yet in the moment it's hard for the rational thoughts to prevail, and you can easily spiral, especially if you're already in a weakened emotional state due to normal stressors. But, if you can identify that those intrusive thoughts are starting, you can combat them. You can combat them by writing down true thoughts in your journal. And you can do something that lowers your anxiety overall, like turning your phone off and reading a book or taking a long shower."

I fake a cough theatrically as I supply my own coping strategy for when I'm teetering on the edge of a panic attack. "Weed gummy."

Jenn cracks a smile. "I recommend nonmedication-based strategies as a first step. But if an edible keeps you from having a panic attack, I see no issue with it."

Jenn and I continue to dive into the nitty gritty of cognitive behavioral therapy, panic attacks, how anxiety presents in different ways, and how I've progressed over time, for two more hours. I'll have to cut this episode down, since once Finn's in the room with us we spend another hour doing Questions of the Week. But at the end of it I can't stop smiling, despite all the tough things we've talked about, because I know that this episode is going to help people. So many people can't afford therapy, and while I know the real goal is to make therapy accessible to all, in the meantime I'm glad that I can fill that gap in some way.

TWENTY-EIGHT

Maeve

The past few weeks I've felt alarmingly calm. It's unusual for me to feel *truly* calm. Typically, I have a low-level underlying hum of anxiety, that with the right elixir of relaxation techniques stays there, and with the wrong cocktail of stress and triggers turns into a full on panic attack. But ever since Finn and I really fixed things it's like my body and mind breathed a huge sigh of relief and suddenly I feel calm.

Not just calm. Happy. For the first time since getting this deal, it feels like something I can actually be excited about. This big murder scene of a house is *mine*—after months of living in it I went ahead and made an offer—we've been number one for weeks, and I'm going to show little girls all over the world that yes, we *can* beat out a misogynist prick and make podcast deal history. I take my laptop out to the back deck and open a new document.

Maeve's Solo Show

I've tried not to think too hard about the show, because I don't know if it'll actually happen. But I'm half of the most popular podcast in the world right now. Even if Streamify doesn't want this, I do, so it's happening. My initial vision for this show was pretty simple, just recording therapy sessions. And I still want that to be the crux of the show. But now that I've had some time away from the rough start to this season, and the rejection I felt when I pitched this . . . doing this as a sort of reality TV show doesn't sound so bad. Maybe I do solo sessions with each person, sessions with them together, *and* we get a glimpse into their real life. And instead of going at warp speed through one couple an episode and piecing together clips from a six-month journey . . . maybe I work with five or six couples experiencing the same core issue and the episodes intercut clips of all of them. So, over the course of a ten-episode season, we see all of the journeys, and where some couples struggle others may succeed. We could even put hidden cameras in their homes to capture B-roll, instead of having a camera crew, so that they act more natural.

This is much more ambitious than *Tell Me How You Really Feel*. Even though we have guests now, I'm still completely capable of recording and editing our show basically solo. There's not B-roll to overlay, different locations to go to, anything like that. For this show—maybe I'll call it *The Couch* or *On the Couch*—I'd need a whole crew, probably a network backing me.

I text Finn, excited about this new idea.

Want to come over later and talk solo show?

DUH

I'm in my pajamas, eating my half of the Thai food I ordered for us, when Finn finally shows up at eight thirty. Finn walks in without knocking. I added him to my digital lock a week after we got back from the trip, and I've woken up to him in the kitchen eating my cereal, thinking I have a ghost, three times since. "You're abusing your lock privileges. At least ring before you come in," I shout without looking up from *The Bachelor*.

"I brought Ben & Jerry's and Thai." Finn laughs when he walks into the living room and sees me already eating food from our new favorite Thai place in LA. "Well, leftover Thai food is a great breakfast."

"What flavor ice cream?" I ask, tilting my head back to look at him upside down.

"Half Baked?"

"Already in the freezer."

"How am I supposed to make up for being late when you already have everything?" Finn puts the ice cream in the freezer, then brings his Thai food into the living room. He's ordered all the same things, but about one and a half times the quantities I have, meaning we now have enough for six to eight people, instead of four.

"Buy yourself a nice watch and be timely," I retort.

I spend the next fifteen minutes filling him in on every detail of what I'm thinking for the show, not stopping until I'm breathless and have not one good idea left to say. I've turned completely away from the TV, which is still running, although I haven't heard one word of the group date. My knee is resting on his thigh, and he's angled toward me too, half-finished food forgotten on the table. I can smell his fresh-from-the-shower scent, could count his stubble. His arm is along the back of the couch, and if I shifted just the tiniest bit, we'd be cuddling. Which we're pointedly not doing.

"Maeve, I think that would be brilliant. I've never seen a show like that. And I've watched *a lot* of TV." Finn smiles at me, flushed with excitement from my idea, and I can't hold back a grin. "I mean, when does it start? What network? Streamify might want it to be their first foray into reality TV, but I feel like any network would want this."

"I mean, I wasn't really going to think seriously about that stuff until the end of our contract." I run to the kitchen and grab the pint of Ben & Jerry's and two spoons. "I don't want to lose focus on this initial goal, you know? It's still really important to me."

Finn digs his spoon into the ice cream, which is a bit soft from the drive over here. He takes out a gaping spoonful and shoves it all in his mouth. "The contract is three years long," he says after swallowing.

The side of his mouth has chocolate dripping from it. I reach out and wipe it off with my finger, gently rubbing over his mouth. My stomach twists, and I feel a pull somewhere lower. I probably shouldn't have done that. But it felt really good . . . His eyes are glued to mine, and I think we're both holding our breath. "We need to stay number one for four more months. If we do that, I'll consider multi-tasking."

"And if your solo show takes off? What will you do when our contract is up?" Finn hasn't looked away from me since I touched his mouth, which was way too sensual a thing to do. I almost licked the ice cream off my finger after.

"If everything goes perfectly? Film the show during our holiday or summer breaks, and keep doing *Tell Me How You Really Feel*. As long as you are."

"If you stick with the show, I stick with the show."

"Good," I say. Or try to. It comes out as barely more than a whisper. Something about having Finn's eyes on me makes my heart beat too hard in my chest. I cough, trying to break the mood. "Want to finish this episode? I can rewind?"

"Sure," Finn agrees.

I turn *The Bachelor* back on from the beginning and dim the lights with the remote. Finn holds the ice cream between us with his left hand, his right arm still along the back of the couch. We trade snarky barbs as the show plays, and when two girls start pranking the rest of the house we dissolve into laughter. And move closer together. Suddenly, I'm flush against Finn's chest, his arm still hovering on the back of the couch, not *quite* around my shoulders.

"Can I lean?" I ask, before I can think better of it. Because I know better than to complicate things further between us. But right now, I don't care. I just want to dispel the two inches of space keeping us from where we once were.

"Of course," Finn whispers.

I fully relax against him, and he tentatively drops his arm around me, slowly, as though if he prevents it from being a jump scare, I'll forget that we do *not* cuddle anymore. But I lean into it. I cuddle against him, pull his arm closer, and stretch my legs across the couch so my full weight is against his solid body. The show keeps playing but I barely hear it, and Finn isn't bantering either. I can feel how fast his heart is beating under my head and his hand feels hot on my arm.

This isn't even the most intimate cuddling in our repertoire. Back in New York we used to lie in bed, my leg hiked across him, head tucked against his chest, and arm thrown territorially across his chest. How did we ever tell ourselves we were just friends? That we were actually giving dating a shot, not just doing it for show content? I never *really* believed we would date seriously, because he basically was my boyfriend. Which is why Cassidy was such a shock. Even though I gave him permission . . . he *took* it. And he asked for it, which is what was most heartbreaking.

"You could be the bachelor, you know," I say. "America loves you." I want to break the tense silence, let us collapse into pretending this is normal again.

"They always use people from past seasons now."

"So you'd do it? If that wasn't true? I'm sure for you they'd make an exception. You could film that while I film my show, have your own thing." I know Finn likes doing *Tell Me How You Really Feel*, but I still don't think it's his perfect creative project, it's just a huge improvement on his finance job. He still doesn't seem to be thinking that hard about acting again, or finding that fulfillment in another way, but I don't want to push too much, since I know that's all his parents do.

Finn laughs, the sound a deep rumble against me, his breath hot on my head. He squeezes me tighter. "No. I am not going to be the bachelor. I'm not looking for anyone new." And then all of my thoughts about his career are forgotten because he *said that*. Not looking for anyone *new*. Doesn't say why. Doesn't add anything to that momentous statement. I open my mouth to respond, then just close it.

We don't speak the rest of the episode, and when it fades to credits we let another start, unwilling to move. The remnants of the ice cream are melting on the coffee table, the Thai food is sitting out stinking up the living room and going bad, but I don't care. I would give anything to stay here, to not have reality hit when we separate.

I wake up in the morning and the show is still playing on the TV, the volume muted. I'm covered with a blanket, now completely intertwined with Finn on this ridiculously comfortable couch. And he's sound asleep, remote in hand, muting the TV having evidently been his final move. Every movement of my neck sends shooting pain down my spine, and my left arm is tingling from being crushed under Finn all night. I try to move gingerly and not wake him, but since I'm fully on top of him, the moment I move he half wakes up. And he pulls me closer into him.

He burrows his head into my hair, and I'm suddenly aware that I feel the push of morning wood underneath my thigh. And it should *not* make me feel as turned on as I do. It's unfair. But everything about Finn is like it was designed to be exactly for me. His height, his eyes, his hair, his laugh, his sense of humor, it's all perfect. It's what I've always looked for, but better. He checks boxes I didn't know I could ask for. I let myself be pulled in, subtly pressing closer to him, forgetting about my stiff neck and tingling arm because it feels so good to be held by him. I must fall asleep, because the next thing I know I'm floating, or actually, he's carrying me up to my bed.

Finn stands on one leg and uses the other to push the covers back without missing a beat, then puts me underneath them. My eyelids flutter open. "Stay," I command.

He chuckles. "I was planning on it."

He climbs over me, to the other side of the bed, and gets under the covers. Happily, we're now on the opposite side, so at least the cricks in my neck will be even. He tugs me to him, and I let him wrap his arm around me, cuddling close. And I fall back asleep, so easily.

But when I wake up this time, Finn is gone. I reach over to touch his side of the bed. It's cold. My heart sinks as I climb out of bed and brush my teeth. I pull my most comfortable sweatshirt on and head downstairs, the low hum of anxiety in my head buzzing louder and louder while I wonder whether Finn is still here. Halfway down I hear music and breathe a sigh of relief. Last night was so, so stupid. But maybe I don't care. Maybe getting my hopes wrapped up in the shape of Finn isn't the worst thing I've ever done. Maybe.

Because he's standing in my kitchen making crepes, wearing one of my hoodies, with its too-short sleeves, singing along to "Cruel Summer." He doesn't hear me come in, so I watch him dancing, flipping crepes, carefully cutting strawberries, and arranging them on a plate. When he turns around to put the plate on the kitchen island, he starts.

"You're up!" He holds the plate out toward me, and I see he's arranged the strawberries into an M. And next to them is a strangely shaped blob of crepe. "It's a microphone," he explains sheepishly. "My nanny used to make these, but she was much better at it."

I grab a fork and stab the crepe, taking a huge bite. "Well, it's the taste that counts. And I approve."

Finn finishes cooking and we eat, the tension of cuddling last night lingering. But I don't want things to be like they were. I don't want to cuddle and wonder and not talk about it. Every second it's not addressed is making me more anxious. "Let's do an episode," I blurt out.

"About . . . what?" Finn asks, but the uncertainty in his eyes makes it clear he knows.

I put my fork down, no longer hungry. I'm ready for the answers. I no longer feel so fragile that hearing them might set off the mother of all panic attacks. We've worked through it. We're good. I'm good. "All of it. I want to talk about it. For real."

"Maeve, are you sure? We can talk about it without recording."

I take Finn's hand, and he squeezes mine back immediately. "We started this with our fans, then cut them out. Let's let them hear it. The good, the bad, and the ugly. I'm tired of hiding us just because it's messy. It feels dishonest."

Finn frowns. "I'll record it. But I'm not going to promise we'll release it."

This all feels reckless. But also, maybe, just a little bit right. Until everything went to shit between us, we had shared absolutely *everything* with our fans, and I know that they're dying to know what has happened. Finn cleans up breakfast while I set up the cameras I have from our old setup on tripods in my bedroom. We're taking this back to our roots, recording in bed. This is just the giant, fluffy, high-thread-count version. I grab recorders, unable to find our old mics, and then Finn joins me in the bed.

"Hello, everyone. Things have been different lately on *Tell Me How You Really Feel*, and we appreciate you all sticking with us through the growing pains and giving us our privacy the past few months. We've been working through some personal stuff and we're finally going to hash it out, here, now, with you. I haven't wanted to hear how Finn feels the past few months, but now I'm ready for him to tell me how he really feels. So, Finn, let's hear it. What happened with Cassidy?" We never use people's real names, and now I'm going to have to bleep out her name in post every time we say it. But I want this to feel more like a real conversation than an episode of the podcast.

"You're really going to start there?" he asks. "Start with us."

"Then you do it. Start with us." If he thinks I'm going to put my heart on the line first, he's not thinking clearly.

"Maeve and I were friends in college. But we fell for each other while we were doing the show. Which, just saying, does not make for great content. Wild sexcapades and interesting dates to find our people are what the show was all about. We were supposed to be each other's sounding boards. But I mean, how could I not fall in love with Maeve? She's incredible, you all know that."

I jump in. "And I felt the same. We have so much fun together, and, I mean, I don't know if you've all noticed . . . but Finn is *not* bad to look at." Finn looks at me, waiting to see if I'll really tell all. My breath catches in my throat when I look into his eyes. I always thought it was just something people said in books and movies, that they could read everything someone was feeling in their eyes, that they could feel completely seen. But with Finn, right now, I really can. So I keep going. "One night, we slept together. And it was incredible."

"Mind-blowing. The best night of my life."

I roll my eyes. "Considering you were taking Cassidy out within a month, I highly doubt that."

Finn frowns. "You said you wanted us to be on pause for a month. And a month had passed! I thought you might have just been letting me down gently. And we were on a break, and things just happened to start to play out with Cassidy, and you gave me permission. I didn't realize what I was doing was so . : . wrong. I didn't think it was against the rules."

"Finn. Come on. Is this an apology or not? Because I don't hear you taking responsibility for anything. If you actually cared, you wouldn't go and take out the one that got away. It's not like you even just slept with someone! You took her on a date, like to see if there was a future. And when you realized she was interested, you called to ask permission. I wasn't going to stand in your way, so I called things off. Because *clearly* you weren't serious about me. Your call was everything I needed to know. It was what I *knew* would happen and it hurt so fucking much."

Finn shuts his eyes and takes a deep breath. "Maeve, I'm sorry. We've always been up-front with each other and I really thought that since you said I should see things through with her that it was okay with you."

I can't help but interrupt. "If you *actually* liked me—or loved me like you said—you wouldn't have *wanted* to try with her at all. That is really it. I knew you didn't like me so I didn't stand in your way."

Finn groans. "Fine! I'm sorry! I'm stupid. I thought you were pulling away and it got weird. But if you had said, 'No, Finn, don't do it, I really want to try,' then I would have walked away and tried with you. And the only reason I even considered it is that she isn't just 'other people' . . . she was my first kiss and someone I've known for so long and always wondered about, and maybe would always wonder about if I didn't see it through, and I also kind of thought it would be silly not to try. When that's what we'd been doing for two years! Trying to find the one. And when I asked, you told me to do it."

"I thought we'd found each other already." I sound bitter and try to blink back my tears. I resent him for ever making me feel this way. And I hate that all of the incredible feelings I have for him are polluted by this situation. Finn starts to speak again, but I hold up a hand to stop whatever he's about to say, in an effort try to steer the conversation back toward productivity. "Circular breathing. Let's do circular breathing." We both do a few rounds of breathing independently, then Finn starts talking.

"I understand why you're upset. Do I think I behaved my best? Toward either of you? No. But I am sorry. And you haven't let me say that."

I let out a frustrated huff of air. I forgot that part of what I love about Finn is that he calls me out on all of my bullshit. He doesn't tiptoe around me like some exes did, afraid to make me cry after they found out about the panic attacks. Finn knows I'm a grown woman that can take care of myself, but is also there to take care of me when I need him. "Fine. I am sorry for that. I wasn't ready to have the conversation. I felt like your actions showed me everything I needed to know."

"I know. But dating Cassidy, the one person I'd always kind of wondered if I might end up with . . . that made me realize that you're the only person for me. Cassidy and I had no chemistry. We were just checking off the 'What if?' box so that we could both move forward knowing with one hundred percent certainty that we are meant to be with other people. That I'm meant to be with you. And, Maeve . . . I really did feel worried that *you* didn't want to be with *me*. It feels like you think you're the only one who can feel insecure. But I care about you so much. I really did doubt that you felt as strongly for me. Because, Maeve, you are *everything*."

I want to just believe him. But it's not that simple. "Finn, I don't want to be your second choice. And I know we're going in circles now, but I can't help but keep thinking that if you actually loved me you wouldn't have wanted to be with anyone else. You were cuddling in bed with me five nights a week, we were practically already in a relationship. I felt discarded. And even worse, discarded for someone of your pedigree. Shinier, richer, more famous, more beautiful. Someone that made more *sense* for you. And you didn't just go on a date. You *dated*. You frolicked all over Europe for like two months." If he'd slept with some random person, that would be easier to accept. But he and Cassidy were the love story of the decade, plastered all over every magazine in town. I'm spiraling and I don't know if anything he says can pull me back from this abyss of insecurity.

Finn takes a deep breath. "Maeve, Cassidy is not some random date. She is a good friend. Our families are friends. I felt rejected and made a poor choice. I thought, you know, the girl you love doesn't want you. Maybe you should really *try* dating the one that got away. And it was easy! We know the same people, live in the same worlds, travel to the same places. It was fun."

"So why did you break up?" I am trying so hard to actually hear him. To let his words penetrate my own swirling thoughts.

"You! You are why we broke up." Now my eyes are smarting, but Finn keeps going. "Because Cassidy is great, but she just isn't you. On the surface we were perfect. And the first month was fun, so I really thought maybe I should lean in, you know? But after the thrill wore off . . . it was clear to both of us that we were friends, not in love. And I realized I had just given up what might have been my only chance to be with my soulmate. I can only date other people and have them feel halfway right when you're in the picture. Because all the things that make me tick, make you tick. We challenge each other, and ever since I met you I couldn't imagine a world without you. I didn't want to, ever again. Maeve, I love every fucking thing about you. So much. And without you? A piece of me was missing. We are perfect together, and I don't want another day to go by without getting to say I love you. I love you, Maeve."

I feel like I've stopped breathing. Time has stopped. I don't know what to say, how to go on. Finn is crying as he speaks, looking at me like I'm the only girl in the world. I hold up the mic. "Finn, I love you too."

TWENTY-NINE

Finn

I hit Pause on my mic, then reach over and press the same button on Maeve's. The cameras are still rolling, but there's no more audio. Because I want this moment to exist only for us, now, for real. Maeve is looking at me, her eyes wet, but no tears actually falling. But the gray bed sheets are spattered with flecks of dark, like rain drops, from my own fallen tears. Once everything is off I stare at her, waiting. *Say it again*, my eyes are begging her.

"I love you," Maeve whispers. "And I loved you then too."

"I'm sorry I hurt you," I say softly. And I am. I've never regretted anything as much as trying to move on from Maeve. Not just because it wasn't possible. But because I hurt her, and told myself I was giving her what she wanted. I was insecure and Cassidy was the easier choice because I knew exactly where I stood with her. But I regret not doing the bold thing and putting my heart on the line.

"Why did you say all those things?"

I don't ask what. Because I know. "Because I felt rejected. I acted like the worst version of myself. I'm so sorry, Maeve."

The silence is heavy. I'm afraid that despite all the push and pull and tentative progress of the last few months, Maeve will turn away from me again. Kick me out. And if she did, I would understand. I *felt* rejected and acted out of fear. But I actually did reject her first. After claiming to love her.

Maeve puts her mic down and takes my free hand. "I forgive you. Let's try to put it behind us."

This must be what winning the lottery feels like. My heart is soaring and I can barely believe that I could be this lucky. I put down my mic and clasp both of her hands in mine. "Thank you. And Maeve, now I get to say it. I love you too. Not as a friend. Not like family. Well, kind of like family, because you *are* family. To me, you are my whole world. You sometimes act like you're a supporting character that got pulled up to the main spot. But that's not true. You're the sun and I'm just happy to be in your orbit."

Maeve smiles as she wipes her eyes and nose on her sweatshirt. "You're lucky the mic's off. Because that was so cheesy."

"I don't care. For you, I'm cheesy." I scooch closer to her on the bed, where we're still sitting cross-legged facing each other. Scooching is not romantic. But it doesn't matter. There's something pretty magical about the person that you helped puke in a dorm-room stall freshman year of college being the person that years later you still love. Because I think I may have loved her since the beginning. I threw out every rule I had about being in the spotlight and working in entertainment in an instant to spend more time with her. And I never made a move on her all those years. Because Maeve was too perfect, too smart, too amazing to make a move on and risk losing

if the nineteen-year-old version of me screwed it up. Although . . .
I still managed to do that now. But I'm glad that I didn't fall for a
girl that I met now, because I've loved getting to know Maeve before
she figured out how she likes to do her hair, back when ultra-low-
rise jeans were in and everyone looked irreversibly cringe. I love her
through the trends and fads. I just want to be by her side as we watch
everything come and go.

"Can I kiss you now?" Guys always write in to the show saying
how cheesy it is to say that. But I think they're wrong. Waiting with
bated breath for her answer is something I want to cherish. That feeling, knowing in the back of my head that probably, hopefully, she will
say yes. But that I can't be sure of it.

The way my heart soars when she nods and reaches for me is
everything. "Yes," Maeve whispers.

She pulls me toward her, her hand on the back of my neck, and I
run my fingers through her hair, tug her closer to me. Our lips connect, hard. We had our share of tentative kisses the first time around.
Now I want her as close to me as possible. I pull Maeve into my lap and
hold her tight. There should be something slightly ridiculous about
making out in our matching sweat suits. Maeve's is so oversized she's
swimming in it, the sleeves falling down her forearms now that her
hands are laced in my hair. But while seeing her in her amazing gala
and awards show dresses is so fucking hot, I love the intimacy of this
moment at home.

I could keep kissing her forever. If this was all she ever let me do,
I would still be happy. Because talking to her, laughing with her,
that's better than sex for me. And I know *exactly* how great our sex
is. Maeve presses into me, and I grab her hips, grinding against her.
She moans, and I slide my thumb up under her sweatshirt, run it over
her stomach. She kisses me harder and I never want to let go of her.

And then she pulls back. Her lips are swollen from me biting and sucking on them, her chin red where my day-old stubble has grazed her face. I love seeing her cheeks flushed and knowing it's from me. "Are you okay?" I ask immediately.

She kisses me once, softly, sweetly now. "I'm better than okay. I just . . . let's wait."

"We can wait. Whatever you want." I kiss her again and squeeze her close, toppling us both over so we're lying down, still intertwined.

"Today was just emotional. I want to take our time this time."

"Of course. And Maeve, you never need to explain to me why you want to wait. You say wait, and I'm waiting. And I'll never get tired of it."

Maeve burrows her head deeper into my shoulder and I hold her tightly. She fits into me perfectly, and the feeling of her soft curves against me is incredible. Holding her is somehow both calming and also the hottest thing ever. Eventually she wriggles lightly away from me, and I release my grip for a moment. She takes a dramatic gulp of air. "You need to tell me if I'm crushing you!" I exclaim.

She latches back on to me. "I didn't want you to let go yet." We lie there cuddling for so long that I doze off, and when I wake up Maeve is gone, her side of the bed cold. For a moment I wonder if this was all a dream, but then I see the cameras trained on the bed, which is actually a bit creepy when you wake up to it, but I'm elated because it means that this is *real*. We're good again.

I spring out of bed and head directly to Maeve's editing bay. Sure enough, she's there, cutting the episode together. She doesn't hear me through her giant headphones, and so I touch her shoulder gently, not wanting to scare her. She turns toward me and when she smiles, it's like everything I've ever worried about is gone. I really think this is what has been missing the past few months. With her

I won't have *maybe I should try acting* in the back of my mind as I fall asleep. I'll just be content again, finally. I take her headphones off gently and lean down to kiss her.

She meets me and stands, still kissing me. "Sit," she commands between kisses. I sit in the chair and she tucks herself onto my lap, then unplugs the headphones and hits play on the beginning of the episode we filmed in bed. It's short, with no Questions of the Week, but at the end of our conversation she sped up the video of us talking privately and blurred it, then included the shot of us kissing, no longer blurred, at regular speed.

"Did we just make a sex tape?" I joke.

She hits Pause. "I wanted to see it, even if we don't use it."

I kiss her cheek. "It's very honest. More honest than we've ever been. And slightly messy." I've never cried on camera before, even though I've told our listeners countless times that men should be able to be vulnerable and emotional. "Well, pros and cons. Why should we put it out?"

"To beat *The Paul Myers Show* and make history, pro. We're pretty close to the goal, and this is such good content that I think our agents could renegotiate the length of time we have to be number one if we put out something like this, which is basically guaranteed to go viral."

"Like, if we break the streaming record by X amount, we cut off a month?"

"Exactly." Maeve nods. I wrap my arms tighter around her. I'll put out whatever episode she wants if I get to stay here with her. "Con, Paul Myers's entire fan base will definitely tear apart our most delicate moment and say awful things. I think you'll get the brunt of it."

"Pro, we help redefine what's appropriate for men to express on camera."

"Con, you get cyberbullied and memeified."

I tuck my face into her neck and inhale the scent of her shampoo and perfume. "We've dealt with that for the last two years. I can handle it. What are the other cons for you?"

"We lose an intimate moment. It becomes a part of the public narrative. I don't know if it's worth trading. Why do we have to be that honest now, just because we were before?"

"If you think it'll be too hard or will affect your anxiety too much, let's not do it."

Maeve turns partway so she can see me. "Pro, we need the ratings. We slipped a bit last week. We only made number one by a few hundred downloads."

I lean my forehead on hers so that our faces are only an inch apart and give her the softest whisper of a kiss before pulling back to respond. "It's up to you. If you want to release it, let's release it."

Maeve takes a deep breath and kisses me once more, slowly, before speaking. "I mean, we recorded it for a reason, right?"

Within twenty-four hours it is the most downloaded episode in Streamify history. Maeve's place and my parents' house (according to the pictures my dad is texting me) are full of fruit baskets and flowers from our agents and advertisers. Streamify agreed that if we stay number one for just two more weeks, we can get the pay bump, and that this extra episode can count toward a missed week. And the numbers on this bonus episode just keep going up.

We're floating in Maeve's pool, our interlocked hands keeping the pool floats close enough together to kiss for each hundred thousand streams. Maeve downloaded a browser extension so that every time we pass a hundred thousand new views, a confetti cannon sound goes off. The celebratory pops are alarmingly close together, and as one goes off I swear Maeve flinches. It's a weird feeling when you know that your success is also tied to scrutiny.

I tug on her hand and pull her closer to me. "Want to go to Disney?"

"What?"

"Let's go to Disneyland. Leave our phones here. Forget about winning, and the ratings, and whatever awful stuff Paul Myers's groupies are saying online." I wonder if Paul Myers knows about the incentive in our contract. He's always been vicious, so it's hard to say if he knows or is just an asshole. This morning he brought up our episode during his morning live sesh and called me a variety of homophobic slurs because I cried, and he called Maeve ugly. So the same old.

Maeve slides off her float and wades up to mine, resting her arms on it and letting some water leak on. "That's so random. Since when are you a Disney adult?"

I roll off the float and into the water, then pick her up and she wraps her legs around my waist. "You like rides. I like rides. We used to have a blast at Kennywood back in college, so let's go to Disney and go on some roller coasters. Forget about the episode for a while." Kennywood was the local amusement park in Pittsburgh that we used to go to all the time back in college with our friends.

"Would it be outrageous of us to fly to Pittsburgh and go to Kennywood instead? I could see my family, and then there's no lines. We can go just for a night."

I walk us deeper into the water. "It's what, four hours direct?"

Maeve nods. "Four and half. And the only airline that goes there direct is Spirit."

"Want me to charter a jet?"

Maeve splashes me in the face. "Absolutely not. That is way too expensive. And the emissions!"

"We can afford it . . ." I counter.

"I know. I really do. But the thought of spending that much money makes me feel physically ill."

"Just think of it as free money, because the interest your money is making will pay for it in like hours or whatever." I wait, hoping she'll change her mind. But she just grimaces and shakes her head. "Fine, we can do Spirit."

It takes approximately three hours for me to realize exactly *why* I've never flown Spirit. From the moment we get to LAX there are problems. First off, they don't let us use the special celebrity entrance, because we're flying a budget airline. They turn us away at the door and we have to go in the regular entrance. Then I wait in line for an hour to spend more than the cost of the tickets on our bags, because I didn't realize I was only allowed on the plane with my cell phone and wallet. I hand over my credit card with an eye roll, and Maeve giggles.

"What's so funny? This is outrageous." I put the tags on our carry-ons and we head over to security, where, thank god, they at least let us use PreCheck. Since we thought we were using the private entrance, we're both in full *Tell Me How You Really Feel* sweat suits and horribly conspicuous. We've posed for at least five selfies, and I catch people recording us here and there.

"This is what budget airlines are like. How did you even get home from Pittsburgh all through college?"

"I flew private," I mutter.

"What was that?" Maeve bumps my suitcase with hers. Rimowa sent us pink luggage sets after our Met Gala outfits made *Vogue*'s roundup.

I glare at her. "You heard me! I'm not a man of the people, okay? I'm a fraud."

Maeve throws her head back and laughs, and I crack a smile.

We make it through security and I rush us to the airport lounge, since after that baggage line we only have forty-five minutes before boarding. From the safety of the lounge, Maeve calls her parents and tells them that we'll be there tonight. I arranged for a car service to take us directly to Kennywood and hold our luggage while we go on the rides, and then we'll head to Maeve's and stay the night, leaving the next morning, after what Maeve has assured me with be a *lengthy* interrogation-style breakfast.

The lounge is a brief respite from the organized chaos that is Spirit Airlines. There isn't an organized boarding system when we get to the gate, and when we finally get on the plane we're rushed to the very last row, where the seats don't recline. Or maybe none of the seats recline. To make matters worse, the seats are comically small. My legs are folded like pretzels in the tiny chair, and even Maeve has difficulty maneuvering into a comfortable position.

"If you told me how bad it would be, I would have gotten us a plane," I whisper to her aggressively. "This looks like a flying soda can. I think I feel a breeze right now, and we could definitely combust and die."

Maeve takes my hand and squeezes it. We didn't do any PDA in the airport, to avoid photographs, but now that we're on the plane she leans against me and I start to relax. "This is how us commoners fly, Finn. And you know what? This flight was only twenty-seven dollars. Does that mean nothing to you?"

"Plus a hundred fifty in bags."

"We make eight figures. Relax on the bags."

I must miss whatever passes for the safety announcement because suddenly the plane is moving. And I mean *moving*. We basically jump into the sky, no taxiing here, and the pressure drop has my ears popping over and over. "Do they give us water?" I ask Maeve. The lounge didn't have any to-go bottles.

She shrugs. "Maybe if you bribe them. On this short a flight they may not even do the paid beverage service."

"This flight is over four hours."

Maeve nods gravely. "They were selling water for ten dollars at the gate, you know."

I let my head drop back to the headrest in defeat, only to catapult forward with a jolt. "That's just a patch of rough air," the flight attendant says into the intercom.

"What a rebrand. 'Rough air' sounds so much nicer than 'turbulence,'" Maeve muses.

"Yeah, and way nicer than you're on a budget airline that can't handle wind."

"You're being a diva," Maeve chastises.

"We're flying to Pittsburgh because you want to go to an amusement park with less lines. You're the diva!" Maeve kisses me deeply. "Comment withdrawn," I amend. "You have impeccable taste and spend your twenty-seven ninety-five with wisdom beyond your years."

"That's what I thought."

I'm about to get up and try to secure bottles of water for each of us when a college-age girl pauses hesitantly in front of our seat. I look up and squeeze Maeve's hand. So tightly that she can't drop mine because, come on, we're not doing this again.

Maeve sees the fan and drops her neck pillow. "Hi! Oh my god, how are you!" From her tone you'd think she and this girl were life-long friends.

The girl lights up. "Ohmygodhi!" she says in a rush. "I am such a big fan. My friends and I are coming back from a bachelorette party and were wondering if we could take a TikTok with you? And give you some Questions of the Week?"

I glance at the SEATBELT sign above us, then crane my neck behind us and clock the flight attendant, who's reading a book and sipping a Coke.

"Of course!" Maeve agrees readily. "Why don't you all come back here! Or should we come to you?"

"I'll go get them!"

Within moments there are eight women in full makeup and travel outfits, but also visibly hungover, clustered by the bathroom around us. I guess this is the one perk of sitting at the back of the plane. Plenty of room for fans. I switch places with Maeve and cram myself into the window seat, and for the next hour I participate when instructed, but mainly watch Maeve interact with these women. It's clear they view her advice as invaluable, crucial, priceless. The way they act, it's almost like they think she's one of their best friends too. Maeve answers all of their questions, full of conspiratorial eyebrow raises and advice, and it's not until half of them have returned to their seats that one of them finally mentions yesterday's episode.

"I think it's really cool that you released that episode of you two kind of fighting? Or getting back together? You're so real to do that, and we're really happy for you two." The other girls nod in agreement.

"Thank you," Maeve says quietly. She reaches over and squeezes my hand. "It wasn't easy. But we owe everything to you all, and we wanted to be honest."

By the time they leave we're both exhausted. I put my arm around Maeve, and she leans into me, drifting off. I stay awake, ready to ward off fans while she sleeps, and she crashes for the rest of the flight, jolting awake only at our rough landing. She cuddles back into me, and we stay that way until everyone else has deplaned; then I grab our bags from the overhead and we exit.

We'd had to take our phones to the airport for the boarding passes, but once we made it on the plane we'd turned them off and stowed them in our carry-ons. I itch to check my phone to see if there are any tabloid photos of us at the airport or press coverage of our episode. But instead, I take Maeve's hand and we stride through the airport and find the man waiting with my last name on a sign. If this was New York, that might be enough for someone to call paparazzi and would definitely be enough for random people to pull out their cell phones and film us. But in Pittsburgh, no one cares, and our ride to Kennywood is smooth sailing.

We get to the park in the late afternoon, and, per usual, it's largely empty even though it's a Saturday. The admission is the price of a drink at any other amusement park, and just like that we're in business. Maeve and I walk through the winding entrance to the start of the rides, and Maeve throws her arms out wide. "Isn't this better than Disney?"

I pick her up and spin her around until we're dizzy and stumbling, then plant a giant kiss on her cheek. "Absolutely. Especially now that it's not Fright Night."

"I forgot about that," she exclaims. "You were so scared!"

"Startled! I was slightly startled as anyone would be." The first time we went to Kennywood with friends from CMU we were there in October for Fright Night, which meant that all over the park people dressed as monsters and ghouls were doing jump scares. It was never-ending. Some might call it torturous. But Maeve loved it.

"Eh, we can call it that, for your vanity." Maeve takes my hand and leads me to her favorite ride, the Thunderbolt. It's a wooden coaster, and not as big as the Steel Curtain, the premiere Steelers ride, but still large and fast enough to make your stomach drop out from under you.

Our first ride, we sprint up the steps, but by the third time in a row on the Thunderbolt our pace is more of a trudge. The amount of stairs at an amusement park is the kind of thing you only notice when there are no lines. Otherwise, it just feels like standing at different places on the stairs. But now we're really getting a calf workout as we race up, eventually queuing behind the six other people in line. After riding that for the fourth time, Maeve turns to me. "Your pick!"

I lead her to the Steel Curtain, and we vault over and duck under the line barriers the park optimistically installed. Kennywood is an extremely robust amusement park. The rides are plentiful and big, the food options are great, and the parking is free. But it's half an hour outside Pittsburgh, surrounded by tiny, middle-of-nowhere towns, and with tough competition in Ohio, so not many people actually come here as compared with a Six Flags or Disneyland. Which Maeve would argue makes it better, and I would say makes it at serious risk of becoming a ghost park.

"Why this one? I feel like you barely even feel it, too much centripetal force or whatever."

I shrug. "It's fun to ride the biggest fanciest ride without waiting in line." Although, once we get up the stairs we see this one has a solid fourteen people in line, since it *is* the premiere ride. "And you say there's no lines here," I tease. "False advertising."

Maeve leans over the railing and surveys the entire park. "How much do you think this would go for?"

I bracket my arms around her and kiss the side of her neck. "Kennywood?"

"Yeah. Like a hundred million or something?"

"Less. Maybe fifty mil? It's hard to say. And it's probably part of a parks group. I don't know that they'd sell you just Kennywood."

Maeve turns so that her back is against the railing. The line has shortened, but we haven't moved. I press against her and kiss her. "After we beat *The Paul Myers Show*, you could buy it."

"That would be crazy," she argues between kisses.

"So let it be. It's your money. You earned it. And after the therapy show you'll have so much more between the residuals and the contract." I kiss her, longer, until I feel her relax against me. "So if you want to buy an amusement park that no one goes to, do it. You'll still have plenty of money to pay for all your sisters' extracurriculars and go on vacations and renovate your creepy house and all that."

"Next!" the teenager staffing the ride calls down to us.

Maeve breaks away with a giggle, and I chase her up the stairs. "Front or back?"

She's ignoring what I said. I don't think the whole being rich thing has hit her yet, because the only thing she's really spent any money on is her house. But I let her ignore it right now. It's not like she's actually serious about buying this place; she's way too responsible for that. She'd feel pressure to make it profitable and it would lose all its charm. "Front. And we're riding with our eyes open."

"You are," Maeve says. "I'd like to keep my eyeballs."

We ride three times, and I buy the plastic-framed photos of us on the ride each time. They're horrendous, our faces pressed back by the force of the ride, Maeve's eyes squeezed shut, my arms up and teeth bared because my lips are forced wide open. They're incredible.

"What next?"

"I think we should do the jukebox," Maeve exclaims decisively.

The sun is setting, and we stroll through the park to the Johnny Rockets. There are families with children eating dripping Millie's ice cream cones, and a few groups of teenagers and college students. Inside, I order an outrageous amount of diner food, and Maeve sits at the counter and starts selecting songs. There are miniature free jukeboxes all over, and she flips through the catalogue, laser focused. After I order, I join her.

"What'd you pick?"

Maeve tilts her head, waiting for the current song to change. As the last few bars fade away, her pick starts and she jumps up and offers me a hand. I don't recognize it at first. And then Elvis's deep voice starts crooning. "I can't help falling in love," I echo softly, a smile creeping over my face. Normally I wouldn't start dancing in a diner. Even a fake one like this, that's made for a small town amusement park. I'm not a dancer and I don't want videos of my horrendous moves on TMZ for the rest of time, accompanied by headlines like *Is Finn Sutton Losing It* and *When Did Finn Sutton Start Using?* because my dance moves are so atrocious. But now, I take her hand and let her lead me to the center of the room.

We start slow dancing, pressed tight together, and it feels like we're the only people in the room. When the lyrics start, I spin Maeve gently and then pull her back into me, and we keep dancing slowly, tenderly, until the end of the song. We don't break apart when it ends, and I stare into her eyes. "Maeve, you make me—" Suddenly, the next song cuts in. "Dancing Queen" by ABBA. Maeve's face twitches while she tries to suppress a laugh at the change in mood while I'm trying to be sentimental. "So happy," I finish, before she starts to giggle.

The server further interrupts things by aggressively dinging the bell by our seat as he leaves our food, but Maeve grabs my arm when I move to sit. "One more."

I raise an eyebrow. "I mean, it *is* ABBA."

Maeve silently holds up three fingers, dropping to two, then one. And then we start dancing, as though we're in the tiny closet of a bedroom back in New York and no one is watching. And it just might be the most fun I've ever had in my life.

THIRTY

Maeve

Having Finn in my childhood home is like watching my past and present converge in one instant. They're almost impossible to align, but I'm doing my best to swallow the discomfort. We've never had the space for a dining room table in our tiny one-story house—despite my repeated offers, my parents would only let me pay off their home, not buy them a bigger one—and so we grew up taking our plates to the living room and eating on the couch, more often than not with a show running in the background. We'd talk over it, and the sounds of everything from *New Girl* to *Ozark* were our room tone.

Now, when my mom serves Finn his plate first, his eyes dart around frantically while he tries to figure out where to sit. Our house, like many houses in the desolate towns surrounding Pittsburgh, is a tiny box. When you walk inside, you can see the kitchen, the living room, and the one bathroom without turning your head. Walk down a hallway and there's my parents' bedroom, and two minuscule rooms that my sisters and I shared. Now that I'm coming from my sizable house, this feels tiny. I think that our hotel room for Fashion Week may have had more square footage. Finn hovers uncomfortably until Tiffany is served, then follows her lead to our beat up leather sectional. All in all, he takes the couch eating situation in stride.

Claude and I join them, and Finn smiles broadly. "So, any embarrassing childhood photos of Maeve here?" Finn asks with a grin.

Claude glares at him. "For you? No."

Tiffany is also eyeing him like he's a bug she'd like to squish. Although I'm closer to Sarah, both in sheer proximity and understanding what it felt like to grow up in our sisters' shadows—which is how it felt (even though we'd be considered the more successful ones for some time now, by people outside our town)—Tiffany and Claude are well versed in the saga that is Finn. And they don't pull punches.

Tiffany stabs a piece of melon aggressively. "Why are you even here?"

Finn looks hesitantly between me and my sisters. I shrug. I'm not helping him out of this one. And since my parents are in the kitchen making their plates, my sisters are taking full advantage. "Have you two listened to the latest episode yet?"

Claude's eye roll is a lesson in pageant queen sass. "Duh. Do you think we're fake fans? Obviously Maeve believes you, she's been into you since college." Now I'm the one shooting Claude dirty looks, but she continues anyway. "As far as *we're* concerned? You're bullshit central. How hard is it to lay out your feelings, ask our *sister* to Carbone, and make things official? And then you took another girl instead. Disgusting. *Why* would she be expected to lay her feelings out on the line when you called and asked permission to see someone else? It's giving . . . disrespect."

"And you're fucking famous," Tiffany chimes in. "Like, grow a pair already."

"I *know*!" Claude seconds, momentum building. "Why should we think you're committed to Maeve *now*? What is it that you like about our sister?"

For all the complicated feelings I had growing up, when it felt like all that mattered was my siblings and not me or my mental health, I've always been grateful that I have them. We have each other's backs until the very end and are absolutely relentless in our support of each other. I would run into a burning building for them, and I know they'd do the same for me.

My mom and dad return for that final question only, and squeeze onto the couch. We're wedged in like sardines, with Finn in the center and the rest of us leaning out to peer toward him. "I'd like to know the answer to that one too, actually," my dad remarks. My mom raises an eyebrow at me, clearly more in tune with the dynamic that's unfolded between Finn and me. She's on my side no matter what. Despite her not knowing how to do what I needed as a kid, I know she's always tried to do her best and she can tell that I care about Finn. But my sisters and dad want to make Finn suffer a little bit before they welcome him to the family, given how upset I've been the past few months.

Finn puts his plate down on the coffee table and smiles. "Well, *that* is an easy question. First and foremost, Maeve is brilliant. Smarter than me, every day of the week. If I were to become stranded on a deserted island, she's who I'd want to be with because I know she'd think of a million ways out that I never could. She's so creative too. So innovative. And funny! She gives me all the credit for humor on the show, but she makes me laugh the hardest. Oh, and she's kind."

Finn started his speech looking between my family members, but now his eyes are locked on me. "No one is kinder. To strangers, friends, family. She is generous and caring and the best listener. She actually listens, instead of just waiting to respond. I love everything about her. She's easily the best person I know. When she wasn't in my life the past few months, it felt like all the best parts were missing. And obviously it doesn't hurt that she's completely gorgeous. Ever since the first day I saw her, our freshman year of college, she's taken my breath away. She is so beautiful. *Way* out of my league."

I wasn't sure whether Finn would be able to hold his own around my family. His parents are cultured and elegant, polite at all costs, used to everything they say and do being potential media fodder. My family is a bit rougher around the edges and *not* into media-trained responses to their questions. But it appears that Finn's soliloquy may have won them over.

My sisters have gone from angry to swooning, and my mom is smiling to herself looking between us. Even my dad looks like Finn's words have taken the edge off his distrust.

I take Finn's hand and squeeze it. "He's not all bad," I joke. "But for real, guys. We're good here."

There's a collective pause as Finn and I wait for my family's response, and they take in what I said. I've never brought someone home like this. I've dated, just not seriously enough to all sit on the couch and stare at him, unlike Sarah and Claude, who have a new "serious boyfriend" every year. After a moment, it's like everyone exhales, and my family members all start firing at once.

"Can we FaceTime your mom?" Claude asks. "She's, like, an icon."

"Do you know any pro women's soccer players?" Tiffany jumps in.

"What kind of car do you drive? I'm working on one in the back if you want to take a look," my dad says simultaneously.

My mom reaches over and squeezes my knee. "Help me in the kitchen?" she asks. I follow her to our tiny kitchen, with the peeling tile floor and sagging wooden cabinets. She and my dad have turned down my offers to buy them a new house three times so far. I paid off this one the second I got my first Streamify payment. When I got that first deposit, my bank account suddenly had more zeros than I had ever imagined. I still don't know exactly what to do with the money, but I know that I want them to live somewhere nicer. And a McMansion here is $300K.

Our kitchen is practically in the living room, but everyone is so focused on Finn that they're not paying attention to us. I turn to my mom, eager to hear what she has to say. "So?"

She looks at Finn. "He seems like a nice boy. And you know how proud of you we are. But are you sure about this?"

My gut twists. I want to hear that my *mom* is sure, so that I can be. Even though I know that I shouldn't let her words hold weight because she has never *really* understood me. "Why? Just tell me what you're actually thinking."

My mom smiles sagely. "How I really feel, you mean?" She looks over at Finn, who's still holding court on the couch. "Your whole life, you've been a team player. Helping everyone around you. I shouldn't have relied on you so much when you were a kid. You were just a kid, and I expected you to be like a mini-parent to your sisters because I was strapped so thin working. I wish I had known how to be more of what you needed. But now you've finally gotten to be the star. And honey, I am so proud of you. You're still my baby, and whether you've seen it or not, I always knew once you found your thing you'd be a superstar. I want the world for you because I know you've been striving for it all since you were a kid. But with him, I don't know that you'll get to be the superstar. Because he already is one."

I tear my eyes away from hers and toward Finn. "He's happy supporting me. Helping me shine."

"It's a rare man that actually wants to help a woman shine, once he's done winning her over. Or back. I want to make sure that you finally get to be a star in your own right. Because sweetie, you deserve it. More than anyone. So I'm just saying be careful."

"I will be," I agree quietly, my stomach churning despite all the vows I've made not to trust my mom's advice over my own gut, when I'm the one who's spent years of work on figuring out how I work and what makes me happy and healthy. She means well, but she has such a smaller view of the world. I believe that Finn is one of the rare men. My mom doesn't know him like I do. She doesn't know him at all! But the doubt running through my mind now isn't just about Finn . . . Would I have been able to do this without him? Am I worthy like my mom thinks? Or just lucky enough to have proximity to Finn like his agent thinks? It's hard for me to shut down these thoughts when I'm at home, where I always feel most vulnerable because I spent so many years here watching everyone else's needs get met before my own. Just being here makes me feel like I don't matter.

When we squeeze back onto the couch, I try to repeat my affirmations and push the lingering doubt out of my mind. I plant a kiss on Finn's cheek, and he turns toward me and kisses me quickly on the lips, leaving both of us smiling like idiots. His hand on my back is like a weighted blanket, firm and reassuring.

After we eat I practically drag Finn away from my family and into my childhood bedroom. The room is so small that we could reach out and hold hands across the beds, and the walls so thin that I could hear Claude and Tiffany giggling until we fell asleep. Finn stumbles into the room after me, and I slam the door behind us.

"I think that went well—" I swallow Finn's words with a kiss.

I'm tired of playing it safe. Of holding back. Of being the responsible one. I want to go all in and forget my worries.

Finn kisses me back like his life depends on it. He presses me against the wall, his hands roving over me. They feel like a memory. The best sort of déjà vu. I press into him and run my hands up and down his back, under his shirt, the skin I haven't let myself touch for months. The skin that I know as well as my own.

And then suddenly I feel a thump resound through the wall, directly into my back, followed by footsteps and my sisters giggling. Finn pulls back, his eyes dark with longing, his arms bracketed around me. I laugh softly and he smiles and kisses me, over and over and over until I duck away. He pulls me to him and we collapse onto one of the beds.

"Maybe we should get a room," he suggests.

I nuzzle into him. "I agree. Let's go home. To my murder scene of a house."

And that is what feels like home now. Despite my struggles with anxiety, I never wanted to leave my hometown behind until I had already moved on. Looking at our house now—it's tiny, we ate melon instead of berries to save money, there was no AC in the summer, and it was cold in the winter. But all of my friends lived the same way, so I never felt I lacked anything. Once I went to college, though, then to New York, and continued to learn and work on myself, I realized that back home everyone's thinking was small. There was so much more out there than pageants and soccer and having kids by twenty-five. And that it was reasonable to expect people to hold my feelings carefully, to respond with care, and to have emotional intelligence. My thinking isn't limited to survival, so I can think about what is fulfilling. And when I started the show with Finn, I finally started to dare to dream. I don't think that my family understands exactly what my life looks like, but they love me and that's enough. I know they're there with me no matter what I do, and I'm deciding to be bold and dream bigger. To hope. To believe in myself. And to love hard enough to fall and trust Finn will catch me.

THIRTY-ONE

Finn

Maeve had told me her family was middle class. But I had pictured middle class looking different. Maeve has never complained about how she grew up, and issues with how they handled her anxiety aside, she largely has good things to say about her family. But I was always a bit concerned by the amount of financial responsibility she felt for them. Until now, I never realized just how differently we grew up. I realize that I've never wanted for anything, but I had assumed Maeve's family also lived in a big house here and that she never had to go without anything. Now it makes more sense that first thing she did when we started making real money was send it to her family.

I've never felt that weight. That responsibility. In fact, I don't think I've even checked that the Streamify payment came through, because my trust provides plenty to pay for everything I want to do.

Risking everything, her job, her reputation, her employability, on

Tell Me How You Really Feel also hits differently now that I know how much of a risk it really was. Maeve hasn't had a safety net. And I respect her even for more her creative certainty and her belief in this idea, having seen what a huge leap of faith it was.

I can't think of a time I've ever done *anything* like that.

It makes me love her even more. And it seems like I've passed the family interrogation, because Maeve's family has transitioned from suspicion to smiles as they bid us goodbye. We head to the airport and take another Spirit Airlines flight back to Los Angeles. And we can't get there fast enough. I can't keep my hands off her, and she seems to feel the same way, keeping one hand touching me at all times, even as we stride through LAX and risk being photographed.

The moment we're back at Maeve's place she slams the door shut behind us. I leave our bags on the floor and pick Maeve up. She wraps her legs around me, kisses me deeply, then pulls back. "Are we totally reckless to do this? With the show? And how badly it went last time?"

I shake my head immediately. "If it's with you, then I don't mind being reckless." I kiss her, and she melts into me. "But this is pretty fucking premeditated. I'd call it the most thought-out thing I've ever done, actually."

I start walking into the living room, still carrying Maeve. "Upstairs," she whispers.

"Are you sure?" I don't want her to think I'm rushing this. Rushing us. "I told you. I'm happy to wait. In fact, I love waiting. Let's go to Carbone. To Italy. Spain. Japan. Wherever you want. Every date we could do. I'm happy to do it all first and have the world's longest courtship."

"I'm sure," she says. And so I carry her upstairs to her bedroom and lay her on the bed. Holding her, it feels like the rest of my life starting. Like I would do anything to make this moment last.

I know that this is just the beginning for us, really. But it sure as hell doesn't feel like it.

I undress Maeve slowly, lingering to kiss each part of her that I unveil as I discard her sweat suit. Once she's just wearing her delicate lace bra and underwear, I inhale sharply. "Maeve, fuck. You're so gorgeous," I say, my voice thick with longing and admiration. I can't help but think of our first time, how intimate and desperate and hopeful it was. This is better because now I know we can and will work through everything. I know, with absolute certainty, that this is the start of forever.

Maeve tugs me down by my sweatshirt and kisses me, then lets her hands rove downward, pulling my sweatshirt up ineffectually. I yank it off, leaving our clothes in a heap on the ground. I lower myself back over Maeve and we kiss, no longer heedful, knowing already just the slightest bit about what the other likes.

I could keep kissing Maeve, just kissing, forever, but when she arches into me with a gasp, I groan. I start kissing my way down, sliding her bra off, taking my time with each breast until her nipples are peaking. I go lower, lower, until I'm circling her clit, not quite meeting it, until she's breathless and moaning. I take her hips firmly when I finally lower my mouth to her, and after that it feels like seconds, although I know it's longer, until she's crying out and I'm painfully hard, not letting up on her. Her orgasm keeps going, seeming to intensify and wane and intensify, and I continue until she runs her hands through my hair and pulls me up, relaxed and breathless.

I wipe my mouth on the pillowcase and kiss her, gently. I'm straining against my boxers, and when Maeve reaches down and pulls them off in one smooth movement, I groan. "We don't have to do more," I manage to choke out. "I'm completely satisfied with seeing you like that."

"Finn. I want you inside of me."

That's all I need to hear. I reach over to her nightstand and fumble, looking for a condom, until Maeve reaches over and grabs one, shoving it toward me. I put it on, add a pump of lube, and bring myself to meet her, stopping just at her entrance, trying to ease in, until suddenly I just have to be *in* her and push in all at once. She's so wet from coming, and I slide in and out, faster, leaning down close to her, kissing her face, her mouth, her cheek, her neck, pulling back every few moments so I can look at her.

"You're so beautiful," I whisper. "Absolutely fucking gorgeous."

Maeve starts grinding into me, and suddenly it's almost too much. It feels like we're one, moving, feeling. I try to hold on longer, but then I'm coming apart in her, and it's the best feeling. We lie there, me still in her, until she wants to pee to avoid a UTI. When she comes back, I wrap her in my arms and hold her tightly.

After a few minutes, I turn to Maeve, both of us slick with sweat, but not caring. "You know, I remember the first time I saw you."

"Oh yeah? The dorm meet and greet, right? I kind of remember it."

I tuck a stray strand of hair behind Maeve's ear. "That's when you first met me. But not the first time I saw you."

"Am I supposed to guess?" she whispers with a smile.

I kiss her. "You won't. I switched to your dorm. I saw your family moving you in, your sisters were fighting. You were mediating, even then, and your dad was moving furniture with the RA. Your mom was talking to another woman—"

"My roommate's mom," Maeve says. "We didn't know yet that my roommate would be a terror. You'd think living with three sisters in that tiny house would've prepared me for anything."

"Your roommate's mom," I amend the story. "It was a million degrees out, and you were sweaty. You kept pushing your hair off your forehead, but some of it was stuck there, darker than the rest. You were wearing a cutoff pink T-shirt and shorts. Oh, and your dad had absolutely parked illegally."

Maeve's brown eyes are locked on mine, listening. I keep going. This is one thing I've never told her. "I had moved in already. My parents couldn't make it, so they sent a whole crew of assistants. They'd hand selected my roommate. And once I saw you, I walked back across campus and persuaded their team to move me into your dorm. I said it was a better location, closer to classes, less dangerous at night, anything but that I was chasing a girl I hadn't even talked to."

"You were in a forced triple, though."

"Yeah. My parents paid the room and board for the other two guys so they'd let me join the room." I kiss Maeve once, slowly. "The other guys on your hall refused to trade with me; they were already moved in. And we made the triple work."

Maeve sits up, climbs on top of me. "I don't think I believe you. It doesn't make sense—you never talked to me, really. You didn't ask me out. We were just friends."

"We were in the same dorm all four years, though. How many other people did you happen to be on the same hall with every year?"

Maeve tilts her head, thinking, then lies down on me, her head resting on my shoulder. I run my fingers up and down her back slowly. "Why? Why do that, just to be friends? I just don't get it."

I can't see her face, but I can feel her breath on my cheek, the tickle of her eyelashes, our heartbeats pressed together. We're a perfect fit, as always. "Because I realized you were too good for me. That I'd ruin it if I tried to win you over then. Because you weren't just the most beautiful girl I'd ever met . . . you were *you*. So I guess it was for this. In hopes that one day I'd get this with you."

"A multi-multi-multimillion-dollar podcast deal and sex in a bedroom where someone once murdered their lover?" she whispers.

"*Exactly.* I play the long game. I told you this was all premeditated."

She giggles, and for a few minutes we just listen to the sound of each other's breathing. Slow. Steady. Calm. "Finn. I don't know what to say. That's so romantic it's almost creepy."

"I stopped listening at romantic," I say, then kiss the side of her head.

We lie there for a moment until suddenly Maeve sits up, fast. "Wait. Did you steal that from a movie? I think the guy in *Call Me Crazy* did that!"

She's leaning over me, and I tuck her thick auburn hair behind her ears again, rest my hands on her hips. "Think about who wrote that movie."

Her eyes widen. "No."

I nod. "Yes. I told my parents over Christmas break. And my dad stole it for a movie. Please consider that evidence, Exhibit A. Call him, right now, or my mom; they'll back me up. I was always gone for you."

Maeve leans down and kisses me, in a way no one else ever has.

THIRTY-TWO

Maeve

"I'm thinking about pitching the therapy show next week." It's been a week since we fell back into being together, *really* being together, and Finn and I have spent all day today in bed. This morning he got up and made French toast and coffee and brought it back to bed. Now, it's almost two and our plates are discarded on the floor, but we're still here.

I've never been a stay-in-bed-all-day kind of person. Even with other people I dated, I always would get up at a reasonable time so I could start the day and get things done. But with Finn, doing nothing in bed is the thing I most want to be doing on a Sunday. Every moment feels so perfect that it should be illegal and I want to bottle this feeling so I never lose it.

"Why next week?" Finn asks as he traces lazy circles on my back.

"We're going to break the record next Sunday," I say as I rap on the wooden nightstand with my knuckles. Our agents did a fantastic job renegotiating the terms of the bonus incentive in exchange for the personal—and therefore super viral—bonus episode. "Maximum leverage power. And Shazia has preemptively set up a magazine shoot."

"Oh really? I haven't heard about it yet," Finn remarks casually.

I stiffen slightly, without meaning to. Finn has always done separate press, because he's famous and the media loves him. But I've never done anything without him. I roll over so I'm looking at him. "Just for me. *W Magazine* is doing a feature on how I broke the glass ceiling in podcasting."

I don't know why I worried for an instant that because Finn assumed he would be included, he would be jealous not to be. He just smiles and kisses me, genuinely so happy for me. "That's amazing."

I kiss him again, lingering for a moment to take in his scent, his stubble on my cheek, the firm weight of his body next to mine. He's *so* attractive. And it's not just how he looks, it's everything about the way he carries himself. He has this charisma and confidence that makes him light up any room he's in. Knowing that he's my person in every way feels surreal. "Do you want to edit together?"

Although we're in a great place now, I've still been mainly editing by myself. I got used to doing it that way while we were fighting and it's much more efficient. I know I don't need to, but *Tell Me How You Really Feel* still feels like my baby and I don't know that anyone else would have the same attention to detail with it that I do. I can tell Finn's been a bit bored lately, though. He's been texting me constantly and stopping by my place unexpectedly with flowers or food, then looking like a crushed puppy when I'm too busy working to hang for more than a few minutes. So even though I don't need his help, I want to extend the invitation.

"Absolutely," Finn agrees. We head over to my editing bay without getting dressed, me still in his giant T-shirt and a lace thong, and him in just boxers.

Our episode this past week was with a former Olympic gymnast, who talked about the sexual abuse warning signs. It was more serious subject matter than many of our episodes, but at the end, during the Questions of the Week, we kept it lighthearted. I sit at the computer and start playing the episode, stopping here and there to cut pauses, or to pause it and hear Finn's thoughts.

About ten minutes in the gymnast stumbles over her words. "Should I cut around it, do you think?" Typically we would. But since this is such a personal story from her, one she's never talked about to the press, I feel a bit hesitant to touch it.

Finn exhales. "Hmm. I'm really not sure. I wouldn't want to edit anything out, but also I feel like it's bad to let her stumble like that. I got the vibe that she wanted to sound confident and in control."

I play back her audio again. "I just . . . well, you know, I think that he . . . actually, you know, *forget him*, really, we are who everyone should be talking about. Like, center the narrative."

I like the way Finn's thinking. I don't want to edit her either, but I do want to make her sound like the most confident version of herself. I start splicing and rearranging, dragging clips and adding cross fades, then play it back. "You know, *forget him*. Center the narrative. We are who everyone should be talking about. Our resilience."

"I like that. Where did you get the 'our resilience' line?"

I glance over at him. "I took it from later on in the episode. Think it's too much of a stretch? It's what she was getting at."

"She gets approval for the episode, right?"

We don't typically let guests approve our episodes, but given what she's been through and the intensity of the subject matter here, I offered to send her the edit after we finished recording. "Yeah, I felt like it was the right thing to do."

"Then I'd keep it. If she doesn't like it, we can change it. But I think she will."

The next three hours of editing pass in a blur as we continue to spitball ideas and play off of each other. By the end, I'm completely confident this is a great episode. An episode that will get press, and not for talking about blow jobs. Plus I think it'll be another episode that will help the conversations about my solo show, since I want that to be elevated content as well.

"You know, this is so different from where we started. I kind of like that it's *the* episode," Finn remarks.

"I almost wish we did more of a sure thing for this week, so we'd *know* that we hit the mark and are getting the pay bump. This is so serious, you know? What if people don't listen through to the end. Maybe we should just talk about blow jobs one last time." I'm exporting it from Premiere via media encoder, so I can create the face out graphic in Photoshop while the export runs, and my computer is humming with effort.

Finn has been walking around the living room, but now he drops into the chair next to me and takes my hand. "Maeve, it's a great episode. I think it's our best yet, it's serious content, yeah, but it really *matters*. We've got this."

A week later the episode drops, and Finn is completely right. *The To-day Show* covers the episode in their nine a.m. segment, *The New York Times* jumps on it and publishes an op ed interviewing all of us, and clips are reposted right and left. It takes twenty-four hours for the ratings to roll in, but I feel good about what they'll say.

So good, that instead of anxiously waiting for the call to come in from Shazia, I let Finn persuade me to go to Carbon Beach, the celebrity-studded stretch of ocean directly outside his parents' house.

"Let's go in," Finn exclaims the moment we step onto the sand. It's high tide, so there's almost no beach exposed, and he shucks off his shoes and shirt and leaves them on the sand in front of the house.

"Why don't we just sit here and look for a bit?" I argue. "The call is going to come any second. Then the swim can be celebratory!"

I so badly want to find out whether we beat *The Paul Myers Show*. Paul Myers gets paid so much more than us, the gap between what he makes and what we do isn't even funny. Right now, we're paid like a really good podcast. We make around what the other top solely female-hosted shows do, although our ratings are on par with *The Paul Myers Show*. This raise will mean that not only do I become the highest-paid female podcaster, I completely shatter the glass ceiling and show women everywhere that women *can* be paid commensurately with men when they are just as successful. Our salaries weren't public during the initial deal, but if we get this, the article will tell the whole world what I make, and how it's making history.

"The call could come in two hours. It's not an exact science, and who knows how long it'll take Streamify to tell them. They're probably cross comparing all the ranking sites, trying to find one that ranks us lower so they don't have to pay up. It could be tomorrow for all we know! Let's just—"

The sound of my phone ringing cuts Finn off, and I shriek in delight. "It's Shazia!" I pick up, and Finn steps close to me to listen. "Shazia? Did we get it?"

We wait with bated breath. "You got it," she confirms. "Congratulations, Maeve. You're officially the highest paid female podcast host. You two have beaten *The Paul Myers Show* to be the highest paid show. Now go celebrate!"

I end the call and Finn wraps me in a huge bear hug, swinging me around in circles until we both collapse in the sand, laughing. And, okay, crying, just a tiny bit. The water breaks over us, getting our legs wet, but we don't move.

"I can't believe it," I whisper. And I can't. This feels too good to be true. I have the deal, I have Finn. My anxiety is whispering in my ear, telling me it's not possible to have it all like this. But we really fucking do.

"I can," Finn says firmly. He leans on one arm so he can look down at me, my hair frizzy and full of sand, and my face wet with water and salt and happy tears. "You deserve it."

THIRTY-THREE

Finn

I am so happy for Maeve. That's all I can think about in the days following our big win. I got a sizable raise too, but it doesn't mean all that it does for Maeve. I'm just making more money. Not history.

I've been trying to dream up a way to show Maeve how much I care about her. How special she is to me because I know saying it only means so much. I always notice she's used to having to do everything herself, or at least having to take point on it to make sure it's done right, and I have a surprise in mind that I think will really show her that I see and appreciate her.

"Do you think he'll be able to do it so last-minute?" I ask my mom.

"Honey, he's a friend. I'm sure that if it's at all possible, he'll do it. Or at least have his assistant do it." My mom sounds mildly exasperated. Her new movie is lacking a male lead, and I can tell it's wearing on both her and my dad. She's costarring in the movie with Cassidy, and my dad wrote the script during the brief period in which I was dating Cassidy. It's a movie about a mom who pays a young woman to date her son, because he's never had a girlfriend that they like. Lots of great actors want the role, but my parents have been disappointed with all of the screen tests and chemistry reads.

Before I can ask more questions, my mom's interior designer, Luca, walks in with an assistant in tow. He kisses my mom once on each cheek, then shakes my hand. "Evangeline. It is always my pleasure. And Finn! You look . . . dare I say . . . grown up!" We exchange pleasantries, then all sit back down. "Now, what is this emergency?"

My mom raises an eyebrow at me. "I want to build my girlfriend, Maeve, her dream podcasting studio," I say. "I know exactly how she envisions it, more or less, but want to add a light-up floor that has testimonials from fans. Or something like that, anyway."

I thought it would be nice to add a more personalized touch. But the moment I say light-up floor, both my mom and Luca flinch. "I see!" Luca says politely. "Do you have sketches? Swatches? A location? Anything like that?"

"So, not exactly . . . she has described what she wants to me, and I wrote down a list of the color chairs and brand of the rugs she likes and all that. And I found a few *Tell Me How You Really Feel* mood boards she made for the studio this year in our old emails. But she hates the studio Streamify made; she thinks it's super tacky."

"It is, honey," my mom interjects. She looks knowingly toward Luca. "The table . . . it's a vagina. An *obvious* vagina. So tacky."

Luca throws up his hands and shakes his head in horror as he looks through the papers I've passed to him. "And the . . . light-up floor? And location?"

This is where things get tricky. "Well . . . I want it to be a surprise. So I was hoping we could make like a shed-type thing that we can just cart over to her place afterward? Like those Home Depot sheds that get delivered?"

"Where in the world did *you* learn about Home Depot sheds?" Luca asks witheringly. "Because I *know* it wasn't from your parents."

I press on. "Pittsburgh. People love them. But anyways, I wanted the floor to be normal-looking at first glance . . . but maybe if she flips a switch, she can see testimonials from fans about how much the show means to them."

Luca and my mom exchange glances. "Why the floor?" the assistant asks suddenly.

I shrug. "I don't know. I don't really care where it is; I just want it to have a personalized element."

The assistant nods thoughtfully. "What if we lose the light-up floor idea. And instead, we make a custom desk with the quotes on it. Or put them on the ceiling? It could be in the handwriting of the person who said it."

"That works," I agree readily. "Really, I leave it to you guys. I just want to make it as close to what she described as possible with the personal touches added, and then if there's things she wants to change, obviously help her do whatever she wants. Does the moveable shed idea work?"

Luca flinches again at the word *shed*. "We'll look into what's possible. Just stop saying 'shed.'" He chokes out the word as though it's poisonous and sighs heavily. "Maybe . . . an elevated shipping container. We'll see what's available. There's potential to cut down on construction time significantly if one of my partners can source the right one."

"You can do the construction, or furnishing? Whatever really, on our property as needed," my mom interjects. "Just in the yard or somewhere. When you did the pool house, your team was phenomenal; we barely knew they were here."

I roll my eyes. "You were filming in Maui."

"Well, hopefully, by the time this is truly underway, I'll be filming in the studio."

We bid Luca and his assistant goodbye, and my mom starts throwing things in her giant bag. "You're in a rush," I remark lightly.

"We have another screen test today. I really hope this is the one. Well, the one we pick anyway, since you're *the* one."

I sit at the kitchen island while she transfers her coffee to a to-go cup. "Come on, Mom. You both knew when Dad wrote it that I wasn't going to act in it."

My mom takes a long sip of her coffee, then finally stands still for a moment. "Finn. *Why?* You said you wanted a normal life and to avoid the paps and fame. But that time is long gone now thanks to the podcast. You're such a talented actor! And really, what else are you doing, sweetie?"

"I'm doing the podcast!" I argue defensively. We've had this fight a million times, but more often with my dad.

"Honey. You are doing the podcast. But one day a week. The rest of the time you're wandering around like a ghost, working out, swimming, trying recipes, it's just . . ." She trails off. My mom's tone is gentle and searching, like she's trying to figure out where she went wrong, how she can help. "I don't think the podcast is the end goal for you. Keep doing it; I know it's fun. But I don't want you to be like all of my friends' kids, who spend decades trying to scramble together meaning out of money, looking hot and partying."

I exhale deeply. She's not wrong. I thought that once Maeve and I were back together everything would just click into place. But it hasn't. She has the show, and soon her new show, and she's *so* passionate about it. It's like as long as she has that she knows she'll be happy and fulfilled. I really do want that. "I know," I say softly. "But acting . . . I never told you this, but I had a panic attack when we first started the show, and started getting death threats and hate messages. It was like a flashback to when we would get chased by paps all the time when I was a kid. I've just always felt like if I act again it will unleash this hellhole. Like, ten times worse than back in the day or anything that could happen from a podcast. Harsher criticism, more aggressive paps and fans. I remember how scared you were of them when I was a kid."

My mom walks around the counter and wraps me in a hug. "Darling. I was scared because I was concerned for *you*. I've learned to deal with them on my own. But I was not going to let anyone chase my little boy. As for the criticism, we already know you're talented. A movie or show is an epic collaboration, and with that comes risk, although given that your dad and I are working on it the risk is mitigated. With your talent, your dad's writing, me and Cassidy costarring . . . you have the goods to back it up. You already proved yourself once, all you have to do now is come back with a splash." I don't say anything, and my mom pulls back from her embrace to look at me. "You don't have to do anything you don't want to. But the reason we keep pushing this is because you *loved* acting. It was your dream and you were phenomenal in that movie and had the time of your life until the fame hit. The way the media treated you was a completely unfair way to treat a child. But times have changed. And you've grown up. You can handle it. I just want you to try, because you've looked all this time and not found any other passion. We just want you to be happy. Why don't you ask Cassidy how it's been for her? You've built this up in your head for a long time. Maybe the reasons not to do it aren't as scary as you think."

I hug my mom back suddenly, fiercely. "I will think about it. Just don't tell Dad, please."

THIRTY-FOUR

Maeve

"So, have you heard anything?" I'm sitting in hair and makeup at the magazine shoot, and Shazia has stopped by to give me an update on the meetings we've been doing to pitch my solo show. But by the look on her face, it hasn't gone well.

She takes a long sip of coffee before speaking. And to her credit, she doesn't wince or smile sympathetically while delivering the news. It's more like ripping off a Band-Aid. "They all passed."

I turn my head, taking the hair stylist's hands with me. "All of them?"

We sat down with each major network within three days last week, hoping it would create a bidding war situation and lead to better offers. The question that came up in every meeting was: What is *Finn's* place in the show going to be? In *my* show. Based on that, I had tried to convince myself the offers just might not be as good as we'd hoped. Now I wish I felt disbelief, but it's more like resignation. I *knew* this would happen, deep in my gut.

"Did they say why?" I ask. The makeup artist starts tilting my face, combing through my eyebrows and adding fake lashes. In my gut, I know why they passed. They want me, sure, but only if I'm with Finn. On my own, I'm not considered talent. Just his barrier to entry.

"Just the usual bullshit," Shazia says nonchalantly. "They're worried the show is too serious for people to watch. 'Where's the drama?' Not confident there's enough appetite. Not risqué enough."

The disappointment is crushing. I knew the show would be a tough sell because I've never seen anything like it. And when you first hear about it, a show where people go to therapy doesn't sound like fun. But this is *real* drama. People love seeing other people's problems play out, plus with this I would get to help people and show viewers there's a healthy way forward through their problems. I know I could make this show awesome and that our *Tell Me How You Really Feel* fans would watch it.

"What now?" I ask. The makeup artist starts applying a bold red lip and I watch her in the mirror. I can see Shazia analyzing me, and know that she sees how disappointed I am. And that if she offers condolences right now I *will* break down. So thankfully she sticks to facts.

"Evangeline reached out. She's interested in producing. You could partner with an individual producer like her and create the show yourselves, exactly how you want, then sell it to a network."

I love Evangeline. But I don't want this show to also be attached to Finn through his mom, since I know that it was shot down because he's not involved and all of these entertainment execs are tying my worth to him. "Could I self-produce solo?"

"You could. You definitely have the money to do it. But I don't think you have the experience you need, if I'm being completely honest." Shazia's words have no bite, but they still sting.

"All set." The makeup artist calls out toward the creative director and photographer. "She's all set!"

"What?" I turn around. I've totally forgotten that I'm here for a magazine shoot. *The* magazine shoot. This is probably why Shazia asked if we could talk later. Which I refused. I knew I would be anxious the entire shoot, waiting to hear what she said. But now I'm anxious because I know.

The photographer walks up to my chair. "You ready? Once you're changed we'll start on the main cover set, then do an outfit change for the smaller alt sets. But those pictures probably won't be used on the cover, unless we love them."

"Just give us two minutes," Shazia interjects. She's always ready to be the bad guy for me.

The photographer walks off and starts setting up, and Shazia looks me in the eye directly, instead of via the mirror like we've been doing during hair and makeup. "It's a great idea, Maeve. We'll get it made, and you'll crush it. I would consider working with Evangeline, but either way, we *will* get the show done."

I have so many questions about how I would self-produce a reality show. Where would our set be? Would I have to pay everything out of pocket? Why would a network buy it later, if they won't buy in now? And a small anxious part of myself wonders, does Shazia believe in me? Separate from Finn and Evangeline and Streamify? But instead of asking any of that, I just nod. "Okay."

Inside the changing area, which is made of three extra tall foam bounce cards that create a triangle against a real wall, I change into the hot pink power suit. The suit has been tailored to me and I know I look great in it. Feminine, powerful, like a boss. But I feel like a fraud.

I walk onto set with my heart pounding in my chest, so loudly that I can barely hear the photographer. Music is blasting to get us in the mood, but it's overwhelmingly loud, and once I'm standing on the main set, a simple white sweep with a mic, the lights are blindingly bright. Just as I'm about to ask what to do, because really, photoshoots are not my forte, we've only done the one with Streamify for our podcast's cover art, the entire crew bursts into applause.

I glance around set, confused. "What are you clapping for?"

The photographer snaps a few photos, then lowers the camera. "You. You're breaking glass ceilings. For *all of us*. Not just podcasters. This is an all-female set today, which *never* happens, and we're so fucking excited about what you're doing."

I smile, my anxiety fading away, and she takes a photo of the moment my tense frown turns into a genuine grin. In the crushing disappointment about my show, I forgot for a moment that I've done something big. Something meaningful.

We get into it, me posing with the mic, without it, smiling, smizing, stern. I don't really know how to pose, but the photographer directs me and it feels effortless. After a few minutes she gestures to me to come over. "Let's see how they look."

I step over the cord that tethers her to the monitor, and we peer over the digi-tech's shoulder at the images. I look *good*. More confident than I've probably ever felt. But also like myself. And the first one, where I'm breaking into that smile, is my favorite.

Suddenly I feel a hand on my shoulder, a familiar weight behind me. "Surprise!" I turn around and am face-to-face with Finn, who's holding coffee from my favorite shop. He gives me a quick kiss. "Maeve, those photos . . . they look amazing."

"Thank you," I say. I should be happy that my boyfriend, who I've wanted to be my boyfriend for literally *years* now, is thoughtfully surprising me. But instead, I feel a slight sense of discomfort. Because we were just making a big thing of the all-female crew. And because this is my moment. And now when I glance around set, all eyes are on him.

The creative director has joined us at the monitor. "Maybe we should get one of you two together. Just in case, you know . . . since he's here."

Finn shrugs and looks to me. "Whatever you want."

I will look like the biggest bitch right now if I say no. And Shazia left after the clapping so she's no longer here to run interference. I force a smile. "Sounds great."

Finn heads over to hair and makeup and I follow the crew over to the next set. They've gotten our vagina table, or a replica of it anyway, and I'm directed to sit directly on it. We do a series of strong poses, less goofy, and then Finn appears. From somewhere, they've procured a matching pink suit and it fits him *really* well. It makes my pulse rise. Did they always plan for him to be in this? That's paranoid. My anxiety talking. Actually, is it *that* improbable?

I must be making a face, because the stylist jumps in. "We had an oversized option for you, and the tailor was able to adjust for Finn."

"That's amazing!" I say. I can't tell if my tone sounds hollow or happy.

We walk over to another set, that's a black sweep, with brightly colored sex toys scattered throughout. I'm getting nervous again, but right when we step onto the set, while they're still setting up the lighting and wheeling over the digi-tech cart, Finn pulls me in for a kiss. And that kiss . . . despite my anxieties about him being here, it feels like all of my worries melt away for a moment while his lips are on mine. I probably am letting my anxiety talk. There's no reason to think everyone is plotting to make the shoot actually about both of us, or about Finn. They probably won't even use the images in the real article; it wouldn't make sense. Maybe they're just for social. And having him here centers me.

We start posing and together the shoot goes from good to genuinely *fun*. Within minutes he has me laughing, as he picks me up, playfully examines sex toys, kisses me. He's a natural on camera. I've always been respectful of his decision not to act, although I believe it was one made out of trauma more than logic. But every time I see him in front of a camera it makes me wonder if he's *sure* he shouldn't try it.

Finn stays for the rest of the shoot, although after that set and a few pickup shots with him on the main one, he steps back and watches. Having him there relaxes me, and I can tell the photographer is pleased with the shots she's gotten at the end of the day. I look more lighthearted with him around. Although, is lighthearted really the vibe for a serious conversation about the importance of paying women equitably?

"Which one will be the cover?" I ask the creative director on our way out, Finn carrying my things, both of us in *Tell Me How You Really Feel* sweat suits.

"We'll review internally and decide!" she chirps. "But don't worry, we got so many amazing shots today. You will *love* it."

I look at Finn as we walk out of the set and into the industrial hallway. "That should make me nervous. But I actually think she's right."

"Of course she is. You looked incredible in there." He kisses me, and we walk out hand in hand, all of my nagging worries fading away, at least for the time being.

THIRTY-FIVE

Finn

Maeve is working 24/7 to get her therapy reality show off the ground, and it's left me with way too much free time in between *Tell Me How You Really Feel* episode recordings. Which is how I've been roped into going to the set of my parents' new movie for the day, to look at their latest option for the male lead. And to talk to Cassidy about acting.

My dad has been on set since five a.m., but my mom's call time wasn't until ten. I trail after her as we walk through set, until we get to the living room that they're using for the screen test. This is actually a set that another show uses periodically, but since it's not in use this week, they've moved to this soundstage instead of using a plain room for these tests. It's unusual, but not unheard of, for a lead role, especially given how much trouble casting this is giving them.

"Who is this guy, again?" I ask as we walk into the living room set.

Cassidy is sitting on the couch on her phone, and my dad is at a table behind the camera monitor. Instead of watching *them*, he'll watch through the monitor, to see how they show up on camera.

"He was on some shitty CW show," Cassidy says without looking up.

My mom nods emphatically while my dad interjects. "It wasn't shitty! The writing could have used a little touch-up, is all. And he was quite good. But being a vampire shape-shifter is a tough role to add grit to."

"So you're saying . . . this isn't the bottom of the barrel quite yet," I joke.

My mom and Cassidy laugh, and my dad glares at me. I join Cassidy on the couch as we wait for the actor. And wait. And wait some more.

"Want to check out crafty?" I ask Cassidy after twenty minutes.

She glances at me. "Sure."

The craft services table is a folding table, or several folding tables when we have a full crew, that production covers with snacks, baked goods, sandwiches, drinks, candy, and sometimes charcuterie. Some things are always there, and everyone develops their go-to snacks as production wears on. As kids, raiding the craft services table was a huge thrill, and so even though now I'm sure Cassidy has her full rider in her trailer, and Streamify always stocks mine, it still feels a bit illicit to go over to the table together while my parents are waiting to film.

"Your mom said I should sell you on acting," Cassidy says bluntly once we're out of earshot, picking through fun-size organic candy bars and a mix of artisanal chips and Classic Lays and Cheetos. "Should I?"

I rip open a bag of veggie straws and inspect the contents for way too long. "Yeah," I say finally.

She arches an eyebrow, clearly shocked. "Well, okay, then. First, forget the things you already know because they don't really matter. The money is great. Your fame will grow. Brand partnerships will appear. But you basically already have that. What will change your life is that you love acting. You'll be happy doing it again. I fucking know it. You get to be someone else. You get to do something that will matter to the people who watch, at least for two hours. I think it'll make you feel . . . I don't know. I liked modeling fine. But acting makes me feel *alive*. Like there's nothing else I'd rather be doing. Maeve has that already. And I *know* that you don't. But you can if you just let yourself."

I offer her a few straws while I contemplate. "And the fans? The paparazzi?"

She stops, the straws not yet in her mouth. "I can't believe you're still on that. You were okay when we were in Europe, and that was the most intense coverage I've experienced since we were kids. The rules are stricter now, especially here in LA. Back then they could do anything they wanted. Now, if you'll work with them here and there . . . you can arrange to be alone when you want to be."

"*Really?*" I say, intrigued.

Cassidy nods and digs into a mini bag of white cheddar ridged Cheez-Its. "Totally. Every month or two my team offers them something decent—me leaving a bar, in a bikini, whatever. And then I get to live without them for a while. But even without that they've really cut back on the chases. We didn't get chased once last summer. Think about it." She narrows her eyebrows when I don't answer, aware her hard sell is slipping. "Trust me. Just try acting. Once you try, it'll feel worth it. And you only need to get over the hump of the first movie—which, *bonus*, will be great since your dad wrote it—and face your fears, and then you'll have a whole new life that you actually love. Swear on the crafty table."

A PA runs over and interrupts us nervously. "Um, excuse me?

Miss . . . Cassidy? And Mr. Sutton? They want you in the screen-test area."

Cassidy tosses the rest of her Cheez-Its, and I shove the veggie straws into my mouth in one massive bite. Back in the living room set, my dad is venting to my mom. "These people. Doesn't he know he should have left hours early? This is LA. There's always an accident on the freeway."

"Unprofessional," I agree blandly as we walk in. My dad barely hears me as he keeps talking to my mom, who's eyeing Cassidy and me, waiting to jump in at the right moment. We drop onto the couch to wait out my dad's venting. When he's finally worn himself down, I move to get up so we can all head out.

"Stop!" my mom blurts out. I lean back against the cushions. She grabs my dad's arm. "Just . . . look."

The camera is on and trained on Cassidy and me. Based on the expressions on my parents' faces as they look at us through the monitor, I can already see where this is going. And I don't feel totally opposed. "Did you set this up?"

"Absolutely not," my dad barks. "I would never let a full day's work ride on you—too fickle. But now that we're here and have wasted a day . . . why not just read for it?"

My mom looks at me pleadingly. "Honey, why not? Just try it, and if it's awful and you hate it, we will never bother you about acting again. How's that?"

"I don't believe you," I argue halfheartedly. But I haven't walked away, and I know that's telling in and of itself.

"I swear," my mom promises. "No more scripts written specifically for you either."

"Ignore that," my dad argues. "I'm not making any promises. Inspiration is what it is."

Cassidy jumps in. "What's the worst that can happen?"

I groan and sit back down. "This feels like a reverse intervention."

My dad reaches over and hits Record on the camera, and my mom passes me the script. Cassidy waves hers off. "I've done this like fifty times," she says when I raise an eyebrow. "If I don't have it memorized by now, just fire me."

My parents cluster behind the monitor, and Cassidy and I start running the scene. It's the first time we meet in the script, when Cassidy has been hired by my mom to date me, but I don't know it yet. My role is funny, but in the subtle way my dad does so well, where it depends on the actor *getting it*, and isn't just cheap laughs. It's another in a long string of mother–son roles he's written for my mom and me.

At first, I feel clunky, since I'm reading, bouncing between the page and Cassidy. But by the end of the scene I'm into it, and it feels like this is something I never stopped doing. It's easy to slip into a role that was written for me, and opposite Cassidy, who I have so much natural chemistry with, I know I'm hitting all the right notes with the jokes. I'm able to take the material further since I already half know how she'll react, and that she'll be able to build on what I do. In the back of my mind I remember the vacations we used to go on as families, and how Cassidy and I would act out elaborate renditions of our moms' movies after dinner on the last night every year, until we did the movie for real, and then suddenly we didn't do that anymore, because acting felt like the bad thing, when, really, the bad thing was the harassment by the media. And now I really wish we'd never stopped.

When we wrap the scene, the sound stage is quiet. Then a slow clap starts. I turn and see that various PAs and gaffers have gathered to watch. My dad waves them off with one stern look, then walks over to me. "Finn. Just watch it back before you say anything. Before you even *think* anything."

I shut my mouth, although I'm actually not sure what I was going to say. Because I loved it. And I hate that I loved it. It feels too stupid to admit, when I've been so adamant about not acting my entire life. I follow my dad to the monitor and let Cassidy and my mom crowd in tight behind me to watch it back.

We're good. *I'm* good. When it stops, everyone waits for my response, the room silent. I don't say anything.

Finally, my mom can't take anymore. "Just say you'll do it! Come on! We'll film around the *Tell Me How You Really Feel* schedule. Have the release and press tour during your summer hiatus. Just do it!"

I look between them all, and Cassidy squeezes my arm encouragingly. And then I can't hold back my smile any longer. "Fine. I'll do it."

My dad wraps us all in a giant hug. "*Finally*, Finn."

I pull away. "But no bragging! Or badgering me about how long I held off. And for now, until we see how it all plays out, it's just this one."

My mom mimes zipping her lips. "Not a word out of us. We're just happy to all do this together as a family."

"Me too," I agree. And I mean it. I've resisted this for so long, laser focused on building my own path and staying out of the spotlight. But Cassidy's right. At this point, I'm in entertainment. There's no reason to hide anymore. I enjoy doing the show, which is akin to acting, and even though I've resisted it my whole life . . . I think my parents might be right. Acting might be what I was meant to do.

It's not until we're walking out of the studio that I wonder if I should have talked to Maeve before agreeing to do a movie opposite Cassidy.

THIRTY-SIX

Maeve

When I run into the gas station to get gum, I find myself staring at two dueling magazine covers. One has me on the cover in a pink suit. The other has Finn and Cassidy, hand in hand, on the set of his parents' latest movie. His first movie since his award-winning performance as a child.

I buy both.

Back in my car I have a moment of pause over which to flip through first. My gut instinct is to look at the photos of Finn and Cassidy. Finn told me he was doing the movie with her, and although I wish we had talked about it together before he committed, that he went to me instead of her to get the pep talk about conquering his fears, I can see how embarrassed he is to love acting after refusing to do it all this time. So I'm trying to support him, like he would do for me. And I really am happy that he's found his way back to his passion! I've wanted this for him for a long time. But every anxiety I had over the two of them—how much better suited to each other they are, how much the press loves them together, how well they know each other—has come flooding back. It's like I'm looking at that first photo outside of Carbone. And every photo that came afterward: on Instagram, in magazines, and on social media. But I force myself to push aside the deluge of intrusive thoughts and open my own magazine spread first.

The cover photo is gorgeous. And the headline—*She's On Top*—is both provocative and flattering. I got an early copy of the text component, and the article itself is thoughtful and kind. Friendly press, as Shazia called it. It's meant to serve as a beacon of hope for women everywhere. When I open the magazine, the text is as described, with lovely pull quotes featuring my most empowering quotes from the interview. But the pictures . . . they're all of Finn and me. And in the middle of the article, I see they've bolded a quote from Finn that wasn't in the initial draft.

Maeve is the most brilliant person I know. She deserves all of the credit for Tell Me How You Really Feel. *And trust me when I say this, you will be blown away by what she has coming next . . .*

He was being kind. Trying to give my solo show a boost. But the article takes a detour to praise him for being supportive, for saying I'm the "most brilliant person" (note: not *woman*) he knows. Men are constantly lauded for just being decent. This is supposed to be my article, but once again Finn is given the spotlight because he is just *so* famous, *so* much more appealing, and will get *so many clicks*.

Anxiety is burning in my throat as I put my magazine down and open the tabloid. I should just throw it out. There's a trash bin about two feet away, directly in front of my car, and I know I'm only feeding my anxiety by reading this. But I open it. *Obviously.*

It's nothing I don't already know. They're doing a movie together, where they play romantic leads. I *know* that's why there's a photo of them kissing. Finn came home the night before and told me it was technically possible to CGI the kiss, if they stayed an inch apart, but it would cost a huge amount and would it be okay if he just kissed her? It's not like they hadn't already. My heart hurt when I said yes.

For a while it felt like everyone wanted *us* together. But really, that was just our fans. The *world* wants Finn and Cassidy. It's an old story, and I hate that I'm anxious over it. But this is all combining into a perfect storm, one that plays on my worst fears. That I'm not enough. That I'm no one without Finn. That he wants a bigger, better life than the one he has with me. I throw *People* onto the passenger seat, my own magazine now obscured, and head to the studio.

I've gotten over our jump scare of a set, no longer flinching when I see the dick mics and vagina table. And today, right on top of the clitoris, is a cake, with an edible photo of my magazine cover.

I look up to Finn's smiling face. My first thought should be, *Wow, my boyfriend is so caring and amazing.* But what I'm really thinking is, *How did he get this photo early?* I couldn't see the photos early, and I'm the fucking cover. Does this mean he knew that they overhauled my solo article that was supposed to be a celebration of women crushing the patriarchy, of me shattering the glass ceiling, with quotes and photos of him?

"Wow," is all I say.

Finn walks around the table and pulls me in for a kiss. It's a perfect kiss. Tender and deep and loving. And I wonder if it's the same kiss Cassidy gets. I don't know how I'm going to be able to turn off this part of my brain.

"Congratulations," Finn says when he breaks away. "I know we already knew you did it . . . but you did it. And now everyone knows how incredible you are. So let's eat your face." He picks up a knife and starts cutting us slices of the cake, clearly trying to sculpt out the best piece for me.

I should feel happy. This is what I've been striving for, after all. But instead I feel the dull throb of anxiety. A slight sense of dread. Regardless, I paste on a smile, or at least try for an approximation of it. "Thank you. This is so nice."

Finn stops what he's doing, putting the piece of cake he was plating back on the platter. "What's wrong?"

I don't want to ruin this moment. But my anxiety is threatening to overwhelm me, and I don't know how to hide it from him. I just shake my head mutely, focusing on holding back the tears.

Finn walks around the table and puts his arm around me, guiding me toward a chair. "Maeve, just talk to me. It's okay. I'm here, I'm with you." I sit down, his grip on me tight. "I'm going to reschedule today's interview, okay?"

"No," I choke out. "It's unprofessional." My voice cracks on the words, and I swallow hard.

"It's okay," Finn murmurs. "I'll say I got food poisoning. And I know the guest; she'll be okay. She'll probably be secretly glad to do it tomorrow. I saw she was out partying last night. I'll take the blame. Okay?"

We've never canceled an episode. If I was the cause of cancelation, I would be unprofessional. But I know no one will mind if Finn is. And that's the problem. I'll always be held to a double standard that I don't think he will ever really understand. Finn steps out to cancel the episode and comes back in, a cold glass of water and tissues in hand. The tissues, no surprise, are in a container shaped like boobs.

I take one and pat underneath my eyes, trying to soak up the tears while they're still light and I have a chance of preserving my mascara. "Do you want to talk about it?" he asks gently.

I take a shuddering breath. "It's nothing, really. I'm just feeling anxious. The article was a little different than I thought it would be, and the photos of Cassidy just made me feel stressed, even though I know it's stupid. I don't know."

It's hard for me to pull my thoughts together when I'm feeling anxious like this. Finn rubs my back gently. "The article is my fault. I never should have let them take photos of me. And I didn't realize they were going to use that quote. The focus should have stayed on what your accomplishment means for other women."

He's so understanding. So *nice*. But why did he let them integrate him into the shoot if he's so self-aware now? I don't know if this is a problem we'll ever be able to solve. But I'll just have to learn how to live with it, because really, it's about the world around us more than his actions. "I appreciate you saying that. I'm just feeling insecure, I think, because all those networks wanted you to be part of my solo show . . . I just feel like I'm not enough, I don't know." I hate that I'm punctuating my feelings with uncertainty. It's something women are trained to do. Usually I make a point not to do it, but in these vulnerable moments I can't think clearly enough to monitor my own speech. And really, I shouldn't have to.

"Maeve, you are so talented. I'm so sorry; those networks are idiots. And I'm sorry I took away from this huge accomplishment, at all. Especially when you've been so nice and generous about me working with Cassidy. What can I do to try to turn this around, to make this moment about the awesome thing you've done?"

He always says the right thing. His palm rubbing my back is rhythmic and soothing, and I can feel my heartbeat slowing back down to normal. The threat of tears subsiding. "Let's just have a nice night at home. Takeout from our favorite place. We can try the cake, then. I want to go to the gym, then we can meet back up." Working out is the one thing guaranteed to help my anxiety.

"Sounds perfect." Finn kisses me sweetly on the forehead. "And do you want them to change the digital edition of the article? They can sub the quote and pictures."

"Finn, they wouldn't even show me the pictures. I don't think they're going to change the article."

Finn pulls me closer. "My mom is a good friend of the magazine. If it would make us all feel better, I think they would. Let me do this for you."

"I'm afraid they'll think I'm being difficult to work with," I argue halfheartedly.

He kisses me, not caring about my snotty nose and running mascara. "Let me be a diva. It's good acting practice."

I nod, agreeing, like I almost always do with him. And by the time we're eating the cake, the digital version of the article is perfect.

THIRTY-SEVEN

Finn

I wake up to the sound of my mom banging on the door of the pool house. I still haven't gotten my own place, but to be fair, I have been spending most nights at Maeve's. Last night, though, Sarah stayed over with her, since she's been struggling with her anxiety. I feel like it's mostly my fault, for taking away part of her big moment with the show and the article, and for doing this movie with Cassidy.

"Finn! Get up and get into the kitchen. Right now!"

My mom sounds pissed, but I can't think of anything I've done. I rack my brain as I pull sweats and a T-shirt over my boxers. Did I leave the seat up? Break something? Forget to lock the house? I'm still mulling over what it could be when I walk into the kitchen and am stunned to find not just my mom and dad, but our family publicist, Sandra.

"What's happening?"

My dad turns his computer screen around toward me. "*Tell Me How You Really Feel*'s Finn Sutton Is Paid Nearly Double His Female Cohost's Salary."

If this were *Daily Mail*, *Page Six*, even *People*, it wouldn't be the end of the world. But it's a *New York Times* article.

I grab the computer and start reading, my stomach dropping. The article says that I was always paid commensurately with rival host Paul Myers, while Maeve was paid roughly sixty percent of our salaries. The pay jump incentive we accomplished was percentage based and did make Maeve the highest-paid female podcaster or higher paid than Paul Myers, but still left her lagging behind my salary.

"Who did they reach out to for comment?" I mutter as I read. It said Streamify and my team declined to comment.

"Derek and Mark," Sandra says curtly.

"Did you know about this?" my mom asks. She sounds angry, justifiably so. She took a huge stand over the pay gap a few years ago, and my dad backed her up. Since then, the pay on every single one of their projects has been not just equal, but public, and her foundation has been championing the issue in different industries.

"No!" I protest. "I had no idea. I assumed we were getting paid the same."

My mom and Sandra shoot each other a look. "You know better than to assume that," my mom says tightly.

In my gut I *know* that's true . . . but I also didn't really think about it. I rack my mind, thinking back to how all this went down. Derek gave me the contract, and I asked if Maeve was good with the contract. I think he said she'd already signed hers? That he got me a good deal? "Fuck," I mutter. "You're right. This is my fault. I just . . . didn't think. I know that I should know; it's just didn't occur to me."

"It didn't occur to you because it doesn't have to. Men always use that excuse: they don't think, don't notice, don't know. I raised you better than this, Finn." My mom's disappointment is crushing. I can only imagine how I'll feel when I experience Maeve's.

"What do I do? Actually, wait . . ." I don't have my phone. Without another word I run back to the pool house. I need to talk to Maeve. My mom is mad, but Maeve must be furious. When I see I have no texts or calls from her, I don't know whether to be scared or relieved. Maybe she hasn't read it. Maybe this can be contained. This is going to be humiliating for her and send her anxiety through the roof, and I *really* want to stop it if it's at all possible.

I run back into the kitchen. "How do I fix this? Can we kill the article? I could talk to Mark and Derek and release a statement."

Sandra smiles wanly. "I spoke to Mark, and he says you knew about the disparity. Would you mind opening your emails?"

"That's impossible," I rush to say. But my gut is sinking. "I would never have been okay with that."

I start scrolling back through old emails. I barely remember those weeks. I was lost in a fog, trying to get Maeve to talk to me and beating myself up over my decision to date and then dump Cassidy. But eventually I find the email with the contract.

I got you a nice bump up from what was discussed in the meeting. Good to sign. Like I said previously, Maeve's contract is already signed.

"He doesn't say I was being paid more exactly," I say quietly. But reading it now, it's clear what he was saying. I hand the offensive email over to my parents and Sandra to read. "How do I fix this?"

Sandra screenshots the email and texts it to herself. "This reflects badly on the entire family. I'll draft a statement saying ignorance isn't an excuse, but you are working directly with Streamify to make this right. We'll have to get them to bump Maeve to your pay grade. And then you can donate all of the extra money you've made to your mom's equal pay foundation and pledge to make your contracts public from here on out. We need to release the contracts for the movie too."

"Done."

"I'll get right on that statement." Sandra opens her computer and starts typing. "I think you should part ways with Mark as well."

My dad winces. "Are you sure? We've been with him for a long time. We went to USC together . . ."

"It's done," my mom says, throwing my dad a sharp look. "He never should have done that to Maeve. The negotiation should have been a collaboration between him and Shazia."

"You're right," my dad agrees reluctantly. "I'll talk to him myself. And Sandra, can you set up a meeting between Derek, all of us, Shazia, and our entertainment attorney?"

"On it," she agrees. She's typing rapidly, clearly planning on turning our kitchen into a crisis and triage center for this.

I look to my mom. "What about Maeve? What should I do?"

My voice cracks on the last word, and my mom's eyes soften slightly as she looks at me. "Finn, you're an adult. We just cleaned up the bulk of your mess. But only you can fix things with Maeve."

"But don't forget flowers," my dad adds. "You'll need the basics, on top of everything else."

My mom and Sandra both roll their eyes. But I'll take any advice I can get. Maeve still hasn't said anything, and I want to try to intercept her seeing the article. Maybe she's busy with Sarah, making breakfast and getting manicures or something. Maybe I can talk to her before she reads the article, which is unforgiving, and the comments, Threads, and TikToks, which are scathing.

I text Maeve. I'm coming over with coffee ♡

I get no response.

THIRTY-EIGHT

Maeve

I turn to Sarah, my stomach filled with dread. "He's coming here."

"When? Now?! Let *me* talk to him." She moves to snatch my phone, and I pull it away. "I do not want to hear this man use being an idiot as an excuse one more time," she gripes.

I put my phone under my leg so it's safe from Sarah, then go back to staring at the article. I don't believe Finn would screw me over like this. That can't be possible.

I text Shazia.

Anything?

I asked her to find out if Finn knew about this. I want the answer to be *Of course not*, but I have a sinking feeling in my gut that says otherwise. In response to my text, my phone starts ringing.

"Did he know?" I say, the words tumbling out before I can manage pleasantries.

I hear Shazia's hesitation, her intake of air. It's unlike her. "Derek told him that he had a more favorable deal, via email. He also had both versions of the contract. Are you sure he knew your salary?"

"Yes," I say confidently. "I mentioned it many times when discussing the Paul Myers situation." It makes me feel physically ill to think Finn was being paid commensurately all this time while pretending to support my quest for equality. Even if he missed the email, he *sees* the money landing in his bank account and knows what I make. There's no way he could have just overlooked this. He's not that stupid. His mom's charity is centered on equal pay; one of her big talking points is how male costars need to advocate for their female counterparts to be paid equitably for it to ever happen. Did he think this was just business, like Paul Myers would say?

"His family attorney has already requested we meet with Streamify as a united front; they want to get you paid equitably. And I'll negotiate for back pay. On the bright side, this article will make you much richer."

I know it's Shazia's job to think of the financials. But it's hard to care about the extra money when this article is going to be the dissolution of our relationship. Before I can respond, I hear the doorbell ring. "Thank you for checking, Shazia. I've got to go."

I don't move, and the doorbell rings again. Sarah looks between the door and me. "Want me to kill him? I know *exactly* where in the yard to put him."

I shake my head and walk to the door. Finn is standing there, a giant bouquet of roses in hand, along with three iced coffees. His face falls as he looks at me. "You saw it," he says. It's not a question. I nod anyway. "There's no excuse here. But can I try to explain?"

Sarah walks over and takes all three coffees and the flowers from him, glaring the entire time.

"Talk," I command, without letting him in. Maybe I shouldn't let him explain. But I want to hear it. I want some inkling to hold on to, that can make me believe he isn't this disappointing.

"It never occurred to me that we might be being paid different amounts. I barely read my emails, but I know you probably already know by now that the contract was there, and Derek told me it was more. Although, just saying, he didn't outright say it. It was confusing wording. Especially when you're just skimming. I assumed if I got more, you did too! Which is wrong. I am so sorry I was not more aware of the pay gap, and I will make this right." He's out of breath when he finishes, his cheeks flushed and eyes earnest.

When he reaches for my hand, I pull it away. "Finn, don't play dumb. You *know* about the pay gap. *Everyone* knows about the pay gap. You just have the privilege to ignore it. To choose to ignore it. You can't undo this."

He nods emphatically. "You're absolutely right. Like I said, it's no excuse. I am in the wrong here, and Maeve, I'm so sorry. I'm an idiot. I've always said you're smarter than me, and—"

"Finn, just stop talking!" Suddenly I'm yelling without meaning to. "You talk a good game, but you can't undo this. You can't claim ignorance on this. You know better! I am so tired of you doing the wrong thing, then just expecting me to forgive you. Please, just leave."

"Maeve, come on. Is it really so bad that I assumed we'd be paid equally? Let's call it stupidly positive thinking. I really think—"

"How nice for you that you can pick and choose when to care. It's not stupidity, it's sexism. And laziness. And your fucking privilege that you are *never* going to outgrow. You are always going to be some rich kid nepo baby that never has to work for anything, but gets credit for *everything* at the expense of people like me, who work *so fucking hard*."

I slam the door in his face, cutting off whatever excuse he's offering next. "Leave!" I shout through the door.

I can hear him yelling through the door. "Are you serious? Maeve, I'm apologizing! I thought we were a team. Why can't this be a real conversation?"

I walk away while he's still talking. I am so tired of always adapting to him. Of being second. This article is the manifestation of all my anxieties. Does it even count as anxieties if it's *true*? I am valued less than him despite being the one doing most of the work for the show. My mom was right, Finn will always outshine me. And I was okay with it! Back when I thought we were a team. In public, where he gets credit for it, he's always been a great man, giving me credit, saying no to golf course meetings, taking the blame for anything that's wrong since it rolls off him. But all that is just performative if when it counts he's not actually advocating for equality. And he let me look like an absolute idiot in front of the entire world. First with Cassidy, then Cassidy again, then this article. Again, and again, and again.

I walk back into the living room and collapse onto the couch with Sarah. She has thrown out the flowers and assembled a wide array of junk food and beverages. "I can't believe he did this," I moan. "It just makes me so angry! He is never going to understand what it feels like to take responsibility. To not have everything go perfectly. He never has to work for anything and wants applause for just being a decent guy, which is actually so much worse than the average woman."

"Men are trash. All of them," Sarah agrees. "Like, what is *wrong* with him? Evangeline is, like, the gender-pay-gap queen; he can't claim ignorance. And actions are what matters, not intent. If he's dead to you, he's dead to me."

"Well, right now, he is dead to me."

Sarah grabs my phone and goes to Finn's contact, changing his name to the graveyard emoji. My sisters do that with all our exes that we're completely done with, so that if they text us, we don't even know who it is.

"Am I overreacting?" I ask. Sometimes I wonder if my feelings are real. Or if my anxiety is building a mountain out of a molehill, loosening my grip on reality.

Sarah shakes her head. "One hundred percent not. This isn't forgetting to take out the trash. This is your career. Your real life. And he doesn't even need the money. You fucking fought to get here."

I start to cry, softly. These aren't the tears of a panic attack; these are tears over the fear that something I love might be ending. Of doubting the man I love. Of sadness that something I accomplished has been stolen from me. "I was just so happy to have done this. To finally get recognized. It's all ruined now."

Sarah wraps me in a huge hug. My face is buried in her shoulder when suddenly I feel more arms around me. I look up and see it's Claude and Tiffany. "Sarah added us to your lock," Claude murmurs without breaking her hold.

"How did you get here so fast?" I ask through tears.

Tiffany rolls her eyes. "Spirit and a time difference. We saw the article before you. Now fuck that stupid fucking man. Let's watch rom-coms and eat our weight in junk food. Or health food. Whatever is available here in LA. You are so much better and smarter than that idiot."

"I just feel so *stupid* for thinking that I did something with the glass ceiling."

Claude pulls back to look at me. "Maeve. You *did*. And I'm sure that as a result of this you'll do even more. You shouldn't have to leverage a painful moment to drag the fight for equality forward. But that's what women, people of color, queer people—that's what we're all forced to do. And it sucks, but it's true, and more *will* get done here. You were betrayed, pure and simple. But don't discount how much your pain is being used for."

Her speech wipes my tears away for a moment. "You're like ten. Where did you learn to talk like that?"

"Shut up, you're barely older than me. Pageants aren't all dresses and bikinis now, bitch. You're not the only one who knows how to talk."

I pull my sisters back in for a huge hug. "Thank you for coming." And now my tears aren't over the article, over Finn. They're over how happy I am that no matter how big and scary my life gets, my sisters are always going to be here.

THIRTY-NINE

Finn

Set has been a decidedly somber affair ever since the pay gap exposé and my blowout with Maeve. Both my mom and Cassidy clearly blame me for what happened. And it is my fault, but it was an honest mistake! That I apologized for sincerely and profusely. I'm starting to get annoyed that Maeve still won't talk to me, and that everyone is still mad at me. I've done the apology song and dance, we've negotiated way more money for Maeve from Streamify, I've done everything asked of me. So let's move on from me being persona non grata.

"Maybe the sex scenes could be what we end with." Cassidy is talking to my mom and dad, ignoring me completely. "Right now . . . it's just not the best time, chemistry wise."

"We could revisit the idea of body doubles," my mom offers.

My dad nods thoughtfully. They're about five feet away from me, acting as though I'm not there. "Are you serious right now?" I burst out finally. "I've apologized! Why isn't that enough? Can we just move on? It wasn't even your contract."

My mom narrows her eyes, and Cassidy responds with an epic eye roll and biting tone. "Yeah, *you* can just move on. You won't ever have to feel the repercussions of your actions."

"What is that supposed to mean? Trust me, I feel them. My girlfriend won't talk to me—actually, I don't even know if she still is my girlfriend. The internet hates me. And I've spent the last week apologizing."

"You got a few negative tweets. And a bunch of positive ones from misogynistic assholes. At the end of the day, the press tide has turned positive and people are *commending* you for supporting women." Cassidy's tone is full of disgust.

"And why is that so awful?"

My dad walks over and puts a hand on my shoulder, trying to calm me down. "Because you shouldn't be commended for just doing the right thing after making a huge mistake. Women pay for everyone's mistakes and never get commended for it. And think about how Maeve is feeling."

"Better, I hope, she just got a heck of a lot more money." But more pinpricks of guilt are popping up. "Listen, I know she must feel betrayed. But I don't know what more I can do here. And I am *so sorry.*"

"You don't get a medal for being sorry Finn. Not from us," my dad responds calmly.

"Why don't we all take ten," my dad commands, and around us lighting techs and assistants clear out as fast as they can. Cassidy stalks off to her trailer.

"She's right you know," my mom says firmly. "You expect to be rewarded for apologizing, because the press makes such a fuss when you, or any man, does anything right. Apologizing is the minimum. Making things right financially is just what you should do."

"I don't think she's ever going to forgive me," I say quietly. "I really was just being stupid. So stupid. But it wasn't intentional."

"But Finn, women don't get to be stupid. If you really want to be a good team, a good partner, you have to be fighting against all the ass-holes and unfairness in the world with her because you're in the most privileged position possible. I know you try. But the little things don't matter much if you get the big fights wrong." My dad's tone is gentle, and that makes his words hurt even more.

"I know, you're right. And I feel awful. I *will* do better. I never want anyone to screw Maeve like they did. But I feel like I'm never going to be able to get past this with her."

My dad opens his mouth to give me more advice, but my mom squeezes his hand, stopping him. "Honey, you love her. And you *know* her. If we help you fix this, we're not doing you any favors."

Once set wraps, I drive straight home and do what I've done for the past seven nights straight. I walk to Maeve's now almost-finished recording studio shipping container, which is temporarily housed in our yard, and lie on the floor. Sometimes when she's editing or brainstorming and having a hard time, Maeve will lie down on the carpet to think. And so I asked Luca to put the messages from friends, family, and fans on the ceiling, so now when she looks up she'll see a million reasons why she's brilliant and impactful.

I hate that my actions made her doubt herself even more than I know she already does.

I know that the pay-gap reveal hit her right in the gut. From her solo show getting turned down to the article's focus on me, it was a series of blows that broke the camel's back. I've been nursing my wounds all week, upset that she wouldn't just forgive me, when really, I should have been thinking more about how closely this hits on all of her biggest anxieties.

My mom and Cassidy are right. Even though all this time I've claimed to want to be normal . . . I'm used to special treatment. And that's why I'm waiting for a gold star for apologizing rather than groveling or doing the work to learn and do better in the future like I should be. Maeve is the most important person in the world to me. Even when I started acting in this movie, which I *knew* would bother her, she never said a word. She supported me, without pushing me, like always. She makes me think more deeply, take risks, face my fears, be the best version of me. And while I've done the basics to be a good guy, I haven't truly taken into account just how hard she's had to work to get here, and that for everything I've been born entitled to, she had to work a million times harder to just get a shot at. That to level the playing field I need to be behind her one million percent, even if sometimes that means staying behind the scenes, like my dad does for my mom at times. I need to apologize again. Properly this time. With grace and humility and no righteous remorse turned to anger.

It's time for me to make sure she knows that I *do* see her.

FORTY

Maeve

I am now the highest paid podcaster. Full stop. At everyone's urging, Streamify raised my compensation a hundred thousand over Finn just to make a point. It's another glass ceiling, but although I've done the press for it, it doesn't feel the same. Getting a pay raise Streamify was forced into doesn't feel like earning it, even though the game is rigged and I know, logically, I *did* earn this. Far more than Finn did.

During this epic negotiation, we skipped putting out an episode, and according to reports Streamify lost half a million in ad spend just from that one week. We have influence. And now, I have more money than I ever imagined I would, so it's time to take my destiny into my own hands and produce my show.

"Thanks for meeting with me," Evangeline says as I walk into her office. It feels strange to be at Finn's house but to see his mom rather than him. "And let me say, I am so sorry about everything that has happened with the Streamify deal. And for my son's behavior."

"Thank you," I say quietly. Finn and I haven't talked this past week and a half. It still feels so raw—I have nothing more to say right now. My sisters went home last night, after a week and a half of take-out sushi, phone interviews followed by tears, and wallowing. I know I'll have to see Finn next week to record, but until then . . . I don't know where we stand. What I want us to be.

"So, I hear you want to start a female-focused production company," I say, a statement, not a question. Shazia has told me Evangeline really wants to work with me. At first, I worried she was just trying to patch things up for Finn. But I sat with my feelings and talked to my therapist and eventually logic prevailed. Evangeline is a creative I deeply respect, and those worries are my own imposter syndrome talking. I want to hear her out.

Evangeline nods. "I do. I want to be able to produce the projects that the studios turn down. The ones with female leads over fifty, and movies that don't end with the guy getting the girl. Or the girl getting the guy. I want to focus on empowered women, flaws and all, because I think the studios are overlooking the spending power of women."

"That's extremely cool. And smart," I add. "I'm slightly surprised that you want a reality TV show in the mix."

"I want *you* in the mix. And, yes, I want reality TV. Especially reality TV that doesn't revolve around women competing for a man." Evangeline noticeably shudders when she says this. "But mostly, I want you. I've listened to every episode of *Tell Me How You Really Feel*, and I think you're brilliant. You don't need me to back this new show; you have the means to do that yourself. But I want us to be a team. The old and the new, combining forces, to tell stories."

This is a lot to wrap my head around. "Are you . . . are you sure?" I'm not used to someone with this much power telling me that I'm smart. Typically, when we have a meeting people are falling all over themselves to compliment Finn, since he's the famous one. "I still have to do the show with Streamify. So I'd be spending two days a week as talent."

"As you should. You're very talented. But I am completely sure. This will be a lot of work, no doubt about it, but the logistics of most of the productions will all be outsourced. I know everyone in the industry for that. I can find you an incredible editor for the show, a woman you can trust. And then when you're not on camera, you can be finding the projects that deserve to be made and putting together the teams to do it with me."

I'm quiet for a moment, considering. This sounds too good to be true. "Why aren't you doing this with Cassidy? Or Finn?"

"Maeve, we don't need to give men more. They already have enough. Finn will be fine. More than fine. And Cassidy is a lovely woman. A talented, kind model and actress. But you are incredibly smart. You have vision, guts, determination. You deserve this and are exactly the person I want involved. Your therapy reality show can be the first show we announce, start all this with a bang, because I want you to know, I *believe* in your ideas."

"Okay," I say finally, tentatively, after another moment of hesitation. But then a smile breaks across my face and I speak confidently. "Okay. Let's do it."

On my drive home I feel calm, for possibly the first time since I started pitching my show. Hearing that someone else believes in me completely is just so *nice*. And my self talk must be working lately because I actually believe Evangeline means what she says. This change will be a lot, but it feels like a next step I'm excited about. A year ago, I would probably have said no. I was having fun podcasting with Finn, hanging out, building the show. But I'm excited to do something totally separate from him, to get out from the shadow of my male cohost. Although I know Evangeline is much more famous

than I am, I feel like this will actually feel and be perceived as a collaboration, and there's a sense of relief in that. In not having to fight
for what I deserve every second of the day. I'll still have the show with
Finn, but I like knowing that my entire career isn't hinging on it.
That I'm doing something bigger.

Back at home I change into a bikini and lie on a pool float, staring
into nothingness, at the hat that I have thrown over my eyes to hide
from the sun. I have four days until I see Finn. And I still don't know
what I want to say. After speaking with Evangeline today, then with
Shazia about how the negotiations went down, and reading all the
news reports of what Finn has committed to doing with public contracts and money donated, I do think he understands that he fucked
up. I believe that he's sorry. And I'm starting to wonder if *maybe* I was
looking for a red flag. A flaw in the picture that is us. A reason for it
not to work.

I love Finn. I feel in my gut that he's who I'm meant to be with.
But at the same time, this whole thing made me so angry! I felt not
just betrayed, but humiliated. The past few weeks have heightened
every anxiety I've had since starting this. Since childhood, really,
when I first saw my sisters' talents and wondered why I wasn't as
special. But even though Finn overlooking the pay discrepancy was
the giant problem my anxiety was looking for . . . I don't believe it
has to be what ends us. We know how to communicate, and it's time
for me to start fighting for our relationship too.

FORTY-ONE

Finn

I start to enact my plan by calling Sarah.

"What do you want, asshole?" she asks, her tone harsh. If this is an indicator of Maeve's feelings toward me right now, it's not a promising sign. I can feel the nerves starting and my armpits are suddenly moist. I wipe my upper lip, glad this isn't a FaceTime.

"Hi, Sarah! It's great to talk to you. I was wondering if you could help me with something?"

"And why would I do that?"

I take a deep breath. "Because even though I realize my actions have been disappointing and that I fucked up . . . like so badly . . . I love Maeve. I want to make things right with her. And I want your help surprising her."

Sarah suddenly sounds more alert. "If you're thinking of proposing, don't. I know guys think that's romantic, but she *will* say no."

"I'm not!" I say defensively. "I just have something to give her that I think will show her how much I see her and appreciate her." The line is quiet while Sarah mulls over my words. I jump back in, sensing her hesitation. "Sarah, I love your sister. And I really think that she loves me. I know that making my mistake right isn't an apology. It's just doing the right thing, and it doesn't deserve any thanks or praise. I did that, and now I want to apologize."

"Why can't you just ask Maeve yourself?"

"Do you really think she'd come to my place right now?"

Sarah laughs. "No way." There's another long pause. "You know what? Fine. But only this one time. And *only* because I see how happy you've made Maeve. And this is your one fuckup. It is now officially used up, just so you're aware."

"Trust me, I know this is already my second strike, and I don't get a third."

"Fine. Then tell me what it is and what you need from me."

And that's how, the next day, I get Maeve to come over to my place. I open the door to the pool house before Maeve can knock because I recognize the jingle of her keys as she walks up the lawn. I know all of her little sounds, smells, and mannerisms. I could teach a whole course on what makes Maeve *Maeve*.

She looks surprised to see me. And I can't help but notice that she's wearing the red dress. My favorite dress. Is it a revenge dress now? "You didn't need to enlist Sarah to get me here you know."

It's the first thing out of her mouth and takes me by surprise. "I thought she was going to tell you I needed help! That I had a broken limb or something."

Maeve rolls her eyes. "Come on. She's my *sister*. No secrets. But I'm here, aren't I? And what she said was probably better."

"Do I get to know what it was?"

She smiles and it feels like my heart skips a beat. "Absolutely not."

"Well, can we take a walk?" She nods and we stroll toward the water, toward the same beach where we found out we beat *The Paul Myers Show*. I let my palm brush hers and am shocked when she slips her hand into mine. I lead her around the back of the house, to the now fancified shipping container that's overlooking the ocean. The walls are glass on the ocean side so the view is almost completely uninterrupted. I hand Maeve the key.

"This is for you. But before you say anything, I want to say my piece. Because I'm not just giving you a gift because I messed up."

Maeve opens the door to the shipping container studio—which is *much* nicer than a Home Depot shed—and we step inside. At first, she's scanning the interior, taking in the chairs and the desk and the colors with a soft smile on her face. But when I start talking, her eyes lock on mine.

"Maeve, I have been working on this place ever since we got back together. It's not an apology gift. It's just a gift. Because you deserve the perfect studio that you've always wanted. You deserve everything you've ever wanted. And you'll need it for your new show, which will be incredible no matter who produces it.

"I am so sorry that I acted in such a disappointing way. I *know* that our industry is sexist, and I chose not to pay attention because I don't have to. It's wrong. And making it right is just doing the right thing, not an apology. So please, let me apologize. I'm sorry I betrayed your trust. We're a team, and we should have been one even when we weren't together. I didn't act like it. I'm in the most privileged position, and I know that means I should be the one worried about how women, queer people, people of color, anyone disadvantaged by this shitshow of an industry, is treated. But this is also about *you*, and I'm sorry that I haven't been thinking about how things would make you feel. How much harder you've had to work to get any recognition. I promise that moving forward I'm ready to be a true teammate, even when that means taking a step back to make sure that you have your own lane.

"Maeve, I love you. You are smart, and creative, and talented, and so hardworking, and so fucking gorgeous. You bring out the best in everyone around you. You help me become the best version of myself, to look for my purpose, to overcome my fears, and try to both be happy and make change. You're more than I deserve right now, when I still have so much growing to do. But I will spend the rest of my life trying to be the best version of myself and the person you deserve. And I want you to know that I'm not the only one who sees how incredible you are."

FORTY-TWO

Maeve

Finn reaches out and takes my hand, guiding me to lie on the carpet. Tears are already sneaking out of my eyes. This studio is exactly what I've always dreamed of recording in, right down to the furnishings. And what he's saying . . . I can tell he really gets it. I don't expect him to be perfect. But I needed him to be self-aware, and he's showing me that he is, that we can work together, through all the challenges that will come our way.

We lie down on the carpet, shoulder to shoulder, and when I see the ceiling, I gasp. It's full of quotes from fans, in their own handwriting. Some are people we interviewed, a few are my family members, but most are people I've never heard of.

I came out to my best friend because of Maeve. She helped me realize my sexuality was nothing to be ashamed of. -Carla D.

I left my abusive husband. I didn't really believe that I could until Maeve laid out the resources available and really hammered home that it wasn't my fault. Maeve, you changed me and my daughter's lives. -Gen F.

I didn't think I would be here today. I never thought I'd live to be twenty, but because of Maeve I found a therapist. You saved my life. -Chris J.

I had my first orgasm after you walked me through how to touch myself. OMG THANK YOU MAEVE. -Jennifer H.

Now I am *definitely* crying. I've always known people liked the show. But we stopped reading most of the messages we got after Paul Myers's fans started threatening us and Finn had his panic attack, and I forgot how much those kind messages meant. Knowing that I'm doing something for all of these people . . . it's incredible.

"I see you. And so do they. You are the most special person," Finn says quietly. He squeezes my hand and I squeeze back.

I sit up and he joins me, turning so we're sitting face-to-face on the carpet. "Finn. Thank you. Thank you so much for this. You know how much I've worried I don't deserve this. That I just got lucky, or only got here because of you. Even though, logically, I try to tell myself that's not true. This . . . it means so much."

He opens his mouth to talk, and this time I stop him with a hand on his chest. "And the studio, it's everything I've dreamt of. But first, I need to apologize to you. Because even though I *thought* I was all in . . . I wasn't. I was waiting for the thing that would ruin us. I wasn't being totally honest with you and that doesn't make for a good team. I should have talked to you about my anxieties about Cassidy. Even though I am so excited that you're acting again! I should have been honest about how I was feeling. And told you at the shoot, privately, that it wasn't the time for you to jump in. I was holding too much in because I was afraid of pushing you away, or that what we had was too fragile to withstand all of my anxieties. Because even though I tell everyone else not to, even though I've had years of therapy, deep down I view my anxiety as an imperfection.

"You've always loved me for who I am. And I'm sorry I let my anxiety run my brain, making me pull away in fear before giving you the chance to reassure me. I was hurt by the pay-gap exposé. And I listened to all of my worst thoughts and convinced myself that you weren't actually on my side, that you just acted like it. I know that's not true. You've always seen me, even when I couldn't see myself. It means everything to know you're committed to getting it right going forward. I don't expect you to be perfect or never make another mistake. I just need to know we're both always trying together."

"I'm here with you, Maeve, every step." Finn's voice is low and earnest. "I want us to spend the rest of our lives together, as a team."

"Me too," I say.

I lean forward and press my forehead to Finn's. He cups my jaw in his palm, so gently, and I tilt my face toward his. Our mouths lock in a kiss, and it feels as charged as our first one. There is a lifetime of promise and possibility in this kiss. I thread my hands through his hair and pull him closer to me.

We topple from sitting to the ground and he kisses me as though he'll never get enough. It's passionate, it's sexy as fuck, but it's also slow. We don't need urgency. We have all the time in the world. When he finally pulls away to look at me I can't stop smiling.

"What?" he says, grinning reflexively in return. His eyes are dark and focused, looking at me in a way no one else ever has.

"I think we've finally gotten it right this time."

FORTY-THREE

Two years later

Maeve

Finn and I are sitting in the back of the limo on the way back from the launch of season two of my solo show, *Not Okay*. Over the last two years Evangeline and I have partnered on a wide range of female-fronted projects, from movies to docuseries to reality TV, and slowly but surely we've become a force to be reckoned with.

"Think they liked it?" I ask Finn, half joking. We're sitting pressed against each other in the very back seat. I've kicked off my heels, and his arm is around my shoulder.

"I think they *loved* it."

The crowds gathered outside the event were loud and enthusiastic, and the first episode of season two that was screened tonight got a standing ovation. I've been both shocked and thrilled by the success of this show. I never thought I would be doing a reality show, but last season we won the Emmy for Outstanding Structured Reality Program, and I've been having my assistant go through DMs and fan mail so that I actually hear from people who are positively impacted by the show, while avoiding any negativity. It's gratifying to see the world excited about therapy.

And it was pretty incredible that we *both* won Emmys the same year, in different categories. Finn and his mother both won supporting actor Emmys for their ensemble drama, which was produced by us and cowritten and codirected by a talented young female screenwriter and Finn's dad, as part of the mentorship program we launched. I have never seen Finn as happy as when he accepted that award. It's amazing to see the man I love finally find his purpose.

We still do *Tell Me How You Really Feel* and have candid conversations with celebrities. But when our Streamify contract ends, our show is moving under Evangeline's and my production company.

"They did love it," I agree happily. "I can't believe I'm this lucky."

"I can. Because it's not luck. *You're* the luck. Your hard work, intelligence, and passion made this happen." Finn takes his arm out from behind me and pours out two glasses of champagne. He hands me one, and we clink our glasses carefully in the moving car. "To the most amazing woman in the world. I am constantly in awe of you and everything you do."

We each take a sip of the champagne, and then he takes the glasses and puts them on the bar area to the right. I hold out my hand, eager for him to wrap his arm back around me. It's incredible celebrating with everyone like we just did, but it means even more to share this moment with Finn.

But Finn doesn't wrap his arm back around me. Instead, he turns to me and pulls a small pink box out of his suit jacket pocket. His hands are visibly shaking when he starts to talk.

"Maeve. I love you. I have loved you since the moment I met you, and fall deeper in love every day because you are the most brilliant person I know. You are changing the world, and I know you don't need me for that, but I love being able to do it with you. Maeve . . . will you marry me?"

"Yes! Yes, yes, yes!" I'm agreeing before he can even open the box. I throw my arms around him, crying and kissing him anyway, undoubtedly smearing my makeup all over his face.

He kisses me firmly, then pulls away just enough to open the box and slide the ring onto my finger. It's perfect. A classic square diamond on an impossibly thin gold band. Exactly what I wanted.

"Do you like it?"

"I love it. Did my sisters help?"

Finn shakes his head proudly. "I know you, remember?"

I kiss him. "You really do. I love you so much."

"I love you too," he says quietly. He wraps his arm around me, so we're sitting how we were before, but this time both admiring the ring on my finger.

We've shared so much with the world. I'm really happy that this moment was just for us. Two years ago, I think we both would have felt pressure to have this happen during an episode, at the premiere, somewhere our fans can experience it too. But now it feels right for this moment to be *ours*. I love giving them so much of ourselves. But it's important to keep some things for just us.

When we pull up to my house, which Finn has moved into, I practically jump out of the car, excited to call my sisters and tell them the news. Finn takes my shoes and we walk up the drive hand in hand. But when I go to open the front door, Finn stops me. "Let's go around the back."

Something about the look on his face makes me follow him instead of begging off for the FaceTime call first. We walk around to the yard, and I gasp. String lights and candles are everywhere, illuminating hundreds of roses. There's champagne and diner milkshakes, and just as I'm about to tell him how lovely it is, I jump.

"Surprise!" My sisters, my parents, and Finn's family jump out from behind the bushes. They all have lit sparklers and look over-joyed, but also slightly terrifying in the candlelight.

"Tell me you said yes!" Sarah yells.

"Yes!" I hold up my hand, still wrapped up in Finn's. He is so thoughtful. Saving the proposal for just us, but still bringing my family and his? I reach up and wrap him in a huge hug and kiss.

"So, Maeve, tell me how you really feel," Finn teases.

I throw my head back and laugh. "Like I love you more than humanly possible. I love you so much, Finn. Now, tell me, how do *you* really feel?"

"Like the luckiest guy in the world."

I pull Finn down to me and he wraps me in his arms for a kiss.

ACKNOWLEDGMENTS

I had the most fantastic time writing and revising *Tell Me How You Really Feel*, and first and foremost I want to thank everyone who picks it up and reads it. I so appreciate you spending time with this story that I have loved working on so much.

This was the second book I wrote with my incredible editor, Eileen Rothschild, and I am so grateful to her for all her guidance. Eileen, you have made me a better writer. Working on this book with you was such a fantastic experience, I can't wait for the next one.

A huge thank-you to my amazing agent, Lauren Spieller. I so appreciate you encouraging me and guiding all of my projects. Your support is invaluable and I'm so grateful that we get to work together.

To all of the people on BookTok, Bookstagram, and BookTube who have watched my videos the past few years and supported my first book—thank you so much for everything. I am eternally grateful to you all for giving me a platform and reading and supporting my work.

I was lucky enough to work with many of the same people from my first book on this second one, and I so appreciate all of their amazing work. To Kejana Ayala, Alexis Neuville and Alyssa Gammello, from the St. Martin's marketing and publicity teams, thank you for helping readers discover my books. Michael Clark, my production editor, and Michael McConnell, my copy editor, thank you for making sure this book is clear and beautifully laid out. And Char Dreyer, my associate editor, thank you for your notes and help along the way.

I owe a tremendous thanks to the audiobook team. Elishia Merricks, EmmaPaige West, Chloe Nosan, and Isabella Narvaez, you made the best audiobook I could ever dream of. I had so much fun in the studio with you. Thank you so much for helping me film social content.

I am also constantly grateful for my writing group, because their notes on my earliest drafts help make it the book it ultimately becomes. I can't wait until our books are alongside each other on the shelves. I also want to give a huge thank-you to my mom, Susan, for absolutely everything, and to my sister, my partner, and my friends.

And thank you to my friend Ashley, because when I was completely stuck drafting the ending to this book, your suggestions changed everything. Thank you so much for your willingness to brainstorm, and your friendship.

ABOUT THE AUTHOR

Betty Cayouette is an author and viral video content creator. She graduated summa cum laude from Brandeis University and currently lives in Salem, Massachusetts. Betty created @bettysbooklist, the viral TikTok/Instagram/YouTube account that is featured in outlets such as *The Boston Globe*, Euronews, Fox News, Boston.com, and *The Times* (London). Her debut novel, *One Last Shot*, released in May 2024. *Tell Me How You Real Feel* is her second novel.